GHOST FLOWER

GHOST
FLOWER

SPACE ✴ TIME ◈ DESTINY

WILLIAM F. MERCK II

MERCK II PRESS

Ghost Flower - Space ✳ Time ✦ Destiny

© 2024 William F. Merck II

ISBN: 979-8-9879768-7-6

First Edition
Published in the United States
Merck II Press

Original artwork © 2024 Ksenia J. Merck. All rights reserved.

For more information, please visit merckiipress.com.

E-book and audiobook editions also available.

Please explore *The Ghost Flower Companion Journal* by Ksenia J. Merck, as well as William F. Merck II's earlier works:
So, You Want to Be a Leader: Secrets of a Lifetime of Success and
Breadcrumbs: Finding a Philosophy of Life.

For Ksenia:
It's my hand you hold
my heart you own ...
It's a beautiful life
because of you.

2200 BCE
EARTH

A SONIC BOOM PIERCED THE SILENCE of a clear, otherwise quiet, peaceful spring day. Grazing animals lifted their heads in surprise, birds took panicked flight, and then an eerie silence settled over the rolling plain. If there had been anyone present in the surrounding area to be curious about this sound—like the crack of thunder but not quite the same—they would have witnessed an incredible sight. But no living person was around to see what happened. Not to say there weren't people in the distance who heard the sound and wondered what the boom could be in the absence of a thunderstorm. Momentarily distracted, they shrugged it off and went back to the tasks at hand.

If someone had been present to see the source of the thunderous sound, they would have witnessed the sudden appearance of twelve strange-looking apparitions, stepping out of a clear bubble that burst out of nowhere, on a peaceful plain. The place would later be referred to by many names, one of which would be the Salisbury Plain of England. In one moment, it was an empty land, covered with grass, some of it tall but most of it short from the grazing of both domesticated and wild animals. The plain was also home to heather and small shrubs, occupied by colorful birds, a few rabbits, and the occasional fox. In the next moment, appearing from the source of the boom, stood twelve human-appearing forms, their general appearance similar but not quite like the local inhabitants of the area. But they weren't human in the Earth sense of human.

One of this strange party, unsteady from the sudden change in atmosphere and gravity from that in their arrival craft, slowly regained his balance and focused on his surroundings, looking with concern for the other eleven of his companions. As the commander of this mission, he quickly looked for each in turn, accounted for them all, and saw that other than minor discomfort, they appeared to be normal and functional. He looked over at a female member of the group, his second in command, and in a voice that revealed his sense of relief, exclaimed, "Lieka, we made it!"

"Yes, Aiela, it worked!" she replied.

Similar exclamations broke out from other members of the group as they excitedly checked over their bodies and those of their comrades for any unusual anomalies resulting from their novel journey. The excitement was palpable, but faded as they began to notice a strangeness in breathing, and an odd sense of lightness in their bodies. Their commander, Aiela, known only by one name as was the custom on their planet, a sturdy-looking male about five feet, six inches tall, with almond-colored skin and black hair cut to a level an inch below the bottom of his ears, saw their reaction, and offered reassurance. He reminded them that they were experiencing what scientists on their home planet, Golan, had told them to expect.

The original scientists, who had lived a thousand years earlier, sent an unmanned probe towards a planet of interest to them. When it reached its destination after hundreds of years, the probe transmitted data about the planet back across space, eventually reaching current scientists on Golan. That data transmission was the last sent before communications with the probe permanently ceased. Scientists studying the transmittal found it contained an inconclusive but intriguing message of life forms detected on the planet all those years ago, suggesting some were likely humanoid. Simulations generating possible scenarios from the data offered the possibility that the planet's humanoid forms may have been very similar to Golan's, but results were inconclusive in details as to what physical differences there might be due to the differences in gravity and atmosphere. They also acknowledged there would probably be unfamiliar leadership structures and economic factors on that planet.

The Andromeda Galaxy, home to the space travelers' sphere of Golan, is a system containing approximately a trillion stars. Golan has an atmosphere with less oxygen and a little more methane and nitrogen than that of their mission's landing site. The lightheadedness being experienced by the strange party appearing out of nowhere on the plain was a result of continuing their normal breathing pattern as they would on their home planet. Their respiration rate was suffusing their red blood cells with more oxygen than they were accustomed to.

The second in command, Lieka, continued the explanation to the crew that the commander had initiated.

"Our normal breathing pattern at home is too fast on this planet, causing us to hyperventilate. We must slow it down a little when we are at rest. The abundance of oxygen here, more than we are used to, may allow our endurance, under stress, to be maintained for a longer period of time than on Golan. The lightness we are feeling is caused by our home planet being larger than this one, resulting in our bodies being stronger to counter the greater force of gravity there than necessary on this smaller world. We were told that we would experience about thirty percent more strength here.

"Additionally, our sun bombards us with more ultraviolet rays than we find on this planet, causing our skin and eyes to have developed a greater resistance to that harm than the residents of this dimmer place. Paradoxically, even with brighter sunlight in the days, we developed an ability over thousands of years to see better in darkness than what we were advised we would observe here in the native population. Unfortunately, while we need to blend in with those who live here, our scientists suggested that because of the difference in light, our eyes may appear to be a little larger and our pupils will dilate in a manner not exactly like the natives we might encounter. It is a concern for blending in."

Lieka had eyes that were indeed slightly larger than those they would be encountering on this strange new planet. They were an emerald green and seemed to have a faint luminescence that contrasted nicely with her soft, almost shimmering, black hair. Just as her commander's hair, hers was cut to a length an inch below her ears, a current style shared by both females and males on Golan.

With that, the party of twelve spent the rest of the day acclimating themselves to breathing in the unfamiliar atmosphere and enjoying a new feeling of lightness in this lesser pull of gravity. While they suspected their eyes would not be helpful in their efforts to blend in, they would later find that their five foot, four inch average height plus the extreme density of their bone structure and musculature would give them an outward appearance of weighing the same as a similarly-sized human. However, the Golans were aware they would actually weigh about thirty percent more due to the dense nature of their bones, muscles, and connective tissues—giving them an advantage over the locals in the strength and durability of their bodies on this new world.

As the day passed, they slowly began to acclimate to their new environment. Night soon approached, leading to a decision to move to a more protected place they discovered a hundred yards or so from their landing site. It was an unusual spot, with a curious circular mound of earth surrounding a series of upright stones. Once gathered there, they prepared some of the meager rations and spices they had brought with them. Following the meal, Aiela announced his decision to send a small reconnaissance team out that night into the surrounding area to learn what they could to help them plan their next move.

The small band of interplanetary castaways had no idea, on this first day on a foreign world, the chain of events being triggered that would ultimately affect the survival of millions.

CHAPTER 1

2034 CE ARCTIC CIRCLE, NORTHERN HEMISPHERE

"WHO WOULD HAVE THOUGHT A FEW years ago that we would be here in the northern reaches of the Arctic, digging up Mastodon bones?" This question was posed by Gary Sorensen, a graduate student standing on a cold, rocky outcrop jutting from the remains of recently melted ancient ice, brightly lit by sunlight in the thinner high-altitude air.

Maggie, a smiling student member of the dig team, wearing her university sweatshirt above tan cargo pants, their pockets loaded with archeological brushes and small picks, responded rhetorically with a question of her own.

"Well, Gary, my fearless team leader, who would have thought that extreme climate variations would have come upon us as fast as it has, releasing the secrets of eons locked up until now, frozen in time, but suddenly being freed by the melting glaciers?"

Gary, thinking about what Maggie had just said and ignoring the "fearless" part, unwittingly offered a prophetic comment as much to himself as to her. "In one of my classes, before budget cuts closed my environmental professor's program, she suggested that this rapid melting might be like opening Pandora's box, releasing things to the world after being locked up for thousands of years under a mile of glacier ice. Some of what is released might not be as welcome as our discovery of this trove of Mastodon bones. I'm pleased to say, so far at least, we have seen nothing like that."

Maggie, pushing a strand of red hair away from her freckled face, her hereditary Irish skin sunburned from the bright Arctic sun, began brushing off a bone fragment she had just photographed and meticulously logged into her handheld smart device. She gave a little laugh as she said, "Only a day or two more before our merry band of student researchers will all be going home for summer break! I've decided to spend that time with my new friend, Nataly, in her home in Uzbekistan."

"Sounds great! I'll be going to Boston, but in a reverse of what you are doing, our friend Jack from Stratford-upon-Avon will be coming to visit with me for a couple of weeks."

"You know, just the name of his home town sounds intriguing," replied Maggie as she put her hand, no longer soft after the weeks on the dig, over her mouth to cover a cough. Wrapping up the long day, she turned away from Gary to begin packing up her equipment to head back to the small tent city the twenty-five international students and their university professors had lived in for spring research activities in the Arctic.

CHAPTER 2

2035 CE
BOSTON, MASSACHUSETTS

FAR FROM THE ARCTIC, AND A year later, the atmosphere in a Boston teaching hospital was not as jovial.

"This virus has mutated again in less than a month! So, once again, our vaccines are losing ground in potency. I'm sure our hospital will see a higher mortality rate among incoming patients as a result of the declining effectiveness of the shots they took just a few months ago."

Dr. Ada Sendall, wearing her knee-length white lab coat and seated on a wheeled stool pulled up to a lab bench, looked up in frustration at her assistant from her computer screen displaying the results of the latest blood sample from a recently-admitted patient.

"We can't develop new vaccines at anything near the speed of the new mutations we are seeing. The new strains are multiplying at a rate I've not seen in my twenty years of experience as a virologist and physician, and each one seems to add to the severity of the pandemic as the older strains don't seem to be fading away as these new ones appear."

"I wish I had a useful comment I could make at this point," responded Joel Larsen, her gifted graduate assistant, "but I'm at a loss. We need a miracle."

"Or," Ada suggested, "perhaps we need to look at this problem with fresh eyes and an open mind for some approach unlike anything we were exposed to as students in med school or from the lessons we have since learned in the real world. None of our experiences seem to be giving us any helpful answers to deal with what we are facing now."

She looked away from Joel, and although he was attentively listening, it seemed as if she was only talking to herself as she began reviewing what she knew. "About all we are reasonably sure of is this new virus with its shockingly-fast mutations started when an ancient pathogen, long frozen in the Arctic glaciers, was released as the ice locking it up melted. A team of professors and their students spent two months at a dig where we suspect the melt released the virus and, unknown to them at the time, infected them all. A very virulent virus as it turned out."

Ada continued, "As their dig ended for the season, they all departed for home. As fate would have it, they were an international team, and home for the twenty-five individual members and their two professors was spread over several countries in Asia, Europe, and North America. Within a week of arriving at their respective destinations, all of them became ill, and shockingly, half of those died within a month of their return. The others slowly recovered after a time but with lingering medical issues that don't seem to be going away. At first, the medical community thought it might be a new mutation of the MCV31 virus, emerging in strength after its predecessor strains were beaten down—but not defeated—by current preventative measures and newer, more effective vaccines. But they quickly surmised this virus was something different and was not responding well to any of the available treatments. There seems to be virtually no protection offered by existing vaccines and little symptomatic relief offered by the usual palliative treatments. The spread of infection to people who the returning Arctic research team came in contact with is not yet a large number, but that number is growing and growing fast."

As she reflected on the situation, but now looking directly at Joel and speaking a little louder, Ada added, "We have a little time to work on a solution before this virus is totally out of hand but since the spread is growing rapidly, it is imperative that we find some answers before we reach a point similar to what happened sporadically during the fourteenth, fifteenth, and sixteenth centuries with the bacterium, *Yersinia pestis*, or the Black Death as it was sometimes called, that wiped out half of Europe. As you know, that was a bacterium. What we are dealing with here is a virus— with death certainly common to both. I'm possibly being overly pessimistic but, unfortunately, my experience as a doctor tells me I'm simply being realistic."

"I have a cousin, a research assistant and lecturer at a small college in the Midwest," Joel said. "She mentioned a project she was involved with in Spain; Salamanca, to be precise. She is a medieval scholar, with a particular interest in art history. A few years ago, her college received permission for her to examine the ancient illuminated manuscripts housed in the rare book archives at the University of Salamanca. While her interest focused on the amazing artwork and drawings on the margins of the page, she was accompanied by a linguist specializing in the classical Latin used in the writings penned on the pages by the monks who recorded the history and stories of their times. His translations helped her to determine the meaning of the accompanying marginal drawings and symbols on the pages she was interested in."

"What does that have to do with what we are talking about?" Ada injected.

"She, her name is Melinda Ramsey, was musing about one of the drawings she had seen in the University of Salamanca archives. This was during a dinner at our house roughly three years ago when she was taking time off from work. I only remember it because I was struck by a mysterious name she mentioned, designating a particular flower on one of the page margins. It was referred to in the Latin script as the Ghost Flower, and reputed to have some medicinal benefits. A passage on the page mentioned a village in England, I don't recall the village's name now, but there was reference to how the small population there were spared the Black Death as well as other maladies with unknown origins that seemed to be everywhere else. Naturally, given the times, superstition abounded. Some of the folks in the countryside who were losing loved ones to the plague did not see even one of the twenty or so residents of the village she mentioned ever get sick. Witchcraft, sorcery, deals with the devil, all of these were suspect as reasons for their immunity to disease."

Joel became more animated as he relayed the rest of the story to Ada. "However, in addition to these suspicions, the script on the page with the Ghost Flower drawing suggested that there was some connection between this particular flower and their protection from disease. Magic? Who knows what they attributed this connection to but a few believed there *was* a connection. Obviously, this potential nexus was mentioned frequently enough in the information given the monk— considering he wrote in this particular text that it was worthy of mention. Later, his parchment manuscripts were acquired for inclusion in the University of Salamanca's collection."

"How long has that university been around?" Ada asked.

"The University of Salamanca, or the Universidad de Salamanca, was founded in 1258 by King Alfonso IX. It's one of the oldest in the world that is still in operation today. They have accumulated quite a trove of ancient documents in their time, with many now stored in their rare book archive. The archive is built like a vault with an entry door that is every bit as formidable as one you would expect to find in a bank. As Melinda was leaving after one of her days reviewing documents in the vault, she asked one of the librarians accompanying her about the sign over the exit door. Written in Latin, the librarian loosely translated it for her as, 'Those who are caught taking books from this library will be excommunicated from the Church—by order of the Pope.' Quite the library fine, don't you think?"

"Where is Melinda now?"

"She's here in Boston on a short break before heading back to college in Ohio, where she is still teaching classes in art history as far as I know. I'll check to see if she's still around."

"Well, it's a slim reed to grasp, probably at best only an interesting story for us to hear without any benefit to our current problem," Ada sighed. "But, as I said, 'fresh eyes and an open mind' are possibly our best hope now. Do you think she would be able to meet us for drinks and dinner Wednesday night? There is a small restaurant and bar upstairs in the Boston Marriott Cambridge that would be convenient for both of us. If nothing else, we can enjoy good company and a great view of the Charles River. If we are there before dark, we will enjoy watching the various university rowing teams practicing with their shells accompanied by coaches in their launches. Always interesting to see."

* * *

Melinda was delighted when Joel called and was there to meet them at the Marriott a little before sunset on Wednesday. Being first to arrive, she had commandeered a table for the three of them with a great view, and sure enough, there were university teams rowing on the river as part of their afternoon practices.

"Great spot, Melinda!" Joel exclaimed as he and Ada arrived and he pulled out a chair for his boss.

"Pleased to meet you, Dr. Sendall," Melinda said as she rose from her chair to greet them. "Joel has said great things about you and is certainly happy with the opportunity to be your research assistant."

Melinda smiled as she noticed the professor obviously looking at her slim, strong build and weathered face and hands. She saw she was correct when Ada spoke.

"For an art historian, you don't look like you spend all of your time in the classroom. I would guess you enjoy the outdoors and spend time there in some manual pursuit."

"Very good observation for us just meeting but then you are a research scientist so quickly absorbing details in your environment must be a valuable skill," she smiled.

"Okay," Ada returned her smile and relaxed a bit, "So, what's the story?"

"I'm an art historian, interested in medieval times and the following Renaissance period. I have a passion for archeology, particularly in work being done unearthing the secrets buried in the earth dating to time periods that have a bearing on my art interests. I volunteer to spend my time away from classroom obligations with research teams in the field."

"Interesting," Ada observed as she turned to ask the server, just arriving at their table with menus, about specialties of the house. The woman, who from her age, bearing, and confident look, seemed to be a reliable source for offering knowledgeable recommendations for the most desirable fare on the menu.

"For a starter, we have a Boston chowder that I love and is a favorite of the regulars here. For the main course we have a number of excellent choices but you won't go wrong with our pan-seared salmon."

After hearing about the other choices, all of which sounded excellent, they each settled on the chowder to be followed by the main course of salmon, accompanied by a steamed broccoli side dish. A suggested Argentine chardonnay completed the order.

As the bowls of chowder were delivered, the rich aroma of the fresh whole clams, the creamy broth, and solid roux told them the recommended starter was truly an excellent choice. While enjoying the taste of the rich flavors of the chowder, they watched and commented on the rowers beginning to depart the river. The sun had just dropped below the horizon and the buildings across the river were beginning to light up from within. Their soft glow was sparkling on the soft ripples of the waters below. As the diners watched the romantic scene unfolding below, the conversation at their table turned to the reason for the meeting.

Ada began with a recap of the dilemma they were facing with the mysterious new virus and told of Joel's revelation about Melinda's work in Salamanca. "Melinda, tell us more about those ancient documents you were poring over in the archives—particularly the notice you took of the Ghost Flower. What can you tell us about that?"

A faraway look came into Melinda's soft brown eyes as she began recalling the time, those years ago, when she was in the presence of the documents in question. In her mind, she could feel the old parchment through the protective covering of the thin blue nitrile gloves she was wearing, peering at the beautifully preserved writing and colorful inks used in the monk's hand and the illustrator's drawings on the pages; drawings both interspersed in the script and on margins of each page. She was remembering the thoughts and emotions she had at the time, imagining herself being present ages ago with the monk as the words and drawings were so meticulously being recorded. Thinking how painstaking and time-consuming it would be to record information in this way, she was confident the monk would not have spent this precious time recording events or opinions that were inconsequential. This was not some modern-day blog that could be typed out on a keyboard in a matter of an afternoon, using emojis and public domain art work to illustrate points. No, this was important work that was believed worthy of the time and effort expended to create a record for posterity.

"The story of events in far off Brittan, accompanied by a description of the flower, were the equivalent of breaking news to the monk, even though the information was delayed reaching him by the story's long journey from the British Isles, south over the Pyrenees mountains and finally to the monk's convent near the University of Salamanca in Spain. By the time the stories and reports of the white Ghost Flower were recounted to the monk, they had been told and retold a number of times, with the versions he heard being subject to the vagaries of memory, the interpretations of the tellers to the listeners, and the understanding of the listeners based on their experiences in life. "I believe," continued Melinda, "the monk was an intelligent person and no stranger to academic rigor as practiced at the time. Therefore, he reduced the story he was told to the basics as he understood them, leaving out some of the more dubious parts, at least in his mind, that were told. Let me be clear that what I'll tell you, is what I, Melinda, gleaned from my linguist's interpretation from the original Latin to English."

She paused to take a sip of wine. "See, even my linguist's translation of the monk's iteration of the story provides an opportunity for a slight variation from the monk's intended meaning. Remember, too, the story was originated by English speaking peoples around 1200 CE during one of the early onslaughts of the Black Death. It was retold in Spanish sometime later and then the monk heard that version and recorded it in Latin, in which he was fluent, but still, Spanish was his native tongue."

Ada observed, "Modern day religious practices are often based on stories passed down through the centuries and subject to similar distortions based on their telling and retelling, especially when those with knowledge of the events were unable to write them down so they were passed on by word-of-mouth for generations. That does not discount the basic truth in the stories, but leaves some questionable details that should be discounted in searching for those basic truths. I believe we should take this understanding into account when we examine what we know of the monk's recitation of the Ghost Flower tale."

"Dr. Sendall, you are absolutely correct!" exclaimed Melinda. "Let me tell you what I recall as we sit here at this dining table. I will go over what you asked but first let me plant a seed in your imagination to consider. I'm itching for an excuse to go back into the field, so what would you think about an expedition to beautiful

Spain and a visit to Salamanca?"

"Worth a thought," Ada replied. "I *am* interested but I'd like us to hear more of your interpretation of what you saw on the book's parchment pages and your linguist's translation of the Latin."

"Okay, realize this is from memory as I don't have my detailed notes with me but here goes: There is a small village on what is now called the Salisbury Plain in southwest England. I'm sure you are familiar with Stonehenge; you have probably visited there. It dates back to roughly 3000 BCE. Just north of Stonehenge, about twenty or so miles, lies the village of Avebury. It's the site of the Avebury Henge and Stone Circles. The village was established late in the life of this ancient place and was built partially within the henge. The stone circles of Avebury are considered by some to be older than Stonehenge by a few hundred years but the construction at both sites spanned centuries. With each century that passed, there was more complexity added and then, in later centuries, the sites' grandeur diminished due to weathering over the ages and destruction caused by humans.

"Now, more to the specifics I believe you are interested in," Melinda continued. "Even though the evidence is scant from the early times, it seems these sites had religious significance, or maybe better put in a general way, spiritual significance, as different cultures of people used the sites over thousands of years. Burying the dead became a common practice in the nearby barrows and even, apparently in some cases, in the henge ditches and maybe within the stone circles themselves. It also seemed in ancient times that people with infirmities or various sicknesses would be brought to spend time within the circles because they believed there was a healing energy present. Nothing I am aware of suggests a scientific backing of those beliefs regarding healing bodily infirmities but the beliefs were certainly handed down in folklore.

"Now, imagine how I felt in the University of Salamanca library, when my linguist began reading a story for me from one of the old documents about a time around 1200 CE. It was a story regarding a small number of residents living near the Avebury stone circles who never became sick when the Black Death was ravaging the countryside. I told you I believed the author recounting the stories was probably a fairly intelligent individual who applied a certain amount of academic rigor to his work. He was also a monk, which makes me think he would have spent a great deal of time pondering the spiritual possibilities suggested in the stories regarding the folks in Avebury who were seemingly immune to diseases everywhere around them at the time."

Melinda continued, "I don't know what the monk would have thought about the rumors of witchcraft, the influence of the Devil, or other reasons attributed to the immunity of this small group of people living near what is now called Avebury. I believe the oldest known record of the name "Avebury" was a reference in the Domesday Book of 1066. However, the monk did refer to those suspicions, as they were a big part of the stories, but his writing appeared to be an unbiased reporting of what people were saying without opining on the validity of their suspicions.

"And, finally, what really struck me in his recounting of the stories about the people of Avebury was his reference to a small white flower referred to as the Ghost Flower. The seeds of which, along with the petals and stems, were used as a garnishment in the popular stews of the time and often prepared for a special holiday. There was some speculation in a few of the stories that these flowers may have had some effect in warding off the plague as a natural defense against bacterium and other diseases. The flower story was just one of many speculations for the odd fact that the residents did not become deathly ill from any of the seemingly endless epidemics of the time. The other explanations ran the gamut from sheer luck to supernatural forces controlled by Satan. Of course, no one at the time understood anything about chemistry, viruses, bacteria, or immunity. So, in the story of the flower, its suspected disease-fighting properties were lumped in with all of the other stories tied to witchcraft, magic, or some other force limited only by the creativity of the various storytellers. However, the flower story piqued the interest of the monk to the point that he directed his illustrator to draw, on the margin of the page in this particular document, a representation of how that particular flower might look from what he gleaned from the old stories. The illustration of the flower appeared to resemble the white flowers I have seen on dogwood trees, with two notable exceptions. One, if the flower on the page was drawn to scale, and that I must say I have no idea if true, then it would be about a third smaller than a dogwood flower. Second, it had six petals, not four."

Ada interrupted at that point, "Your attention was captured by the possibility, with your twenty-first century knowledge of things unknown in the thirteenth century, that this flower's chemistry might impart an immunity to those diseases when they were used as a garnish. A garnish possibly used as an ingredient in a common stew served in those days consisting of a mix of lamb and mutton."

"Exactly! But I didn't consciously connect the possibility that the flower's chemistry might be used to attack the causes of the pandemic we are faced with today. Particularly so, as the plague in those times was bacterial and what we are facing today is a virus. Then, I got Joel's call inviting me to join you for dinner. In a flash, a possible connection between your research and mine came together! I'm excited to pursue this!"

"Me, too," Ada added, which was quickly seconded by Joel. "Now, let's think about what we have discussed, get back together very soon, and map out a plan of action. Considering the speed of the spread of the virus and its mutations, there's no time to lose."

After dinner had concluded and the party split up, Ada was in her ten-year-old BMW, driving home, some forty minutes away. As was becoming more and more frequent, she began contemplating her life goals. This was not her first time down this path. At forty-five years of age, she had recently gone through a painful divorce and, to some extent, had attempted to lose herself in her academic work—without much success. Five years ago, a tragic traffic accident on an icy road had resulted in the death of her only daughter, barely nineteen at the time and a promising student and outstanding soccer player at Boston College. She reflected on her daughter's athletic abilities and saw much of herself in her. Athletically inclined in her own college years, Ada had been a star point guard on the basketball team. A very attractive woman, she was still in excellent shape in her mid-forties. She was an avid jogger, frequenting the running paths along the banks of the Charles River, and spent time working out in a local gym. Not seeking to develop a body-builder's physique, she simply wanted to keep her muscles toned from a general health perspective.

However, Ada's mental state was not nearly as healthy. She had begun to seriously question her purpose on this earth. While she enjoyed the academic life that she tried to immerse herself in, that focus and distraction dimmed whenever she was alone, which was becoming more and more the case. She could feel herself slowly descending into depression. But tonight's dinner conversation was newly inspiring, sparking her interest in a way she thought had left her forever.

CHAPTER 3

2200 BCE
EARTH

As the landing party from their planet in the Andromeda system slowly finished their meal while sitting among the assortment of huge stones encircled by a deep ditch, Aiela looked over at Lieka, his second in command, as she poured the final residue from her dinner bowl on the ground. "This is a strange place, don't you think?" she asked. "The trench surrounding this place has a high earthen mound on the outward-facing side of the ditch, just the opposite of what would be constructed for defensive purposes."

"I noticed that as well," Aiela said. "I'm thinking this place is for ceremonial purposes, not a defensive military site. Plus, there is no sign of habitation anywhere nearby. The passageway we followed to come in here runs through an opening in the earthen berm and then crosses a fill in the ditch. It appears well traveled, suggesting this place is heavily used on occasion, even though deserted at the moment. I suggest we stay here for a day or so until we get our bearings and then move on." Aiela's tone was more of a decision and command than a mere suggestion.

Then he changed the subject. "We left our transport bubble a few hundred yards away and the light is beginning to dim as our first night on this planet is approaching. But have you noticed the bubble seems to be fading more than can be accounted for by the changing light?

"I'm sorry you said that because I am noticing the same

phenomenon and was hoping it was just me," Lieka admitted.

He then commanded her, "Tell the others to stay here while we go check it out. I want to see what's happening while there is still decent light. Remember, we brought no artificial light sources with us as our plan is to blend in with the locals. We don't want to exhibit any technology they don't have."

As they neared the vessel they arrived in—a clear bubble composed of an electromagnetic force field creating an impenetrable barrier when the entry and exit portal was closed—they saw that indeed it appeared to be fading away. "Uh, this is a problem," the commander observed.

Lieka quickly responded to Aiela's comment with a similar concern. "It's a big problem. This is the first use of this type of interplanetary transport. Part of our mission was to calibrate its functions for a return trip. If it disintegrates, we are here to stay. There will be no way back! Even if we could find the resources on this planet to build a new one, which I doubt, the huge scientific and engineering team that developed this one is all on Golan, six light years away."

The two Golans stood in shocked silence as they watched their transport bubble slowly disintegrate and fade into nothingness. In just a few minutes it was completely gone, leaving no trace that it ever existed.

Lieka, a tough individual who had recently been through heavy conflict on her home planet, seemed unsurprised watching the evaporation of their transportation. She whispered to Aiela, "We will never return to Golan."

"I think you're right," the commander acknowledged. "Those who sent us don't know what happened here. They will wait for us to return as planned. When that doesn't happen, they will be afraid to send another sphere. They don't know if we successfully arrived, were lost in the newly understood dimension, or landed in the middle of a rock. I think they will ultimately abandon this program—at least in our lifetime."

"That means it's critical to do the best we can to blend in with the locals and learn how to live here, because this is now our home planet," Lieka affirmed. She began to think of the newfound freedom this turn of events would mean for her. As that thought sunk in, she decided she would wait to tell Aiela things about her past that he was unaware of until the right time came. She was beginning to like this handsome leader of the group and the way he respected her was something she had not experienced with others she had known on Golan.

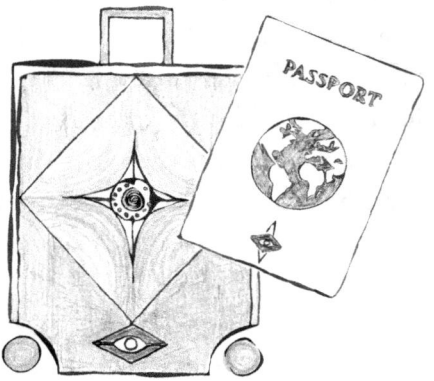

CHAPTER 4

2035 CE
BOSTON, MASSACHUSETTS

THE MONDAY FOLLOWING THEIR DINNER MEETING the preceding week, Ada, Joel, and Melinda met again in a small conference room in the university hospital. They had each had the intervening few days to think about next steps.

Joel spent the time with his closest friend from childhood, who also had found a research internship at a local college. Their lengthy conversations included thoughts about inflection points in people's lives—unexpected encounters that offered the possibility of a new path to be considered. Joel's upbringing had been in a family with interest in many things, including a love of the outdoors that led to many camping trips in several of the national forests. His dad had served in the military and his mom was a nurse working in a local hospital. Their skills had been very useful during those times in his childhood when they embarked on trips to experience roughing it, hiking during the days, and sleeping in tents in all types of weather during nights on the trail. Joel and his brother, four years younger, and his sister, two years younger, bonded on these trips and developed a joy in finding ways to adapt to new and challenging surroundings, leaving the normal comforts of civilization temporarily behind.

One such trip he fondly recalled was a ten day vacation the family spent hiking on the Appalachian Trail where it meandered through the mountains of North Carolina and Virginia. He recalled the time during that trip when a planned stop at a spring to refill their canteens did not go well—a severe drought had left only a cracked mudflat where streaming water once flowed. As a result, no water was available on their arrival. There was only a forlorn frog sitting on a stone where water had cooled him a few days before, giving out a plaintive "croak" as they approached before hopping off and disappearing. That night, it began raining so they rigged one of the small tarps they had brought to sleep under as a way to catch rainwater and funnel it into their cooking pot. The next morning, they refilled their canteens from the pot of rainwater. Problem solved.

Joel's childhood had a number of such adventures and he enjoyed the experience of facing difficulties and finding solutions. He also believed in keeping himself physically fit, maintaining his weight around 155 pounds on his five foot, eight inch, frame. He enjoyed basketball and had a regularly scheduled game once a week with his fellow research assistants. That, and weekend co-ed flag football contests, kept his flexibility, endurance, and hand-eye coordination sharp. He spent five years after college working with a small pharmaceutical company prior to the firm being absorbed by a larger conglomerate. At that point, he decided to pursue a graduate education at Harvard and soon landed the gig as Ada's research assistant.

His cousin, Melinda, was about the same age, around thirty years old, and in similarly good physical shape but not so much from sports as from her interest in archeology, spending many months each year in the field, often in harsh conditions. She was not particularly tall, about five feet, two inches, with sun-bleached brown hair and a physical quickness sharpened by her practice of martial arts. This activity was chosen not from paranoia but more from a sense that she wanted to be able to take care of herself if something went sideways on one of her frequent field trips to remote locations, often in the presence of other researchers she did not meet until she arrived at a particular site.

Melinda had planned to marry in her early twenties but the engagement ended as she slowly realized her future mate, Howard, was actually boring to be around for any extended time. He had little interest in learning about other cultures or, frankly, anyone different from those he had grown up with. The one time they traveled to Europe together, he continually complained about the different foods that were available and longed to return to a familiar environment. She couldn't believe that while spending a few days in Paris, of all cool places, he couldn't wait to leave. Among the many experiences he complained about was the rudeness of the French. Maybe they did seem rude to him, she thought at the time, but that was in reaction to his behavior that did not work in his favor with the locals. He would sit in a cozy, Left Bank bistro, talking to her in a disturbingly loud voice, frustrated because he couldn't find something resembling a burger and fries on the menu. He would keep his little ball cap on while he ate with the brim turned backwards and turn up his nose at the small demitasse cups a strong, after-meal espresso was served in.

The breaking point for Melinda came when she had arranged a romantic dinner at Le Jules Verne on the second level of the Eiffel Tower. She donned a very *haute couture* outfit she had purchased earlier at a fabulous women's wear shop, called Eva, on the Boulevard Saint-Germain earlier that day. Howard insisted on wearing pants he insisted were "designer jeans." Her guess was that they were designed in a high school sewing class by fourteen-year-olds. He couldn't speak French and didn't spend any time trying to pick up a few words from an English-to-French dictionary for tourists she brought on the trip for him. He seemed to think if he spoke *very* slowly and distinctly with a *very* loud voice, surely the Jules Verne *sommelier*, who had arrived at their table after they were seated, would understand him. Melinda quickly saw by the wine steward's facial expression that she indeed understood English quite well.

But with Howard speaking to her as if she were stupid, she refused to acknowledge she understood and instead pointed to the most expensive wine, smiling, and repeating *"oui, oui"* as though she was acknowledging that he agreed with the wine she was pointing to. She then turned and left to place the outrageously expensive order. Since that ill-fated relationship, Melinda had yet to return to the dating scene.

* * *

As Ada, Joel, and Melinda gathered that morning at the hospital, their enthusiasm and excitement were palpable. Ada, being the senior member of the now forming team, started with a declaration, "When do we leave!" followed by a hearty chorus from the other two.

"Immediately!"

Which was quickly followed up by Joel with a sheepishly quizzical, "Where exactly are we going?"

Ada clarified, "Well, we certainly need to flesh out our plan of action before we pack our bags. My thought is that we start with the University of Salamanca library, then we travel north to Avebury in England to check out the stone circle and the village. I think what we learn from those visits will shape our thinking for the next steps. Since this pandemic is showing no signs of letting up, actually just the opposite, I think we should be on our way as soon as we possibly can. I've already arranged with my dean to take a leave of absence and, between us, we arranged for someone to take over my classes."

Joel then spoke up, "Since I work for you, I suppose I'm covered for the trip."

This was followed by Melinda smiling and adding, "I jumped to a conclusion right after our dinner meeting that this is what we would be doing. So, I have been on the phone with my folks at work and arranged for a substitute to cover my research assistant and teaching duties. I hope you won't be upset with me but I took the liberty of contacting Thomas White, the linguist I told you about. I gave him a brief—but somewhat vague—intimation that I might be returning to Salamanca for another look at the rare manuscripts and asked if he might be available to accompany me. If that's okay with you and Joel, I'll check back with him and firm up a commitment for him to accompany us as well as fill him in on who you are and more about what we are planning."

"It seems to me that his skill set will be invaluable to us, so I say, yes. Okay, with you Joel?" Ada asked.

"Absolutely."

"That's good then," Melinda began to show her excitement. "Just so you know, in addition to being a talented linguist, Thomas is also a student of ancient cultures, cultures whose history was passed down through the generations by word of mouth before ever being recorded in a written language. Sharing his insights into ancient cultures helped me better understand the true intent of the messages of the ancients that were recorded many generations after they had passed away. Based on his understanding of those long-gone peoples, he has an uncanny knack for seeing what others miss in old manuscripts, clouded by time, multiple retellings, and translated from one language to another before being recorded in written form."

"Alright then," Ada confirmed. "Melinda, will you make hotel arrangements in Madrid and Salamanca since you have been there before? I'll line up the air travel from here to Madrid, then we will rent a car and make the drive west to Salamanca."

Melinda interrupted her with a suggestion. "Just for fun, the route we will take goes through Segovia, about half way to Salamanca. When we get there, I would like us to stop at a restaurant that is known for their specialty, young roast pig, *cochinillo asaado*, that maybe sounds unappetizing to our American ears but their presentation of this regional dish is actually quite fabulous. The restaurant is located on the north side of the road and adjacent to an old Roman aqueduct that is still in place spanning the space between two small hills on either side. That alone is worth the stop to see."

"I like that idea. I'm looking forward to it already," responded Ada.

Then she informed them, "I convinced my dean to provide me with a small research grant to at least cover this part of our planned trip, so Melinda, I'll pick up the tab on what we have discussed so far." Addressing them all, she added, "This is Monday. When do you think we can leave?"

After discussing many details about what each needed to accomplish, they decided on Thursday of the following week for departure. After going over a few finer points concerning what they each needed to pack for the trip, how many days they should plan to be away, and a time for a virtual coordination call on Friday, the meeting adjourned.

Chapter 5

2035 CE
SPAIN

THE RESEARCH AND TRAVEL PARTY, NOW numbering four as Melinda's talented young linguist, Thomas, had enthusiastically agreed to join the group, had successfully organized the trip, and departed on the first leg of their journey on Thursday, only ten days after they had made their decision to go. In the early hours of Friday morning, they arrived in Madrid, having endured a night flight with little sleep over the Atlantic. After arranging for a rental car, they checked in to the Hotel Madrid Alameda Aeropuerto as soon as their rooms were ready and all took a long nap to acclimate to the time change and exhaustion from the flight. That evening, they had dinner in the hotel restaurant and went to bed early.

The next morning, they regrouped for a light breakfast in the hotel, saving themselves room for *cochinillo asaado* in Segovia. They were now convinced by Melinda it would be worth their time. They climbed in their rented Ateca compact SUV, a product of the Spanish motor company, SEAT, and departed for Salamanca. The drive would be about two hours and forty-five minutes but the stop in Segovia would add nearly two hours to their journey. But this lunch diversion would still get them to Salamanca early enough to check in their hotel, meet with Melinda's local contact, have dinner, and be ready to go to the University's library on Sunday to gain access to the rare book archives.

After arriving in Segovia and partaking of the *cochinillo*, which everyone agreed was even better than advertised by Melinda, Thomas went outside to take a closer look at the amazing Roman aqueduct. He wanted to see firsthand the skill and care that it took to design and build this enormous structure, with the stonework so perfectly cut that no mortar was necessary to bind the stones together. The trough on top of the aqueduct that originally carried water across the space between two hills, now contained a modern pipe that had been laid in the trough to carry the town's potable water. His knowledge that the structure was constructed *sans* mortar led him to jokingly caution the driver of their SUV, Melinda, to be careful driving under it as they left the restaurant and continued their journey to Salamanca. "I don't want you to wreck into it and have tons of rock crashing down on us!" This resulted in a not-too-easy punch to his shoulder.

CHAPTER 6

2200 BCE
EARTH

ANDROMEDA IS 2.5 MILLION LIGHT YEARS from Earth. Traveling at the speed of light, it would take a craft 2.5 million years to get to Earth from Andromeda—not remotely reasonable. The Golan scientists had learned that within the universe, there exists a dimension, unseen, unmeasurable, but there nonetheless, that had not been discovered by scientists before. They had studied the curious phenomenon of virtual particles, such as gluons, disappearing and reappearing. It would be the *same* particle, coming and going, not simply one disappearing and a new one appearing. So, where did it go to and come back from? That led them to theorize about an unknown dimension that could be that place. Further study over several generations of Golan scientists led to the revelation of an astounding fact about that dimension: *it was devoid of time and space*. A particle going in and, *in the same instant*, coming back out but at a distance removed, led to the conclusion that no time existed during the travel inside the dimension. This also meant that the distance traveled was irrelevant, distance being a concept that doesn't exist in that dimension.

Later study and experimentation in the realm of particle physics led the scientists to understand that a vessel made of a unique combination of electromagnetic energy, sensitivity to light photons and gravitational waves, could be used to pierce the unseen barrier into this dimension having no time or space and then instantly reappear in a spot programmed to receive it, based on instructions for the destination being a map of nuances in light emitted by cosmic entities and the relative strength of gravitational waves at the intended destination. In their research, Golan scientists used massive computing technology and power sources far beyond anything developed on other planets in their observable universe.

The directions in the program they developed were limited to line-of-sight calculations that considered light bending by the gravitational pull of large objects, stars, planets, and so on. However, if the view of a destination star or a planet was completely blocked from a direct line of sight, the scientists planned for transmission of a transport vessel be done in two stages. The first stage would get it to a point within a few million miles of the target whose visibility has been blocked but at an oblique angle from the target so it would then be visible to the vessel. Then, the program was designed to recalculate using the direct visual line on the target.

The next step for the Golan scientists was to design and construct an appropriate vehicle to transport living creatures. They developed a spherical container, composed of a localized and powerful gravitational field, combined with an embedded electromagnetic energy, to contain the elusive particles and their comings and goings within the thickness of the gravitational skin of the sphere. The scientists introduced computing functions contained within the sphere's skin for navigating the craft. When arriving at the final destination of the voyage, the central programming included instructions for calculating a precise spot for a reappearance of the sphere at the specified target location. These calculations included input data at the location regarding altitude, breathable atmosphere, water, solids, and habitable temperatures so as to ensure the craft would reappear just a foot above solid ground and not in water or other situations unconducive to life; such as in a wall of rock or in a tree trunk.

The final product, a vehicle capable of carrying living beings on the journey, would depart the trip's point of origin and arrive at the destination virtually instantaneously, even at a distance, measured by realities in this dimension, six light years away. Instantaneously, other than the few milliseconds needed to appear, the vehicle could recalculate if the journey was a two-stage trip, and disappear into the subject dimension again prior to arriving at the destination.

The integrity of the sphere's structure designed and developed for use by Aiela and his companions had unanticipated vulnerabilities. One of those was the difference in Earth's atmosphere from what was expected and the second was the unusual electromagnetic energy around the final target site derived by the onboard central brain's second calculation that sent them to a spot near present-day Avebury. These unexpected conditions had a corrosive effect on the sensitive gravitational field unique to the sphere's skin. Over a relatively short time, the sphere simply dissipated into the space around it. The scientists on Golan did not predict these two variables in their design of the sphere.

The travelers from Golan could not comprehend the reason for the failure but it was quite obvious to them that an irreparable failure had occurred. After some emotional back and forth, the landing party understood they were on Earth to stay. With the stunned group reaching that conclusion, Aiela laid out a plan for the immediate future.

"The supply of food we brought with us will last two days at most. That becomes our timeline for beginning our transitioning to this planet. Our scientists and astronomers back on Golan determined that the conditions on this planet were conducive to life similar to ours, including the likely existence of humanoid creatures. Based on what we have already seen with the stone structure we are standing in, the passageway leading to it, and the humanoid footprints we see, I believe their assumptions were correct. I'll go so far as to say they are essentially like us unless we learn otherwise."

Aiela continued, "We need to reconnoiter the nearest human

habitation we can find, without being observed, to verify this hypothesis. Anticipating our assumption would be correct, or at least reasonably close, we brought a handheld device with translation capabilities. All we need to do is to allow the device to record enough of their speech to decipher the patterns, inflections, and repetitions until it can create something akin to a dictionary for us with a pronunciation guide. Our training with this translator device before we left Golan should allow us to be reasonably proficient in a short time. We will cover the difference in our speech as the locals will hear it for a while with the guise that we are travelers from a distant land on this planet. Not perfect … but it should buy us some time."

Lieka spoke next. "We need to observe what the people clothe themselves with here. Is it some manner of cloth, animal skins, or something else? Then we need to find a way to appropriate enough of these coverings for us to wear as we make our first appearance to them as travelers from far away. Our numbers are too great, at twelve, to do this clandestinely, so we will send a scouting group of four of us out tonight under cover of darkness to see what we can accomplish. The rest of you will devise a camouflaged, temporary base camp a half mile from this place and wait for our return. With Aiela's approval, the four will be me, Aiela, our crew member, Abeda, carrying the translator device, and Liebeda, who has the skills to move quickly, silently, and almost invisibly in low light conditions. If the opportunity presents itself, she will help me in acquiring and carrying any supplies and clothing we can scavenge. Abeda's task, in addition to getting language samples for the translator, will be to use his talents in assessing this new environment we are in and informing our medical officer of everything he learns on his return."

"Good plan, Lieka," the commander confirmed. "As it is already dusk, we will leave shortly and be back here before sunrise."

The medical officer then spoke up with some not-so-good news. "Five of our team have developed an illness in this new environment that I have not yet been able to diagnose for prescribing a treatment. It came on rapidly, only in the last two hours. The good news is that no one else is showing any of the same symptoms yet."

"Do what you can for them, doctor, and keep an eye on everybody else for similar symptoms. Maybe you will have some idea what caused this sudden illness by the time we return before morning light."

With that, the four members of the scouting team gathered up what they needed and headed for a hilltop not too far away, beginning their first night in this alien place searching for anything that might give them a visual clue as to which direction a place inhabited by the locals might be found.

CHAPTER 7

2035 CE
SPAIN

DURING THE DRIVE FROM SEGOVIA TO Salamanca, Ada, who was now being called Doc by her companions, turned the conversation to getting to know the newest member of the team, Thomas, the linguist. "We know you have a facility for languages and an interest in the cultures of ancient civilizations, Thomas, but what else interests you? I've noticed that even when we were eating, though you were engaged in the conversation, some part of you was always alert to what was going on around us, even to the activities you could see from the window into the parking area." Even though she was their leader, there was a growing sense of equality, something they believed to be important for their mission. Each one brought an essential but different skill and knowledge base to the effort. In a sense, Doc was becoming thought of as "first among equals."

Thomas sat quietly for a few moments before answering. "I spent some time in my childhood in an orphanage. My parents were not married, my mother was very young, with no family support or job to support us. My dad was, frankly, irresponsible, refused to marry my mother, and split, never to be seen again. My mother was desperate. She saw our future as two homeless people in New York City and did not believe she would survive very long in that environment. Looking back on it, I think it probably broke her heart to do it but through private assistance services, she arranged for me to go to an orphanage. I learned later that her fears were realized as she did end up homeless and was found dead in an alley one winter Sunday morning by police officers responding to an anonymous tip."

Doc saw a wetness beginning to form in his eyes, and tried to change the subject. Thomas told her it was okay, he wanted to finish the story.

"The orphanage was run rather well, as orphanages go, I guess, but it was understaffed and so often there were times when us kids were left unsupervised. Being one of the youngest there and not as big or strong as the older ones, it was not uncommon for me to be the recipient of taunts and physical abuse from the older boys and occasionally the older girls. I was afraid to report any of this behavior as I was pretty sure that if I did, the kids would make my life a living hell. I learned to be keenly situationally aware; I became very good at reading the clues from body language and the tiniest changes in facial expressions that would signal a danger to me. I suppose I never lost the need to be aware of my surroundings and keep my guard up. Oddly, that indoctrination has made me feel almost clairvoyant. It's like an early warning bell goes off in my head as I sense someone's intent is to do me harm. But strangely, it also allows me to anticipate benign actions of others as well. Weird, I suppose, but there it is."

"I'm sorry to hear the painful background to this sense you have developed but, on the other hand, you have a gift that can serve you well and may indeed turn out to be helpful to us on our current quest," Doc reassured him.

Shortly afterwards, the team arrived in Salamanca and made their way to a small hotel near the city center and the Plaza Mayor. Melinda called her contact, a man she had gotten to know on her earlier visit to Salamanca who, with his family, owned and operated a jewelry store not far from their hotel. The man, *Señor* Javier Fernandez, invited them to come by his shop after the traditional siesta time and then accompany his family to dinner that night.

When they arrived at his shop, he gave his friend Melinda a big hug, followed by the same from his wife, Maria. Introductions were made all around by a smiling Melinda, followed by a "get-to-know-you" conversation.

Señor Fernandez, a distinguished looking gentleman, about fifty-five years of age with silver highlights starting to grow in his immaculately-brushed black hair, raised his arms with his palms out and exclaimed, "My old friend and my new friends, I can't let you leave my humble shop without a gift!" At which point it was apparently not the first time he had made such an offer to guests because his wife brought a hand from behind her back holding four silver stick pins, featuring the Spanish Salamanca charro button, or *el boton charro*, a traditional button with the central silver bead representing Salamanca surrounded by eight smaller silver beads representing the eight *comarcas*, or districts, that compose Salamanca.

The folklore around the *boton* was explained by *Señor* Fernandez. "It serves as a protective amulet for one choosing to wear it. You will no doubt see it displayed in rings, necklaces, stickpins, or other jewelry worn by the locals you see at dinner tonight. You may also see it adorning the attire of some of our many tourists but they will have no doubt purchased it from one of our shops, hopefully mine! They will just think of it as a little bright, shiny souvenir they acquired on holiday. I have no scientific basis for this but I think the protective power of the boton is only energized by those who believe."

Quite an appropriate gift for what they were undertaking, both Doc and Melinda thought. They were already contemplating a plan far beyond what their comrades believed they had signed up for. However, both kept their thinking to themselves.

Dinner that night, hosted by the Fernandez family, was a little different from what they had experienced in Boston. Arriving at their restaurant location, they in their Ateca, *Señor* Fernandez and

Maria arriving in their black Mercedes, or *coche*, as they referred to it, all entered the front door of the restaurant.

At first glance around the interior of the restaurant, the American party was somewhat surprised. They were thinking it would be something unusual but the place looked like any ordinary restaurant, a little larger perhaps, but not inspiring in their quick look around. It was evident that this spot was on the list of places tourists to Salamanca would frequent. They didn't see many diners who appeared to be local citizens.

Señor Fernandez stifled a smile at their reaction. This was all part of the show he had planned. The first one through the door, after a slight hesitation for the group to assemble inside and get a look around, he stood there in his immaculately-tailored black suit and motioned with an outstretched arm for them to follow him to one side of the dining area to a nondescript door. Opening it, he led them down a flight of stairs that opened into another dining room below the one on the first floor. A smiling host met them on landing, who grasped Señor Fernandez outstretched hand in a friendly grip while giving Maria a quick kiss on both cheeks as was customary among friends.

The Americans quickly realized the Fernandez family were regulars and had arranged for a table for them in the middle of the basement dining area. They also quickly saw there were no tourists in sight down here. The place was filled with what they could only surmise were the people who lived here in lovely Salamanca. The table conversations they could hear all around them were lively, happy, and imbued with a sense of familiarity that could only come from a tight-knit community that frequently saw each other here on Saturday nights.

"Wow," exclaimed Doc, followed by a quick "This is so cool!" coming from Joel.

"I hope you won't mind but I've taken the liberty to have the owner tell his staff to take care of us—no need for menus tonight!"

their host explained.

Shortly after that declaration came a parade of servers with appetizers, water, bottomless pitchers of Sangria and then, a little later, the main course—if it could be called that as it was actually a sampler of all the restaurant's special dishes. After more than an hour of feasting, interrupted only by great conversation and repeated compliments for the superb culinary delights, desserts came in an endless stream, each more delicious than the last.

Finally, about 11:00 p.m. or so, Doc declared it time to call an end to the beautiful evening. With a big grin, *Señor* Fernandez, suggested that they all head over to the Plaza Mayor for dancing, where all of the other restaurant patrons were heading.

"Thanks for the invitation," an amazed Doc responded, "But we need to get back to our hotel to get our beauty rest. Big day for us tomorrow."

As they were driving back to the hotel, Thomas, being a linguist and student of ancient cultures, observed, "I was thinking back over our restaurant experience tonight. If we had not been the guests of *Señor* Fernandez, our night out would have been that of the average tourist, nothing at all like what we experienced. However, because we were taken under the wing of a local, we saw a side of Salamanca that few outsiders see. That is a lesson for us tomorrow as we review the ancient parchments and read about life in an older time—reading just what someone wrote, perhaps only a version for tourists. We need to read between the lines and watchful we don't take what we read literally—but instead have the presence of mind to understand the information may only be a surface view of a deeper reality."

⋯⊷⊶⊷⊷

Chapter 8

2200 BCE
EARTH

As Aiela and Lieka reached their destination hilltop with the two others, Abeda and Liebeda, night had fallen and darkness was upon them. Pausing as they reached the top, Aiela and Lieka looked up at the heavens. Puzzled, and then alarmed, they saw a totally alien starscape. Lieka spoke first. "Umm ... unless I am hallucinating, if we are six light years from Golan, I would expect the night sky to be different but this is *completely* different! I see *nothing* familiar."

Aiela was still staring, transfixed into the night sky. After a full minute of silence, the commander replied with what was becoming quite obvious to all four of them. "Something went very wrong with our transport here. We are not on the planet in our galaxy that was supposed to be our destination. And not only are we not on that planet but it appears we're not even in the same star system as our Golan. Based on what we are seeing or, better put, *not* seeing, we are way, way farther than six light years from Golan.

"We seem to be fortunate that the miscalculation, or whatever it was, still allowed us to land on a planet similar to the one we had targeted. We were mistaken as to our location when we landed since the atmosphere and the gravity on this planet was what we expected. Now, I'm worried that the illness five of our crew are experiencing is a result of some other difference in this place that was not accounted for."

Lieka responded, "Yes, and I said earlier today that we were here to stay because our Golan scientists would not be able to send a rescue expedition for us because our sphere unexpectedly disintegrated, leaving us without the planned way back and no way to communicate what happened. It seems now that it is even worse than that. They have no idea where in the entire universe we might be."

The stunned party of four, reeling from the dawning reality that they would never return to Golan and the lives they left behind, sat on the hilltop, lost in their individual thoughts, gazing at the stars above them. After a time, Aiela slowly came to the realization that his role as a leader of this expedition had abruptly ended. He was suddenly only the nominal leader of not a scientific team but a group of shocked individuals who were showing the beginning signs of fear and panic.

He knew he must not reveal his own fears to the others. His role as their leader was intact for the moment but, only if, in the next few critical minutes, he could summon control of his emotions and demonstrate that he was capable of continuing as their leader in a new mission—not the scientific mission they all envisioned but a mission of survival on this alien planet.

As Aiela was contemplating his next move, he noticed Lieka looking at him in a strange, calm way. He pulled her away from the other two so they wouldn't be overheard.

"You look like you are about to say something. Something that will help, I hope," he added.

Lieka shook her head slightly. "I'm thinking about a lot of things, most of which can wait. But for now, as your second in command, I think you and I must maintain control of our scouting mission—and quickly. No doubt the others at base camp will be looking at the sky and coming to the same conclusions we have. They will have to deal with it on their own temporarily. Our medical officer is there. She is accustomed to dealing with emotionally upset people in her line of work so my sense is she will keep some order until we return. For us, as I see it, the immediate goal should be to complete this investigative expedition and learn as much as we can about what is around us, including putting eyes on some of the locals."

Aiela took in a deep breath, instinctively testing the strange oxygen pressure on his body. "I agree. We have the advantage of darkness for several more hours. Let's get the most out of it we can, then head back to the base camp and use what we learn tonight to develop a plan to blend into the local environment, whatever we determine it to be!"

The two of them moved back within earshot of the others and as they did, Aiela spotted a dim light in the distance. He explained their need for haste in learning what they could before daylight and said he would share with them his understanding of the situation as they double-timed their pace toward the light.

About an hour after they set out, they could see that the light was from a small wood fire in the center of five structures that was clearly occupied by indigenous life. As they closed in, slowing their approach and then finally crawling through low, purple-and-green-colored vegetation that grew about two feet above the ground, they were rewarded with a decent view of four or five humanoid-looking creatures, some sitting, one standing tending the fire, and one of short stature that most likely was a child. The small structures were round, with walls that appeared to be only about two-feet high but with tall, thatched roofs above that would give adequate head height inside.

The walls appeared to be made from bent tree limbs that had obviously been carried in from some other place as there were no trees in sight. These limbs, interlaced to form the round walls, had grasses and other vegetation woven around and through the limbs. What looked like moistened earth mixed with some other unknown material had been daubed onto the entire exterior of the walls, protected to some extent from rain by the overhang of the thatched roof.

Almost inaudibly, Aiela whispered to Lieka. "This looks promising. From what I can see, these locals look very much like us, though their clothing is different. It appears to be made from animal skins and some primitive looking cloth."

Turning to Abeda, their tech with the translation device, Aiela instructed him to silently move in a little closer and record enough of the local inhabitants' speech to allow the device to be able to convert the words into the Golan language. Hopefully, it would produce a primitive teaching program to help them learn to speak the local language, even if only in a very limited and rudimentary fashion. When it came time to meet these creatures, the cover story they had planned to relay—that they were travelers from a distant tribe whose native speech was a little different—should buy them some time if they could pull it off.

After about an hour of laying completely still and recording the native's conversations, Abeda silently crawled back in the darkness to his companions.

"I thought once or twice the young one somehow sensed my presence but didn't act on it. Made me quite conscious of myself. Anyway, I have recorded enough to have what we need. Let's go."

The four of them began a slow crawl back the way they had come until it was safe to stand and begin jogging back to their base camp.

"Liebeda," Lieka said to her stealthy crewmember who was along to confiscate some local clothes and supplies, "you could never have infiltrated that small village, illuminated by their fire, tonight. We will need to come up with some other means of clothing ourselves to blend in. However, we did learn much about the locals, their dress, and their language, so I call our mission a success."

＊ ＊ ＊

They were back sometime after midnight, finding everyone awake and excited to hear what they had learned. After the relieved greetings on their return were finished, the medical officer, Kala, informed them of some bad news. The five crew members who had taken ill had only gotten worse in their absence. Kala said she only had some simple pain-relieving drops she had brought along to offer them. Her opinion was that the atmosphere on this planet was not allowing them to absorb the oxygen they needed, even though the percentage of oxygen on this planet was greater than found on Golan. It seems, she opined, their particular DNA was just different enough from the other travelers to be a fatal mismatch with this planet. The others in the party were not experiencing the same oxygen absorption problem. She said that if she had access to the medical equipment in her clinic in Golan, she could probably find a way to help the ill ones, but not here.

Further, Kala informed them, "When we embarked on this scientific mission, the plan was to be here no more than two weeks. Without recharge, the stored energy in my medical devices will be depleted about two weeks after that. In our planning before we left Golan, we believed the extra two weeks of compacted fuel pellets were a good safety margin. I suspect our other technical devices that we brought along will suffer the same fate about four weeks from now."

"I agree, Kala," responded Aiela. "Our translator equipment is one of those devices. We will need to use it to learn the language of the local population as quickly as we can. I'm sure there are other languages on this planet but this one will give us the start we need and we will have that completed well before the translator equipment becomes useless."

Turning to the others, Aiela reminded them of the primitive nature of the local culture. "When the energy powering the translator is depleted—along with the medical equipment and any other sophisticated tools we brought with us from Golan—we must destroy all of it, leaving no trace. Universally, people are suspicious of things they don't understand. I don't expect the inhabitants on this planet to be any different. If something alien is examined and its purpose and composition can't be explained in a factual way, then, and maybe this is an evolutionary survival trait, unless something can be deemed safe, it is a danger. Our tools will not be understood and, since they belong to us, the suspicion will encompass us as well as the tools. I repeat, this means when our tools are no longer usable when their energy is depleted and it's the same for any other devices or equipment that might seem strange to the indigenous population, we must destroy them, leaving no evidence behind. It could mean our lives since we don't know how violent they might become when sensing a threat. In fact, even if we had a way to reenergize our tools, it would still be in our best interest to have them disappear soon."

One of the crew members who had taken ill brought up the topic on all of their minds; "Why are we here and not on the planet we were programmed to land on?" As she was articulating that question, there was a uniform mumbling of agreement with that question from the others. Aiela opened his mouth but before he could speak, Kala, unofficially the closest member of the surviving team to be a science officer, spoke first.

"I've been thinking about that question all night and I believe I know what happened. Our planned flight path from Golan to our target planet six light years away involved a two-step process. The target programming for our journey required a direct line of sight to our target. The target planet, it was referred to as planet 'x' in briefings, so I'll call it 'x,' was not in a direct line of sight from our departure point on Golan. After we entered the dimension being used by our scientists to provide relatively instantaneous transport, our programming required an exit at a point that would give the required direct line of sight to the target—planet x. Then, the central input processor—what I often call the brain of the sphere—

recalibrated to send us to x, having the necessary direct line of sight. When that was done, we went back into the timeless dimension for the second and last leg of the journey.

Kala then came to her conclusion. "Well, here is where the plan went awry. The Golan scientists described the target using what they knew of the planet's size, atmosphere, gravity, and other descriptors. This information was fed into our sphere's brain. After the first leg of the journey was complete, going into the dimension and then popping out at a point for the recalibration to the target, what was not anticipated was that in the same general direction as x, there was another planet that met the programmed parameters more precisely than planet x. Since time and distance are not existing concepts in the dimension that allowed us to travel here, the recalibration was literal in complying with the description of the target, and since this planet was a better fit, we ended up here. The difference in time and distance was irrelevant to the recalculation since those concepts didn't exist in this dimension. So, here we are, on a planet apparently millions of light years from Golan, not six light years."

Aiela, still asserting his leadership status with the crew, agreed with Kala's explanation of what had happened and suggested they all get some needed rest for the remainder of the night. After appointing two of the crew to alternate watch for the rest of the dark hours and speaking some words of comfort to those who had taken sick, he asked Lieka to meet with him to develop their plan of action to begin when dawn broke.

Walking slowly away from the others in the direction of the strange stone circles, Lieka figured this was the moment to reveal why she had been appointed as his second in command prior to their departure.

"At first, I was surprised by that decision, which was made by the project leaders without my input," slowly offered Aiela, "But you seemed competent and knowledgeable regarding our mission, so, while I was offended by not being involved, I decided not to object."

Lieka, feeling uncomfortable but considering the circumstances in which they found themselves, needed to be forthcoming. As they continued strolling into the starlit night, she began telling Aiela what he needed to know, including her background and reason for her selection.

"This interplanetary mission we trained for was, in fact, a scientific mission to study planet x, gather data on its atmosphere, indigenous life, and all of the other details we could glean in a two-week mission. What was not known to the science committee and our immediate bosses, was the military interest in our findings. They were interested in the same things our science bosses were but for a different purpose."

She stopped in front of him and looked at him squarely. "As you are aware, Aiela, Golan has a strong military, a military that only grew stronger as the different, previously independent, regions on Golan created a planetwide federation. This all occurred after Golan was repeatedly surveilled at a distance by other civilizations in our galaxy, generating a plausible case that the greatest threat was not internal but instead posed from external forces. Over time, the military leadership of the strongest region on Golan convinced the other nations that for planetary survival, they should consolidate their national military forces in the new federation under one unified command to better counter the threat from alien forces. This induced fear proved to be strong enough to convince the competing forces on Golan to put their differences aside and agree to create one global, unified military command to combat the perceived external threat."

In an extensive explanation, Lieka revealed information to the commander that was clearly of a high-knowledge level. As she spoke, in his mind he was turning over all the details she was sharing. Some he was aware of but other nuances covered new ground for him to absorb.

Concurrent with this action of a unified command, she claimed, was growing concern that Golan was becoming overpopulated and would soon outgrow its ability to sustain life in its present state. The political and military leadership did not want to deal with this problem in any way that would require changes to the status quo, changes that would lead to upheaval in the political and military leadership. An upheaval that would result in the current leadership risking loss of control of the world's economy and with it their ability to continue to enrich themselves beyond imagination.

The top military leaders met with their political counterparts in the strongest nations comprising the Golan federation to come up with a plan to retain their positions and wealth. The *secret* solution they agreed to was expanding to other planets, eliminating the inhabitants to make room for colonization, relieving pressure on Golan, and keeping them in charge. This Golan Interplanetary Council, or GIC, *publicly* fostered the idea that Golan needed to explore other sparsely inhabited planets that could be a new home for many of Golan's citizens. A relief valve, so to speak, for the growing home planet population. This was a reasonable action in the public's view. However, the secret plan was to find another planet that could be militarily conquered and ruled by the GIC. But the story concocted and sold to everyone outside of the small political and military group of planners was that planet x was one of the planets that could be peacefully settled by Golans. But they needed more information to be sure. The cover story for the collection of that information would be a visit to that planet under the guise of a scientific mission, carried out by a science-based entity ignorant of the true reason for the expedition.

"That science mission is us," Lieka stressed. I'm the only one on this crew who knows the true reason for us being here. The scientists on the mission were to believe that theirs was an information gathering expedition, to be done quickly and clandestinely so as to not unnecessarily alarm any indigenous population encountered. Of course, all this was with peaceful intent. However, that information

could give confirmation to the leadership that the planet could be easily conquered and they would then initiate final planning for a strike, with devastating consequences for the population there."

She then said something that shocked Aiela. "When our crew on this mission returned to Golan, I'm sure all of us would be eliminated, including me, even though I had been promised otherwise. That would allow the leadership to announce to Golan's population that planet x was suitable for peaceful colonization with no one from our mission to contradict them. One of the many terrible consequences of their plan would not only be the elimination of a majority of x's population but enslavement of the survivors—all under the pretext of happily discovering a new land to support Golan's growing population."

Aiela's tone turned very serious. "This information is fascinating and horrifying. So, I think you are leading up to sharing with me your involvement in all of this?"

"Yes, and here it is," Lieka shuffled a bit and tried to steady her voice. "My credentials as a scientist and value to this mission were all fabricated. I am a colonel in the armed forces under the command of the GIC. I saw combat in many bad places prior to all of the different nations of Golan consolidating their military forces under a unified command. I was chosen for this mission as a cover to assess the conditions, on the ground, so to speak, for our strike, hitting them before they could mount any type of meaningful defense. The data our so-called science mission was to collect would be invaluable knowledge for use in preparing our strike force with appropriate gear and training for an invasion. The transport we used, our sphere, was developed by the military, not a peaceful group of scientists as you were led to believe. It was a prototype and we were the test subjects to evaluate how it worked. Based on our experiment, if it were successful, the military would complete plans already underway to construct much larger vessels to ferry troops and equipment, incorporating design modifications based on what they learned from our mission."

Aiela inwardly was outraged but tried to temper his emotions as a leader should. "This is incredible! I find it hard to believe you would consent to be a part of this horror show that is unfolding! And keeping this mission-critical information from me is nothing short of betrayal and collusion. I have good reason to confine you to quarters on the spot. What possessed you to be a part of this?"

"I know this may be difficult for you to absorb. And, believe me, there were plenty of times I wanted to tell you the truth," Lieka's tone became sharper. "The short answer is blackmail. I told you I had participated in many combat actions before the world's militaries were consolidated under the GIC. One of my earlier assignments, years ago, was fighting in an area controlled by the future deputy director of the GIC. In that action, I was the platoon leader leading an attack on an enemy headquarters. In the command structure we were attacking was a man named Gerrd, a general in their army. Gerrd was the brother of the future deputy. The resistance in the firefight was intense and, as we broke through the outer perimeter of their HQ, I was the one who fired the shot that killed Gerrd."

She continued. "A few short years later, after all of the consolidation I told you about, the GIC deputy director had gained access to all of our after-action reports which were now housed with the GIC. The deputy found out it was me who had killed his brother. Enraged, he was determined to have revenge but was prevented from doing anything about it by his boss, the supreme director. The supreme director saw a chance to use me for this mission. He had learned of my combat abilities and leadership qualities, so he decided to leverage this knowledge to his benefit. I was called in to a secret meeting with the two of them. I was given the choice of a life sentence at hard labor in a prison camp that was legendary in its reputation. Inmates sent there endured inhumane conditions until they finally died an agonizing death from the constant brutal labor that slowly drained the life from their bodies. I was given the choice of that short future, or accepting this assignment with the inducement that if I returned with sufficient, actionable intel, I would be spared internment in the death camp. Instead, I would be given an assignment in a safe, but remote place, with the promise that if I ever revealed any of this, they would do something to me even worse than the death camp."

Now things were beginning to make more sense to Aiela. Still, he had a growing suspicion that Lieka sabotaged their mission—destroying the sphere on purpose—so she would not have to face the consequences of a return to Golan. "I need a little time to absorb this revelation and understand what it means for our future on this planet," he said abruptly and turned on her to be alone with his thoughts.

"Well, Aiela, you may now understand why I'm not upset as the others are at the prospect of never returning to Golan," she called after him. "When I accepted this assignment, I knew I could not return and use what I would have learned to facilitate what could only be described as a crime of unimaginable proportions. So, I decided my best option was to pretend to go along until I could find a way out. If I chose not to go along with them, I knew they would have killed me and they would have found someone else who would have been fine doing their bidding. I also suspected that the choice of going along with them would only delay my execution as I would most likely be killed after the crew was debriefed when we returned to Golan. I knew their promises to take care of me when I returned were false. I was a dead woman walking. So, now, here I am with you, out of their reach. The hard fact that we are missing will derail their plans. As I said, our ship was the prototype for larger ships to ferry troops and supplies. As far as they are concerned, the prototype has disappeared without a trace and they have absolutely zero idea why. The plan to invade planet x under false pretenses has failed."

Then Lieka added with a grim smile, "It appears, like awaking from a horrible dream, I have escaped the nightmare and can live a free life, in a place unknown to those in my past."

Aiela looked at her with contempt, though he felt her anguish in having to face an impossible situation, too. *Does she care nothing for the damning predicament she put me and her fellow passengers in?* He headed back to camp at a steady pace.

Lieka thought it best to linger behind, letting him think through all that she had said and hoping she had not been mistaken in trusting him. She had a sense of both relief and dread.

As he walked, Aiela's mind wrestled with conflicting thoughts. He had been appointed commander of this expedition with a crew assigned to him that he was unfamiliar with and that included Lieka. Should he believe all that she had just unloaded on him? Should he simply trust that she was telling him the truth about the real purpose of this mission? If all she said was true, he was feeling a rising anger, not only at being misled by her but for both of them being used by those who appointed him to lead this expedition.

Back at camp, Aiela decided that his focus must turn to what was necessary to their survival on this alien planet. He could not let his questions and doubts cloud his judgement. He decided that his best course of action was to continue to rely on Lieka as his second in command for the time being. Instinctively, he knew her support was critical for what he would decide to do next. And, to her credit, he was impressed by what he had seen in her demeanor and her obvious experience in leadership on this mission so far. But he was far from trusting her yet.

>•)ↈ··

CHAPTER 9

2035 CE
SPAIN

THE PARTY OF FOUR WERE FINALLY in the University of Salamanca archives with Melinda and Thomas leading the way. They quickly found the document they were looking for. Thomas located the page with the Ghost Flower drawn in the margin. Doc asked him to interpret the Latin script that was associated with it along with anything else that pertained to the Avebury location and what was going on there at the time.

Using his translation, they zeroed in on the time being described as the year 1585 CE. They were able to estimate the population of the small village as being around twenty-five souls, primarily involved in farming. There was some, rather sparse, description of the farmers breaking up some of the stones in the circle to use when constructing their homes and building stone walls. There was, obviously, no mention of structures that were built later, like the Red Lion Pub, licensed in 1802, currently within the Avebury circle of stones.

Melinda explained that the Inn was built over the village well, which was dug some eighty-feet deep, that served the village in earlier times. One of the villagers found his wife, Florrie, in bed with another man and in a rage killed her and threw her body into the well. "Makes one wonder about the water quality after that," she added. "Legend has it that to this day her ghost is still occasionally seen near the well."

Thomas said that he was not clear from the monk's writing much about the life in the village or the nearby area around the 1585 CE timeframe, so that was not helpful. However, as Doc took several pictures of the Ghost Flower drawing with her smart device, she muttered to herself, "*This* will be useful."

Following the review of documents, the team went outside into the beautiful, sunny Sunday morning on the grounds of the University of Salamanca. "What now?" offered Thomas, their linguist. "I was excited to be here with you and have a chance to revisit some historical documents but now that we have done it, I'm feeling a little let down. I'm not clear what this visit has gotten us in our search for an antidote to the virus."

Doc looked up into the blue of the sky and smiled. "More than you think. I needed to see the drawing of the Ghost Flower for myself and take pictures of it. It will be of great use to us in identifying the flower when we see it."

"How will that help? The flower no longer exists anywhere as far as anyone knows," Thomas protested.

Doc flashed a momentary enigmatic smile and responded, "It does exist, it's just the matter of getting there."

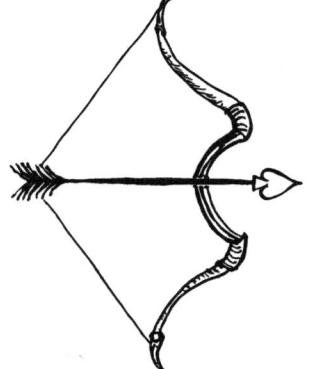

CHAPTER 10

2200 BCE
EARTH

FIVE DAYS AFTER AIELA AND LIEKA had their conversation revealing more about Lieka's background and the deceptiveness of their mission, the two of them relaxed the tension between them a bit. They tried to rely on each other as equals, given all they were facing. Aiela's concerns had not fully faded but he continued to see and appreciate how much she had to offer. They kept a formal relationship in the presence of others, never discussing the matter, since they needed to keep order and discipline in making the transition to living in an alien environment. Having clear leadership was crucial in calming the fears of the others. They provided structure and purpose to the crew's daily activities and were successful in encouraging a positive outlook for the future.

Unfortunately, the five crewmembers who had become ill within hours of their arrival had died, despite Kala's best efforts. That left seven marooned Golans to find a way to live in this new place. In addition to commanding officers Aiela and Lieka, there was Kala, the medical officer, Abeda their technician and translator operator, Liebeda, the crew member who went on the first night's recon mission, Obria, a female officer who was skilled in martial arts and, as a hobby, competed in archery tournaments utilizing arrows and bows that replicated ancient versions of those implements used in Golan's history. Completing the seven was Jabreen, a male second officer with prior military experience. His specialty was training soldiers in survival techniques in hostile surroundings. Of the five who died, three of them were specifically on the team to take readings of the environmental conditions on the planet for their debriefing on return to Golan.

Since this was the first time the deceased members of the team had met and worked with the others, personal relations had not yet had a chance to form. During a moment of reflection led by Aiela after their deaths, the remaining survivors showed little emotion, except for the unspoken fear that what had happened to their teammates might befall them as well. Aiela knew this dread would fade as time passed and stronger personal bonds had a chance to develop.

After the death of the crew members, Aiela held a meeting to reassure everyone that according to Kala's observation, no one else was showing any of the symptoms presented by the five who were now dead. It was a solemn occasion but with a nervous energy emanating from the group. Aiela could sense the feeling of relief they would not be next, mixed with a little guilt for feeling that relief while wanting to show concern for the others.

Kala spoke first about what they were all thinking. Honoring the deceased with a funeral ceremony that was traditional on Golan would definitely not be appropriate here. Ultimately, they decided the best plan was cremation, with the ashes scattered near the stone circle. They had come to realize that they would not be the first to do so. They believed the stone circle would be a fitting memorial place as it seemed to be for many of the natives of this planet before them. Importantly, this action would not leave any evidence of their presence, with the unknown ramifications of a discovery of their physical remains. That solution being agreeable to all, over the next few days their interment was accomplished with the care and solemnity it deserved. At least here, fires would not be seen as suspicious to the locals. Following this closing event, the crew's efforts turned to the practical matters at hand, with each person finding their niche based on the skills they possessed.

The task of outfitting the group with suitable clothing fell to Jabreen. In several additional nighttime scouting missions, it became apparent that while there were a number of settlements not far away, the families were all too small and intimate for the Golans to steal some of their sparse supply of clothes and not have them recognized by their owners when the Golans showed up later. Jabreen's skills in survival included adapting outerwear to blend into a different environment. Based on his clandestine observations of the local garments, with their creative cuts and tucks, and aided by the use of different colors of berry juice coming from indigenous plant material, he was able to make the crew's presentation reasonably close to what the locals wore. Again, when making first contact, the key to explaining their accents and clothing differences would be their cover story of being from a distant tribe.

In their first few days, the crew had been able to gather enough berries and succulent plant leaves, supplemented by roasting rabbits that had been procured using snares Jabreen had taught them to use to provide food for the group. Thank goodness, they all agreed, Jabreen was part of the crew. Making fire to cook with and keep them warm at night was not a problem they thought it might be considering their plan to destroy all of their modern equipment. Jabreen had found a couple of stones—flints—and a piece of iron pyrite. He showed them how to use those two items to strike a spark to generate a fire. The pyrite he found near the stone circles he assumed was something left behind years before as a gift for the dead.

As a backup plan to procure meat for their diet, Obria had fashioned a reasonably powerful bow from a local tree that proved suitable along with six handcrafted arrows. The feathers used for fletching the arrows came from the wings of a medium-sized bird she found near their camp. Since they had not observed any locals using bows and arrows, they decided to be on the safe side in showing these until they learned otherwise, assuming this technology had yet to be developed on this planet. So, Obria left the bow unstrung, which was appropriate to protect the structure of the bow. But that move also made the bow appear to resemble a staff for walking rather than the weapon it actually was. The bowstring she had woven from wool was cut from a nearby wild animal resembling a sheep. She attached the bowstring to the unstrung bow in a way as to make the whole assembly look like a walking staff with the string appearing to simply be a sling for carrying the "staff" over her shoulder when not in use.

For arrowheads, she fashioned very small, elongated points from shards of rock she found nearby. She made them thin and small, so they protruded from the arrow shaft just enough to be effective but unobtrusive such that a casual glance would not make someone curious about what they were intended for. Altogether, her creations were not nearly as suitable as the ones she had made with the materials on Golan. But they were fine enough for the limited use she anticipated here. If they found the locals using bows and arrows, then she could replace hers with better arrowheads made from the same material used by the archers here.

At night, when seeing was next to impossible, Obria's mind took to comparing life on Golan to this primitive land, wondering how long it might be before she didn't have to think so hard about any detail that might give them away.

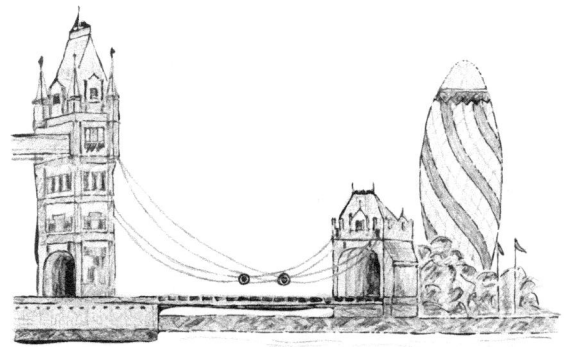

CHAPTER 11

2035 CE ENGLAND

THE NEXT DAY, MONDAY, THE TEAM left Salamanca for the airport in Madrid to catch their flight to the next stop on their journey, London's Heathrow airport. Renting another SUV at the airport, this time a Mercedes, they started the drive to a small inn in the country about five miles from Avebury. Melinda had again used her knowledge of the local area to book them in a place that had air-conditioning. She discovered that air-conditioning was not available in all of the local places during her visit several years before. With continual climate changes recently impacting the area nothing was certain but she didn't want to chance it.

As they cruised west on the M40 motorway, Doc decided this was as good a time as any to get their reaction to an outrageous plan she and Melinda had privately cooked up while they were in Salamanca. Slowly easing into it, she started by asking how they were enjoying their adventure so far. After a few minutes of animated conversation about what they were doing, she began talking about the Ghost Flower and how it was extinct—as far as anyone knew.

That reminded Thomas of the comments he had made in the Salamanca library when Doc was taking pictures of the Ghost Flower drawn on the margin of the manuscript.

"You said your picture would help you identify it when you saw it. But now you are saying it's extinct."

"Yes, I did say that," Doc admitted. "I also said it *did* exist but it was just a matter of getting there."

After a little pause, she went on, "Getting there is what I want to talk with all of you about now. The Ghost Flower exists in the past, quite a while back actually, and there may be a way to return to that time in the past." Doc watched their reactions. She noticed a mixture of wonder as if she was losing it, joking, or maybe they just didn't hear her correctly.

With the hint of a Mona Lisa smile, Melinda was silent for a moment, then spoke up. "She is quite serious. Let me fill you in on something in my background I haven't mentioned before. Because of my archeological work, I was recruited as a consultant by a branch of the military to assist with a top secret project. After passing extensive background vetting, they took me to a black research site they have in a remote part of the western United States. There, they briefed me on a project to travel back in time."

Melinda paused for a few seconds to let that last sentence sink in. Then she continued. "Their interest in me was to become part of the team that would investigate what the ground conditions would be like for receiving a research party 'popping' into existence in a particular place at a particular time. As you think through what I just said and wonder if it's not just Doc losing it but me, too, you may be thinking, *if all this is secret stuff, why are you sharing it with us? Aren't you guilty of unauthorized sharing of classified information?*"

Melinda was quiet for a minute, as they stared at her in stunned silence. Then she added, "The team at the site are contemplating a live test of their time travel theory. Full disclosure, they are confident, at least as anyone could be about something this outrageously bold, that they can send people back in time, to a particular place at a particular time in history. The catch is—and it is a big one—they don't know how, at this point, to bring them back.

"Two other consultants and I have been charged with recommending the specific members of a team to take this leap into the past, lay down some markers that will survive hundreds of years so they can read them in the present, in order to know if what they have developed to date works. We are to share our recommendations of candidates for the experiment to the research team. They will vet the candidates for the experiment and choose the individuals they believe best suited for the travel.

"While we were in Salamanca, unbeknownst to all of you other than Doc, I called the researchers and received permission to share all of this with you. When I told them about the possibility of incorporating information about developing a potential vaccine to fight the current pandemic as content in a message to be sent to the future proving the time travel experiment worked, they were very excited about the concept. They immediately began to refine their plan to pinpoint an appropriate time and location for the destination. Frankly, I don't know if they were more excited about the opportunity to fight the pandemic or the marketing possibilities of using that story to strengthen their pitch for more government funding. In any case, that narrowed their focus on who would be the best candidates for the travel, meaning probably us."

Silence filled the SUV as Joel and Thomas tried desperately to wrap their heads around what they had just been told. Their thoughts were interrupted when Doc spoke up.

"Let this all sink in and we will answer your questions as best we can. Then, while we are in Avebury, you can tell us what you think—whether you are interested in pursuing this or not."

Not long after the silence that followed the shocking revelations, Joel and Thomas erupted with excited chatter, questions, and speculation. Then, a quiet settled over the group with each lost in their own thoughts for the rest of the drive to Avebury. Upon arrival, after they had checked into their respective rooms, they got back together in the inn's eating area just off the kitchen. The inn was a small one, only catering to a maximum capacity of twelve visitors on any given night. On this particular night there were only six other customers who had already finished their meals and gone out to experience the local night life at the Red Lion Pub.

Doc's team sat in the cozy eating area, surrounded by old oil paintings on the white plaster walls beneath a very interesting vaulted ceiling, the dark beams of which seemed to have been repurposed from some much older structure. Sitting on a trestle bench on her side of an old farm table, Doc looked at the stew she had ordered and smiled. "I wonder what was used as condiments to give this stew its unusual but very appealing taste!"

She got the impression that Melinda, at least, had caught her suggestion. But rather than comment, Melinda raised a proposal instead. "I think tomorrow we tackle two objectives. First, let's see if we can arrange to join a tour of the stones to see what a local guide says about them. Next, I would like for us to explore the surrounding area by car to the extent we want and then explore on foot the village and immediate area.

"I like it," responded Doc. And with that, the conversation turned back to whispered questions for Doc and Melinda about time travel.

∗ ∗ ∗

Early the next morning, the small group gathered again in the eating area of the inn for a simple breakfast of fabulous hot-cross scones, smothered in clotted cream, with two pots of steeping tea. Within the hour, they were entering the visitor reception in the Old Farmyard of Avebury to arrange for a tour of the stones. They were able to organize a noon departure and purchased their tickets. With that taken care of, they decided to visit the Alexander Keiller Museum to review the archeological finds and other artifacts from the past on display. Then, they planned a walking recon of the village followed by an early lunch at the Red Lion Pub prior to their scheduled tour of the stone circle.

"Quite a history to this place," remarked Melinda as the four of them entered the front door to the Red Lion. "There is another place to eat but, somehow, since we are looking back in time, this pub seems more appropriate, even though as old as it is, it doesn't go back far enough to help us."

Doc spied a table that seemed a bit out of easy earshot of the other diners, even though there weren't many seated for lunch yet. "Here's a good one. We can sit here and talk about what we saw this morning at the museum and on our walk."

Just as Doc finished saying that and they were settling in to their seats, their server arrived at their table. She was eyeing them curiously but broke her gaze as she proffered four menus for them to review. After making their selections and the server had walked away, Thomas quietly spoke to the others.

"You remember I mentioned I am tuned in more than most to body language and micro facial expressions in the people I am around? Well, I picked up something unusual in our server's demeanor as she came to our table. Nothing at all suggesting a threat or anything like that, just a look of curiosity as she glanced at each of us, a fraction longer than I'm accustomed to in similar circumstances. She sees many tourists in the everyday course of her work, so we should not stand out as anything special. But I sensed she saw something about us that was different."

Doc took a peek over at their server, now occupied with a couple seated on the far side of the room. "Now that you mention it, I was noticing her general appearance as she came up to our table. I couldn't quite tell her age. The wait staff in restaurants are all ages, young, old and everything in-between but something about her was just a little off. She has a few streaks of gray in her otherwise jet-black hair but she moves like a young person. At our table, the look in her eyes was the maturity of one who has seen much in their life. A lot of contradictions."

Melinda added to the appraisal. "I was struck by her emerald green eyes and how they seemed a little larger than average. A good look if you ask me."

As they finished their conversations and the meal, the woman of indeterminate age came back to ask them about dessert. She stood there, about five feet, two inches in height, dressed no differently than the other servers in the restaurant. As they had been discussing her appearance earlier, they were discreet but now all four were checking her out a little more carefully. Maybe because they were all physically fit, they were more conscious of the smooth skin and muscular definition in this woman's arm as she held out the dessert menus. Her arm was attached to a slim but what appeared to be a very firm frame. That was one more aspect of the woman of indeterminate age that didn't quite conform to their perception of normal.

After the four took the menus and began to glance down at the dessert options, the woman casually commented that she had overheard their comments when they first arrived at the restaurant.

"You mentioned, 'the Red Lion as old as it is, is not old enough to go back in time to help with your interests.' Are you planning to take one of the tours of Avebury this afternoon? If you are planning to visit the stone circles, they go back way beyond this place and may be of interest to you."

"Yes, that is the plan," Doc replied. "You must live around here, right?"

"I do. Over time, I have been quite interested in the history here as well. Occasionally, I fill in for some of the tour guides when they take time off. I enjoy sharing what I know about the stones and their history. There is more here than meets the eye."

That last sentence hit the sensitive Thomas like a hammer blow. To the surprise of the others at the table, he suddenly blurted out, "It would be great to have a person who lives around here and has heard—and probably told—many of the stories about the place, accompany us on our tour this afternoon."

Picking up where Thomas was going with this, Doc added, "Too bad you are working today. We are tourists, I guess, but we are also a research team trying to learn as much as we can to help a larger project. Art history and archeology are a couple of our specialties. We may not be able to get answers to all of our questions on a regular tour."

"I'm on the early shift today," the server explained, "so I'll be finished about the same time you are with your desserts. It would please me to walk with you and add anything I can to what your assigned guide covers. I'm allowed to accompany some of the tours without a ticket since I'm the occasional guide and I do that from time to time. I find it sharpens my presentations when it's my turn to lead a group. So, if you are serious, give me a few minutes to change into something more suitable for going with you. This sounds like fun!"

Thomas, listening intently, didn't quite buy the "fun" comment. But he was very interested in having the woman of indeterminate age accompany them.

With dessert finished and the bill paid, the four gathered outside the Red Lion. A few minutes later, their server, now changed into jeans and a light denim shirt, finished off with sturdy brown walking shoes that seemed to have seen much use, introduced herself. "My name is Jane, by the way."

"Hi, Jane, pleased to meet you. My name is Ada Sendall, Dr. Sendall, so they call me Doc. I hope you will, too. This is Thomas, Melinda, and Joel," she said as she pointed out each in turn. "Our tour is just about to begin, so let's walk over to join the others. It's a beautiful day so I'm surprised there seems to be only two other couples joining us."

Jane explained, "The size of a group varies from day to day and tour to tour. We seem to be fortunate since our assigned group will be a small one."

The tour of the stone circle was much more informal than

those held at the better known, and more popular, Stonehenge. The stones aren't as imposing as those at Stonehenge, not as dramatic, and many stones at Avebury are missing from where it was clear there would have been some in the past. The young man assigned as their tour guide explained the cause of the missing sarsen stones was largely a result of local residents over the years taking them down and breaking them up to use as building materials in houses and fence rows. Doc and her group were not hearing a lot they didn't already know until they reached what appeared to be the end of the tour.

The guide produced two L-shaped metal divining rods, holding one in each hand, shoulder width apart. He then proceeded to walk through two of the upright twelve-foot-high sarsen stones, each about five-feet thick. As he took a few steps and crossed between the two stones, the divining rods crossed. The entire group, watching this, became fascinated.

A woman from one of the other couples on the tour, seeming somewhat skeptical, asked if she could walk through the stones with the rods to see if the rods would cross for her. The guide responded, "Sure," and handed over the rods.

Indeed, as the woman walked through, the rods crossed just as they had with the guide, Robby. After retrieving his metal rods, he gave a somewhat mystical explanation of the energy flowing from the rocks as part of the Avebury vortex. He was admittedly overly theatrical with his explanation of the mysteries of the site but all were entertained, as was his purpose. With that, Robby announced the tour was concluded and the two couples started to head back, apparently to join a separate tour of the village.

Once they were out of earshot, Jane asked Robby if she could take the divining rods to show her guests a little more about the physics of what they had seen. Since Robby knew Jane both as a local resident and a part-time tour guide, he simply asked that she return them when she was finished to the origin point of the tours for the next guide to use.

Once Robby was gone, Jane said she would like to add something to the demonstration they had seen earlier. She instructed Doc, "Take these rods and walk between the stones, holding them about waist level."

Doc took the rods and the rods crossed each other as she went between the stones.

"Now, Doc, walk back through. But this time, hold the rods higher, about level with your head."

Doc again walked as instructed. This time, however, the rods didn't cross, but each flared out to the side.

"Thanks, Doc. The energy flowing in the stones is actually an electromagnetic force that flows from the earth here. Due to the elemental composition of the stones, it flows up into them but in an uneven pattern ... layers, if you will."

Joel and Melinda looked a bit confused so Jane continued to try to explain what was going on.

"One layer affected the metal rods in a way that pushed them away from the stone each was closest to, making them cross. At a little higher level on the stones, the next higher layer of electromagnetic energy pulled at the rods, making them point outwards, each toward the closest stone. The reason I'm going into this is because of what you said about a larger research project and the sense I have that you are not being open with me about that larger project. The reason I am being so blunt is that I think I may have an interest in the same objective as you."

Silence ensued. Then Thomas, with his heightened awareness of the motives and intents of others, spoke up.

"This may seem weird to you, Jane, but my senses are telling me that you can be trusted and that you, indeed, do have something you want to tell us. You seem to already know more about what we are looking for than we have told you so far. Am I wrong? Further, when you talk, especially when you are looking at me, I can feel a connection, almost as if you can read my thoughts."

Jane looked straight into his eyes with a piercing intensity like none other in his experience. "I'm not clairvoyant but I am possessed with a hereditary ability to grasp the essence of what someone is thinking if I focus on them. I try to be careful not to show it because I know that ability will frighten people. You, however, seemed to slip through my defenses. And, surprisingly, you don't seem afraid."

"My senses aren't inherited; they were developed out of necessity to survive," Thomas explained. "I think I understood you have something similar soon after we came in contact in the Red Lion and that feeling has grown the more I am around you. So, no, it doesn't scare me, I'm intrigued by your ability and I am very curious in learning more. If we tell you what we are about, I expect you to do the same. I really believe we can help each other."

Thomas turned to the other three and asked if they were comfortable with his offer to share their stories. With a hint of reluctance in her voice, Melinda said she was okay with his offer but suggested they go back to the inn where they were staying and have a talk in the privacy of one of their rooms.

"I agree," was the simultaneous reply from Doc and Joel.

❋ ❋ ❋

Once back in Doc's room, which was a wee bit larger than the others with a small wooden game table and chairs, plus a worn but serviceable, two-seater couch, Melinda started the conversation with some background for Jane. She began with a description of the pandemic that was threatening to balloon out of control and already spreading to many places in the world. Melinda went into how extreme climate conditions had melted glaciers, with one in particular unleashing an ancient virus that infected a team of international research students. The students had returned to their homes in America, Europe, and Asia for a holiday break before becoming symptomatic.

Doc took over from there, describing the failure of current vaccines used to treat the infection, the rapid mutations, and the very high death rate.

Joel mentioned the comparison with the direction this pandemic was taking and what happened in Europe with the Black Death. "That was caused by a bacterium, not a virus, but the devastation to the population was horrific. We don't want this pandemic to reach those proportions but we are heading in that direction if we don't act fast."

"Our research with vaccines is getting us nowhere," added Doc, "so, out of desperation, we began to rack our brains for alternative ways to attack the problem. This is where Melinda's research in art history and archeology comes into play. Several years back, she and Thomas, acting as her interpreter and her informal cultural historian, were researching old illustrated manuscripts in the rare book collection of the University of Salamanca. As an art historian, Melinda was particularly interested in the drawings on the margins of the parchment pages."

Melinda picked up the story from there. "One particular drawing was of a white flower. Asking Thomas to interpret the Latin script associated with the flower, he read the stories of the times recorded on that particular page. They were chronicling a period in the 1500s, about a small village that seemed immune to the plague that was otherwise destroying the surrounding population. Many speculations as to why they were always spared were recorded by the monk who authored the page in question. They ranged from witchcraft, work of the Devil, the grace of God, or other unknowable reasons. But one story hinted that a local flower and its stems and seeds used to garnish food in the village may have had special properties. They referred to it as the Ghost Flower. Based on the description of the flower, the monk had his illustrator draw what he gathered it looked like in the margin of the page. The drawing was of a small flower with six white petals surrounding a light brown center."

Melinda told Jane she had not thought much more about it until Joel remembered she had mentioned it to him at a dinner party some time back.

Then Doc took the story over again. "As I said, we were seriously reaching out for any ideas that will lead to some antidote to the awful pandemic that is about to engulf the world. That's when we invited Melinda to join us for dinner and tell us more. She convinced us to add Thomas, her interpreter to our group, and together we developed a plan to pursue this mysterious flower. And that, my new friend, led us here to Avebury by way of Salamanca. While at the university there, I took this picture of the monk's drawing of the flower."

Doc pulled her smart device out and scrolled to the image. There was an audible gasp as Jane turned to see it. Thomas jerked forward in his chair, visibly affected by Jane's reaction.

Until that moment, Jane had been someone who exhibited an almost unworldly calmness and control over her speech and mannerisms. For about ten seconds, that calm demeanor disappeared and a look of shock and disbelief swept over her face.

"I haven't seen that flower … but I know it."

CHAPTER 12

2200 BCE
EARTH

THREE MONTHS HAD PASSED SINCE THE stranded research party arrived from Golan. During that time, they had made further contact with the locals they observed on their first night on the planet. At their first meeting, they had slowly walked up to the small encampment in the middle of a day, talking among themselves as they approached so as to not startle the group by suddenly appearing. They made sure their hands were visible and not holding anything that might be mistaken as a weapon. As they approached, a single male, appearing to be in his mid- to late-twenties, walked toward them and stopped some ten paces away. He looked curious, somewhat defensive in the way he held himself but not threatening in any way. As they had planned earlier, Lieka spoke first. They thought maybe having a woman in their party be the first to make contact would lessen any sense of hostile intentions on their part.

Lieka spoke softly and with the language she had learned from their translator. She offered what she hoped was an appropriate greeting and was relieved when the male responded with a reply that she could understand. His accent was not terribly different from hers. The clothes the Golans were wearing that Jabreen had fashioned for them to mimic theirs seemed to be convincing enough. At least if they weren't examined too closely. After Lieka went through their cover story of traveling from a distant place to explain their accent not being like the young man's who greeted them, as well as not understanding a few of the words he spoke, an easy introduction to the rest of the locals ensued. They were curious about these strangers, where they came from and what they were doing here.

Lieka explained that they were in search of materials to make sturdier and more useful instruments for hunting, preparing food, and cutting the materials used in making their lodges. They seemed to understand and conveyed that they, too, were interested in the same things to make their lives a little easier. Their young leader, in a show of friendship, introduced himself as Harold.

After that first meeting, Aiela and Lieka returned to their home camp, now some four miles away. The landing party sat by their small evening fire, now only numbering seven after the unfortunate deaths of their other companions shortly after their arrival. After a few minutes of idle chatter, Lieka spoke about a topic she knew was on all of their minds.

"We must decide how we are going to assimilate into this place, our new home. The people here are very primitive compared to the civilization we left behind on Golan. They are at a point we were two or more millennia in the past. We understand science, technology, and medicine beyond anything here. We also understand the evolution of society in an advanced culture like Golan. We know what works and we know what the failures have been. For a short time, using what we know, we could be like deities or idols here, what some on Golan call gods. I say a short time, because I know a fear of our power would develop. But once they found we are mortal and can be killed, I believe that is exactly what would happen to us."

Everyone listened closely as Lieka went on. "We *could* use our advanced knowledge to introduce these people to technologies that would speed their understanding of such things by generations. But I believe that would be a tragic mistake. A civilization grows best by growing with balance across all of its population; a balance only achieved by having people develop an ethical, moral, and compassionate practice in living together. That takes time. On Golan, in its history at a time where we are on this planet now, worship of supernatural forces was widespread. The beliefs were all over the map. Some individuals used those beliefs for self-serving ends, not for the good of all. Power was accumulated in different parts of our world there and religious beliefs were appropriated for use by those in power to control their subjects. Conflicts over natural resources developed and wars ensued, killing millions over time in pursuing the goals of the leaders of the rival factions."

Aiela was compelled to weigh in on the matter. "What we are seeing here, now, is something similar to Golan's early days. In our short time on this planet, we are seeing spiritual beliefs developing, based on interpretations of phenomena and natural events. They have no concept or understanding as to the how or why these things they see or experience happen. Lightning on a stormy night? People dying from causes they can't see or save? They have no knowledge of electricity, viruses, or bacteria. The night sky is something they look up at with wonder and awe. They marvel at the star-filled heavens, making up stories about what they are seeing."

He continued, "It takes generations of research, study, observation, and wisdom to advance knowledge and create viable civilizations. And, for the best outcomes, this advance needs to come slowly … slowly enough to give time for all of the planet's inhabitants to absorb an understanding of the world around them, to develop positive life philosophies to guide their actions in productive, meaningful ways, instead of living destructive, greed-filled lives."

Kala, their medical officer spoke next. "We must be vigilant in our contact with the people here so that we don't introduce anything that will be misunderstood, misused, or because of ignorance, used in a way that causes them harm rather than something helpful. We need to blend in, living as they do. We can use our knowledge to help each other when we are physically hurt or ill, we can prepare our

food in ways that will not poison us due to bacterial contamination
and other realities of which they are not yet aware. But we cannot
begin to explain the whys of these practices to others as they will
be seen as supernatural powers. That goes back to Lieka's comment
that if they begin to believe we have powers they cannot fathom,
they will become suspicious, leading to nothing good for us."

They all nodded in agreement as Kala went on. "We need to be
very conscious of exposing them to something they are unfamiliar
with and haven't yet gained the basic knowledge to understand. For
example, the provisions we brought with us for our first few days
here contained some flower seeds that we use on Golan to spice our
foods and bring us health benefits. It adds a distinctly unique flavor,
one which I certainly appreciate, but this flower doesn't grow here. If
we want to continue to have the comfort it brings, I suggest we plant
the remaining seeds we have in a place—somewhere we know is not
on any ordinary route of travel—and harvest the flowers and their
seeds in secret so we can sustain and extend their growth. The less
we have to explain about something we do that they don't, the fewer
times we will have to invent cover stories that will eventually be
hard for us to keep track of. The flower cultivation shouldn't really
be difficult to do, as the people here forage in the nearby forests for
mushrooms and other foods on a regular basis, just as we will. Even
if they happened upon our flowers, they probably wouldn't think to
add them to their foods. And if they happen to see us with them,
we can simply say they were picked for decoration or flavor. They
do, fortunately, look similar to some other wild flowers I have seen
growing here, so they really don't appear unusual."

Jabreen, their survivalist, suggested a place for planting the
seeds. "Remember when we first arrived and visited the strange
stone circles that seemed to be erected as a place of spiritual value?
It is respected as such and the people don't seem to want to hang
around after their rituals are completed. I think there may be some
fear of being alone in the place, so unless they are in a group, they

stay away. On one of my scouting trips of the area, I came across a much smaller circle that appears to have been abandoned generations ago. While falling apart and becoming somewhat overgrown, it still has open space in some areas that allows the sun in. Even though abandoned, I suspect the locals would avoid going into the circle when they are foraging out of the fear they have of the unknown spiritual powers of the place. It's a small circle, really not that imposing, so I doubt it has much historical value, if anyone is even interested in that sort of thing now.

"I know when I was a boy on Golan, there was a forest near where I grew up that I often frequented on my youthful hunting trips. There was an old hand-dug well near some particularly large trees, planted, I'm sure, from the long-gone residents of the area. I had seen the old well on some of my earliest visits and noticed that someone had placed a piece of metal over the well's opening to prevent someone from accidentally falling in. Over the years, leaves from the surrounding trees covered the metal lid which, by then, had rusted to the point I think it would have collapsed had someone stepped on it.

"So, in my later years visiting that particular area, and no longer being able to see exactly where the old well was from the leaves covering the area, I avoided going even near there when I saw the big trees that identified the spot. My point is I believe the same trepidation I had about going near a place that could pose a danger to me applies to the local residents regarding the old, broken-down stone circle. They avoid getting too close to the site for fear of encountering some lingering spirit there making this an *excellent* place to plant our flower seeds."

"Done!" remarked Aiela. "Hiding the location where we grow our flowers seems like overkill to me but I agree with the idea that we need to continue developing a habit of being conscious of not acting or doing things that are different from local practice."

The commander added with a bit of gallows humor and a smile

on his face, "Let me change the subject from flowers to something more important. I think as newcomers to this world, new to us, we should keep a record of what we think and do. It may well be useful in the future to those who follow us. That is … if we survive long enough to have offspring in this place!"

Lieka had a suggestion. "For now, at least, we should keep the record written in our native Golan language in case it falls into the hands of others. And, in the spirit of what we just said about not being different, the record should be kept secret."

Tensions had eased considerably between the first and second in command after Lieka had shocked Aiela by revealing her undercover mission. She hoped he was developing warm feelings for her as she was for him. Risking a furtive glance at her potential future mate, she continued her thoughts.

"I'm going to be so bold as to predict that we will have offspring. In a few generations, as we assimilate into the culture here, our writings need to include an instruction to the last of us who remembers how to speak Golan. That day will come. We must ensure our Golan writings are handed down and translated into the language of the time so they will not be lost forever."

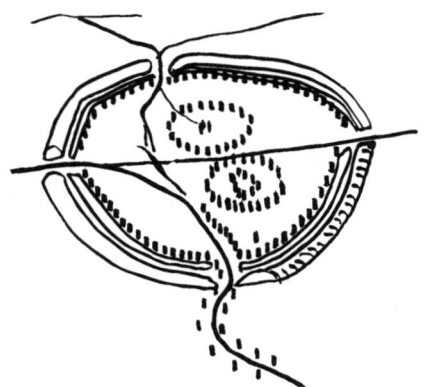

CHAPTER 13

2035 CE
ENGLAND

AFTER JANE REGAINED CONTROL OF HER emotional response to the picture of the white Ghost Flower that Doc had shown her while they were gathered in her room in the Inn, the conversation paused for what seemed an eternity. Then Doc spoke up.

"Look, we are all dancing around the big question of who shares what they know first. Jane, you obviously know something about the flower that now has us all curious. I'll start with what we are really involved in beyond what we have said so far. Some of what I am about to tell you is classified information. I'm going to take a leap of faith that if you swear to keep it secret, I'll explain."

Jane did not hesitate in her reply.

"I will also take a leap of faith and agree to keep what you reveal to me as secret. And I will in turn tell you things that you must keep to yourself. Agreed?"

"Yes, I agree. And the rest of you?" Doc asked.

Melinda, Joel, and Thomas pledged themselves to keep the confidence.

"Well, I suppose that even if you did reveal something about what I am going to tell you, no one would believe you anyway, and I would just say you were delusional," Doc said as a way of beginning her story.

"I told you about our theory, based on a long dead monk's writing, that the Ghost Flower, the flower in the picture I showed you, had some pretty miraculous medicinal properties that kept people who ingested it immune to the pandemics of the time. But the flower has long gone extinct. Now, here is the classified part of the story. There is a closely held project being developed in a black site by the United States military in conjunction with some of the country's most talented academics in the field of quantum physics, astrophysics, and a few other technology specialties to send someone, or a small group, back in time."

Melinda then joined in. "Our research tells us that the flower and its seeds apparently had the effect of amping up the natural immune system of anyone eating them. This became amplified to the point of effectively fighting off infection due to exposure to harmful bacteria or viruses. Further, unlike other experiments attempting to boost one's immune system to such high levels, this boost does not result in the antibodies going beyond the target infection and attacking healthy cells, resulting in death to the patient. The reward of learning the chemistry of the flower is incalculably greater than the risk involved in attempting to go back in time to learn its secrets. When I say risk, to be more precise, the time travel system has yet to be tested with human subjects. The reward is the possibility of finding a solution to defeat the pandemic currently threatening millions of lives across the globe. Doc and I are two of those willing to take the risk."

"Joel and I are still thinking this through. We just learned what Doc is telling you only a couple of days ago," added Thomas.

Jane, now visibly back in control of her emotions, sat forward in her chair and began to tell her side of the bargain.

"My ancestors came from far away, so far that I suspect you are not going to believe me, but if you are seriously contemplating a trip back in time, maybe you possibly will. I don't know anything about traveling back in time but I am familiar with the stories passed down from the distant past that involve traveling unheard of distances in the blink of an eye. Stories that involve people being transported from a distant galaxy to this one in a way that I have never heard of in my many years of life in this place.

"These stories tell of an experiment that went wrong—more than four thousand years ago—when people from the planet Golan attempted to send a team from the Andromeda Galaxy to Earth. The project utilized a journey through a newly discovered dimension. This theoretical dimension was only written about in science fiction novels here on this planet but on Golan, it was actually understood enough to be applied as a portal from there to here, making travel virtually instantaneous. My ancestors were a part of that team. The picture you showed me of the Ghost Flower is exactly like a drawing I have that was passed down over the generations in a record of our history here. I've not seen one in my lifetime but I know where the ancients grew that particular plant. And I can show you the location."

Thomas took a breath before responding. "I sensed from almost the minute we met you that you were different in a way I couldn't understand. Not friendly or hostile, but at the same time I felt a connection, like you were somehow privy to my thoughts. I sensed you saw something in us that piqued your curiosity in a way that was different from the other tourists you see in the Red Lion every day. I have no factual basis for believing your story but I do. I want to hear more."

"Let me ease your mind on one point right away," Jane reassured him. "As I mentioned to you earlier, I'm not clairvoyant. I can't read your minds. What I have is an uncommon ability to sense what people are thinking based on micro facial expressions, body language, tone of voice and choice of words used. This, in general, is something most people here do but my sensitivity is tenfold that of what others seem to have. You, Thomas, are above normal in that regard and that is why you picked up on my abilities."

Doc chimed in, "We all noticed something about your appearance early on that has us puzzled. You have striking eyes, a fit body that seems unusually toned for a person that seems older in other ways, such as the maturity you display that only comes from time. Is this something you inherited or is it something else?"

"You are all very astute," Jane replied. "I suppose that comes with your inquisitive backgrounds as research scientists. I am indeed older than I look. In fact, I recently celebrated my 110th birthday. My ancestors' normal longevity was around two-hundred Earth years. Many centuries have passed since their arrival here. Their numbers were small; only seven of the original party survived their arrival on Earth. Some had children between them but, as you can imagine, with that small original party, they began mating with the locals.

"As you know, this mingling of genetics could not be passed on uniformly. Instead, it is mixed in the offspring with varying outcomes. I am one of the few who was born much later with a dominance of the genes that were present in the first arrivals. That gave me some of the characteristics you have noticed. I think the fact I am descended from those who stayed in this area, around Avebury, means that the gene pool I am descended from is a little stronger here than elsewhere for the descendants who moved away."

After Jane answered a few excited questions following her mesmerizing story, Melinda brought the conversation back to their pressing mission.

"You said you know where your ancestors planted the Ghost Flower plants? Could you show us? And on the way, let's continue this conversation."

"Sure, I can take you there," Jane stood up, ready for action. "It's a few miles from here in the general direction of Stonehenge but it's off the beaten track. We can drive part of the way, then walk maybe a mile and be there. It's the site of a really old stone circle. Not much is left of it. If you didn't know that it once existed you probably could walk right through the middle of it and not realize what had once been there."

Anxious to go, the group left the inn about twenty minutes later, all the while continuing to fill each other in on their respective stories. They arrived near the old circle and hiked in.

"Well, here it is," Jane said as they slowed their walk to a stop about a mile from where they had parked their car on the roadside. She waved her hand in a general way toward a nondescript opening in a small stand of woods. Most of the surrounding area was devoted to pasture land where they could see some cattle grazing in the distance.

Melinda noticed a few large stones scattered haphazardly through the trees, some partially covered with shrubs and earth, others broken into smaller stones and scattered about.

"I have always thought the reason there are trees still here," Jane explained, "that weren't cut down so the land could be used for more agrarian use is because for generations, farmers would come here to gather the stones for their pasture fences or for building material, much as they did with some of the stones in Avebury. These farmers were not from the older time that considered the place to be sacred. They saw this place as a valuable source for stones that they found scattered through the trees. So they didn't clear the area to use as a field for crops. As a result, the trees were left in place."

Looking over at Melinda, Doc told her, "Use your smart device to call up the GPS coordinates for this place, right in the center where there would have been an open space in the past. Also, record the elevation at ground level—which today is probably pretty close to where it would have been in the sixteenth century."

"Okay, I'll take care of it," Melinda replied. "But looking about, I don't see any signs of flowering plants or shrubs that might be left from the Ghost Flower days."

Overhearing this last bit, Jane spoke up, "There are no remnants. This circle has not been used for cultivating anything in centuries. Any cultivated plants left from my ancestors would have died out long ago, or been devoured by wild grazing animals."

By this time, the sun was approaching the horizon with darkness beginning to fall soon. Doc suggested they start their walk back to the car while they still had light and return to the inn for dinner and a continuation of talking about next steps in their quest.

* * *

A few hours later, after finishing a comforting meal of Shepherd's pie along with a simple salad accompanied by two bottles of Chardonnay supplied by the inn keeper from his stock, they resumed their conversation about next steps. Doc kicked it off looking directly at Joel and then Thomas.

"Well, you two have had some time now to think about accompanying Melinda and me on our trip to the past. You know it is dangerous. I have no rational basis for gauging our chances of success. We will be the first to attempt what has not been done before. And, here is a big consideration for you, I doubt we will ever be able to return. With this scary invitation, what's your pleasure?"

Joel spoke first. "I can't begin to say enough about how brave I think you two are, and what an exciting adventure it will be if you pull it off. But I have decided not to go. I don't see this as my future. However, I think I can still be useful as you will need someone here in the present to retrieve whatever messages you are able to send back, interpret them, and make sure the data you send gets to the hands of appropriate pharmaceutical companies to begin production of life-saving vaccines for the world's population. Remember, before becoming your research assistant, Doc, I spent eight years working in the pharmaceutical industry. I can use my contacts to save a lot of time finding one or two select firms that are ethical, swiftly cutting through bureaucratic red tape, making sure the data are analyzed properly, and getting production and distribution underway."

Thomas added, "I, too, don't see that I would add that much

to the team going back with you. But if there is any difficulty in determining what and how you left a message for us to find in the present time, I think I would be useful in that. As for the classified nature of what is happening, Joel and I will volunteer to be a part of the military science team here to help them. Right Joel?"

"Yes, it's a good plan for us," he replied.

Jane had been listening intently to all that was being said.

"Would you consider this? I have been here for 110 years. All of the people I grew up with have passed away. Spending another century here has little appeal for me. But the idea that I could go back in time and be with others like me who may still exist in the sixteenth century … now that is very interesting. It would be the most meaningful thing I could do with the rest of my life. Not only would it be an incredible adventure but my background would be invaluable to you in locating my ancestors and providing a bridge for you to more easily and quickly find what you are looking for. I definitely want to be included."

CHAPTER 14

2200 BCE
EARTH

By establishing themselves as friendly with the native people, Lieka and Aiela were able to learn quite a bit about their local customs and culture. They also learned that not all was peaceful in this new land. More than occasionally, hunting parties from one tribe would intersect with another and disputes over who had the right to the game would ensue. There were also grudges that developed when a member of one tribe, competing for the attention of a potential spouse in another tribe, ran afoul of a local suitor. These were rare but sometimes these clashes would develop into physical fights, some leading to injury or death. The chieftains of the competing tribes would do their best to settle the quarrels to keep outright war from starting.

On one of their visits to the group they had first met and gotten to know, they were gathered by a cooking pit late in the afternoon just before the sun had begun to set when several men approached their camp. One of them called out to the young leader sitting around the fire.

"Harold! Your people have been hunting in territory you know is ours. We warned you about this and told you there would be trouble if it continued. Well, it has continued and we are here to make an example of you to the others."

The only adult male of the tribe was Harold. His sister, and a young boy of about five, looked on in fear. When three of the visiting men advanced, it was clear from the clubs they were holding that they intended to inflict some serious damage to Harold, if not kill him outright.

As Harold stood, Lieka quickly stood and moved to his side. Aiela stood as well but did not move to join them. A strange smile was etched on his face as he simply stood there. Lieka spoke with a low voice but her tone was menacing.

"If you come for my friend, Harold, you will need to deal with me first."

She took another two steps to put herself between a surprised Harold and the three men spreading out to attack. She took their measure and decided the one doing the talking would make the first move.

"Move out of the way, woman!" he shouted.

The man quickly moved forward and raised his club to strike. To his surprise, rather than take a step back in fear, Lieka moved towards him faster than he had seen anyone move before. As his arm began the downward swing to bash his club into her head, she was already in so close that only his arm hit her on the shoulder. At that same moment, she hit him with a ferocious blow to his midsection, followed by a knee to his groin. Before he hit the ground, Lieka had moved to her left, shoved the left arm of the man there upwards and delivered another lightning-quick punch to his kidney, followed by a left fist to his gut. The third man, still standing a little way to the right, his eyes wide in disbelief, backed off, dropped his club, and raised his hands in a universally understood gesture of defeat. With both of the men she had put down in a matter of maybe two seconds, three at the most, lying in the dirt, retching, and holding their injuries, Lieka took a step back to meet the astonished Harold. Without even breathing hard, she asked if he was okay with her injecting herself into a tribal squabble.

Harold mumbled something that sounded like he was good with that but the look on his face was that of someone trying to understand what had just happened. Lieka looked at the third man, still standing in shock and invited him to have a seat at their fire.

"Your two companions can join us when they are able. We were about to have something to eat."

She then turned to Harold, who was still just standing there, trying unsuccessfully to speak. Lieka, facing Harold and Aiela with her back to the other three so they couldn't make out what she was saying, whispered, "I think it is best for Harold and his small band to start making alliances with his neighbors. In our short time here, we have noticed that while there aren't that many people in this area, there are a number of small bands, or tribes milling around. They have cut down most of the forests that appeared to have been in this area and are cultivating the land. I think there will be increasing rivalries for the good arable land and the strong will push out the weak. There is strength in numbers. Our friend, Harold, would be well advised to form an alliance with these men rather than have them as enemies going forward."

Then she added a further comment to Aiela as they moved out of earshot of the others, speaking in their native tongue.

"I saw your confidence that I could take care of those men on my own. I appreciate that. My combat training and experience on Golan was to seriously disable or kill my opponents. We have learned the population on this planet is relatively primitive and they have little in the way of medical knowledge. What would have been a disabling blow on Golan would probably be a lethal blow here. If I had done something as simple as breaking a jaw, snapping an arm or leg bone, or even hit them in the head too hard, it may well have led to their death through infection, internal bleeding, or inability to perform tasks necessary for survival. That would not have augured well for Harold in developing an alliance. So, I went for their soft spots and tempered my blows."

Aiela listened to her in silence. But he was thinking about what he had seen and how Lieka had explained her actions. He realized he was becoming more impressed with her abilities and her wisdom as time passed. He wondered if he had forgiven her completely by now for her betrayal, considering they were stranded here together—for better or worse. He was also acutely aware of the way he was looking forward to her company each day and how he was increasingly missing her presence when they were apart. Aiela was conflicted by being the leader of the group and aware of the taboo against becoming romantically involved with a subordinate, even though in private they considered themselves equals. However, he sensed that his restraint in following reason and good judgement over his growing feelings for her was going to end with emotion triumphing. Oddly, he thought, *I am not as troubled by that as others might be.*

By this time, the two men on the ground had recovered sufficiently to learn from their uninjured companion they had been invited to dinner. Stunned by the turn of events and still somewhat dazed from the encounter with Lieka, they stumbled forward and dropped to a seating position on two short pieces of a log cut to form seating near the fire. When they were able to speak, the one who seemed to be the leader stared at Lieka with a look of total puzzlement.

"I have never encountered a faster fighter, or one so accomplished. Where did you learn this?"

Lieka, obviously not wanting to reveal the truth of her status as a seasoned combat veteran, simply answered, "The women where we come from are trained early in their lives to take care of themselves. There are many who would do them harm if they were perceived as weak. But rather than talk about me, tell us more about yourselves and your tribe."

Harold's wife had come out during this conversation with a stew of mutton and vegetables, pouring it from a large pot for each of them into small, bowl-shaped clay pots, to be used for individual servings. She also gave them spoons, cleverly carved from wood. As they ate and continued to talk, Lieka was pleased to see the hostility they had arrived with was dissipating and being replaced by a mutual curiosity about Harold and his family as well as the strangers who were visiting his camp.

Harold learned their rival tribe numbered about thirty and were successfully farming land they had cleared nearby. They also supplemented their food stocks by hunting and that had been the beginning of the anger toward Harold. After he had told them he didn't realize they saw the land he had killed a deer on as theirs, explaining it with a sincerity that was compelling, he offered in the future to hunt with them and possibly trade with their tribe. He went into his small hut and came back out with a very serviceable copper hatchet.

"I have learned the skill necessary to separate the copper from the raw ore, melt it down, and then pour it into a mold to form to the shape I want. Perhaps this skill is something I could contribute to an alliance between our two peoples?"

The larger male, whose name they learned was Tom, or something that at least sounded like Tom, seemed very interested. Before the night was over, they had begun plans for more of the people of their tribe to meet with Harold and his tribe to sort out what they could do for each other.

* * *

On their return to their camp later that night, Lieka shared some of her thinking with Aiela.

"We know sharing our knowledge about things they are not ready for is a bad, bad idea. However, based on our experience on Golan, we can possibly use our influence to help shape a peaceful society to some degree, even if it is limited to the local area. I have a very distinct feeling the population in this part of the world is growing. There will be increasing competition for the good farming land and areas that are good for hunting. As we saw tonight, the first reaction to competition is not cooperation for the greater good but open hostility instead. We can use our experience on Golan, having seen what constant war does, to try to direct their competition into something productive rather than destructive."

"I agree," Aiela responded. "Based on our life experiences, we know that people are slow to adapt to new ideas that challenge old ways of doing things. It often takes several generations for consequential social change to occur. We have also seen, on Golan, how technological advances made available to the general population, before they understood the potential for negative outcomes associated with new powers put in their hands, led to some pretty awful consequences. I'm confident our decision to destroy the advanced equipment we brought with us was the right thing to do."

"Yes, I feel the same way. Obria disguised her bow as a walking stick. Now that we have seen that the locals have and use bows and arrows, she can openly carry hers and discover the best local materials to improve upon what she has. We can use our experience to aid in fostering peace. But for other advances, we will follow a practice of adopting the tools and other devices they use rather than offer ways we know would work better. We just don't grasp enough about their social and intellectual development to know if we would be helping or hurting."

Back at camp, the pair was met by the medical officer, Kala. "I have a surprising discovery to share with you. When we first arrived here, I ran several tests on the physical reaction of the environment we are experiencing here on this planet on our crew's bodily chemistry and functions. I also ran an analysis of the chemistry of the food we were eating on arrival. Then, several weeks later, just before I destroyed my medical equipment as we had planned, I repeated the tests of our crew and the local foods we have been eating after our arrival here. The results of one of the tests showed something I did not expect, leading me on a hunch to take some measurements of the planet's electromagnetic energy and gravitational fields since we learned that was a cause of the deterioration of the craft we arrived in. It seems that there is an anomaly in those fields, particularly in and around the stone circles. I also noted a slight change in the immune systems of the crew from readings I had taken for each of them before we left Golan. Their immunity appears stronger than before. I haven't discovered a reason for the change but I suspect it may be associated with our diet. I'm still working on an answer for that."

"Very interesting," observed Lieka. "We are still learning about the nature of the diseases that afflict the population here. Without the advanced medical resources we enjoyed on Golan, and with vaccines unknown here, we will be vulnerable to a similar illness and mortality rate as the indigenous population. If there is something unique in our diet or atmosphere giving our immune systems a boost or some type of insulation to these illness conditions, we need to find what it is and make it a permanent supplement."

CHAPTER 15

2035 CE ENGLAND

WITH THE TEAM'S TIME IN AVEBURY coming to an end, Doc and Melinda were first out of the inn early one bright morning and standing near their Mercedes waiting for Thomas, Joel, and their new partner, Jane, to join them for the trip back to London's Heathrow airport.

"It's unbelievable what has happened during our visit here," Doc exclaimed to Melinda. "You and I are committed to the trip back in time—if it actually works! And, we have a new member of the team to travel with us, Jane, plus we've established a base crew of Thomas and Joel who will remain here to recover whatever we can send back. Jane has put in her notice to the National Trust that she is resigning as a part-time tour guide as well as having given notice to her employer at The Red Lion pub. When we meet with your military research team, I have no doubt they will be excited to have Jane as a part of our crew. That will leave one more crew member for them to assign to us for the trip. My guess is that it will be someone who can analyze the Ghost Flower's chemical properties and give us instruction as to exactly what we should transmit back. Honestly, the transmit back part troubles me, as I don't yet have a good plan for how to accomplish that."

The night before was filled with conversation about what was coming next. Thomas and Joel were discussing ideas for how Doc's team could encode the Ghost Flower chemistry information in a form that would survive four hundred and fifty years between the time Doc's team would create the message in 1585 CE and when the two of them would retrieve it in 2035 CE. They all knew that any places they came up with to leave information before their twenty-first century departure may not turn out to be feasible locations when Doc's team arrived in the sixteenth century. They believed it worthwhile to have several potential locations to search.

Jane arrived outside, ready to go and travelling light. After greeting Doc and Melinda, she said with a smile of amusement on her face, "It's so weird to think that if we are successful in sending forward in time usable information on the Ghost Flower that it will be here for Thomas and Joel the instant we leave it. However, for us, we have years to put the information in place when we travel back. Blows one's mind to just think about it. Knowing that, Thomas, Joel, and I figured out some likely places in Avebury yesterday where we might leave the info. Then, we went to those places and the information wasn't there, of course, because we haven't left it yet!"

Joel and Thomas came out of the inn while they were talking and caught the last part of the conversation.

"Yes, Thomas and I will come back here to Avebury to start the search after you depart from the military site. We will use all of our detective skills to figure out where to look," Joel said. "The scary part is if your part of the plan doesn't work, we will have no way to know that and we could look forever for something that was never sent."

"But we have faith that you will be successful," added Thomas. "We will just have to look for clues you may have left behind to figure it out. Another possibility is that if we are unsuccessful in Avebury, we may go back to Salamanca to see if you left a message in one of the manuscripts there through some communication with the monk who wrote the passage in the book we looked through earlier. Your message won't be there now; only after you depart will it appear—if you are successful. Another mind-bender. Don't forget the University of Salamanca archives as a possibility for us to find a message from you!

"A difficulty with that plan is that it will be quite challenging for you to get from Avebury, England, to Salamanca, Spain, in 1585 CE in order to leave a message. Something equally challenging to contemplate is if you don't travel there yourself, you would be attempting to somehow get a message to a monk you have never met and hope he would include your Ghost Flower information in his writing. You would be relying on others to get your message to him in an age when most of the population can't read … and the distance between the two places is more than 1,100 miles. It requires crossing the English Channel and the Alps. That is, unless you can catch a ride on a boat from England to Portugal and then travel overland to the east into central Spain. Either way, a difficult journey in 1585. Please try very hard to leave something in Avebury!"

✳ ✳ ✳

Upon arrival in the United States, the next part of the journey for Doc, Melinda, Joel, Thomas, and Jane was to get to the military site where the time travel project was underway. This involved Melinda contacting the team there for instruction. Since it was a top-secret project, communication was limited. From Boston, they were advised to go to nearby Hanscomb Field, a general-aviation airport adjacent to an Air Force base. The military—Melinda said they would not reveal to her what particular branches or divisions were involved—was to arrange for a Gulfstream G500 to pick them up and transport them to the undisclosed research location somewhere in the western United States. The plane would be a civilian aircraft, chartered by a nondescript shell company but flown by military personnel.

Two days later, Doc's team arrived at Hanscomb Field, where they were recognized upon entering the airport departure area by a nice-looking, late twenty-something year-old woman dressed in faded jeans, hiking boots, and a well-worn brown leather bomber jacket. With a big smile on her tanned face, topped with a colorful blue and red wool sherpa cap complete with ear flaps hanging to the sides, she held out a hand to Melinda, and announced, "Welcome cousin! Glad you could make it."

Melinda, without batting an eye, followed through with the charade performed for the few other strangers within earshot.

"Yes, glad to be here as well. You are looking great!"

The blond young woman turned to the others. "The plane is ready to go, so please just follow me out on to the tarmac." Without any further conversation, the five marched out into the open air behind her like a row of little ducks following their mother.

Once they had boarded and settled into seats assigned by the young woman, she introduced herself as Captain Caroline Mabry and congratulated them on picking up on her subterfuge in the airport lounge and carrying it through.

"As this project is top secret, myself, the pilot, and co-pilot are all dressed in civilian clothes. Please don't take offense but you will find the window shades are locked down for the flight, so you won't be able to see anything as we go, just another precaution we are taking to keep this all on the down low. When we reach our destination, we will taxi into a hanger. When the hanger door is closed you will be escorted into the back of a deuce-and-a-half, a common military truck, also enclosed to block view, and taken to the site of our operation. This may seem extreme but when you see what we have built there you will understand the significance to national security for it to be operating as a black site. Melinda has been to this site before. But until vetting is complete on the rest of you, we will keep a strict security protocol in effect."

The captain then changed her tone to a slightly louder and lighter one. "We had the plane catered with a great lunch for you later in the flight. For now, how about I get you some coffee, tea, or water?" she said with a smile, perfectly emulating a professional flight attendant.

Jane was the first to speak, "Very impressive! How informed are you, Captain Mabry, as to what is going on? I'm naturally curious as to what we can discuss on what I'm assuming will be a several hour flight, based on the type of plane we are in and your comment about lunch later."

"Excellent question. I'm part of the research team at the site and I will be accompanying you throughout your training and preparation for the trip. I've been assigned to this project for about three years now and have been briefed on Melinda's recent report on the possibility of incorporating information into the proof-of-concept message to be sent back, relating to a potential vaccine for the pandemic. I agreed that it was a great idea. I was hopeful Melinda would quickly recognize me in this outfit, as I have always been in uniform in her presence before, and go along with my cousin routine. Melinda, you did great!"

"Thanks. And, good job, cousin, meeting us at the airport," Melinda laughed.

She followed up with some background information on the others for Captain Mabry. When she got to Jane, she explained, "This introduction is going to take a little longer and certainly will have surprises for you that were not part of my earlier report. You may want to buckle-up for this."

Twenty minutes later, Captain Mabry had not uttered a word. She simply sat listening with a thousand questions welling up in her head. Finally, she spoke.

"The only reason I am giving this wild story about aliens from Andromeda living among us any credibility is the fact that Melinda vouches for you and we are on the verge of making our first jump back in time. That suggests to me that this technology could have been developed in the past, somewhere else in the universe. Of course, Melinda, you realize on a sensitive secret project like ours, with all sorts of national security ramifications, we will need to *thoroughly* vet Jane before we include her on the team."

"Yes, I expect nothing less," Melinda replied. "I think you should start with a physical exam, looking at DNA for sure, and see what that tells you. It will surprise you I think."

Captain Mabry looked at Jane, who simply nodded her head and smiled.

CHAPTER 16

2200 BCE
EARTH

SIX MONTHS HAD GONE BY SINCE landing on this giant, foreign rock. Aiela and Lieka had not heard a consistent reference name for the planet. They assumed it was because the people they were in contact with had no idea that it was a planet in the universe, circling a star. They only knew what they could see in their daily lives and that was really not much from a limited perspective.

There were various ideas about the lights and the big, white moving sphere in the night sky, and the bright yellow light that shined on them in the daytime. Lieka and Aiela decided it was in their best interest not to attempt to explain anything they were not ready for … and that certainly applied to the cosmos. In their conversations they picked up a local expression they couldn't quite pronounce that seemed to indicate that locals referred to the land they lived on as their piece of reality. The name they used was simply "earth," or something similar that the Golans could never quite understand. So, they simply translated the name into something close to the word ground in their language and among themselves, began calling the place they now lived the Earth.

During the time they had been on the Earth, Aiela had finally decided to share his feelings for Lieka. Overjoyed, he learned that Lieka felt the same for him but had tried to disguise those feelings for the same reasons he had. They were both somewhat surprised that the other members of the crew, and the whole village for that matter, were not blind to what was happening and were not phased at all when the two of them publicly acknowledged their romance and the desire to make their status as a couple permanent.

Ultimately, they worked with Harold to engage in a public ceremony practiced in the village's culture to signify they were bound to each other. With the help of the villagers who had grown attached to them, they built a dome-shaped dwelling for the couple to live in similar to other shelters in the area. The two of them believed it important in shaping their new relationship with the residents of the Earth, so they begin living with them and continued to assimilate into their society. Not wanting to overwhelm the small village with the five other Golan crew members, they worked out an arrangement for a small patch of land about a half mile away where they begin their own settlement, abandoning the landing party's earlier, more primitive campsite.

Possibly influenced by the union of Aiela and Lieka, another romance had bloomed among the crew. Not surprisingly, it was between Jabreen and Obria. Jabreen, the ex-soldier and survivalist trainer and Obria, skilled in martial arts and an expert archer were a natural match. Not long after, another public ceremony was held, officiated by Harold, to cement the union between the two.

As time passed, relationships between the remaining three crew members and members of Harold's tribe began to form. Over the course of the next two years, other unions began to be formalized but these were between the Golans and the native population. Not surprisingly, the Golan settlement that was created at some distance from Harold's small village began to be abandoned as the two groups merged into one village. Life in 2200 BCE was not the easiest and mortality rates were high among the indigenous population, not the least causes of which were from infections resulting from physical injury, or from diseases that were not understood and which had no known cures.

Aiela and Lieka, with input from their medical officer Kala, wrestled with the dilemma of using their knowledge of such things to help. They weighed this against being perceived as having some magical powers which would put them in a position of compromising their physical safety to those who might decide to eliminate them as evil spirits they could not understand.

Kala continued to notice that the Golan crew, after the unfortunate death of several of them soon after arrival, were experiencing an unusual degree of boosted immunity from local diseases that were common to the indigenous population. She began a meticulous review of their habits, including their new diet on this planet. After a time, she discovered a single dietary difference between them and the locals. Some of the seeds from the flowers they had propagated near the old stone circle for their soups had been poured out on the ground after their meals and taken root. After questioning them, Kala found out the surviving crew members had later noticed the sprouts and recognized them as something they were familiar with. They had picked the green stems before the flowers had even developed. Crushing up the sprouts, they included them in salads they had made from nearby leafy plants. She further found out that picking these new sprouts for garnishment was not being done by anyone other than the Golan crew.

She deduced, it was really more of a guess, that the seeds in the garnishment they had brought from Golan into this new environment had been altered in some way by the convergence of the different gravitational field on the Earth and by what she had determined was an unusual electromagnetic vortex in the vicinity of the stone circles in the immediate area. The genetic makeup of the discarded flower seeds, she thought, may have been altered in some way as they germinated and sprouted to bring extra-protective healing properties to them. Kala made the connection between ingesting the newly grown flowers with their food and an almost miraculous boost to their immune systems, giving them protection from attacks by harmful bacteria as well as viral infections that swirled around the local populations.

As a result, in the early stages of their assimilation into Harold's small band, the Golans ensured that the communal meals they shared, which were frequent, included the spice they ground up using the white flower petals, stems, and seeds. The shared immunity was successful. Illness and mortality rates in their small village declined dramatically. With the intermarriage and bonding that occurred, the story of their arrival from another world was slowly learned and accepted by the residents of the very small village, most of whom were now direct or indirect family members of the Golans in their midst. They also understood the value of not sharing this information with anyone from the outside world. They did not want to be suspected of having supernatural powers that would be feared.

Time and again, Aiela and Lieka decided not to try to teach the others about science and technology methods that were familiar to them, although situations often presented themselves that tempted them to break their rule. They knew the Earth people were not ready for their mysterious ways and would not be for generations to come. It was clear that kind of knowledge would need time to develop across various cultures. Any effort on their part to share information that would be of a fractional nature of the whole of the body of science they were familiar with would only lead to confusion, if not wholesale disbelief, and their original fear of being seen as witches or evil spirits would come to pass and they, in turn, would most likely be destroyed.

What they could do, they decided, was to help their little village become early adopters of advances they knew were occurring in small pockets of the population in the Earth. An example that revealed itself to them was when Harold had shown Tom, in that early encounter after they had arrived, his copper axe. Aiela and Lieka realized they already had the means to extract copper from rock, heat it to a temperature that would liquefy the metal, then pour the liquid metal into molds they had fashioned to dry until hardened. So, this technology was not unknown, though rare. They knew from their Golan history that from this advancement, it would only be a small step to figure out how to mix the copper with tin to generate the next advance in metallurgy, bronze. But rather than explain or demonstrate any of this, they simply kept their eyes and ears open for signs that advancements were being made anywhere and subtly convey those methods to Harold, encouraging him to check it out.

What more they could do, they determined, was foster a positive social environment to help create a safe and productive place for them. They learned that other villages within traveling distance of theirs—and farther away, for that matter—were all led by independent village chieftains who were highly competitive. This village-by-village independence and competitiveness was further entrenched by the fact that many different and competing religions had sprung into existence, complicating attempts to unify the broader population in any semblance of agreed upon governance for the greater good.

Aiela and Lieka shared some of their thinking with Harold, who seemed to be more thoughtful and introspective than the other chieftains they had encountered. He saw the wisdom of forging alliances with some of the nearby villages for mutual benefit, something that was reinforced by the early encounter with Tom that became a worthwhile alliance. These moves proved to be timely, as a rumor had been picked up from travelers through their area that a large band of marauders had been moving into their proximity from the north, coming in from the sea, to raid and plunder the small villages in their path.

After the second such rumor had been passed on to Harold, he went to Aiela for advice and counsel. Knowing her military background, Aiela quickly included Lieka in the conversation and she expressed her first thoughts.

"Information is key to preparing for what may be to come.

I suggest we send a small number, two at most, on a trip north to gather intelligence on what is actually occurring and get some reliable information about this band of marauders. How many are they? How are they equipped? How fast do they travel? How likely is it that we are in their path? I believe Jabreen and Obria would be the best suited for this task. We have shared with you, Harold, some of their background. Jabreen being a trainer of soldiers in his past to survive in hostile surroundings and live off the land. Obria is skilled in martial arts and an expert archer. Considering their training and skill sets, they are perfectly suited for this reconnaissance mission.

"I would include Liebeda to go with them but I want to keep her in reserve, so that if these marauders get closer, and we have not heard from Jabreen and Obria, we have someone else we can send out to surveil the situation. I have spent enough time with her to have developed confidence that her military skills coupled with her uncanny ability to move quickly and silently in nighttime environments make her a perfect backup for Jabreen and Obria. If word is that we are in the path of harm, I will certainly volunteer my talents toward preparing this village and those with whom we have developed alliances to give anyone who would do us harm a very unpleasant welcome."

Aiela responded by addressing Harold. "I have no one I would trust more than my wife to lead the resistance to any attack on our people. If you agree, when the time is right, you will be instrumental in arranging with the other chieftains in our alliance for her to be appointed head of our defense."

After a moment of thought, Harold responded, "Agreed. And send Jabreen and Obria out immediately."

Jabreen and Obria were quick to agree to the plan. "Obria and I were some miles from here several weeks back on a hunting expedition. We were surprised to see two rival hunters, who did not see us, riding on small horses. We didn't know that practice was known here yet but apparently it is by some. Our first objective will be to go back to that place, locate and acquire horses for ourselves. We were both skilled riders in our homeland so that will be helpful. The horses will give us the ability to move considerably faster than we would by foot. We should be only a matter of days out from learning what is going on and be back with useful information."

* * *

A day-and-a-half later, Jabreen and Obria had arrived at the location where they had observed the horseback riders. Within a mile of that location, they came upon a small village with a corral containing six horses. After a quick discussion, they decided against simply taking the horses. Thinking they may need something to barter with on their mission, they had brought some copper jewelry and a copper axe. After a meeting with the local chief and several of his people and describing their mission, they learned the rumor of a marauding force had reached this village as well.

Jabreen used the opportunity to gain their support for their undertaking. The chief said that on their way back, if they agreed to inform him of what they learned and introduce him to Harold to become part of an overall plan of defense, they could keep two horses for their use. He further said to keep the axe and jewelry in case they needed it for some trade later. The horses, he allowed with a shrug of his shoulders, were runaways from some travelers passing through a year ago, so they had cost him nothing.

The chief gave them some simple rawhide bridles he had made and two small blankets to use over the horses' backs. Both Jabreen and Obria had experience riding without saddles, so this presented no problem for them. After some further conversation, the two scouts rode off to the north, not to waste the remaining daylight.

"This is a lucky break!" exclaimed Obria. "The chief gave us the direction to the next village to his in this direction, so that can be our next stop. Perhaps the people there will have more information on the direction we should head next. I believe the closer we get to our objective, the more rumors we will hear and the more accurate the details."

"Agreed," Jabreen replied. "I appreciate the gift of a meal the chief gave us to travel with. That will save us time in not needing to forage tomorrow."

Two days of hard riding later, armed with the directions they had obtained at two other stops on the way, they approached a small ridge just before sunset, beyond which they could see wisps of smoke rising into the sky.

"Good thing we got to this point before dark," Jabreen observed, "or we would not be able to see the smoke ahead. It seems too much for cooking fires, so it may be a sign of trouble. Let's tie our horses just before the ridgeline and go by foot to the top to see what's what."

"Jabreen, I am thinking exactly what you are. That smoke is most likely from a burning village. Whatever has happened here may be finished based on the lack of noise I hear coming from that direction. If it was our marauders, they are probably going to encamp there for the night, giving us the perfect opportunity for checking them out."

Twenty minutes later, crouching in the low grasses at the top of the slight ridge, they saw what they expected. What had been five structures were now smoldering ruins. It appeared that the villagers living there had been killed and their meager possessions collected and piled into a nearby wagon. About a hundred yards away, an encampment consisting of about thirty tents had been set up. Armed men, accompanied by what appeared to be women with them, similarly armed, were going about beginning to light small fires for cooking. From the lack of sentries, other than one lone figure standing about fifty yards out perched on a rock, it appeared they were expecting no threats.

Obria softly spoke as she kneeled, looking intently at the encampment in the distance through the top of the grasses.

"It seems we have found our enemy. Their casual attitude tells me they are traveling through the countryside meeting little resistance from a population ill prepared to defend themselves against larger numbers of fighting men and women. Jabreen, how many of them do you estimate are there?"

"From what I can see—and I'm assuming there are several I can't see in the tents—my best guess is about sixty-five or seventy. I see three horses and some sort of cattle they use to pull wagons. I'd say they are traveling at a walking speed with those numbers of people and the few horses. The horses are probably used by their scouts. I would like to get a better look at their armaments and the general condition of their troops. If we can ascertain anything about their future route of travel, that would be a real bonus. Let's see what we can learn tonight. After midnight, the moon will be gone, they should be asleep, and as we have learned about our superior night vision, we should be able to get in and out of their camp undetected. If we are fortunate, we may be able to allow their scouts' horses to escape—which will be a true plus for us in the days ahead."

"Good plan," Obria agreed. "Let's see if we can sleep a little now. It's going to be a long night."

Having no time-keeping or mechanical devices to waken them, the two scouts used a technique they had learned from the native hunters who needed to awaken early for hunting trips. That trick was to simply drink a prodigious amount of water before bedding down, knowing their bodies would awaken them after a few hours to relieve themselves. Sure enough, they both opened their eyes sometime after the moon had disappeared, sometime after midnight.

After arising and taking care of nature's call, they pulled over their clothes lightweight garments Jabreen had brought for this purpose, made from brown and green woolen threads woven into a loose netting with threads hanging down from all of the seams. Then, using some moistened earth, they smeared dirt on each other's faces and hands, cutting any reflection and obscuring the shape of their faces. Now, practically invisible and using their ability to see in the darkness better than the native population, they began their descent down the low ridge to the position of the lone sentry.

Neither was interested in ending a life unnecessarily. Jabreen silently came up behind the sentry and locked his neck in a hold cutting off the supply of blood from his jugular vein to his brain, causing him to pass out. In a few seconds, Obria had tied his hands and feet behind him and together, stuffing a piece of his own clothing she sliced off with her knife in his mouth and binding it in place with another piece of cloth she stripped from his shirt.

"He should be out for a minute or two and he's far enough away from the others. I don't think anyone will hear his muffled grunts when he awakens," Jabreen whispered as they began moving toward the tents and the sleeping marauders. One of the tents was somewhat larger than the others and shaped a little differently. They decided this must be where the leader slept.

Obria softly said, "I can get in there without being seen or heard. Let's see what I can turn up."

"Okay, I'll keep an ear tuned in case you have trouble. I'll find what I can about how they are equipped. Let's meet back here in about eight or ten minutes and turn our attention to the horses. Plan?"

"Confirmed," she replied.

In nine minutes, they were back where they started. There had been no noise. It was as if they had been invisible in their movements. Without a word, they moved to a small corral that had been established for the night by tying a rope around a circle made of eight poles driven in the ground. They simply cut the rope, then led the horses out using the bridles that had been left on them. Luck was with them again; the horses appeared well trained and simply followed them away from the camp.

As they led the horses out of earshot, Jabreen said to Obria, "We will not be able to do anything like that again. These people have obviously not met resistance in their march through the country and so their guard was down. When they realize what happened tonight, they will have more than one sleepy sentry in the future and their fighters will work in shifts. Having all their horses now will give us a tremendous advantage in getting back without them being able to follow. Plus, we can return the two that were loaned to us, keep two of the three that we just took and have one extra for someone else when we get back."

"Yes, Jabreen, and look what I found in the leader's tent. It appears to be a map, drawn on a thin piece of cured animal skin. We have not seen anything like this since we arrived here. Maybe this will tell us more about where we are on this planet, as well as an idea of the marauders' plans. My observation, based on what I saw in the camp and in the leader's tent I slipped into, is that this group of marauders is made up of several different ethnic groups. I saw blond hair, brown hair, and black hair. The skin colors were similar but different. The weaponry I saw consisted of bows and arrows, short fighting knives, and longer swords. The fighters looked to be reasonably fit and their footwear was that of foot soldiers. Since they only had three horses—now none—I think they rely on assault by foot, possibly presaged with an attack by their archers. It appeared they were well stocked with arrows. However, their bows did not look as strong as those we have. And the archers didn't appear to be particularly strong in the upper body. That means their range is limited, which will work to our advantage," observed Obria.

"I got the same impression from what I saw," replied Jabreen. "They have a far superior numerical advantage when they attack the small villages in their path. The villagers that we have seen are not trained in military tactics. My advice to Harold, Aiela, and Lieka when we return will be to use aggressive tactics to harass and weaken them before they reach any of the next villages in their path. We cannot afford to let them make a full-out assault on any more of these virtually defenseless villagers. What do you make of the map you picked up in the leader's tent?"

"I think it is very significant," Obria replied. "We haven't been able to ascertain much about the area surrounding where we are on this planet. This map shows that we are located on what appears to be an extremely large island, with an ocean to the west, and separated from a larger land mass to the east by a large channel that connects to the ocean at the north and south points of this island we appear to be on. From the markings on the map, it seems this is a raiding party that disembarked from boats in the north. Their travel plan seems to be to head south, through where Harold's village is located, and then picked up by boats at the southern point of this island. The boats must be of some size, because they transported the three horses, cattle, and the three large wagons that we saw, plus the sixty or so people in the raiding party. I think we can accurately start referring to these people as village raiders since that is what they are about."

* * *

On the way back, Jabreen and Obria stopped at the village where they had been given the horses. After conveying the information they had gathered and returning the two borrowed horses, they suggested the village chief ride with them to meet Harold and begin the formation of an alliance to deal with an attack by the raiders—something they now believed was firmly in their future.

"Welcome back!" exclaimed Harold as he saw the two scouts nearing the village in the golden rays of a late afternoon sun.

"Thanks, Harold," responded Jabreen. "We brought a guest with us, the chief of a nearby village who was good enough to lend us horses for our expedition. We need to tell everyone what we learned on our reconnaissance mission. There is no time to lose. Can you arrange for a village meeting tonight?"

"Consider it done."

Later, after sunset, the assembled villagers met around a fire in the village center. Jabreen and Obria told what they had learned. In turn, they were informed that in their absence, Harold had not waited for them to get back and proceeded with having Lieka appointed as their military leader by a counsel of the nearby village chieftains. Hearing her name, Lieka spoke to the assembled group.

"Based on what we have learned tonight, it is imperative that we do not allow these raiders to attack any of our villages. The map you retrieved tells us their intended path. I will appoint three lieutenants to organize three bands to be in reserve if the primary plan I will share in a moment fails. Our overarching goal will be to establish a story that will be spread far and wide, a story that this land is a place to be feared by anyone thinking of coming here to plunder or subjugate our people. This land is populated, but not overly so. We will use tactics that will not reveal our true numbers or our lack of a large fighting organization. We will rely on their superstitious nature to believe we are protected by spirits and mysterious otherworldly creatures, some of which they are unable to see or protect themselves from, until it is too late."

She continued with urgency, making sure she had everyone's attention as she spoke. "These raiders have killed villagers to the north of us and plundered their towns. Our emotions tell us to seek revenge, to kill the raiders and drive them away. If we control our emotions and think with reason, that is in our best interest. While there are a number of villages in our land, my intuition is that these raiders come from an area that has a larger population. Based on their warlike nature, if we retaliate in kind now, they will send a more organized force with greater numbers to avenge the casualties we inflict upon them. However, I don't believe the nature of the average person in their country is that different from us. Usually, it is the leaders who influence the direction of a country. Often, their direction is to profit themselves. If their subjects suffer or die in the process, that is not of great concern to them. It is critical that we win over the people in these countries to see us as partners in their quest for a better life. It will be up to them to determine whether they will continue to sacrifice their lives to satisfy their current leadership.

"In the short term, we must convince them it is not in their interest to pursue land or wealth in our part of the world. In the longer term, we must find out more about these people, what their dreams and goals are, and convince them that working *with* us is a better way than fighting *against* us. And, during this time, we should strengthen our ability to defend ourselves. Leaders of tribes or countries change and greedy and self-serving types will most likely emerge from time to time. So, we must develop a reputation as an area that they want to avoid in their quest for more power or riches."

"Okay, Lieka, you make a great deal of sense," responded Harold. "Specifically, what do you propose we do now, particularly as these raiders are headed our way and will most likely be here in a matter of days, or weeks at most."

"I am counting on their superstitious nature to be our ally," she explained. "My plan is to use the horses we have now for speed, using the advantage we have of the captured map giving us their general direction. We will intercept their slow-moving force and begin to work on their superstitions with fears that we will generate. We will do this before they ever reach here. Several of us, as you know now, have superior night vision, and a few of us have fighting experience in moving silently through hostile territory at night. I want Liebeda to lead. She is better than anyone I know at moving swiftly and silently in nighttime conditions. She is an excellent archer and proficient in martial arts. I want her to choose a companion and the two of them set out at dawn towards the raiders' position. She and I will talk after this meeting about some of the ideas I have for beginning our campaign to spread fear among their ranks."

"As you were talking, Lieka, I was thinking I might be playing a role similar to what you just said," Liebeda offered, "and I have decided I would like for Matthew, the younger brother of Harold, to accompany me. I have seen his athletic ability, his thoughtful way of solving problems, and I sense he will be of great help to me."

"Done," agreed Lieka. "This village meeting tonight is over. We'll hold another village meeting tomorrow night to go over more details. Liebeda, you and Matthew come with me to go over a plan for your next few days."

Then Lieka spoke to the chief of the village who had ridden in with Jabreen and Obria. "My new friend, it is too late for you to return home, so we welcome you to spend the night here with us. As our plans for dealing with the raiders progress, I will send a messenger to your village to keep you informed. It is important that we are unified in our efforts to avoid harm from outside forces. Welcome to our alliance!"

Matthew approached Liebeda soon after and expressed his surprise at being chosen for such an important mission. Liebeda reminded him that they had been working together on several village projects and she had been impressed. Matthew was a strong young man, in his mid-twenties with average height for the village at five feet, four inches. He moved with a quickness and grace that was noticeable. He had shoulder length brown hair and a lighter complexion than Liebeda, which had resulted in a sprinkling of freckles across his face, a face usually enhanced by a smile that went with his pleasant disposition.

Liebeda stood at five feet, two inches and had the same dark black hair as the other Golans with only a few strands of white starting to show. Given her Golan longevity, she appeared to be about twenty-five years of age, even though she was actually fifty. Her general size and weight would be mistaken for that of a relatively small woman but that was deceptive since she weighed about thirty percent more. A lithe build, with smooth but taught musculature and, like Matthew, she always had a ready smile showing beautiful white teeth. This was not unnoticed by the comrade she chose, who found her quite attractive and was more than pleased to be accompanying her on this adventure.

* * *

Just approaching sundown two days later out on the plain, Liebeda and Matthew saw several wisps of smoke in the distance. There was a small hill between them and the rising cloud they believed to be from the cooking fires of their quarry. Liebeda motioned for Matthew to stop with her.

"We will ride just a few hundred more yards in that direction," she said pointing toward the smoke, "find a place to hide, and tie our horses. We will get closer to their position in what remains of the day's light, locate a concealed site to scope out how they are encamped, and check for sentries I'm sure they will have put in place. There should be just enough remaining light to get settled in. Then, we will stay put until we believe everyone in the camp should be asleep."

"Okay," Matthew said quietly, even though at that distance it was not necessary. "What then?"

"We are in luck in that while it is not a moonless night, there is only the thin sliver of a waning moon, so we will have a little light that will aid you, even though it's unnecessary for me. Once we have the locations of the sentries spotted, we will go for the one between us and this side of the camp. I will quietly disable him and truss him up with the cord we brought with us. We will use Obria's method of using strips of his own clothing to gag him with. I don't want to leave anything that could be used to identify us, other than the few strips of rawhide we will use to tie his hands and feet. Those are ubiquitous so will be of no use in identification. If he has a quiver of arrows, I want us to take those. We will need arrows later and I don't want to use ours. We want to create a fear in them of this part of the world. We will create an illusion of supernatural beings living here, ones they don't understand and are fearful of."

Matthew nodded he understood as she continued.

"Before we left our village, Lieka gave me this pouch of hallucinogenic mushroom powder that she and Kala made for what we will do next. Once we have the sentry secured and temporarily unconscious, we will blindfold him and I will put some of this powder in his water bag. We will leave him to be found by his brethren in the morning. After getting the gag out of his mouth he will want a drink. Then, by the time he is back in their camp and expected to explain to his superiors what happened, he will be a babbling wreck. And I have an idea how we will add to the tale he will tell in his hallucinating state."

Around 1:00 a.m., Liebeda and Matthew began a slow descent down the hill, crawling and crouching down, taking care to move the grasses as little as possible and taking advantage of low-lying bushes for cover. When they reached the sentry, Liebeda moved the remaining twenty yards by herself and slipped behind the man standing there. She quickly took him down while putting him in a choke hold, starving his brain of oxygen.

Once he passed out, Matthew joined her and secured the sentry as they had planned. Liebeda poured some of the mushroom powder into the sentry's water bag that hung from a cord over his shoulder. Matthew took his quiver of arrows and, for good measure, removed his footwear and his bow, both of which they would hide where they could not be found. The other sentries were far enough away on the camp's perimeter they didn't hear the one guard go down.

"Matthew, carry this guard back up to the other side of the hill while he's still unconscious. Wait for me there. I won't be long."

And with that, Liebeda slowly began moving the rest of the way down the hill to the camp. Watching her leave, Matthew was amazed at how quickly she silently disappeared from his sight in the darkness.

As she stealthily made her way down the slope, Liebeda thought, *let's see what I can do to start them thinking something unnatural is happening.*

Their tents had been erected for the night in a loose circle about ten yards apart, with their three wagons in the center. The cattle that pulled them were in a makeshift corral some distance away being guarded by another sentry. Moving silently to the wagons, she found what she was looking for, a big barrel holding their water supply. She emptied the remainder of her pouch of mushrooms into it.

"Not enough to really get them high but enough to create the odd hallucination they will not be able to understand," she mouthed inaudibly to herself.

In another of the wagons she found additional arrows which she took. She also spotted a container of cooking oil that she poured on what appeared to be a dressed deer among their food supply. On another wagon, she loosened the large wooden peg holding one of the wheels in place—not enough to make it come off right away—figuring that sometime tomorrow it should work its way free. Then as a final act, she moved like a wraith to one of the raiders sleeping just outside a tent and removed a dagger he had in a sheath strapped to his waist.

That should worry him when he wakes up in the morning and finds it has disappeared while he slept.

Liebeda moved out of the camp and back up the hill towards where she had left Matthew. When she found him and their prisoner some distance from the horses so the sentry would not be aware of them, she saw that the bound guard was awake but with his head covered in a makeshift bag so he could not see. She motioned to Matthew to follow her out of earshot, then told him the rest of her plan.

"You are going to become a giant! Strap these two short sticks from dead tree limbs I found to your legs under your trousers to make you stand some two feet taller and stuff the shoulders of your jacket to make your shoulders appear wider. Then hang this shaggy, net drape Jabreen made for us to use as camouflage over yourself, hiding your head and making your body appear larger.

"I want you to stand by those trees in the grass where he won't be able to see the sticks protruding from your trousers. Then, walk just a little but with your back to us. I'm going to *accidentally* lift the bag on his head up over his eyes for a second as I pretend to be checking his bindings from the back. I'll have him facing you for that second. What he will see before I quickly pull it back down is a giant creature.

"We want him to think your strange and frightening form represents the one who captured him so he'll tell the others about it in the morning when they find him. I believe before he starts talking, he will drink some of the water we have spiked. His story should get pretty wild when the mushrooms start kicking in."

Matthew smiled at the clever trick. A few minutes later, they pulled off their little subterfuge without a hitch. The sentry got a glance at the giant in the distance, releasing an audible gasp, before Liebeda roughly pulled the bag back over his head without him ever seeing her size. Leaving him lying there, his hands tied behind his back and secured to the bindings around his ankles, he would surely remain there until the other raiders managed to find him.

When Liebeda and Matthew were out of earshot of the hog-tied sentry, she told him to follow her back to the ridge top. Once there, she unslung her bow, a recurved beauty that was stronger than anything the villagers had and with tension she had the strength to draw fully back. Taking one of the stolen arrows, she wrapped the end with a piece of cloth she had torn from their captive's clothes. Using some pitch she had brought with them for just this purpose, she soaked the cloth, generated a spark from her flint and iron pyrite, and ignited it.

Then, with unerring accuracy over a distance that the raiders would think only a giant could achieve, she launched it into the night sky. It landed on the deer carcass she had covered in cooking oil. In short order, the wagon and its contents were ablaze. Mayhem in the camp ensued, with shouting and screaming as all awoke to the blazing fire.

"This is just the beginning," she said with a smile to Matthew as they headed back to their horses and away from the chaos.

CHAPTER 17

2200 BCE
EARTH

THE INITIAL HARASSMENT OF THE RAIDING party started to have the desired effect. Losing their horses limited their ability to scout ahead of their intended route of travel. The leader of the group was mystified by the loss of his map. They eventually found the sentry, trussed up and gagged. He had reacted just as Liebeda had planned.

When the gag was finally removed from his mouth, the first thing he wanted was a drink of water for his parched mouth. It didn't take long for the mushroom-spiked brew to produce hallucinatory effects. The overwhelmed man began explaining what had happened with an increasing difficulty to stay focused. He rambled on about being captured by giant creatures.

Back at the camp, the fire Liebeda had ignited with a flaming arrow, seen by a few to come from a distance too far away for a normal human to have accomplished, made some believe the giant story wasn't so far-fetched. Looking for clues, they couldn't understand how one of their own arrows was found in the remains of the fire. One member of the band was afraid to mention how his dagger, in a sheath on the belt wrapped around him as he slept in the middle of the camp, had disappeared.

Strange things began to happen the next morning after they had eaten their morning meal, washed down with drink from the water barrel attached to one of the remaining wagons. No one made a connection between the water and the strange tricks their eyes played on them as well as the euphoric feeling they seemed to have for no reason. This lasted for the remainder of the morning, causing them to break camp and move on later than normal. Then, about an hour into their travel, a wheel came off one of the wagons, creating another delay in the day's travel.

The following night, after they were settled in the next spot on their journey, the leader of the raiders doubled the camp guard. When the nervous attackers finally fell asleep that night, Liebeda was back. She silently slipped undetected past the guards under a night sky that had enough cloud cover to limit the light coming from the stars after the moon had retreated. She brought with her a leather water bag but rather than water, it was filled with a red dye made from berries.

She quietly crept up to the leader's tent and squeezing out a thin stream of the dye, created a circle on the side of the tent. She then created a jagged red lightning bolt in the center of the circle. It had no particular significance, she just made it up, but her plan was to use the design in the future to mark the presence of an unknown prowler in their night camp. This was all part of their campaign to instill fear among the raiders who dared step foot in this part of the country. Liebeda then found the tent belonging to the man whose dagger she had taken. Unbelievably, he was again sleeping outside of his tent in the dark night. She quietly stuck the dagger in the dirt by his head and quickly moved on.

If that does not strike fear in his heart, I don't know what will.

She moved on to the remaining two wagons and opened the tap on the water barrel strapped to it. The tap was turned on to allow a stream of water escaping just thin enough that it wouldn't awaken anyone splashing on the ground but it would be sufficient to drain the lot by morning.

Her final stop was the makeshift corral for the cattle that pulled the wagons. She cut the rope keeping them in without the sentry, who was half dozing on the other side of the corral, seeing or hearing her. Whether the cattle escaped or not did not matter. Liebeda just wanted the camp to know that they could have.

I doubt there will be much sleeping tomorrow night, she thought. *But I'll sleep soundly and then pay them another visit the following night.*

* * *

Within a week of Liebeda's nocturnal visits, the raider band was becoming a sleepless wreck. They were low on food. Every other day, they found a circle with a lightning bolt in the center, either marked in the dirt on their path or drawn with the red dye on the side of one of their cattle. Adding to their worries was the occasional sighting of one or two "giants" in the distance, paralleling their route of travel.

The leader of the raiding party had decided the best course of action for his band was to move as quickly as possible to their extraction point on the southern tip of the island, create a defensive camp, and wait for the boats that were to arrive to take them away.

On the day Lieka's scouts saw them depart by sea, that evening found Harold's village celebrating. The scout reported seeing the sixty or so marauders looking gaunt and exhausted as they boarded the boats that had come for them. No doubt the loss of their last wagon carrying the remainder of their food being burned two days before was a contributing factor. The cause of the fire was another flaming arrow, fired from a distance in the night. That could only have been accomplished by a person with tremendous strength: a giant, for sure.

The villagers decided during their celebration to spread rumors to the north of a fearsome tribe of giants who frequented their area, with cannibalistic tendencies. The rumors they spread worked for a few years, keeping marauder's away without the need for bloodshed. Over time, other warlike people came that would not be deceived.

But by then, Harold had developed alliances with other tribes in the area and a form of militia had been organized such that they were able to defend themselves. The giant trickery, along with Liebeda's superior night vision, archery prowess, and stealthy capabilities, they knew was not a sustainable deterrent. But it bought them the time they needed to develop an alliance.

CHAPTER 18

2035 CE
WESTERN UNITED STATES

IT ONLY TOOK TWO DAYS OF expedited vetting for the project team at the black site to approve Jane's inclusion on the team. The results of her physical exam showed the dense bone, muscle, and ligament structure that corroborated her story, along with an eye exam that noted the differences in physiology. What really cemented the approval was the fact that they were able to trace her existence in and around Avebury over the past 110 years. The timeline started with a birth certificate and included later documents that she had handled, in various work assignments, that had been stored away in a remote location by the National Archives, all showing through DNA testing that she had touched them going back at least eighty years. A physical abilities test placed her at the level of a forty-five-year-old woman in excellent shape. At least that was the comparison to a female on Earth.

Dr. Samuel Waters, a phytochemist, was chosen as the fourth member of the team to travel back in time. His task was to take the equipment he would need, analyze the composition of the Ghost Flower, and develop the message to leave in the sixteenth century for the twenty-first century pharmaceutical scientists. The chemical code in the message would be key to create an appropriate medical intervention to treat and to immunize the world's population against the virus responsible for the current pandemic.

Sam, as the chemist told them to call him, explained that the practice of analyzing organic materials for their chemical properties was a complicated process requiring special equipment to create cross-sections of a physical object including its internal structure. It involved extraction and determination of the quality and quantity of bioactive constituents at a molecular level prior to biological testing. The item to be tested may be ground into a powder form, subjected to various solvents, and then put through extensive analysis some days later. This all needed to be done in a sterile atmosphere, devoid of contaminants. He gave a briefing to the team.

"The scientists at this black site have developed a piece of equipment that incorporates new and superior technology. They are absolutely not willing to share what that tech entails at this point, but it can perform the analysis in the field with amazingly accurate results. It doesn't require the process I just described. However, since it is newly developed, there is some question about 100 percent reliability. For a mission as critical as this, with no second chances, they tell me they would like to have a sample of the flower if there is a way to get it to them. A form of redundancy if you will. How to do that without taking any modern containment vessels with us, like glass vials, to leave for the future is a problem they are leaving to us. We can't have someone in the sixteenth century digging up a glass vial, clearly not of that time period, containing a vacuum sealed flower. A discovery like that could alter history in some unforeseen catastrophic ways."

In the days before the trip back in time to 1585 CE was scheduled, the four-person team was inoculated against a variety of medical problems they might encounter. This included a shot for tetanus, diphtheria, and whooping cough. Additionally, they received a shot for bubonic plague. Normally, plague vaccines are extremely restricted and available only to people who have a high exposure to the plague because of their jobs. This team certainly qualified. They were also inoculated against malaria and received booster updates for all other vaccinations necessary for anything anticipated they might encounter. A full physical was performed on all, which turned up no impending problems. Dental exams, plus thorough teeth and gums cleaning was accomplished. No one wanted to start their new life in the past with tooth problems.

After waiting a week to make sure none of the vaccines caused adverse reactions, finally, the day arrived for their journey into the past. Captain Mabry had explained what was going to happen on their virtually instantaneous transit to the location they were going to in Avebury. They were to arrive at 3:00 in the morning in hopes of avoiding being seen on arrival. The sphere they were using for transit was designed to materialize over the span of a few seconds when they arrived to avoid a thunderclap noise that would occur if the materialization was instantaneous. The sphere was designed with sensors to detect any material obstructions and the craft could adjust for those at the landing site.

They were told to prepare for a drop of possibly a foot on landing as the scientists wanted to err on the side of caution for anything unexpected the sensors might find difficult to detect on the landing surface. Since they knew a return trip was impossible, the sphere was designed to disintegrate minutes after materializing at their destination, leaving only a pile of nondescript dust. They were told to expect some disorientation and nausea immediately on arrival but that it would pass quickly.

Their clothing was made in the style of the working class of the time and they would carry minimal belongings with them. That would allow each of them to have a single carrying case that appeared typical of those used by travelers in the late sixteenth century. Each case was locked with a combination, disguised to look like an ordinary clasp. If stolen and opened without the combination, the sides of the case were designed to incinerate, destroying everything within. The temperature of the flash incineration would be hot enough to effectively melt any metals in the case rendering them unrecognizable.

Then there was the matter of traveling money. They realized they would need a small stipend to get started but the problem was sourcing coins that wouldn't cast any suspicion. During the late sixteenth century, English currency was not yet standardized. People still used a mix of medieval and early modern coins made out of gold, silver, and base metals. Also, merchants and traders circulated foreign money from the Netherlands and France. After considerable research and ingenuity, the black site's laboratory was able to reproduce a modest assortment of convincing-looking silver and gold coins, all probably amounting to less than twenty-five British pounds.

"Okay," Doc announced, "are we ready—Jane, Melinda, Sam?"

With an affirmative response from all, they were ushered into the sphere, each carrying their own special case, and sealed in. A three-minute countdown ensued and the mission team in the black site pressed the final key to initiate the action. The sphere faded from sight in two seconds rather than instantaneously to prevent the surrounding air from filling the void with an explosive sound.

"Well," one of the technicians said with an exhale of breath he had been holding, "We have done what we planned to do, let's hope it worked."

Joel and Thomas, who had been officially read into operation with the team at the black site, looked at each other in silence, absorbing the incredible moment they found themselves in. Thomas spoke first.

"You and I can now go to Avebury to see if they were successful. If they were, the information we need to develop a vaccine for the pandemic will be there now, or at least someplace where we can find it."

Thomas added, "I still struggle to wrap my head around the idea that they have almost 450 years to get a message in place for us. For us, the message is there now."

As Joel and Thomas stood there talking, Joel heard a sharp

intake of breath from Captain Mabry. He glanced over and saw a look of alarm spreading across her face at the same time he caught a whiff of smoke. Suddenly, the entire room was inundated with cries of shock and surprise.

"What's happening?" Thomas asked of no one in particular as he looked toward the place where the sphere had been a minute or so before.

What he saw was an electrical fire consuming the electronic panels covering the entire wall behind the sphere's launch site. An alarm sounded to evacuate the area prior to the release of fluoroketone, a non-ozone depleting gas, to suppress the flames. Within minutes, the fire was extinguished but the damage was done.

Later, Joel and Thomas sought out Captain Mabry to learn more about the extent of the damage.

"My preliminary understanding of what just happened is that it was an unmitigated disaster," she began. "The lead scientist I just talked to is devastated. He told me that it could be years before what we just accomplished with the launch of the sphere could be replicated. He said the first order of business would be to determine the cause of the fire. The components of the control system that burned were the result of several years of testing various rare earth elements and combinations of gases that were developed specifically for this system, all of which are now suspect as a point, or points, of failure. He has no idea how long it would take to work through the problem, but it could be years."

The Captain looked completely defeated. As she relayed the news to Joel and Thomas, her spoken words became a confirmation of what she didn't want to believe—but knew she must.

"The other complication he admitted to me is that this extremely expensive time travel experiment was not universally supported by the military nor the government officials involved. He is worried they will not appropriate several billion additional dollars to keep it going after today's events. Even if there is some proof the sphere actually transported humans through time, the fears about tampering with the past, possibly changing the course of history in unknown ways, ways that were expressed in the initial deliberations for this project, will be reignited in discussions following today. If a request is made to spend billions more to continue the program, he doesn't think the support will be there for more funds to be expended. Based on his thoughts, which I respect, I think this project is finished."

CHAPTER 19

1585 CE
ENGLAND

THE LANDING SITE FOR THE SPHERE was programmed to be at the precise location, albeit a foot higher, based on the GPS coordinates Melinda had taken at the ancient stone circle in the woods between the Avebury circles and Stonehenge. It wouldn't be quite as rundown as when they visited it in 2035 but they were counting on it still being deserted. The planned 3:00 a.m. arrival time should help prevent running into anyone foraging in the forest.

The landing was perfect. They dropped to the ground a foot below where they materialized. No one spoke for a few moments as they experienced the disorientation they were told to expect. What followed was the wave of nausea, also expected. Melinda and Sam complained of slight headaches. Doc took a breath and looked around.

"It seems we arrived intact. You all look in good shape, all fingers and toes accounted for! We do have a moon tonight so it's not terribly dark and I don't see anyone lurking about. So far, so good."

They all turned to look at the sphere. As programmed, it began to dematerialize as they watched. In minutes there was nothing left to show that it had ever existed.

"It seems that we should say something about the demise of the scientific miracle of the sphere that brought us here but all I can say is that it worked, we are here, and that is that!"

After a moment of absorbing what Doc had just said, Melinda

looked about the moonlit landscape. "The stone circle is more intact than it was when we visited it before but it does look like the locals have begun the scavenging for building material. And look, over here! I think I spy a little stand of Ghost Flowers!"

Jane saw where she was pointing and let out her breath with an audible *whoosh*. "It's just like the drawing I have in the documents my elders passed on to me years ago!"

Sam immediately took a few samples, operated the code on his case, opened it and placed them inside. "Never hurts to move quickly, even though I know we have plenty of time to come back here, since we are here to stay. But I'm excited and I couldn't resist."

"Nothing wrong with that," observed Melinda. "Let's slowly walk around here, get our bearings, and begin the long walk back towards Avebury. With any luck, we should run across an inn at some point after we reach the road. The next piece of luck will be if there is room at the inn for us. It is not necessary to take the first inn we come to and we don't want to waste all day there but it will be a chance for us to find out what accommodations are in the vicinity."

Jane echoed that sentiment. "I want us to see as much as we can this first day. I want to find out if I can pick up a sense of where descendants of some of my ancient relatives might be. It will be a weird meeting when the time comes to reveal ourselves—me in particular."

Ready to embrace whatever was next, the team slowly began wending through the copse of wood, across a field, until they intersected a dirt road that was heading in the direction of Avebury.

"Our shoes," reminded Doc, "were made by the team at home in the style worn here but invisibly, they added modern inserts for arch support. While the exterior looks like leather, it is actually a porous material that allows for our feet to breathe but also keeps water from the outside from penetrating in so we don't get wet feet."

Melinda pointed out another item they were going to need to

deal with in whatever inn they chose.

"Head lice and bedbugs, I believe, may be a problem here. In each of our cases we have a small supply of tea tree oil we can use to wash our hair with while it lasts. Bed bugs … I'm not so sure how to deal with but we will figure that out. Jane, I'm willing to bet when we meet your ancestors, they will be able to advise us on how to deal with these problems in the long term. The sooner we find an alternative to the local public inns to live in, the quicker we can avoid health issues on a daily basis. That's another reason I'm not keen on jumping into the first inn we find."

"We also need to be picky about the food we eat in the local establishments," Sam advised. "Let's make sure we choose foods that appear to have been well cooked or boiled and as fresh as we can find. When we are able to cook our own food, learn more about decent places to eat, and how various food is prepared, the better off we will be."

"If I remember correctly from our recent tour of the place," mused Doc, "Avebury Manor was built around 1555 CE. As the most prominent structure in the village, it was confiscated by the Crown during a civil war, so I have no doubt that the manor will be inhabited now by a family in favor with the English Crown. I think we should start by scoping that out. My sense is anything we do in a small village like Avebury will come to the attention of the residents of the Manor, who, I suggest, because of their connection to the Queen, have the final word on whatever of importance happens there.

"As we continue our walk in that direction, let's recap our cover story to make sure we are all reorientated. We've come from London, which is a place large enough that they wouldn't be surprised not to have heard of us. Our purpose in being here, we will vaguely describe, has to do with historical research on the village and the stones. As it often does, a little flattery goes a long way. So, to quickly help us get on their good side, we should look for opportunities to throw some their way!"

"Good thinking," Jane commented. "The manor house will be a good starting place for me in finding a way to identify my kin who live in the area."

* * *

The party of four walked on into the morning hours until they reached the outskirts of Avebury. Doc, Melinda, and Jane were all familiar with the Tudor manor house from being there in 2035 CE but it was new to Sam.

"Gosh, I think the gardens and the care taken with the topiaries, are even better now in the 1500s than they were when we were here, just a few weeks ago in the future!" Melinda cried.

"It's interesting to see the place that I was giving tours of 450 years in the future!" Jane added. "I know this place, inside and out, or at least as it will be, after it undergoes some additions and changes in how the spaces are used now."

Marveling at what was not in or around the Avebury they had known in the twenty-first century, as well as how new some structures looked that they had only known as centuries-old, historic sites, the party of four made their way up the manor house road.

With their excitement building, they came up to the front door. Doc took the initiative to knock and was rewarded in less than a minute with the door opening. As they looked upon the young-appearing woman who opened the door, they were speechless. She could have been Jane's sister.

About five feet, two inches tall, the woman had flawless, light almond-colored skin and black hair with a few streaks of gray. Jane's same emerald green eyes were staring back at them. The woman looked at Jane and blinked. An almost imperceptible shiver ran over her body.

"I could welcome you in … and I will … but if you don't mind

...." she quickly and quietly said while looking directly at Jane, "if you would kindly wait in the garden, I will come out in a few minutes and join you." Then, she turned her gaze on the others and introduced herself as a staff member assisting the family living there and asked their business.

Melinda, gathering herself from the shock of seeing an almost mirror image of Jane standing in front of her, quickly responded with a version of their cover story.

"We are visiting the area from our home base of London, doing research on the stone circle we have heard so much about. I am an art historian, and my friends here are interested in the stones and the henge. We are all teachers of a sort from London and wanted to learn more about the fascinating history here, which is not as well-known because of the proximity to the more well-known Stonehenge to your south. We believe that the people living here, if they are willing, could favor us with some extremely valuable insight we could get no other place."

"I will ask. Please wait here until I confer with the mistress of the house who is upstairs at the moment." She closed the door.

Looking at Jane, her three companions had a million questions but knew they would have to wait. Jane quickly turned and walked off some distance into the gardens, placing herself behind a beautiful topiary that blocked her from being viewed through the windows of the house.

A short time passed as Doc, Melinda, and Sam waited silently at the door before it was opened again by the same young-appearing woman. This time, she was accompanied by a woman who looked to be in her early twenties. They assumed this was the lady of the house. She looked them all over in an appraising way and her facial expression seemed to signal she was comfortable with them coming in. With a nod, she indicated to the one who looked like Jane, "Please show them to the parlor and ask James to offer them some refreshment. I will join them in a moment."

"Yes, ma'am. And then, if you don't mind, I'll go to the butcher to pick up the venison we are planning for dinner tonight."

"Fine, I'll see you when you get back."

After James, serving as a butler, or something of that sort for the house, escorted them into the parlor, the young Jane lookalike reemerged at the front door and headed through the garden toward the village butcher's place of business. She immediately spotted Jane and walked over to her.

"I'm shocked. I knew the minute I saw you that you are of Golan descent, as am I. What I don't understand is that I know the numbers of us who retain some of the original characteristics of our ancestors are very, very few. I only know of two and they don't live anywhere near here. I didn't want to have the mistress confused as to why there was a person at the door who looked like me! It's difficult enough for me with my differences to blend in as it is. Two of us? Well, that will take some thought before trying to explain. Where do you come from?"

"Excellent question. But first, what should I call you? My name is Jane."

"Hmm, that's good. A common name, not one of the tongue-twister names of the old ones. Mine, too, is not extra-ordinary either. Mary."

"Mary, I had a feeling I would meet some, or at least one, of my ancestors here in Avebury. What I didn't expect was someone who looked so much like me. I appreciate the quick-wittedness you showed at the door to get me out of sight. You asked where I came from—that is a story that will take some explaining. We are not what we seem to be. Oh! Nothing criminal or dangerous or anything like that! It's just not something I can explain properly in a few minutes. We recently arrived and have not yet found a place to stay tonight. If you can recommend something, we can meet there later and tell you our story, a true one, that will stretch the bounds of your belief. I really look forward to spending time with you. I haven't known anyone else with our heritage for decades."

"I work at the manor house during the day," Mary replied. "I have my own small house about a mile from here. It's small, but if you don't mind being a little cozy in the sleeping accommodations with your friends, you are welcome to stay there tonight. Later, I will bring enough food for our dinner and we can talk. Are you familiar at all with Avebury? If not, I can give you directions. You can go there now. I'll tell your friends where to go when I get back to the house after my food shopping for the family is done. The key to the door is in a small crevice in the trunk of the apple tree beside the house."

With a smile, Jane replied, "I'm very familiar with Avebury. That's part of the story I'll tell you tonight." With just a few more words, including the directions to Mary's house, they went their separate ways, both impatient to learn about the other.

※ ※ ※

Sundown found Doc, Melinda, and Sam gathered at the front door of Mary's small cottage. The setting was picturesque. The thatched-roof structure was located thirty yards off a small road passing by the front of it, surrounded by a few tall shade trees, but with open spaces containing flower beds, apple and peach trees, and a small grape arbor. The exterior walls of the Tudor-style cottage were covered with white stucco between the dark wood structural beams. The windows were not overly large, with bevel-edged diamond-shaped glass panels that would give pleasant refraction inside on sunny days. Window boxes were situated under the two windows flanking the front door, which was a sturdy looking affair of heavy oak boards supported by ornate hammered black iron hinges. A single stone step led up to a larger stone landing at the door.

The sturdy door opened to a cheerful, candlelit interior, with a small fire in the fireplace across the large front room. Mary stood there, smiling, and welcoming the travelling party to her home. Jane was just behind her. The first to speak was Doc.

"A beautiful place you have here. It looks like something out of a fairy tale!"

"Thank you. I'm Mary, by the way. I didn't introduce myself earlier at the manor house. Jane and I have had quite the conversation waiting for you to arrive. I will admit that if Jane had not been with you for me to see in the flesh, I might not have believed the fantastical story of your presence here."

"No surprise there," Melinda spoke up, "I probably wouldn't have believed it either. In fact, I'm still pinching myself to prove I'm awake and not just dreaming all of this."

After a little more greeting chatter everyone introducing themselves with some background information on who they were, they gathered around a table while Jane and Mary took the initiative to bring in platters of cooked venison, vegetables, and bread. Mary produced a pottery jug containing wine which she offered all around. She explained she had made the wine herself from the bounty of her grape arbor. Taking in the mouth-watering aromas of the feast, Sam had to hold himself back from reaching out to sample the savory morsels being laid out in front of him. Smiling at Sam, Mary told them all to sit and began serving their plates. After a time consumed by focus on enjoyment of the food and wine and complimenting Mary, the conversation turned to their reason for being there.

Since Jane had told Mary about the pandemic hitting the future world—and their interest in the Ghost Flower—the conversation turned to some questions about the present. Melinda was curious to learn more about the properties of the Ghost Flower. Were they really effective in boosting immunity, and if so, why weren't they used more widely in this time for preventing the diseases that afflicted so many people?

Mary responded, "All good questions. Let me start with some background. My ancestors, and Jane's, came from a planet in the Andromeda Galaxy. When they arrived, it was by accident. They realized that quickly enough but it took decades for them to determine where they were exactly in the cosmos and where Andromeda actually was in the night sky. Remember, they had never seen their galaxy from afar. I know a lot about their early history because of a secret record they decided to keep, chronicling their time here. Over the centuries, this record has grown to seven books. Three are in the original Golan language they decided to use so they wouldn't be interpreted if they fell in the wrong hands. Three other volumes are the translation into English of the first three and the seventh, in English, is the latest record, written in English so no translation needed. The translations were done after a few centuries had passed and the Golan language was no longer being used by newer generations where fewer and fewer of us could even read it. I'm the keeper of these volumes now. I make annual entries and keep them safely hidden away.

"They determined that the chemistry of the Ghost Flower, they called it a different name on Golan, was altered by the environment here once they started growing it. On Golan, it was simply a pleasant tasting garnish for food, believed to have some health benefits, possibly for the heart or blood system. Some seeds were brought on the voyage by the original scientific crew. They found that two aspects of this environment had a profound transforming effect on the plant's unique chemistry: the electromagnetic energy in the vortex here around the Avebury stone henge and the different gravity exhibited by this planet as opposed to that on Golan. Over time, they discovered the ability to alter a person's immune system was only possible by ingesting the flowers grown near Avebury. And, the flowers bloom only once each year. They tried, without success, to propagate them near other stone circles, like the one at Stonehenge. We have never determined why it didn't work but the fact remains it doesn't.

"This led to a simple problem of basic economics—supply and demand. If we tried to help others by sharing what we know about the flower's disease fighting properties, the demand would be overwhelming and the supply would be brought to extinction. The effects of the plant, they found, last for about a year after ingestion. Calculating the extent of the supply they could produce, it appeared the flower, with its slow growth, very limited environment to grow in, would only be sufficient to serve a small number of people— about thirty or so."

Sam, with his chemistry background, immediately understood the problem.

"This is 1585 CE. Science has not developed enough for anyone to even understand, much less develop, a synthetic alternative to the flower itself. It can be done in the time we come from but certainly not now. Even though I understand how to do it, I don't have the pharmaceutical equipment, staff, or anything else necessary to make it happen here. What I did bring with me is a small instrument that will allow me to analyze the chemical properties of the flower, record the chemical make-up and then find a way to record what I find for our team in the twenty-first century to work with. That is the goal of our mission."

"So, with a limited supply, how do you allocate what you have?" Melinda asked Mary.

"Well, human nature being what it is, if the secret of the flower was revealed, there would have been a stampede of desperate people flooding into Avebury and all of the plants would have been ripped from the ground in a panicked frenzy in no time. An extinction event would have been almost immediate. There was another problem faced by my ancestors and, by extension, me too, even today. Not understanding how immunity was gained by ingestion of the flower and its stems and seeds, they would look to someone like me to explain. Not I, or my ancestors, could give an explanation that would be understood by a population existing in this time. Oh, maybe a few would get the gist of it but that would make little difference. Without a knowledge of chemistry, science, immunology, viruses, genetics, or bacteria, any explanation given would have been incredible mumbo jumbo that would have been ultimately ignored. I only know what I do because of what I read in the journals kept by the original Golans here who understood all of that.

"As you know, people are afraid of what they don't understand because they think what they don't understand might harm them in some way. And, there is a *lot* that is not understood in the world today. The voids in understanding are filled in with superstitious beliefs, mythology, and religion, of which there are many beliefs, some at odds with others and some whose beliefs are quite extreme. I could easily be classified as a witch or sorcerer—people here believe in that—so if I began talking about this mysterious healing flower I have, my life would be extinguished pretty quickly, in more than likely some gruesome fashion. You do know that trials for witches are common in this time. Many have been killed in the name of protecting others in the community. I have no interest in being one of them."

Doc offered Mary a glimpse into the future.

"This is yet to happen but in the new world, America, there will be public trials of witches, in a village called Salem. Trials that will be historic in nature. Europe will have many more over time as well. You are wise in being careful not to appear to possess powers beyond the ordinary.

"We gleaned from some old, well, old in our time but new in this time, writings by a monk in Salamanca, Spain, that mentioned the villagers here were rumored to have some protection against disease. Many reasons were given, including witchcraft, work of the devil, and one small mention of the flower referred to as the Ghost Flower. How, then, are the people here protected if the source of the protection is a secret?"

"This was an inquiry that I read in the history I have," Mary nodded her understanding of Doc's question. "The same thing was pondered by the early ones, referred to as Aiela and Lieka, along with a person born of this planet during their time, a tribal chieftain called Harold. What they came up with was an annual celebration where the entire village, which was actually only about thirty people including the Golans, were invited to a feast to commemorate something that was popular at the time. Over the centuries, the celebration was linked to whatever the latest trend was in society to celebrate. I use Christmas now as that time. You know, I work at the manor house in the village. I've been employed there for about twenty-five years. It affords me the opportunity to keep abreast of all of the news of the village and the country because of the notable guests coming and going.

"But I must admit, I'm the one who planted the idea for a *special* party each year at Christmas. There are multiple parties held at the manor house during holidays because of the connection to royalty and others that come here from quite a distance. My part in this was to have one of the parties held by the lords of the manor exclusively for the residents of Avebury. Being part of the staff and involved in preparing the food for the festivities, it is not difficult for me to gift some of my special spices to the chef for the stew he prepares. Fortunately, the spice does add a nice flavor so I've not had any difficulty with their acceptance of my gift."

"Wouldn't the chef ask for it for other parties?" Melinda asked.

"Yes, he does ask," Mary replied. "I tell him I have a cousin; a sailor on a trading ship. Once a year, when I go to Liverpool to visit him, I say, he always has a small amount of this spice for me that he gets from an Indian tribe in the Americas, near one of the Spanish colonies his company trades with. So, I tell him it is very precious to me since I have such a small supply but, as my Christmas gift to the community, I want him to use it—which he does."

Melinda followed up with another question. "The document we saw suggested that no one in the village ever got sick from the plague. How do you get everyone in town to partake of the stew?"

"Hmm, that is a fallacy in the story. Not everyone partakes. There will be one who is away traveling, or one who just doesn't like the stew. One or two of the villagers do come down with whatever deadly disease is going around but everyone else does well for the ensuing year. But other than that, the story is surprisingly accurate."

Sam, who had been quiet up until that point, spoke up.

"This story is getting better all of the time. The fact that the boost to a person's immune system lasts for a year after one ingestion leads me to think we could develop a vaccine that could be given as a single dose each year. Well, I shouldn't have said 'we,' because it will be the team in the future that will develop it. Our task is to get them the exact chemistry to work with. In fact, with your permission, I would like to use a small device I have in my travel bag to run a test tonight in the privacy of your home to determine the chemical makeup of the flower and seeds. I have a couple of the flowers in my bag that I collected near our landing site."

"That's fine and I have a few flowers here in the kitchen you can use as well if you need them," Mary offered.

"Another situation we need to address tonight," observed Melinda, "is how we introduce Jane to the community with her appearance being so similar to Mary's."

"Believe me, I've been worrying about that all evening," responded Mary. "I think I have a plan. What if I said that I was told as a child that my mother had a sister, maybe I could say a twin sister, living in another village around the time I was born. When I was older, I discovered that my aunt had a daughter in the same year I was born but, sadly, both the sister and the baby died in childbirth.

"When you return to the manor house tomorrow under the guise of starting your research work with the family in the manor, you will bring Jane along. They didn't see her earlier today so it will appear to me that it is the first time we are meeting. It won't be hard for me to feign the same surprise I felt earlier today at seeing her. I could ask for a moment alone with you to ask all of the questions the manor family should think I would. Then, after a suitable time, we could return to the house and explain you are the cousin I had been told died in childbirth. We can devise a simple story of your life somewhere else and how your connection with Doc came about through a shared interest in the stones of Avebury. The current family in residence at the manor have only been here for a couple of years after living in London. We should be able to come up with a convincing story. Once they get past the surprise, I don't think they will have much more interest in wondering about our similar appearance."

CHAPTER 20

1585 CE ENGLAND

Doc and her party arrived at the manor house at 10:00 the next morning, this time with Jane clearly part of the group as they arrived. The door was opened by Mary after their knock, just as she had the day before. After a moment, Mary raised her voice, so that others in the house would hear, and expressed her shock at seeing someone who looked so much like her. Jane took her surprised turn at seeing Mary with a performance that would be the envy of any professional actor.

The young woman they had met the day before, Lady Deborah Pilkington Dunch, on hearing the commotion, quickly came up behind Mary, followed by the butler. Taking just a minute to sort out what the alarm was about, in a calm voice appropriate for the lady of the house, she invited them all in. Not appearing to be able to control their interest and curiosity about the other, she suggested they go into the kitchen to continue their conversation while she talked with Doc and the others about their objective in Avebury and how she might help. Jane showed no surprise at the introduction but smiled to herself as now she was seeing, in person, someone whose name she had mentioned so many times as a tour guide when leading her groups through the manor house in the twenty-first century.

Doc's objective was to establish the purpose of the team's visit. She explained they were in the area to do historical and some limited archeological research. She wanted her team to be able to roam around the village, the stones, the henge, and the surrounding countryside and ask questions of the residents without suspicion. If she had judged it right, Lady Dunch and her parents, when they returned, would let the word out about what they were doing. She believed a universal human trait was satisfaction in being the first to have new information or gossip to share.

Having met Mary early on in their mission was hugely beneficial. She could show them around and introduce them since everyone in the village knew her. This would allow the team to work on the problem of how to leave a coded message on the chemistry of the Ghost Flower for the twenty-first century team to find 450 years in the future. Seeing what they had to work with in the village as it existed in 1585 CE and comparing it with what they knew would be there in 2035 CE was critical. She also knew that over the next 450 years, there would be countless archaeologists, historians, and visitors combing every inch of the place. How to hide something that wouldn't be found or destroyed in that long period seemed impossible. But a way just had to be found.

Sam had completed his chemical analysis of the flowers the night before and was satisfied with the result. He announced to the others that he had the notes he needed, including the chemical symbols, ratios, and percentages, and other bits of information that would be useful to the researchers in the twenty-first century. He combined and encrypted all of the data into a string of letters, numbers, and symbols that he said would be understood by the pharmaceutical staff receiving them. After reviewing what he wanted to send, Doc's team agreed it would be difficult to etch all of the coded message on a stone or other artifact that stood the chance of surviving centuries in Avebury without attracting notice or being destroyed. But now that the message to be sent was clear to them, a rough outline of a plan started to take shape.

Doc's team realized Joel and Thomas were immediately

planning to start their search for the message they would leave behind in Avebury. If the team could not find a way to hide it here, they determined they might be able to leave a clue to lead them to where they did embed the coded message. The first place they considered was at the small, abandoned, and overgrown stone circle of their landing site—the same site where the Ghost Flowers had been harvested over the centuries by the Golans.

They had all walked the site before Doc's team left the twenty-first century. *Could that really have been only a few days ago?* And it would be only a few more days from now that Joel and Thomas would arrive there after traveling from the United States to England. Melinda had etched in her memory the site as it stood then. She planned to go back to that site to see what was there in 1585 CE. She hoped that her memory, which was quite good when it came to details, would tell her, at least fairly closely, what remained undisturbed for the next 450 years. That could be the place to leave their clue.

* * *

Doc's team had spent their first night at Mary's cottage in the woods just outside Avebury. They had gone to the manor house the next morning and arranged the faux reunion of Mary and Jane, followed by a day of being introduced to a number of the villagers by Mary and looking over the village they knew from the twenty-first century, comparing what they remembered with what they were seeing now. After returning to Mary's at the end of the day, they spent their second night in her house—the second night of their new lives in the last years of the sixteenth century.

At breakfast, after awakening in this new reality, Doc verbalized what they had all been thinking.

"Our reason for being here, our purpose in choosing a trip in which we knew there would be no return, is to get the formula, the chemistry, of the Ghost Flower to a place it will be found in the twenty-first century by Joel and Thomas. We will focus on that for as long as it takes to be sure we have done the best we can to ensure it is located somewhere they will find it. Then, we have the rest of our lives here, in the world as it is for us now. What will we do? Where will we go? We are all purpose-driven people. What will be our purpose after we accomplish this mission?"

Mary was the first to react to Doc's contemplative statement.

"I have read the record of my ancestors. They faced the same question in their time and I believe they came up with a good answer. They possessed knowledge, gained from living the first part of their lives in an advanced civilization—knowledge that could help or harm. They decided to use what they knew of a society that had moved thousands of years ahead of Earth to help those they could, while not revealing Golan knowledge that needed to develop here organically, the kind of insight that needs to be revealed to people only when they are ready for it. In a sense, they followed the examples, unwittingly, of the teachings of many of the great religions on Earth. They used their experience to do what they could to help people see the value in living together in peace in harmony. They didn't try to inject scientific or technical knowledge into lives if they were not ready but instead found small ways to inspire them to learn and grow at their own pace."

Everyone turned their full attention to Mary.

"On Earth," she continued, "Christianity, Islam, and Buddhism all had great prophets who spoke for their respective deities. Interestingly, the Lords of these religions, and there were many more than these three, were spoken of as all-knowing, all-powerful beings. But think about this. None of these prophets told their followers about specifics like electricity, viruses, bacteria, galaxies, or all of the other scientific knowledge that would come later. It would have been too much, too early in the development of humanity. Rather, they used parables, stories that were timeless metaphors to be interpreted differently over time as society advanced and grew through the centuries. Some of the rules or decrees that came down were simply believed to be divine direction without specific reasons. As an example, some, but not all, Muslim sects were instructed to only eat fish with scales. The unexplained reasoning may have been geographically determined, such as some waterways were polluted and bottom feeding fish, like catfish, were unhealthy to eat in those places. Fish with scales typically feed higher in the bodies of water, so they stood to be healthier for a human diet. My Golan ancestors helped their Earthen countrymen, who they were becoming assimilated with through proximity and intermarriage, in these same ways. They didn't attempt a futile and dangerous course of trying to *explain* magnetism, for example, but simply showed them the reaction of magnetic rocks to iron. They let the determination of *how* these things worked become developed over time by the indigenous population."

Jane continued with Mary's thinking.

"That is what I tried to do here in Avebury, Mary, 450 years after you. I didn't have the Ghost Flowers to help prevent death and illness because they were extinct by my time but I tried to help in other ways, not revealing my differences. By the way, you may be interested to know that this cottage, your cottage, was purchased after you left it and it was added on to in the twenty-first century to became a popular inn. I referred people to it, not knowing it was ever yours, or that I would ever conceivably be staying here in the past! Also, there is no mention of this cottage in the Golan historical records that I kept in 2035."

"No, there wouldn't have been," Mary confirmed. "I wrote the few pages that span the time of my life here. I have lived in other places than this cottage. That type of information just isn't important when condensing important Earth-Golan events into a single line or two summing up each year that passed. Some years were not commented on at all. The history had to be kept small and compact so that it could be safely hidden and easily moved from generation to generation. That brings up a question for me. If you were the keeper of the documents in 2035 CE, and you will never return to that time, what did you do with them? Where are they in the future?"

Jane smiled and answered, "I couldn't leave them behind. The Golan lineage has been so watered down over the centuries I had no one left to which I could hand it over. That being the situation, I brought the books with me. They are in my travel case. When I received the volumes years ago, I was advised in no uncertain terms not to reveal the information they contained to anyone other than a Golan descendant. I haven't even divulged some of what I knew from my reading of the documents to my companions on this team, although I have shared some of it in a general way. I now know there is no longer a need for keeping anything from them."

Mary looked surprised, then said, "Well, I have the documents here with me now, so how can you have them, too?" Then the answer dawned on them simultaneously.

"There are now two sets of the records of our history!" exclaimed Jane. "The set passed down in history to me was yours at one time. The one you have now is the same one, you just hadn't passed it on before I arrived. What happens next will be different than before, because now you have met me. But you obviously will pass it on to someone later to get it to me in the future. Otherwise, I wouldn't have had it to help us get this far. This time travel has some extremely weird consequences."

"Hmm, I need to think about this," Mary said. "Now that I know what I know, I can't write something about meeting you in this time and have you read it in the future. What I may do is write no more history from my time here and ultimately pass it on as it is written before I met you to one of the few other Golan descendants left. Someone who will be unaware of your presence here. They will add to the story from their perspective going forward never knowing what I did not include. That will allow you to get what you have, which will be accurate, but without any mention of your being here now, or anything that I am involved in from this time forward. You recall I said that it is not unusual for years to pass without entries."

Jane understood immediately why that was important and it answered her unspoken questions about how she could possess documents from the past that did not mention her presence and why the documents she had would be the same as Mary's except for the additions made by other Golan descendants who were updating the records over the next 450 years.

"Okay, back to Doc's original question," prompted Melinda. "What will we all do when our mission here is complete and we have the rest of our lives to live at the end of the sixteenth century and into the seventeenth?"

Jane was the first to respond.

"Now that I have met Mary, I would like to continue to have a relationship with her. That means I want to have a future in some proximity to her as she is the only person I know with our heritage. Because of the intermarriages over the centuries, we know that our Golan DNA is here to stay on Earth. But it has been diluted so much that I don't feel a connection to anyone with remnants of that DNA like I do with Mary. I don't want to lose this connection.

"Scientists in the twenty-first century found DNA, passed down through time, in many Earth beings from the early Neanderthal ancestors who have been extinct as a species for thousands of years. But there aren't strong connections between people in the twenty-first century just based on that DNA connection, probably because it comprises such a minute amount of their makeup. It's obvious with Mary that the DNA connection between us is way more than that!

"Beyond keeping in touch with Mary, I am excited to have the opportunity to visit people and places I have only read about in history books. Who are the artists, scholars, and inventors of this time? It would be fabulous for me to meet and talk with them. Needless to say, I understand the dangers involved in revealing that I have had a glimpse of the future. But that future I'm aware of could be changed by the mere fact of my presence here and some of the interactions I want to have with my new contemporaries. That means I could tell someone about the future and be entirely wrong about it, simply because my presence here and talking about it may well change that future. My interest is to see and hear them, certainly not talk about anything that may, or may not, resemble a future reality."

"Interesting and insightful," mused Doc. "Before we go on with this topic, even though I'm the one who brought it up, I'd like to get back to the main issue at hand for now: what are we going to devise as a medium to record the Ghost Flower chemistry Sam has analyzed and recorded? Furthermore, where are we going to hide it undiscovered for the next 450 years, yet still have it placed so Joel and Thomas can find it?"

"I've been giving that a lot of thought," Melinda responded, "I'm not locked in on a medium but a place for Joel and Thomas to find something might be the old stone circle where we landed. We visited it in the twenty-first century so we know what survives from our time now. They are familiar with that place and will look there, straight off on their return to the area, I imagine. I think we may be able to leave a clue there to direct them to another place. However, the down side of that site is that it's a good bet that professional and amateur archaeologists will be looking over that stone circle, even though it is a minor one without the fame and draw of Stonehenge and Avebury.

"So, what clue can we leave there that they will see that others would overlook or, if they see it, would ignore? As for the chemistry code, we can't just chisel it into a stone and leave that. That much information would certainly be noticed and taken by someone long before Joel and Thomas would get to it. We did say before we left that the first place to look would be Avebury, including the old stone circle abandoned near here."

Jane added, "I agree with the old stone circle being a weak possibility but we should check it anyway. We seem to be concluding that we can't leave our coded message about the composition of the Ghost Flower in Avebury but we can leave a clue directing them someplace else, then. What are you thinking Melinda?"

"Well, we agreed that if Avebury didn't work, we would consider the University of Salamanca. We know it's there now and will still be there in the twenty-first century. I say we leave the chemistry code *there* and a clue *here* to tell them that. The clue will be a Salamanca *el boton charro*. It's just a simple, large silver bead with eight smaller beads surrounding it representing the eight districts that compose Salamanca. Jane, we were there before we met you and we were all given a stickpin whose head was this *el boton charro*. Joel and Thomas will get the significance, I'm sure. So, where do we put this clue?"

"We need to assume that some of the places we put the clue may not make it the 450 years for them to find," Mary suggested. "Chances of success will be better if we put the clue in more than one spot. Jane, you were giving tours in Avebury in the time they will be there looking, so let's go over what is in Avebury now that will have been there then. The more I think about it, there are three places that come to mind. The manor house is one and the church next door another. The old dove cote behind the manor is a possibility. The more obvious place we were thinking of earlier, the stone circle and henge, will be frequented by probably millions of people between then and now. Anything we leave there will certainly be seen as unusual and may not stay undisturbed or even remain there over the years. So, while we leave it on our list to check out, the circle and henge may not be a good place."

"I would like to go back to the manor house," Jane suggested, "to see if I recognize any of the artwork or statuary that is there now that I remember from my time taking people on tours of the place later. I know there was one fairly-common looking still life of a flower whose only significance was that it was old ... old as in about 450 years old. That insignificance was why it was never moved to a museum, or sold at auction, or taken down. I don't know when it was acquired but it may be there now. I'll go look for it.

"Also, there are several gravestones adjacent to the church that survived the years and I believe the old dovecote on the grounds of the manor was there then and is there now. Additionally, the public well that is in the circle of stones will later be enclosed in the Red Lion Pub, a structure not there now but will be in the future. We may be able to leave a sign there just inside the well's stonework that they could spot. During the time Joel and Thomas will be there, the old well in the pub is covered with a glass, or plexiglass top, I don't recall which, and used as a table. I think the interior of the well is lit as part of the tourist attraction, so if they sit at that table, they might see something we leave for them."

"This is good thinking," observed Doc. "After we resolve the issue of where to leave a clue directing them to Salamanca, we will go to Salamanca, meet the monk, the author of the old manuscripts that ended up in the University of Salamanca archives and work, somehow, with him to get the chemistry message into the same volume where he mentions the Ghost Flower. A challenge will be to find him and the monastery he lives in now. At least we think we know his name from what we learned when we were there before. Brother Francisco, I think he was called, but I remember only that. Usually that name would be followed by *de something* which we don't know. Unfortunately, I have a feeling Francisco was a popular name so there will probably be more than one Brother Francisco in the area—but then how many will be involved in working on illuminated manuscripts? I'll wager only one! I especially think that will be true because 1585 CE would have been at the end of the era of producing illuminated manuscripts. Printing presses had mostly taken over since their development around 1450 CE."

Melinda joined in with, "I suggest we start with the *Convento San Esteban*, or Convent of San Esteban in Salamanca. If we aren't lucky there, we can branch out to some smaller places."

With a confused look, Sam asked Melinda, "If we are looking for a monk, why are we going to a convent, not a monastery? I thought those were for nuns."

"In later times that would be true," Melinda explained. "But in historical usage, as in 1585, they were often interchangeable."

"Okay," declared Doc, ready to get into action. "Let's plan to put our clues out now while we are in Avebury. Mary, you can get us access to the manor house when the residents are all gone. I'd like to have a few minutes with the old oil painting Jane mentioned was there in 2035. If it's there now, with a little titanium white paint, I think I can retouch the brown center of the flower, the pistil, with dots representing the charro button. Where a signature is normally located, I'll use a darker paint so it won't be too obvious and write in *aqui*, the Spanish word for *here*."

Mary interrupted with, "I think I know the painting you are talking about. It *is* there now."

"Great," continued Doc, "the symbol for Salamanca and the word *aqui* should be something they will figure out. We will put this little combination in several places. If they don't get it at once, when they see it more times, they will figure it out. They are smart guys."

"I agree with the smart part but if our clue is too subtle, the backup plan was for them to go to the University of Salamanca library archives and see if they can find something there. However, I think they will see our clue and not waste too much more time searching Avebury for the message about the flower's chemistry," added Melinda. "At least I hope not."

><)))•••

CHAPTER 21

1585 CE ENGLAND

DOC'S PARTY WAS GREETED BY A beautiful light the next morning; the rising sun shining through the surrounding trees created a dappled light on the interior walls of the cottage. As they woke from a surprisingly restful sleep and congregated in the kitchen area, Doc remarked, "What a nice sleep! No traffic noises, airplanes flying overhead, or streetlights like the time we came from that never lets darkness and quiet completely take over. I know I will get used to this!"

"Okay, where do we start today?" asked Sam.

Mary said she needed to report in to the manor house. "I don't think it is a good idea for all of us to show up there this morning but I don't think it will surprise Lady Dunch if you come with me, Jane. We did such a good job of acting like long lost relatives yesterday, she will understand our desire to spend time together today. I will tell her you agreed to help me with the various errands I will be responsible for."

"Good. Sam, Melinda, and I will head out to the old stone circle to see what's undisturbed. Next, we'll look at the village well option, which in later years will be enclosed in the Red Lion pub," Doc added to the plan.

Mary, and her long lost cousin, arrived in town just as the sun was coming up over Avebury. It looked as though it would be a beautiful, late spring day. The rising sun was lighting up the thin layer of clouds to the east, creating a beautiful display of color. The small village was active already as cooking fires were burning in the cottages, some of the residents were already heading out to tend their fields, and the merchants, such as the local butcher, were preparing to open for their first customers.

At the manor house, it was still quiet except for activity in the kitchen. The middle-aged man they had met as the butler the day before was clearly in charge of the early morning preparations going on in the kitchen. There was a woman about twenty-five who was introduced to Jane as the cook and a much younger girl, around fourteen it appeared, who was helping her out.

When they met, the cook and the young girl tried to be polite but their expressions betrayed a sense of suspicion. They had become used to Mary's slightly unusual appearance. But when confronted with her cousin who looked more like a sister and had the same unusual appearance, their tamped-down suspicions were reignited.

Introductions over, Mary walked Jane out of the kitchen and whispered to her, "I'm afraid bringing you here is going to get complicated. These folks, as good as they are deep down, are a somewhat ignorant lot and they view strangers suspiciously. What they don't understand, they tend to fear. That fear causes them to search for explanations for that fear. When none are obvious, their superstitions begin to overcome their logic. Over time, I have managed to ease those suspicions, at least to a large extent, but now with *two* of us, I'm worried. I think I need to show you around the house as quickly as possible, allowing you a chance to find likely spots to leave clues for our twenty-first century visitors that will come here in the future. You will know what survives the 450 years between now and when you were giving tours of this house then."

"Agreed," Jane said in a quiet voice. "I picked up on their body language immediately and sensed the suspicion they were experiencing. Let's get this done before the others in the house are up and around." They moved through the other rooms of the house quickly, staying clear of the bedrooms where there were clear sounds of early morning movement of those beginning their preparations for the day.

As they quietly moved through the house, Jane was surprised at how little the furnishings, and the rooms themselves, resembled what she knew from her time as a tour guide in the twenty-first century. She spoke to Mary about her observations.

"This is going to be harder than I thought. There is a lot that happens to this Tudor house going forward. In about fifteen or so years from now, new owners, Sir James and Mrs. Devora Mervyn, arrive on the scene and add on to the house. Another major renovation happens in 1740, when the Great Hall, which is where we are now, is remodeled. Then, in the twentieth century, a BBC television series, *The Manor Reborn*—don't ask now, I'll explain what television is later—renovates nine of the rooms to reflect the different historical periods this house survives. That means that virtually everything we are seeing now, by the twenty-first century, will be somewhat shaken and stirred—with some of these furnishings being either restored or replaced with reproductions.

"I'm not certain this is fertile ground for us to leave a clue. However, I do notice something that will survive. See that floral still life oil painting over there? That's the one I told you I saw on my tours in the future. It was moved to a room that was redone to reflect the Tudor period. Probably made it there since it is actually from this time period. Also, while a nice painting, it does not appear to be particularly valuable, meaning its provenance is sketchy ... even more so now. But I know it does survive and will be in the house when Joel and Thomas arrive to look for clues. So, if Doc is able to doctor it up with the clues she mentioned yesterday, I'm sure they will look around carefully when they go into the room designated as Tudor."

Mary looked at Jane with a strange look, hearing about all that happens to the house she is so familiar with years into the future.

"You can tell me more about what is to come, later. But now, I think we have found our target for a clue, the painting, so we better get out of here before the Lady comes down from her bedroom. You meet me at the front door, outside, and I will join you as soon as I tell the butler of an errand we are going to run—a fabricated errand, of course."

In just a few minutes, they were on their way, walking first next door to the old Saxon church, old even in that time. "This is another place we could look for a spot but this structure could be more difficult. There aren't many nooks and crannies here that the priests and others aren't totally familiar with. I say we leave it alone," suggested Mary.

"How about the dovecote. It's here now and will be in 2035," offered Jane. "If we can find a loose brick or two, we can pry them out, make our marks, and replace them. We need a source for some mortar to put them back in place. Perhaps we can obtain some from that building project I saw just a short distance from here. It wouldn't take much to surreptitiously gather up a little after they have mixed it and come back here later to replace the bricks."

"Worth a try," replied Mary. "I know the builder. I think I'll just ask him for some. I'll say it's to repair some brickwork at my cottage. That way, we won't have to be sneaky and risk getting caught and having to explain."

"Better plan," responded Jane, then she added, "Since we have some time together today, tell me a little more about yourself."

"Sure, and then you, Jane, can fill me in with more about your history."

Mary started with the time she was born, which she said was the year 1495 CE, making her ninety years old, even though she looked about forty-five.

"I had a mate once, years ago, a nice young man, a native of Earth, no relation to our Golan ancestors. Our relationship started off well, I really enjoyed his company and the intimacy we shared.

However, as time went on, he had questions about why he seemed to be aging faster than me and how I was so much heavier than I appeared. He was also amazed at how strong I was. I finally decided to tell him about my ancestry, which I had kept secret until then, being quite vague about my parents and other relatives—a vagueness which had become a problem for him.

"When I started to unload all of this," she sighed, "at first, he thought I was kidding. Then, that changed to suspecting I was losing my grip on reality. Finally, I think he begin to see that I was serious in what I was sharing with him. He never believed that my ancestors came from another world. He couldn't begin to fathom something like that with his limited knowledge and experience—being a creature of the sixteenth century. So, in his mind, with his limited understanding of the universe, he began to rely on conspiracy theories of the time about witches and agents of the devil to explain my wild stories. That belief truly frightened him.

"It was not long after when I knew our relationship was over. We split up and he moved on without telling me where he was going. He had developed a true fear of me by that time and wanted to get away from me as fast and far as he could. I was truly fortunate that he didn't widely share his new beliefs about me with the townsfolk, or I could have been in real trouble—mortal trouble. As a result of that experience, I am very cautious about forming personal relationships with men, knowing that it is making me miss out on one of the real joys of being alive."

Jane was quiet for a bit, then shared her own experience.

"I understand what you have confided in me better than most because of my own failed relationships with men and, frankly, I've not even been able to develop real friendships with women. Living in a world where we must be very cautious about revealing who we really are is a tough road to travel. I have recently begun to open up to Doc and her team. It's because they are open-minded, smart, and knowledgeable about the universe beyond Earth, even though they have not traveled beyond here. But the fact that they took a leap of faith to participate in this time travel adventure told me that they were the type people who would believe me when I told them about my past. And, they believe you, Mary, as well."

"That's comforting," Mary nodded. "It is really nice to have someone with a shared history to talk with. I haven't had that for decades. I know more about science and the worlds beyond this from what I learned from my long-deceased parents and the records I have of those that preceded me. They taught me about the existence of viruses, bacteria, food-borne pathogens, and all sorts of science that is unknown by my contemporaries here. I do what I can to help myself and those around me to stay healthy to the extent I can, which, unfortunately, is very limited since I cannot explain *why* I would advise someone about an act they are about to take. For example, a piece of meat that has been left uneaten for a day may still look okay but they can't see the unhealthy bacteria that has grown on it. That's something they don't know about and I would sound to them like a crazy person if I tried to explain."

"Well," Jane added, "a lot more was learned by scientists between now, 1585 CE and 2035 CE. For example, a vaccine was developed to prevent polio from crippling or killing children and adults, almost eradicating that health issue. More vaccines were developed for other ailments, easing human suffering tremendously. However, just like in this present time, 1585, there are a number of people in 2035 who fear what they don't understand. They will also believe bad information if told to them in a way that taps into their emotions. Some things are a constant I'm afraid; one of them being that our politicians seem to clearly understand this and appeal to our emotions rather than logic to sway people into actions and beliefs that further their ends, not necessarily those that are in the best interests of their constituents. Churches are also guilty of this manipulation to serve secular ends, disguised as religious beliefs."

Jane took Mary's hand in hers.

"Our mission here is to discover the chemistry of the Ghost Flower and somehow find a way to leave that information in a place where it will be found 450 years from now by others on our team. Assuming we are successful—and I sincerely believe we will be—scientists in the future will take that information and develop a vaccine that will fight a raging pandemic that has the potential to cause as much harm as the plagues of this time in history. Our team in the future will need to be very circumspect in how they obtained this information for developing a vaccine. If they attempt a truthful story about traveling back in time for the information, the entire plan, even with the potential for the life-saving vaccine, will be scoffed at and no work will be done on its production. Similar to our situation here, *n'est-ce pas?* We know things that will benefit people but if we get too far ahead of mainstream knowledge, we will be in that situation of the public fearing what they don't or can't understand. Sad, but true. However, that's up to our colleagues in 2035 to figure out. We have our part to do here and now."

While Mary was quietly absorbing this information, Jane changed the subject back to the task at hand.

"Let's check out the dovecote and see if we can find a loose brick or two that we can take out. Then, we'll return to your cottage to meet back up with Doc, Melinda, and Sam. Tomorrow, we should be able to replace the bricks with our clue embedded in them. Oh, and we'll tell Doc the painting we talked about is there and we know the exact location in the house now."

On the way back to the dovecote on the manor property, they passed the construction project they had noticed earlier, where they planned to ask for some mortar.

"Look," Mary pointed, "they are in the process of molding clay bricks in preparation for firing them tomorrow. I mentioned I know the man in charge, John Mallow. I have an idea, follow my lead." And with that, Mary walked up to the man she knew.

"Hello, John," Mary said with a big smile to the handsome-looking, blond-haired construction leader. "I'm doing a small repair on my cottage. A few of the bricks are damaged and I wanted to repair them, so I was going to see if you would give me a small pail of the mortar you will be mixing to lay your bricks. But as I see you are just now forming the bricks from the raw clay. Rather than get mortar now, I would like to buy some of the clay mix and form some bricks to replace the ones I was planning to repair. That will give me the opportunity to personalize them with some art of my own!"

With an equally big smile, John allowed, "For you, Mary, I would never charge for such a small ask. I know many times in the past you have given me more on my plate at the pub than was covered by what I paid. How about I give you a wooden mold, a bucket of wet clay, and you can form up two bricks tonight and bring them back to me just after dawn tomorrow when I will be preparing the kiln for firing. You can pick them up when they are done."

"Thank you for being so helpful," Mary smiled.

"This must be your cousin I've heard about standing over there," John said pointing to Jane. "She can carry the pail of wet clay and you can carry this small wooden mold. My, she really does resemble you. Can't help but see the relationship."

After John assembled the pail with clay and the wooden mold and handed them to Mary and Jane, the two "cousins" thanked him profusely and promised to be back first thing in the morning. As they walked away, Jane commented on John's obvious attraction to Mary.

"Yes, you are right in your observation," she confirmed, "but because of what we talked about earlier, I've been afraid to reciprocate in any meaningful way—other than perhaps to load up his plate when he visits the pub."

·∙⊪⫷•⫸

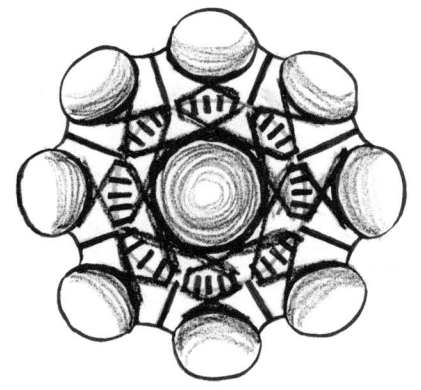

CHAPTER 22

1585 CE ENGLAND

THAT EVENING FOUND THE CREW BACK in Mary's cottage reviewing the accomplishments of the day. Doc, Melinda, and Sam reported on their observations at the community well and their visit to the old stone circle a few miles distant from Avebury. Doc was lukewarm in her report.

"The well is lined with brick but I don't know how anything we put there will hold up over 450 years. I think our activity in replacing a brick there would not escape attention. Further, the well is heavily used, so anything we put there will likely be scrubbed off through use or replaced entirely as routine maintenance is undertaken on the well. I think we should scratch that possibility for hiding a clue off our list."

Melinda added, "I agree. The old stone circle is not much better. There is certainly more stone there now than in 2035. That is the basis for my concern. The fact so much is removed over the next 450 years tells me that many people will be poring over those stones looking for something they need or want. I think anything we put there will draw attention and be long gone before our 2035 team arrives."

"Then," Jane said, "that leaves the two places Mary and I visited today. We think each has real potential for hiding a clue. The first is the painting we discussed earlier. It doesn't get a lot of attention now, according to Mary, and we know it is still in the house, although it will be in a different location in 2035.

"The second, the dovecote, is an excellent choice as well. Mary sweet-talked the construction leader on a project in the village into giving her what we need to make two bricks that we can use to replace two that are there with our special markings on them. Mary and Sam are placing the wet clay into the wooden molds outside now. When they have them ready, they will bring them inside and Doc, you, and the rest of us can put our *boton charro* marks on them with the *aqui* letters. We may disguise what we do for a time by covering our inscription with dirt or clay that will slowly wash off over the years. Sam may have some ideas about what material, other than just raw clay or dirt, we could put on them that would take hundreds of years to dissolve."

Jane continued, "Mary and I will take them back to the construction site in the morning for firing. Mary can tell us a good local source for the paint you will need, Doc, for the modification of the painting in the manor house. Once we have that, Mary can let us know when we will have an opportunity when no one is home to add our clue to the painting.

"Doc, I see from the expression on your face something is troubling you other than what we have discussed so far."

"Yes," admitted Doc. "When Melinda, Sam, and I were making our rounds of the village today, we picked up some local gossip. It appears that word of Mary's "cousin" suddenly appearing has generated an outsized interest. This is a small place without a lot of excitement. So, Jane's appearance has gotten attention. Apparently, there has always been a little curiosity about Mary. She doesn't seem to have aged in the time most here have known her. Her eyes are a departure from the norm and her quickness and strength have been noted. When Jane showed up with almost identical characteristics, well, that has tongues wagging. I'm worried about some of the local superstitions starting to blend into the talk without a good result. I think we need to do what we came here to do: leave our clues and then beat feet out of here."

With an expression of alarm, Jane responded. "Tomorrow, I will ask Mary to go solo taking the bricks to the construction site. No point in me making another appearance with her now that the village's curiosity is aroused, giving them further opportunity to compare the two of us. I think I need to stay here at the cottage. The rest of you can take care of planting the clues and then we leave posthaste for sunny Spain and Salamanca. Sam can go with Mary to replace the bricks at the dovecote and when Mary gives the word, just you, Doc, go to meet her at the manor house and take care of altering the painting."

* * *

The next evening found the group in Mary's cottage discussing their success that day. Doc managed to embed her clue on the painting in the manor and the bricks they had molded were handed over to be fired in the kiln serving the construction site. The construction supervisor had asked Mary about the markings on the raw brick. She satisfied his curiosity by explaining them as a family emblem she thought would be appropriate for her cottage. Since he didn't know Spanish, the *aqui* lettering meant nothing to him.

Mary explained, "I will pick up the fired bricks tomorrow and Sam, you and I will go to the dovecote tomorrow night after mixing some mortar here to make the switch with two bricks currently there. Let's plan to be there after midnight when all should be quiet. I have inherited my ancestors' ability to see relatively well in low light, so I can handle the replacement without need for a lantern to see what we are doing. Your presence with me will be good in the unlikely event someone is about and spots us, they won't be able to see well enough to identify who we are. But seeing a couple out late at night will be assumed to be a romantic liaison, rather than a suspicious lone individual lurking about.

"Mary, have you any suggestions regarding our best route of travel to get from Avebury to Salamanca?" Doc inquired.

"Yes, I have been thinking about that. I'd like to accompany you, at least part way, to help you navigate the territory in these unfamiliar times for you. Traveling overland is an option but a poor one. It is far and we have to cross the channel separating us from the mainland. Plus, there are mountain ranges to cross and we will likely have to deal with thieves more than once along the way.

"That being the case, I believe we should go by sea. The most logical port for us to embark from is to the west of here, a place called Portishead. It is a small port, used for commercial vessels as well as fishermen. We should be able to arrange transport once we are there with one of the commercial ships headed for Gijón, or Xixón, as some call it, in northern Spain. That will cut weeks, if not months, off our travel time compared to travelling the entire distance by land. It won't eliminate our exposure to thieves along the way but it should reduce the frequency."

After thinking about what Mary said for a few moments, Doc announced she agreed with the plan. Melinda and Sam also agreed and were relieved that Mary was willing to accompany them.

Doc directed Mary to develop a map they could use and to begin assembling what supplies they would need for the journey, suggesting that those be kept to a minimum. If she had any ideas about how to get to Portishead other than walking, she wanted to hear it. She further directed Sam to be sure to pack some of the Ghost Flowers. She hadn't totally worked out how they would use them when they got to the monastery in Salamanca but there was an idea she planned to follow up on when they got there.

To arrange for transportation, Mary suggested that she and Jane could ride together in her horse and wagon. She also knew where they could purchase three other horses for Doc, Sam, and Melinda to ride ... horses she was certain they could sell when they reached Portishead.

"Perfect!" exclaimed Doc. "We brought a small amount of money that should be enough for the horses. That's the plan. Now, let's work the plan."

* * *

Two days later, they had achieved all they set out to do in Avebury and were ready to leave. Mary had told her employers that she was going to Liverpool to attend to an old family friend who was like a father to her. She had received word he was gravely ill. She said that being the case, she might be away for an extended period of time. Her cousin, Jane, had agreed to go with her and the other three who had arrived with Jane would go with them for part of the way since they wanted to travel to the southwest side of England for the next phase of their research work.

The next day saw them on the road, headed west on their newly acquired mounts. Jane and Mary rode in Mary's wagon and Melinda and Sam seemed quite comfortable with their rides. But Doc, while not complaining, didn't seem quite as suited to this mode of transportation. She did mumble something about missing her BMW.

The distance to be traveled was something less than fifty miles. Not being in a particular hurry, and not conditioned to riding and needing frequent rest stops, they decided to plan on three days to get to Portishead. Sam suggested they could get there more quickly but was outvoted by the others since the ride would be scenic and they really weren't pressed to get there.

>•)⋙··

CHAPTER 23

1585 CE
ENGLAND

LATE IN THE AFTERNOON ON THE third day of their journey, the party of five reached the top of a rise overlooking the village of Portishead and got their first look at the port and the docks.

"Wow, what a beautiful spot," exclaimed Melinda. "I see several boats in the harbor, some smaller, which I assume are fishing boats, and a couple of larger ones which could be commercial vessels. Let's camp the night here and head down in the morning to see what we can arrange for passage to England."

"I've talked with several tourists over the years in Avebury," spoke Mary, "who came there from Spain by boat and disembarked in Portishead. For the most part, their trips were uneventful but there was one in particular I remember who said they encountered pirates along the way. The only thing that saved them was the appearance of a Royal Navy frigate which, by happenstance, was traveling in that same area at the time. The pirates broke chase on their vessel and headed away before the Royal Navy ship was close enough to cause them harm. I'm only saying this to let you all know this is a possibility."

No one looked pleased at hearing this.

A little later, Doc suggested that they should consider Mary's story of the pirates when they chose a ship to take them to England. "We want a crew who can defend themselves if we run into anything like that!" Little did she know that pirates were becoming a lesser concern than the growing friction between Spain and England.

* * *

The next morning, the party of five rode from their camp in the higher ground to the village of Portishead, searching for a stable to hopefully sell their horses. They eventually found what they were looking for and rode up to the stable entrance. There, they met a very fit-looking young man, pounding a horseshoe on his anvil, sweating from the labor and the proximity to the fire used with his bellows to superheat the metal he worked with.

Looking up, the young man asked, "Well, you are an interesting looking bunch! What can I do for you."

Sam, picking up on the pleasant vibes he was sensing, replied, "Good morning to you, mister! We are travelers, strangers to this village, and looking for a sea captain willing to take on five passengers heading for Spain."

To which the young man replied, "Sure, I can help you. My uncle has a commercial freighter and sometimes does take on passengers for the extra revenue. But going to Spain right now is tricky business, what with the hostilities growing by the day between England and Spain. He may not be making more voyages to Spain with what is going on."

"What do you mean; what is happening?" Sam asked.

"Have you been living in a cave or something?" the young man asked in a somewhat surprised voice. "The animosity between England and Spain is reaching a fever pitch. The war clouds are so thick I'm surprised that even in a cave you would have noticed."

"No," Sam said earnestly, "we are travelers and have been out of touch for some time with the current news." *About 450 years out of touch*, thought Sam, *but I best not get into that.*

"Well, my uncle's name is Charles Henry, he's a sea captain." The blacksmith pointed to the mast of a particular ship in the harbor. "Look for a ship called *The Twin Star* and there you'll find him. Tell him James sent you to talk with him. He may be interested, as he often makes a run between here and the northern Spanish port of Gijón just north of the Picos de Europa. But more to the immediate point, you seem to have come to my stable with more in mind than information."

"Yes," asserted Doc, as she found her voice. "Would you be interested in taking these horses off our hands for a fair price?"

"Well," James mused as he turned his attention from the odd group to their livestock, "there is a growing need for horses, with the impending war and all, so maybe. But first let me take a closer look at them." He inspected each horse in turn, assessing their age and overall health and condition.

"They look healthy enough, all about fourteen-hands high, and fairly young. What are you asking for them?"

Mary spoke up, fishing some papers from her saddlebag, "Here is the bill of sale from our recent purchase of these three mounts and the paper for my horse and wagon. Take a look. It will save time in haggling if you are willing to purchase them at the same price."

Taking the papers, he slowly looked at them, one finger lightly rubbing over his chin as he thought about an offer.

"It looks like you made a decent deal for these horses, so if you are willing to sell them for the same price as it appears you bought them for, we may be able to reach a deal."

"One more thing," said Mary, "Since we are heading for Spain, I'd like to be paid in Spanish *pesos*—pieces of eight as they are sometimes called. Can you arrange that?"

"Lady, this is a port town. Getting the currency you want is easy. If you will include the horses' gear and the wagon, you have a deal."

James directed them to a local tavern for lunch, after which he told them to return and make the exchange. About an hour later, they returned and the deal was completed as arranged.

"Thank you, James," Doc said as she bowed her head in

appreciation of his kindness. "Now, we'll head down to the ship you pointed out to see if we can arrange passage with your uncle, Captain Henry. How will I recognize him?"

"That will be easy enough," James chuckled, "he will be the tall one, standing about six feet, unlike any in his crew. He's around forty-five years old, has long hair, and a short beard. He told me once he fit the description of exactly what he thought a sailing captain should look like! I said he looked more the part of a pirate than a proper English gentleman but he just laughed. I think he actually liked my comparison—he no doubt took it as a compliment."

"Hmm," Doc replied, "sounds like he could be an interesting character."

After wrapping up their business, the travelling party began walking toward the ship. As they neared it, they could see quite a bit of activity in and around the boat.

Doc said, "Looks like they are loading up for a voyage sometime soon. Let's find the captain to see if he's willing to take us on."

A few minutes later, they stood at the foot of the gangplank, looking up at the tall man peering back down at them.

"What is your business here?" he bellowed. "Either spit it out or get out of the way of my men!"

Doc just smiled and said to the others, "I like this guy already." She shouted out, "Captain Henry, your nephew James said we should talk with you about a proposition to take on five passengers for the trip to Spain."

He saw her trying to keep her smile from turning into a grin and thought, *I like a lady who is not easily intimidated, let's see what she has to say.*

"Okay, permission to come aboard *The Twin Star* is granted. Come up and make your pitch—just you, the others can wait."

With that, Doc hopped on the gangplank and quickly made her way to the deck where the captain stood.

"Okay, lady, let's hear it."

"Don't beat around the bush, do you? I admire that. Here's the proposition. We are looking for passage to Gijón and are willing to pay a fair price."

The captain looked at her unwavering gaze, straight into his gray eyes. He gave her a price that was about a third of what they had received on the sale of the horses.

"Done," Doc said.

"You don't want to bargain with me? How do you know what I quoted you is a fair price?" Captain Henry inquired with a wry smile.

"Well, I have a deep sense, my dear Captain," Doc replied in her most polite and formal voice, "that even though we've only just met, you are a man I can trust. So, no, I don't want to debate the price you are charging us. If you say it's fair, I believe you."

"I see," he said matter-of-factly. "Well, then. I don't normally engage with the few passengers I sometimes take along but I'm going to make an exception. The passage will take about two days, depending on the wind. I'd be honored if you would dine with me in my quarters on that one night we should be at sea. And, of course your companions are welcome as well. They look like they could be the source of interesting conversation. Agreed?"

"How could I refuse?" she said with a sincere smile.

"Settled then. We will depart with the outgoing tide in the morning which will be around six. You should plan to board about a half hour before. I'll see you and your party then. What name will you be travelling under?"

"Miss Ada Sendall, plus four," she quickly responded.

The captain raised an eyebrow and then turned back to directing his crew with authority as they loaded their merchandise and supplies for the trip. "Get moving there, mate. We haven't got all day!"

Doc returned to her own mates on the dock and suggested they find accommodations in the town for the night. She took a glance

back at the ship and drew a deep breath for courage. Things were
certainly different in this time!

* * *

Later, after finding lodging at one of the two inns in the village,
they were seated at a trestle table in the dining room, discussing
the day's events and talking about what would come next. Jane,
Mary, Melinda, and Sam had all noticed the interaction between
Doc and the captain.

Jane was the first to comment. "Seems like you and the captain
hit it off pretty well, I think."

"What do you mean by that?" Doc said a little defensively,
inwardly feeling herself start to blush. "I was only being polite and
perhaps just a little flirty to get a good deal for our trip."

"Yea, sure," added Sam "so why do I notice a little flush on your
face as you say that?"

"Okay, I did find the man handsome," she confessed, "and he
has a confidence about him that is contagious. I'll admit, I do think
he is different and interesting, not at all like the men I have been
acquainted with in 2035."

CHAPTER 24

1585 CE
AT SEA

DAWN'S LIGHT THE NEXT MORNING FOUND Doc and her party boarding the ship and being shown their quarters. As they looked around, they could see the ship was fully loaded and had a crew of about twenty able-bodied seamen. Even though relatively young, they seemed seasoned and all appeared to instinctively know their roles and responsibilities.

Melinda commented on the beauty of the small harbor located on the left bank of the Severn River, the quaintness of the village nestled around it, and the beautiful slope of the wild-flowered ground rising up to hills in the distance. As the last of the darkness faded away, the sky appeared clear blue, with little humidity and a few white cumulus clouds drifting by, highlighted by the rising sun causing a gorgeous faintly orange glow on their undersides.

"I could live here," commented Melinda.

"I was thinking the same thing," echoed Doc.

Within an hour, the ship had cast off. With her sails unfurled, she was making good time down the river on its way to the Irish Sea via the Bristol Channel and would soon be headed to the Bay of Biscay north of Spain.

The day passed rather quickly, with Doc's party both trying to stay out of the way and looking to see what was happening with the busy crew managing the sails. In the early afternoon, Captain Henry joined them on deck.

"What do you think of our vessel?" he asked with an obvious pride in his voice. "It's a relatively small boat with a minimal crew but she's fast, she's sturdy, and she's provided me with quite a good living. We have a little time now, so tell me something about yourself and your traveling companions."

After a long hesitation, Doc decided on keeping things a bit mysterious to start. "I have a story about us that I was prepared to tell you but I'm not sure I want to tell it. I have this odd sensation of trust around you and I'm not sure I want to spoil it by telling you a lie. The truth will take some telling, so perhaps I can answer your question tonight at dinner in your quarters?"

Both of Captain Henry's dark eyebrows raised this time and Doc thought he was about to respond, when instead she saw he was looking with concern beyond her into the distance. She turned to see what had caught his attention.

In a low voice he murmured, "That looks like trouble," followed by a loud shout, "First Mate! Call the crew together. We've got a black ship in the distance there and from the look of her sails she will be on us in half an hour."

The crew was assembled in under a minute when the captain gave them the bad news.

"Break out the arms from the locker below deck and prepare to be boarded. We won't be able to outrun her but we can make them pay dearly for trying to take us. They won't fire their cannons at us other than warning shots, because they want to take our ship and cargo as a valuable prize. We've been through this before, mates, and we will survive this attack."

Then to Doc, he commanded, "Take your party to your quarters and stay there."

"Not on your life. My companions are fit and trained in martial arts and I can handle a gun with the best of them. We will not cower in our quarters, Captain, passively waiting on the outcome of the battle."

He glared at her as though she were sea-drunk.

"This is not negotiable!" Doc added firmly.

Surprised by the ferocity in her voice, he replied, "Okay, missy. You have the right to defend yourself, so if that's your choice, so be it!" He turned on his heel and was off to direct his men's preparations.

Doc gathered her companions who had heard the exchange.

"I know I took the liberty to speak for all of us so if any of you disagree, that's up to you. It never came up before now but I was around guns as I grew up, and, not to brag, but I'm a pretty good marksman."

Mary piped up at that point.

"I read the accounts of my ancestors and understood how they survived using fighting skills they tried to hide unless necessary. I took lessons early on in martial arts and I also became an expert archer to follow in their ways."

Jane looked at Mary and added, "There's more alike in us than I thought. I have done the same and I know we both possess a strength and agility that is far superior to most—if not all—of the men I have encountered. I'm sure we can not only hold our own but we can help out the seamen we will be fighting with."

Sam had to admit he was not as skilled as they were, then reminded them they didn't know how brutal these pirates might be. But he told them how he happened to become involved in this project was not only because he was a phytochemist and a Ph.D. but that he was also a captain in the U. S. Army. He had gone through quite a bit of military training in that capacity.

"So, I wouldn't want to match my skills against yours but I did see combat in the Middle East back in the day."

"Wow! That's all I can say," mumbled Melinda, who was starting to stretch her leg muscles in preparation for any swift body blows she might need to land. "Okay, comrades! Let's stick together and make a difference in whatever happens next."

Captain Henry was passing them right at that moment. Doc reached out to him.

"Captain, you don't know much about us but I am telling you we can add to your fighting force. No time to explain but we have two quick requests, if I may. I'm an accomplished marksman. If you have two rifles that can serve as sniper rifles, I can lower the odds as they begin closing. And since they are muzzle loaders, allow me to have a man to load for me. The loader can be relieved from helping me when we are boarded to do his own fighting. Two in our company, Mary and Jane, are expert archers. I don't know if you have anything they can use aboard but if you do, they will be quite formidable."

"First Mate!" the captain yelled. "Quickly, come here! Give this woman what she is asking for. She has my blessing." With that he moved off, shouting more orders to his men.

The surprised first mate, a daring-looking lad with ginger-colored hair who went by Jones, quickly came to Doc's side. After hearing her requests, called over a seaman, relayed what was needed and told him to get with it immediately and to assist Doc with loading. He told another crew member to look in the cargo hold for some hunting bows and arrows in a shipping crate bound for a customer in Spain and to bring those to the two who looked like sisters.

Shortly after, Doc's party was armed with bows and arrows for Jane and Mary, two long rifles with a powder horn, cloth patches, and rounds for her, plus the seaman had given Sam two loaded pistols and a fighting hatchet to use when those pistols had been discharged. The seaman pointed out that the pistols were for close-in fighting and there would be no time to reload them. Doc would be on her own after she had finished with the rifles. Her plan when that happened was to stick near Jane and Mary if she could.

In the next few minutes as everyone was getting into position, the pirate ship fired a warning shot across the bow of Captain

Henry's boat and through a bullhorn, ordered them to surrender. The Captain feigned ignorance to what was being said. He ordered half his men to remain hidden until they were boarded. The other half had their weapons hidden close by each of them and were instructed to mill about in a disorderly fashion, looking panicked.

The ruse seemed to work as the pirate ship closed in and the vandals tossed grappling hooks aboard the merchant vessel in preparation for boarding. At that moment, Doc, lying prone behind a low box on the foredeck, fired the first shot as she was signaled to do so by the captain. That shot took down what appeared to be the first mate on the pirate ship. Quickly taking the second loaded rifle from the seaman helping her, she dispatched the sailor at the helm of the attacking ship. As planned, her seaman had reloaded the first rifle and she took it back and began firing at the first of the attackers leaping on board.

At this point, chaos erupted with the screaming attackers leaping on board and Captain Henry's men now showing none of the faked panic but fighting like banshees to repel the boarders. Outnumbered by almost three to one, the skirmish should have been over in minutes. But to the surprise of the attackers, the anemic response they expected from a merchant ship was not to be.

Jane and Mary had positioned themselves on the quarter deck and began to shoot arrows with amazing speed and power at the wave of attackers coming over the gunwales of the merchant ship. They began falling two-by-two with arrows piercing deep into their bodies. Between Doc's firing and the barrage of arrows, within the first minute of the fight they had reduced the attacking number by nearly twenty, making the odds more two to one rather than three to one.

But the overwhelming numbers still had an effect. Many of the pirates were now on board, including their cowardly captain who reluctantly joined the fight after watching his front men get so pathetically beaten. Out of fire power, they resorted to hand-to-hand combat with the merchant ship's crew.

Melinda and Sam had teamed together and were using their martial arts training to good effect. While they were not able to gain an advantage in taking out a large number of the assailants, they were able to hold their own.

Not so with Jane and Mary. Abandoning their bows and arrows as the attackers closed in, they used their superior quickness and strength, combined with swift offensive moves entirely unknown to their attackers, and were taking down those around them with uncanny speed. Mary quickly identified the panicked pirate captain and delivered a quick death blow to his throat. Despite the chaos, at one point, glancing beyond the attackers directly in front of her, Jane saw one of the pirate crew fighting with a calm and deliberate skill that made her think he was ex-military.

Captain Henry looked over in amazement from his own fighting to notice Jane and Mary standing in the center of a pile of bodies. Just then, while he was back to grappling with one of the pirates, a second man came up behind him with a massive club preparing to bash his skull while he was preoccupied with the man in front.

Mary saw what was about to happen, snatched up a pike that one of her attackers had dropped as he fell and, with a powerful throw, impaled the man behind Captain Henry. It struck with such force that the man was thrown into the wall beside the Captain and suspended there for a moment by the pike that had gone completely through him and into the wall behind before gravity slowly pulled it free and allowed him to fall to the deck.

The captain was losing momentum to the man in front of him because a third pirate appeared out of nowhere and had struck him on the side of his head. Jane, seeing what was happening, picked up a dagger lying close by. Not skilled at throwing a knife, she simply hurled it as hard as she could at the man who had struck the captain. That man had slightly turned his head toward the other pirate who had slammed into the wall with the pike sticking from him.

The knife Jane threw did not turn such that the blade was forward when it struck but rather the brass butt of the handle hit first, striking the man's head with such force that it crushed his right eye socket and rendered him unconscious. Captain Henry, regaining his footing and overcoming the shock from the blow to his head, was able to dispatch the original attacker with a dagger he pulled from his belt.

Jane and Mary worked their way, fighting, over to the dazed captain and faced off two more attackers who were moving in to secure a kill on the merchant ship commander. But it was not to be. With a speed that shocked the two attackers, both went down like sacks of grain, one with his Adam's apple crushed and the other with an elbow strike to his head that cracked his skull.

In only a few more minutes of ferocious fighting, the original attackers had been reduced to fifteen and were surrendering. Captain Henry had lost only four of his crew, with three more wounded but not seriously.

Captain Henry, who was bleeding from a gash on his forehead, called Jones over and told him to assemble the pirate prisoners. They limped forward and huddled in front of the captain, moaning in defeat. The caption stood tall and with a fierce glare, began to speak.

"You have attempted to capture my ship and, in the process, killed four of my crew. But you have failed. You lost most of your comrades and your captain is dead. Your ship is now my ship. I have no idea what your captain believed or where his loyalty lay. I don't think any of you are political but rather in this for the spoils. So, here is my proposition to you. By the law of the sea, I could hang you all now as pirates. I'm very tempted to do that."

The captain paused for a long moment to let that sink in. Then he began again.

"However, I now have your ship and I will take it to port in Spain so I can sell it to the highest bidder. I could use your help in sailing it there. My proposition to you is this: under the direction of Jones here, my First Mate, you will sail your old ship, which is now mine, to the port in Spain, following us there. If any *one* of you—and I mean any single *one*—gives him any trouble, any trouble at all, he has my authority to hang *all* of you on the spot. All of your cannons and personal weapons will be removed from the ship. If you try to take the ship back once you are on board and harm my First Mate, I will use our cannon to blow up the ship and sink it with all aboard. However, if you cooperate without trouble, when we reach port, I will release all of you. No charges will be filed with the local authorities and you will each be given five *pesos* as you leave. What do you say?"

In almost no time at all, one of the men stepped forward.

"I am called Smith. My captain and first mate are dead, leaving me in charge. I will speak for my men and say we accept your offer. If any one of my men go against the agreement, I will personally deal with them to protect the rest from your vengeance. We agree with your terms."

With that, the captured men were led down to a storeroom and locked in for the night. Captain Henry had Jones assemble a party to remove all of the weapons, powder, shot, and cannons from the captured pirate vessel and bring the lot aboard his ship to sort out. He planned to keep what would bring a good price in Spain and throw the rest overboard. He told Jones they would separate the two ships at first light and resume the journey to Spain.

With calm returning, the Captain looked out at the sun about to set over the ocean and announced to Doc and her companions that his invitation to dinner was still on. He said they should come to his cabin two hours from now, giving all time to rest and clean up.

><)>iiii··

CHAPTER 25

2035 CE
ENGLAND

THOMAS AND JOEL HAD DEPARTED THE black ops site in the western United States within hours after Doc's party had departed for the sixteenth century. Without incident, they arrived in Avebury two days later and began to search for clues. They first spent two hours at the deserted stone circle in the woods some distance from Avebury. Not finding anything resembling a clue, they moved back to the same inn from their earlier visit, planning to start their search of Avebury the next morning.

After a restful night, they met for breakfast in the dining area. Joel started the conversation.

"I really didn't think we would discover anything in the old stone circle. Too much activity over 450 years, even for an abandoned site, for that to be a viable place to leave something for us. We should start with the manor house today. It was there in 1585 and its still here now, even though it's been changed in several ways after undergoing renovations, restorations, and maintenance activities through all of that time. I don't see how anything would have survived that was left for us on the walls, floors, or other interior structural elements. We should concentrate on furniture, paintings, or other movable items that would have been reused over time even though the structure was changed. The dovecote is on the manor grounds so we should look at that, too."

"Let's get our tickets for a guided tour of the manor house,"

Thomas suggested. "If we see something promising, we can hang back and look more closely. I don't recall them allowing photographs but I think we can sneak a couple of quick ones with our smart devices set on high definition to look at later more carefully. Then, we will improvise from there."

"Let's do it!" Joel exclaimed with a look of excitement on his face.

By mid-afternoon they were in a group going through the manor house with their guide. Hanging back just a little from the rest of the crowd but not so far away as to be conspicuous, they were able to whisper their impressions to each other.

Joel was first, pointing out a couple of pieces of furniture dating from the sixteenth century. They couldn't determine if those pieces were original to the house or added later during restoration work. Then they entered a room and both saw the nondescript painting Thomas remembered Mary saying was original to the house, though possibly moved to different rooms over time.

Thomas whispered, "That painting is a possibility. I'll get a quick pic and we can examine it more carefully later."

Joel said, "I'm getting a picture of this armoire, I think it may be original as well."

Outside, after the tour of the interior was complete, they were free to walk around the grounds. "Since we are not under the watchful eye of a tour guide, we can take our time looking at the dovecote. I doubt anything would be in the interior but the bricks and woodwork on the exterior are logical places to leave something for us," pointed out Thomas.

As the two walked alone around the dovecote, Joel spotted something interesting about the bricks.

"Look at this. There are some indentations on this brick and, oddly, there is an inscription molded in the brick that looks like Spanish, not English as you would expect."

Bending closer to inspect, Thomas looked quizzical.

"Actually, I think I saw something similar in another brick over here."

He pointed several feet over in a spot further to the back of the cote. Quickly, they moved to the other brick.

"Yes, Thomas, you're right. They are the same. Get some good images of both and we will look at them carefully back at the inn. In the meantime, we have a tour lined up for the Avebury stone circle and an early supper at the Red Lion."

❊ ❊ ❊

Back at the inn late in the day, Joel and Thomas retreated to Joel's room to transfer the pictures they had taken on their rounds to a larger screen for review. Most revealed nothing of interest, except the photo of the painting in the manor house and the bricks at the dovecote.

"I think we have the clue we are looking for in these photos of the painting and the two bricks," mused Joel. "Now, let's think about where they lead us."

Thomas had been quietly studying the picture of the painting.

"Look at this, Joel. The painting is signed *aqui*. That is not a painter's signature, it's Spanish for *here*. We have the same word on both bricks!"

Joel, looking intently at the bricks and then the painting said excitedly, "And these spots in the pistil of the flower in the painting are in the same arrangement as the indentations on the two bricks. That's way too much for coincidence. Hmm, these spots somehow look familiar, I just can't put my finger on why."

"Ah! Try this explanation on for size, Joel," Thomas grinned with his revelation. "Remember the stickpins we were given by the jeweler in Salamanca? He explained that the larger center circle represented Salamanca and the eight smaller circles represented the districts or boroughs around the village. These spots on the center of the flower and the indentations on the bricks are identical to those on our stickpins!"

"Thomas, I think you have deciphered the message. The spots represent Salamanca and the word in Spanish says, *here, this location*! It's clear to me Doc wants us to go to Salamanca. I can only think that she wants us to look at the illuminated manuscripts again. Something was there we missed when we were there before but at that time, we weren't looking beyond the Ghost Flower drawing and the script describing the possibility of the preventive measures offered by the flower's chemistry to the Avebury villagers in the past. I think there was more there in that manuscript than we realized. Something that may have been in plain sight ... but we just didn't know to look for at the time."

"Pack your bag!" Thomas cheered. "Tomorrow, we head for Spain and the Salamanca archives!"

CHAPTER 26

1585 CE
AT SEA

THE GLOW OF CANDLELIGHT SOFTLY ILLUMINATED Captain Henry's quarters. A table covered with a beautiful embroidered cloth in the center of the room was laid out with a very expensive -looking candelabra and silver dining utensils.

"Oh," exclaimed Melinda as she entered the space. "This is so beautiful—and romantic—I must add."

Captain Henry beamed as he ushered his special passengers into the room. He had changed into a surprisingly fine outfit for the evening and looked no worse for wear other than the white bandage around his head protecting the gash he had received earlier, now mended by the ship's medical officer.

"Welcome to my cabin for a dinner that I hope will please you. And I hope you will receive my profuse thanks for all that you did today to provide us with a victory over huge odds!"

After they were formally introduced all around and shown their places, Melinda, having discretely noticed that the captain had arranged the seating so that Doc was next to him, spoke up.

"Captain, this journey has only been a single day in the making but I feel we experienced a once-in-a-lifetime event already. Let's enjoy your hospitality now, relive some of the unbelievable actions of the afternoon and then, when we have finished, perhaps we can have a private conversation with you so we can tell you more about us. Miss Sendall, or Doc, as you've heard us call her, said you asked her to tell you our mission just before the pirate attack. We have agreed with her to share the truth, rather than try to fool you with a concocted cover story. But our true story will take a little time, so, not to disrupt your cook's schedule, may we suggest we wait on that until we have finished what I'm sure will be a fabulous dinner!"

"Fair enough," replied Captain Henry, shaking his head a bit. "I saw some things today that I surely don't understand. I look forward to hearing your story but agree with your request that we hold that until after dinner. Mr. Johns, please begin with some wine for our guests!"

A lively, yet relaxed atmosphere ensued. Captain Henry, at one point during dinner, had one of his seamen come in, who was quite talented with a viola, to play a few tunes for them. Sam surprised everyone by launching into an old Scottish ballad in his excellent baritone. An hour or so later, all of Captain Henry's guests were truly sated and Doc, speaking for all, expressed how much they had enjoyed the music and the dinner conversation.

After Doc had finished her effusive thanks, Captain Henry spoke.

"Okay, now that we have enjoyed our dinner and my crew has taken their leave, I am very interested in hearing your story."

Doc started with a short preamble.

"This story will be hard for you to believe. You may think we are all crazy and dismiss us for a group of deranged souls. But I dare say, some of the events of today that you saw with your own eyes, particularly the fighting skills of Jane and Mary, should lend some credence to our words. If you are ready, I will begin, with each of us in turn adding to the story. I must also say this before we start. I trust you will keep to yourself what we tell you, for if you share it with others, you could easily put all of our lives in jeopardy. I told you earlier today that for some reason I believe I can trust you and I'm willing to test that by putting our safety in your hands with what we will share with you. Am I wrong in my trust?"

"I don't know what you are about to tell me but whether I believe you or not, I will keep what I hear to myself. That I pledge to you."

Doc began her revelation about how she, Sam, Melinda, and Jane came from a time some 450 years in the future. She explained that it was quite common in their time for women to become medical doctors and she was a practicing virologist and physician. Mary, she explained, they met only recently in Avebury in the current time. However, they immediately could see she has a shared heritage with Jane that is quite different.

Captain Henry sat stone still as he listened, only his eyes moved, getting wider as the story of their medical mission and time travel unfolded.

As the five of them completed the story, Doc turned to Captain Henry.

"I know we unloaded a lot on you all at once. What you saw Jane and Mary do today in the fight with the pirates is not something other people you know could possibly accomplish. I hope that goes a small way in proving our sincerity."

Captain Henry was quiet when they finished for what seemed an eternity. Then he spoke.

"I knew before the pirates hit us that there was something unusual going on with all of you. I was intrigued. Jane and Mary saved my life today, not only once; twice. No doubt about that. I have never seen anyone, man, or woman, move as fast, striking the enemy with a brutal force that seemed easy for them. In the end, they weren't even breathing hard but seemed relaxed. Their use of the bows and arrows in the beginning was a surprise to me. Their speed and accuracy were incredible and reduced the attacking force in a meaningful way.

"You, Doc, with your good marksmanship, reduced the odds even further. And Sam, you acquitted yourself well, taking out three pirates before being knocked unconscious from behind. Melinda, your hand-to-hand combat and deft footwork are something I've never seen. Extremely effective. I would treasure an opportunity for you to train me on some of the moves I saw you execute. I thank God that He allowed me to take you on as passengers. Without you being here, I am certain my ship would have been seized and by this time, I, as the captain, would surely have been hanged if not already killed by the pirates you saved me from."

He leaned forward and crossed his arms on the table, his eyes set seriously.

"I'm not saying I can believe all you have told me quite yet. It's a wild lot to contemplate. But this I can confirm: you have earned an equal share in the spoils of the day. When I sell the captured ship with its cargo, you will get your share of the proceeds, which I believe will be considerable."

* * *

The next day saw the end of their journey by boat. They sailed into the Spanish harbor at Gijón, the crew bursting with great satisfaction of their victory. As they departed the ship, Captain Henry called Doc aside from the rest.

"Miss Sendall, I would sincerely enjoy seeing you again. You told me of your destination in Salamanca. I plan to sell our prize, the pirate ship, and its cargo, here in Gijón. You see, our pirates, we learned, are actually English privateers. They are not really loyal to anyone but pretend to be bound to England. This means I could have trouble selling that captured ship if I took it back to England. And I don't want to have any of the crew with me causing a problem with some self-serving story they might concoct. When the sale of the boat is finished here and I've delivered my original cargo to the buyers here in Spain, I will return to England. But I plan to come back here two months from now with the hope that we can continue to share our stories, perhaps some new adventures

... and grow closer."

Doc had tossed and turned the night before. She wasn't sure she should have told the captain everything so quickly. Now, doubtful, part of her wanted to leave and never see him again. She was unsure they could ever have a chance, considering their vast differences. Yet she felt tears coming to her eyes. She couldn't ignore her desire to be close to him, to feel his strength comforting her. She reached out and placed her hand gently on his chest.

"I ... I don't know how ...." she started to explain.

His large, rough hand covered hers. There was a shock of electricity that came over her as he touched her for the first time. Her mind flashed an image of a sky full of stars. She looked into his eyes, which were twinkling, *or it was her own mist that caused light to dance off his chiseled face?* she wondered.

"Think about it," he offered, releasing her hand. "I'll be here then. If it is your desire to see me then, you will be here when I return. Or leave a message for me with the innkeeper where you are staying now. I will go there to see if there is word for me when I return here. If no message, then I wish you the best as you pursue your dreams."

Doc blushed, managed a smile, and tried to compose herself again. "I am honored by your proposition. I have a feeling I will be here."

Captain Henry slowly reached up to her shoulder to brush a bit of dust off her coat. This casual gesture of affection made her realize they a had connection they couldn't deny.

With that, they both turned and departed.

>•)Ⓗ··

CHAPTER 27

1585 CE
SPAIN

GATHERED ON THE SHORE NEAR THE docks in Gijón, Doc's companions looked at her, not suppressing the big grins they were all displaying. "Found a new friend, did you?" joked Sam, accompanied by laughter breaking out from the others.

"Well," replied Doc, "it's been a long time since I have been around a man I find myself attracted to, I'll admit that."

"I believe your feelings were showing and I got the sense that Captain Henry was more than warming up to you," added Melinda, who followed up with, "you know we are curious what he said when he pulled you aside as we were leaving."

"Not that it is any of your business!" Doc scolded. "But I can't help myself sharing it with you! He said he would be back here in two months. He wanted to meet me then if I was interested in furthering our relationship."

"Doc," advised Sam, "I believe you should be here to meet him. We all know we can't go back to the future and we need to make a new life here for ourselves. Testing the waters to see if that life includes Captain Henry seems like a good start. Mary can go back to Avebury but I'm getting the vibes from her that part of her life is going to change in ways she hasn't shared with us. For me and Melinda, I don't yet know what the future holds, nor for Jane, but I think I see a little glimpse of what your future might be! I definitely think you should plan to be here two months from now."

"Based on my feelings today, I will be."

Wanting to change the subject, Doc got back to matters at hand.

"Now, we need to arrange some transportation from here to Salamanca. Perhaps there is some commercial passage we can arrange. I'm not up for buying horses again, even though when we were in England it worked out well. I just don't think we should make this leg of our journey alone. I would like it to be in the company of people who are familiar with this part of the world."

Melinda said she had a plan.

"We are about eighteen miles distance from Oviedo. It's a larger town and there should be commercial wagons taking goods from the port here to there for sale. Let's see if we can pay to hitch a ride. We should plan on a day to get that done. Then, in Oviedo, we may be able to make the same arrangements to get to Salamanca. The terrain may be somewhat difficult to traverse, and it is about 200 miles, so I think we should plan four days minimum for that part of our journey. If it takes more or less, it doesn't matter. It's 450 years from now that Joel and Thomas will be there looking. The only time constraint I see is that we want to get Doc back here in two months!"

The party agreed with the plan, and sure enough, within an hour of their arrival at the port they found a merchant loading two wagons with goods from a ship he planned to take to Oviedo. After some minor haggling, they arrived at a price for the merchant to take them along and for their party to split up, two and three, among the wagons.

They started early the next morning and arrived in Oviedo late that day. They easily found lodging to accommodate them for the night. After talking with the innkeeper the next morning, they learned of another merchant arranging a shipment of goods to Salamanca. Using an introduction provided by the innkeeper, they arranged passage to Salamanca with a convoy of four wagons scheduled to leave for Salamanca that same morning.

They were warned of the potential for highwaymen along the way, with a declaration that the wagon master would not be held accountable for their safety. Doc's group agreed and were soon assigned to their respective wagons. Mary and Jane opted to ride together in the second wagon from the front, with Doc, Melinda, and Sam in the third.

* * *

On the second day of the journey, the terrain was rough and the driver of the wagon Jane and Mary were seated in commented that this was an area that had seen its share of robberies in recent years. He advised them to keep watch. Little did he know he had two incredible fighters riding with him. The pair quickly took note he had a muzzle loader musket in the seat by his side and a pistol in his belt. The drivers of the other wagons were similarly armed.

The wagon they were in was pulled by four draft horses and the bed of the wagon was piled high with the merchandise destined for the buyers in Salamanca. The goods were covered with tarps for protection from rain. The passengers were seated atop two large boxes located between mounds of other crates covered by the tarps. Not luxurious, by any means, but adequate for the purpose.

About midday, just when they were coming around a large outcrop of boulders, four men stepped out in front of the lead wagon and five appeared out of the rocks behind the last of the four wagons.

"Halt! Stand and deliver!" yelled a large muscular man in the lead group. He brandished a short musket, about two feet in length with a flared muzzle.

The driver of Jane and Mary's wagon quietly instructed his two women passengers.

"That weapon he has is loaded with either shot, nails, or something similar. It has an effective range of maybe twenty feet but, if he fires it, the shot or nails will cover a diameter of about ten feet. A nasty weapon. Looks like only about half of the others have muskets, the remainder have edged weapons or clubs. We have been through this before, so stay quiet and keep your heads down. When the wagon master gives the signal, we will open fire. I'm mostly worried about their leader with that scatter gun."

What he didn't realize was that Jane and Mary had been given the bows they used in the attack of the privateers by Captain Henry. While their driver was talking, they had already unwrapped the unstrung bows and clasped their weapons low between the mounds of boxes, out of sight of the highwaymen, and strung them taut. They laid out several arrows between them on the boxes they were seated on.

"Now!" yelled the wagon master.

Before his men had time to bring their weapons to bear, Jane and Mary had stood up and let fly their first two arrows with lightning speed. Both arrows struck the highwaymen's leader holding the scatter gun, which instantly fell harmlessly to the ground. Even as the first two arrows struck their mark, the second two were in flight.

Jane had remained facing forward and Mary had turned to the rear. Jane's arrow took out a second robber in the front and Mary dropped the man nearest the rear wagon. Three down in seconds.

By this time, the drivers had their weapons up and began firing. The advantage had shifted to the caravan as the surprised highwaymen hesitated after the four arrows swiftly took down their leader and two others. It was a fatal hesitation. Less than a minute before it was all over, with only three highwaymen left alive, they turned and fled.

Stunned, Mary and Jane's driver turned to them while reloading his smoking weapons.

"My god, women, who are you? I've never seen anything like that. But I'm blessed that you are with us and on my wagon!"

"We're just a couple of competition archers who happened to be along. I'm glad we could help out." Mary smiled at him.

"Well, I'm not sure I buy that but, nonetheless, thank you, thank you, thank you!"

* * *

Later that day, they stopped for the night and lit a couple of fires for cooking. The conversation turned quickly to the attack earlier in the day. Jane and Mary were the toast of the evening, with both of them doing their best to modestly turn the conversation to the actions of the others who had done quite well in the firefight.

The next two days were relatively uneventful but the scenery was absolutely gorgeous. Doc's party was able to enjoy the rest of the journey. At the end, when they reached Salamanca, the wagon master approached them and addressed Doc.

"I'm a merchant, so I've got to make a profit on my efforts. But, I'm so grateful to your two companions, who *claim* to be just simple archers, that I'm refunding the money you paid me for their passage as a token of my appreciation for what they did. I would give a refund for the rest of you but, as I said, I must make some profit on the trip."

"Well, thank you for that," Doc replied graciously. "The money will come in handy for what we do next. We thank you for bringing us along. Perhaps in the next couple of weeks when our work here is finished, we might make it worth your while to take us back to Oviedo."

"Done. If we are here when you are ready to go back, you will easily find us, and we'll be more than welcome to have you travel with us again."

·∙₩€∙€

CHAPTER 28

1585 CE
SPAIN

AFTER SECURING AN INN ON THE outskirts of Salamanca, Doc's party met in a nearby tavern for supper.

"Okay, our task in the morning will be to track down one Brother Francisco. If we are fortunate, he will be at the Convent of San Esteban. If not, we will keep looking."

"Yes, that's exactly what we need to do, Doc," Melinda responded. "Before we find him, however, we need to come up with a game plan as to exactly what we're going to tell him."

"I agree, Melinda. I've been thinking a lot about the specifics of how to use the monk's manuscript to get Joel and Thomas the information we have for them. These illustrated books usually involve three trades. First, the person producing the vellum which, in this time period, will likely be thin calf-skin that has been stretched on a wooden frame. The scribe is the second in the trio, in this case the monk, and the third person involved is the illustrator.

"My idea is to work with the person making the vellum to produce a special insert page for us. We get him ... well, I suppose it will be a him and not a her although I'm not sure ... to make two extremely thin sheets, such that when the two sheets are glued together, they will approximate the thickness of a normal single sheet. We will press one of the Ghost Flowers Sam has with him and sandwich it between the two sheets."

Sam nodded in approval as Doc continued to relay her plan.

"Then, we will work with the illustrator—and the monk, of course—to take Sam's chemical formula and break it into one symbol per page. We'll work that symbol into the fancy imagery at the bottom of each page. But we'll need to work with the monk to write something in the script on the page with the Ghost Flower drawing. That is where Joel and Thomas will look first, I'm sure. I'm hoping that's what will guide them to the rest of our message. It will have to be cleverly penned so that for the next 450 years, anyone looking at that page will not notice what we want only Joel and Thomas to see."

Melinda quickly added, "This is really mind-blowing but when we looked at the page in the twenty-first century, what we plan to do now would have been there already then ... but we didn't see it!"

"Yes, either we fail now so it isn't there in the future or we do such a good job now that it *is* there and we just didn't pick up on it," Sam said.

"I have a feeling we are going to do a good job," Doc said with a tone of confidence.

"Okay," Melinda said, "but back to my original question. What are we going to tell the monk?"

"I think we should meet him first to see just how sharp he is or," Doc mused, "it's possible he's gullible. I'm betting on sharp so this is going to be difficult. I don't like doing this but maybe we use Mary as the one telling him our story. Here's what I'm thinking.

"If she stands close to him, maybe in a dimly lit place so her pupils dilate and she looks directly into his eyes, he will be intrigued by what he sees. Mary's eyes are larger than most and her pupils expand and contract very differently than a native Earth person's. She could say she was an instrument of God, chosen for an important but mysterious mission on Earth ... and Brother Francisco's work was foretold to her in a vision.

"She could tell him the vision showed her a page in his current work and go on to describe the drawing of the flower on one of the pages and recite some of the writing on that page. He has never met her so I would wager he will be dumbfounded by her ... *how could a stranger to him know that?* And, her eyes, as he looks into them, their expansiveness will add to the surreal nature of the conversation. Then, she can tell him what she has been charged to do for posterity, using him and his work as her instrument."

Doc looked around and asked, "What do you think?"

Mary reacted first.

"I could do this. I will throw in a bit of Golan-speak. I'm not great at it but he won't know that language. Perhaps I can do something that impresses him with my extraordinary quickness and strength if I need to. I'll have to think about what exactly but I believe I can pull this off!"

"Just don't give him a heart attack, Mary. That would doom the mission," added Sam with a chuckle.

"You laugh, Sam, but it's a possibility!" exclaimed Melinda.

"All right," said Doc, pleased her idea was materializing, "tomorrow we will locate the Convent of San Esteban and hope to find our Brother Francisco there."

※ ※ ※

The next morning, after a quick breakfast and purchasing some provisions for their trip, they got directions from the innkeeper and set out on foot for the convent.

"This looks promising," offered Melinda as they approached. "Construction is still underway. As I recall, they started this building in 1524 but it wasn't finished until 1610. There was a predecessor monastery here, founded by the Dominicans, demolished to be replaced by what we are seeing now. In that earlier building, Christopher Columbus stayed for a spell while defending his idea of sailing west in what later was quite an historic voyage. Can you imagine being here then! Let's approach the front door and see what we can find out about our monk."

Before they reached the entrance, they were greeted by a pair of monks who seemed friendly enough. When asking about Brother Francisco, they were told he was a part of the brotherhood here but was on an errand in the nearby shopping area and would be returning soon. They were invited to wait in a garden not too far from where they were standing and were told they would be able to see him returning. After hearing a description of Brother Francisco so they would recognize him as he returned, they began their wait.

After about an hour, Sam pointed and said, "There, I believe that must be him walking up the road, carrying a large parcel of some sort."

Doc took the initiative to venture out into the pathway to make the first contact. She hoped her Spanish would be up to the task. "*Hermano Francisco*," she hailed.

The brother, clothed in a brown robe, cinched at the waist with a plain rope, first hesitated, then seeing the stranger calling him was smiling and seemed friendly enough, he waved and walked over to Doc.

She explained that she was an English historian on a research project in Spain and asked that he excuse her rudimentary Spanish. Doc went into a story about the transition underway from the art of producing illustrated manuscripts to the more modern print forms of documents and how she heard he was one of the old-school experts in the earlier form so she wanted to interview him about his work. She further explained the presence of her companions as part of her team. During this explanation, Jane and Mary were careful not to get too close, saving Mary from close scrutiny prematurely.

Brother Francisco seemed honored by the recognition of his expertise in his craft and agreed to talk with them and show some of his current work. He also revealed that he did understand some English, although he was certainly not fluent.

"*Señora* Sendall, my work is tedious and with the construction in the monastery, I have been given dispensation to work remotely. There is a small home in town, where I have a good friend who has provided me with a room to work and keep my supplies. I think it would be best if we meet there tomorrow, say around noon, and I will answer your questions and show you some of my work."

He gave her some simple directions to the house and a description of it.

"You will have no trouble finding it!" he exclaimed. "But now, I must leave you and deliver these supplies to the convent. I look forward to meeting with you and your companions tomorrow."

As he walked away, Doc whispered to the others, "I can't believe our luck. But then, we were due some after dealing with pirates and highwaymen on our journey to get here."

Sam agreed. "In the morning, I plan to find a printing press somewhere. I'm thinking with a little modification, I might be able to use a press, when the time comes, to flatten one of our flowers to a very thin state to insert between the layers of vellum as you suggested, Doc."

"Alright, let's declare today a success and find a suitable tavern near our inn to celebrate with a good meal and some fine Spanish wine!" declared Doc.

※ ※ ※

The next morning found the party up and in a small dining area in the inn, where a spread of fruits and cheese *bocadillos* were available for the guests of the inn. Following their late breakfast, they began a leisurely walk to the house Brother Francisco had directed them to.

"I think we should spend some time with the monk, letting him show us how he works. I'm interested in that aside from our main mission here," Melinda shared. "Think about it. I've seen this and other works 450 or 500 years after they were completed. Now, I'm

in the improbable situation of being able to see the creation of one
or more of these documents first hand! I can hardly believe it ...
but it's true!"

"And," Doc added, "you will soon meet one of the illustrators
of these documents in the flesh to actually see him work at his art.
In addition, you will be directing him to illustrate some of the work
you saw 450 years in the future. I find it hard to comprehend that
I am actually saying this."

"That house just ahead looks like our destination," observed
Jane. "I think Mary and I will stay in the background behind the
three of you and while we will be engaged in the conversation, we
will try not to get too close allowing the monk to see our faces
clearly until it is time for Mary's performance."

When the three reached the small but tidy home, Doc knocked
on the wooden front door. Shortly after, a woman who appeared
to be the lady of the house opened the door with a smile and
acknowledged the monk had told her to expect them. The woman
turned with a motion for them to follow and led them to a room
down a hallway. She opened the door where Brother Francisco was
standing at a work table, poring over his latest creation.

"Welcome," he greeted them as he looked up, pleased with his
ability to use his rudimentary English for his guests. Shifting to
Spanish, which Doc understood and Mary was surprisingly fluent
in, he apologized for the cramped quarters, which had been taken
up with his papers, writing supplies, and stacks of correspondence
and other documents he was using as references.

"Thank you for seeing us today, Brother Francisco, we are
honored and delighted to be here," responded Doc. "As I told you
yesterday, we are from England and researching the techniques you
use to create the documents that are so informative but at the same
time so beautiful. With the advent and use of the printing press over
the last few decades, your skill is an art form that is slowly coming
to an end. Before that happens, we want to learn all we can about

it from the man we have been told is a master!"

"I will be pleased to answer your questions and show you some of my work. If you like, we can begin with this one I am working on now," he said gesturing towards a sheet of vellum on his work table.

Melinda could hardly contain herself, as the work he pointed to was part of the same volume she had seen in the twenty-first century in the University of Salamanca's rare book archive.

The brother then began to show them how he mixed his inks for writing and the way he shaped the quills he used to create the ornate lettering he applied to the vellum. Different quills were cut in certain ways to achieve his desired results, similar to a painter using different brushes for different effects.

The monk, obviously pleased with the attention, went on for about an hour, only interrupted by questions from the assembled group.

"Fascinating," sighed Melinda. "I can't believe I'm actually seeing an illuminated manuscript being created."

"Who is your illustrator, or do you do those yourself?" asked Sam.

"I do some of my own work but I do have help. I've been doing this a long time so I've developed some artistic skills! I don't advertise this but the person who helps me with the illustrations is the woman who owns this house, Sophia. She is quite talented. Most of the people I know expect women to work in the home and care for children. None of the women I am aware of have an opportunity to earn a living as an artist. I said I don't advertise her helping me. That is because I value her assistance and pay her for her work, which is not the custom here. My experience has taught me that going against the traditional way of doing things seems to upset people. I would prefer not to deal with that."

"Your secret is safe with us," assured Doc. She went on to say that she thought they had taken enough of his time and they would be on their way.

"However, there is one important part of meeting with you that has nothing to do with our research activities. You haven't had the opportunity to talk with Mary, the lady who has been standing near the wall while we have been talking. I would like to leave her with you for a short while to talk with you about something of the utmost importance. Something that a man of God, like yourself, will be astounded and I hope honored, to hear."

Having piqued his interest, Doc turned to Mary and told her they would wait for her outside until she finished her conversation with Brother Francisco.

Doc, Jane, Melinda, and Sam left the house, giving their goodbyes as they passed Sophia who appeared from another room to show them to the door. Nervously, they paced in the street and then walked back and forth in a little garden area nearby while sharing their anxiety with each other. Melinda pointed out the obvious, more than once, to the others.

"Our entire mission is now in the hands of Mary. The outcome of the future pandemic could be determined right here by the conversation going on in that house, twenty feet away!"

"True," observed Sam. "But there have been other points along our journey so far that have been just as pivotal. Think about what could have happened with the pirates, or the highwaymen, or never even finding Mary back in Avebury."

"Okay, if you're trying to calm me down with that, it's not working! Nice try though, thanks."

✳ ✳ ✳

Nearly an hour later, Mary emerged from the house. Behind her at the door was the sixteenth-century monk, standing in shock, but standing at least. As she grew near, she gave a subdued smile and without a word, motioned for them to follow her in the direction of their inn. When they were out of earshot of the monk, Mary's face wrinkled into a huge smile.

"It went very well, better than I dreamed it would. After you left, I suggested to him we sit at the small table in the corner. It looked like a place he sometimes ate, as there was still a bottle of wine and a single glass there, along with an empty bowl. As we sat down, I leaned close to him to make sure he was looking into my eyes, which he did. The slow realization that he had never seen eyes like mine started to sink in. I told him of my vision and of being sent on a mission by a Higher Power to see him ... and him alone. I threw in a little Golan speak and told him some things about his work that had not yet been published; details that only he and Sophia would have known. That got his attention.

"I also did something with my strength and speed that seemed superhuman. He presented the opportunity for me. In his agitation, he gestured with his hand and accidentally knocked the glass that was half-filled with wine off the table. Without taking my eyes from his, I reached into the air, gently caught the glass before it was more than a foot off the table and without breaking cadence in my sentence, placed the glass back on the table. This was all done in the time it took him to glance to his right in the direction of the falling glass. It was back on the table, not a drop spilled, before he could even bring his hand back from knocking it over. He just gasped after it was over. I'm certain he had never seen anyone move so quickly."

"Wow," exclaimed Sam. "That was great! Were you able to do anything else that seemed supernatural?"

"Yes, indeed," Mary went on excitedly. "At one point, he became fearful and dropped off his chair to his knees to pray. I stood up, went over to him, and simply picked him off the floor and sat him back in his chair. He's not an overly large man but he is bigger than me, so he was stunned at how effortlessly I picked him off the floor and sat him back down. Near the end, I could see his skepticism dissolve. He believed me.

"I didn't get into anything about leaving messages about a pandemic or anything beyond what his sixteenth century education and knowledge would have allowed him to comprehend. He believes he is now an instrumental part of a divinely-guided plan to alter documents in a way that will help people in the future. He also knows that it is something to keep to himself, although I suspect he may bring Sophia into the conspiracy. That may actually be helpful to us, since she will be suspicious of what comes next if she is in the house when we are working on the Ghost Flower document and she is not brought into the fold as to why we are suddenly helping them. Somehow, I think Brother Francisco will handle that part well."

✳ ✳ ✳

The next day saw Melinda, Doc, Sam, and Mary return to the house where the monk worked. Jane stayed behind, so as not to confuse things with her similarity to Mary. This time, when the door opened, Sophia had a strange look on her face as she welcomed them. The party could see that the monk had indeed shared at least some, if not all, of what had transpired between Brother Francisco and Mary when they had met privately yesterday.

"From the curious look on your face, *Señora* Sophia, I can tell Brother Francisco told you of our true purpose here," observed Melinda.

"Yes, he shared with me the conversation he had and the sacred importance of assisting you. As well, he swore me to confidence, which I assure you will be kept!"

"Thank you. I know you will be of great help in our work," Doc added.

A few minutes later, they were gathered in Brother Francisco's work space. He was already at the table, looking at the page he was working on the day before that had attracted their interest.

"Perfect," observed Doc, looking at what he had in front of him.

"This is the very page we would like to start with. What we need to do is replace this page with a special one which Sam will explain to you in a moment. But first, who prepares the vellum for you?"

"The man who stretches and cures the calfskin I use lives about an hour's walk from here. He's been supplying me for years. As you are probably aware, this is an art that will soon be lost. The advent of printing presses—and ability to make paper that is cheaper than vellum—are new contributions that are replacing the old methods."

"Well," suggested Doc, "how about taking Sam with you to meet him to ask him for a special order. We need two pages that are very thin. This is so Sam can place a pressed flower, like the one Mary told you about yesterday, between the two sheets, and press and glue them together in such a way that the two would then be about the thickness of a single page. Is it possible?"

"Yes, I think so," the monk confirmed. "He is a true artist. And, as you might imagine, the pages this particular man makes for me are not always the exact same thickness, as you can see from looking at what I have on the table here," he said, pointing to the work in progress. "So, even if someone were to feel the slight difference in the thickness of the page, they wouldn't notice it as being unusual."

"Excellent," Doc responded. "Will you be able to take Sam there tomorrow to tell him what we need?"

"Better yet, I was planning to see him later today. Sam, can you go then?"

"Of course! I'll be ready when you are." Sam added, "While we are out, is there a printer nearby that I could approach for using their press on the flower?"

"There is one just a few minutes away from where we are going. I know the printer very well. He will help us if I ask," Brother Francisco confirmed.

"Great! I will go back to our inn now, pick up the flower, and be back before you are ready to go. Doc, Mary, and Melinda will stay with you to talk about the revised wording on the page we have been looking at." With that, Sam left the house and headed back to the inn.

Melinda had been thinking about the wording they might use.

"We need to be subtle. The changes I am suggesting vary little from what you have already written. In fact, when we get the new, thinner vellum, I think we repeat what you have written here and simply add somewhere at an appropriate place on the page a new sentence."

Melinda fished out a note page from her case with the message that Thomas had translated into Latin: "The knowledge you seek is within the page before you and on the pages that follow."

COGNITIO QUAERIS INTRA PAGINAM CORAM
TE ET IN PAGINIS QUAE SEQUUNTUR.

"Then," she continued, "we will draw an almost imperceptible oval in the center of the page. The oval will be directly over the place where the flower will be, sandwiched between the next page in our special flattened insert. Next, in an almost, but not quite, invisible writing, we'll add the word *aqui* in large letters across the center of the oval. It must be so faint that a reader would not notice it without some special equipment to bring out the lettering. Does it make sense what we are asking?"

"Hmm ... I believe I know what you are trying to achieve but I think I have a better idea," the monk replied. "Instead of using ink to inscribe the oval and the word *aqui*, why don't I press the oval shape and the word into the vellum. A typical reader shouldn't notice something faint, in fact it might take a light at an angle to produce a slight shadowing effect to allow it to be seen."

"Ah! This is a great idea. Two heads are always better than one, of course, as long as they are not on the same set of shoulders!" Melinda was delighted with the monk's idea as were Doc and Jane.

"Then," added Doc, "at the bottom of the following pages, in the same place on each page, buried in artwork there, we have a set of symbols we want to record, one on each page." Doc didn't try to get into the fact that those would be the symbols representing Sam's analysis of the chemistry of the flower and seeds.

"I can do that," replied Brother Francisco.

After another half hour of talking in general about the art of producing Brother Francisco's beautiful works and lamenting the demise of that art being taken over by printing presses, Sam returned. They all said their goodbyes for the day as Sam and the monk began their walk to the workplace of the producer of the vellum.

CHAPTER 29

1585 CE
SPAIN

THREE WEEKS LATER, DOC'S PARTY HAD completed the work they had hoped to achieve. Their final task was to ensure their involvement in producing the manuscript would not affect the eventual path it would need to take to end up in the rare book archives at the University of Salamanca. They were assured that what had transpired with their involvement would not disrupt the delivery schedule, a deadline the monk had promised the wealthy resident of Salamanca who had commissioned the work.

With that delivery, Doc said events would then be out of their control. Her fervent hope was that history would not be altered by their intervention and the document would end up in the library where they had found it 450 years later in the twenty-first century.

One afternoon, some days later, as they had been leisurely strolling down one of the scenic streets in Salamanca, they stopped on a bridge spanning the Rio Tormes. Standing there, looking at a vibrant sunset starting to emerge, lighting up the undersides of a perfect configuration of clouds that had formed to make a gorgeous canvas for the sun to paint, Melinda broke the silence with something that had been on her mind for some time.

"Let's face it. Our mission to come back in time to accomplish the near impossible has been completed. We knew we could never return to the twenty-first century ... meaning we would have to make new lives for ourselves here, in this time. I have no regrets about my choice to do this. While I enjoyed my career then, my personal life was actually pretty empty. After I broke it off with my fiancé, I never formed a romantic relationship again. Perhaps that is something that I might find here in this time.

"There is so much of interest to me, now that I find myself in the very time I studied and researched for so long. I want to go to places I've only read about in history; see the places and meet the people who are actually living here now. One place in particular is Stratford-upon-Avon.

"Call me crazy, but I would like to meet William Shakespeare and Anne Hathaway. From my memory of history—time gone by that has not yet happened—during the period from 1585 until 1592, there is very little knowledge about what William Shakespeare was doing. It is surmised he was living in Stratford; he and Anne had twins who were supposedly baptized in 1585, so it would make sense he was there for a while. He may have also spent some of that time in London as an actor and possibly doing some writing. I don't recall a mention in anything I read that pinned down his writing during that time, other than a few scripts for plays, and it was not uncommon in those days for people associated with theatre to collaborate on a script to sell to a company putting on plays."

Sam studied her intently as Melinda shared her dream with the others and became more animated.

"If I stay in Stratford for a few years, perhaps I could get a bit part in a play with him! I was in the Thespian Club in my high school and, if I say so myself, I wasn't too bad when I was on stage. Or at least I could experience being in the audiences at some of his plays, participating as part of the crowd. Keep in mind that right now, William Shakespeare is only about twenty-one years old. Much of the work he is famous for came in his later years. This leads me in the short term to be interested in going back to England when I might have a chance to get close to his world. Who knows? The love of my life could be a man waiting for me in Stratford and whoever he is, he doesn't even know it!"

Sam gave Melinda a hug and Doc said she was so happy Melinda was so happy that she might cry. Jane and Mary swooped behind Melinda unnoticed and lovingly mussed up her hair.

Then Mary spoke with seriousness.

"I've not left this time on Earth as you left your time, so I can't speak to what that feels like. Nonetheless, this experience with you has awakened me to focusing more on my future and not dwelling so much on the past. Part of my dilemma is age. As you know, my lifespan, barring an accident or some terminal disease, is about 200 years. Right now, I am only ninety but appear to be less than half that. I became attached to a man years ago and it didn't work out. If I allowed myself to become attached to another man, as the relationship progresses, he will age much faster ... and die long before me. How would that work out? Since my first failure in a romantic relationship, I've been avoiding allowing myself another because of that fear. On this trip, I've decided to put that in the past and move on to see what happens. The status quo in my personal life is an unhappy one now, so what do I have to lose?"

"Well, have you thought about what you want to do?" asked Melinda.

"I want to go back to Avebury," Mary said decisively. "Remember that young man, John, who was the leader of the construction crew who helped us with the bricks? I know he is attracted to me as I am to him. But I put an emotional barrier between us. I'm thinking I will go back to see where the relationship might lead. If and when it starts to get serious, I will share who and what I really am. I know he already suspects something but it hasn't seemed to put him off. Still, the question is: is he a man who can love and respect a woman who, because of my age and experience, is wiser than he, physically stronger, and will always appear younger while he ages? And, will I be content to care for him years from now when he is really old but I'm not? I believe the good times before that happens will be completely worth it. I'm not sure I would have felt this way thirty years ago. It's probably good I've waited as long as I have since my first failed relationship."

Jane embraced her, telling her she could accomplish anything she put her mind to. The others immediately agreed.

"What about you Sam, what are you thinking?" asked Doc.

"Well, I'm still undecided. Like you and Melinda, I have no qualms about choosing to be here in the sixteenth century. I have always had an interest in Paris. You don't know this but one of my hobbies is painting. If I can amass enough money to last me for a while, I would like to try being an artist in Paris—only not a starving artist," he joked.

"Short term, I want to make some money. Long term, I'd like to live in Paris and pursue my passion for painting. Look, I know it's a filthy place now—not to mention the religious wars have wreaked havoc on the population and its people. But if I can find a place in a village within a day's walk of Paris, that might be best for now. I can visit periodically to see how it begins to grow after all the turmoil it has recently been through. If I don't like it, I can move on. You both mentioned your love life. I think my destiny in love awaits me in Paris, or at least somewhere nearby, in France."

"And you can always work in a pub and sing for your supper if nothing else works out," Melinda teased, giving him a kiss on the cheek.

"Okay, Jane. It's your turn … if you are willing to share," Mary said with a smile.

"I'm still thinking about it," she started. "Returning to Avebury is pointless to me. I wouldn't know anyone in this time period. All those who I knew there in the twenty-first century don't exist now. I must say, I completely enjoyed the adventures we have had on this journey. I have done so many exciting things! Fighting pirates and highwaymen, traveling to new places, and meeting people from other cultures. I'm not ready to give up this newfound life just yet.

Perhaps when Captain Henry comes for Doc, I will see what advice he might have for me. He leads a fascinating life."

"Doc, that leaves you. But I think we can all guess what you are going to say," quizzed Sam.

"I'm sure you can," she answered with a sly smile. "As you know, my existence in the twenty-first century was basically all work. My personal life became a shamble and I, frankly, spent all of my free time becoming more and more depressed and unsure of my purpose. I have felt more alive on this journey than I have for years. I don't want to lose this sense of enthusiasm for what comes next in my life away from work. And yes, I am looking forward to what may come of my next meeting with Captain Henry."

Melinda then pointed out there was a commonality in their thinking.

"It seems we all want to leave here and go north. England and France are our destinations. Perhaps we can all travel with Captain Henry back to England and then follow our individual destinies from there. Wherever we go, I am certain we will stay in touch with one another and be there to help if any one of us calls out."

"Indeed," Doc agreed. "Now, we should make plans to work our way back to Gijón to await the arrival of Captain Henry. We still have about a month to make the trip before he arrives there, so let's enjoy Salamanca for a spell while we track down the merchant from Oviedo we came here with. He said he would look forward to our traveling back with him the next time he made a delivery here. Our return to Oviedo will be determined by his schedule over the next month. Once there, we shouldn't have trouble making the last eighteen miles to Gijón. In the meantime, as in today, let's see if we can find another restaurant like the one our jeweler friend, Señor Fernandez, took us to when we dined there in the future."

CHAPTER 30

1585 CE
SPAIN

As **THEY HAD ANTICIPATED, BEFORE THE** week was out, they had found the merchant from Oviedo back in Salamanca. When they met up with him, he was delighted to take Doc's party to Oviedo with him when he returned. He promised his next trip should be less eventful than the last.

The three robbers who had run away from the scene on their first trip had spread the tale of their encounter with the superhuman female warriors far and wide. The merchant said he had not experienced any trouble since then with highwaymen. He was certain that if, on the return to Oviedo, there were any highwaymen on the route they would certainly let them pass when they saw the two archers, now locally famous, were in his company. On his honor because of their skill and bravery, he announced that even though he could use the money, the safety their presence guaranteed was worth giving them free passage back to Oviedo. No one objected to that!

✳ ✳ ✳

A little more than four days later, they were back in Oviedo. Fortunately, the merchant who had given them passage was planning a business trip to Gijón two days after they got there and offered to take them along for the company since it was such a short trip. Doc was thrilled on receiving door-to-door service.

Arriving in Gijón on a beautiful Spanish afternoon, the party headed to a tavern they had found delightful before. They treated the merchant and his second-in-command to join them for a celebratory supper. In the meantime, they checked in to the same inn they had stayed at before.

The next morning found them at the harbor, scouring the waterfront for any sign of Captain Henry or *The Twin Star*. Not seeing either, they discovered a hilltop nearby that was partially secluded by trees and vegetation. There was an opening in the foliage that allowed an unobstructed view of the harbor where they could keep an eye out for Captain Henry's ship. It didn't take them long to notice the unusually high traffic of Spanish naval vessels in and out of the port.

Melinda remarked to the others on the first day they observed this military traffic that her memory of history—history, of course, that had not yet happened—included the fact that an undeclared war would be taking place roughly between 1585 CE, the year they were in now, and 1604 CE, between the Hapsburg Kingdom of Spain and the Kingdom of England. A lot of the activity involved English privateers attacking Spanish ships, as well several full-scale attacks by the Spanish Armada against England and Ireland.

"We experienced one of those attacks by privateers on our voyage here. I think travel by sea will be more dangerous in the next few years. However, I'm not sure overland travel is that much safer. We have been attacked by highwaymen as well. Both routes have their advantages and perils," explained Melinda.

Mary shared a suggestion as to how they could profit from their time waiting for Captain Henry to arrive.

"This little wooded glade we have here is great for observing the harbor and, to some degree, it is not easily visible from the sides or back. This will be a perfect place to exercise, to keep ourselves physically fit and to practice our martial arts and archery. The slight salty smelling breeze coming off the water adds to the pleasant feel of the place."

"Good idea," responded Doc. "In Boston, I had a regular exercise routine that included running, which I have not been doing lately. I would also like to learn a few of the martial arts moves Jane and Mary are so expert in."

"Sign me up for that, too," added Sam, seconded by Melinda.

"We have all been physically active in our personal lives and I, for one, certainly miss that routine."

Over the next two weeks, the party spent much of each day in the little glade, being taught by Jane and Mary, and participating in other cardiovascular exercises as well as strength conditioning. They adopted clothing that mimicked what they saw the locals wearing but with some modifications to allow for freedom of movement without excess material to hamper their martial arts and archery training.

This was a bit harder for the four women, since long dresses or skirts were common attire. Trousers for women were not fashionable. Not wanting to call undue attention to themselves when in public, the four found suitable pants that looked like feminine leggings when slightly protruding from the lower level of a skirt. But when the skirt was released from the waist, the hidden leggings were actually quite attractive slim trousers with pockets and a wide belt with a large silver buckle.

On the morning of the first day of the third week they had been waiting, they came downstairs to the small lobby of their inn to find the clerk had a message for Doc.

"I'm not sure what to say, except that I'm nervous and excited at the same time!" exclaimed Doc. "The message is from Captain Henry. He says he is docked in the harbor and if we are indeed here, he wants us to come down to meet him."

Puzzled, Sam said, "Unless he arrived very early this morning or during the night, I'm surprised we didn't spot his ship. We have been keeping a close eye out."

"Well," Melinda insisted, "we can solve this mystery in short order by getting ourselves down to the docks. Let's go. We can find breakfast later."

As they neared the docks, scouring the area all around, they could not spot Captain Henry's ship. Then suddenly, the tall captain appeared in front of them.

"I'm so pleased to see you! I was afraid you would have found other interests and would not be here when I arrived!"

"We are here and just as pleased to see you," Sam piped up. "But where is your ship? We still don't see it."

"That, my friends, is because when I left you here, I was able to sell the ship we took as a prize from the English privateers," Captain Henry explained. "It fetched a good price, which by the way, shares of the proceeds I owe you. When I returned to England, I was struck by how times had changed for the safety of seafaring merchants, what with the hostilities between England and Spain. So, I sold *The Twin Star* and purchased a new and very different type of vessel. Wait until you hear the story," he promised.

"There was a strange looking boat in the harbor, owned by an aging gentleman from East Asia, a land called the Philippines to be exact. This man had come to England to spend his final years and was considering selling his boat. The style was one I had not seen before but the craft looked extremely interesting to me. So, I had him take me out to show me it's paces.

"It's called a catamaran and we've newly christened her *The Twin Flame*. It measures fifty-five feet in length, with twin hulls. It sails quite differently than my old ship. I find it more stable and it displaces less water so it has less drag. The real selling point to me was its speed. Under sail, it glides across the surface faster than any merchant ship I know. With its shallower draft and twin hulls, it can outrun any big navy ship I've seen. On the spot I decided my days of hauling big standard cargoes by boat was over. Instead, I believe I can profit by transporting small loads of high-value merchandise or well-to-do people who need to get to another destination quickly and safely. Yes, it's a different operation, you see, but promises to be much more lucrative."

"Does it take a large crew to sail her?" asked Sam.

"No, and that's another big advantage," the captain smiled with a wink. "I can sail her with a sea crew of four, Jones is still with me at the lead, of course, without having to take on many duties myself. I've added a cook and a cook's helper, so that makes six crew. The passenger accommodations are very comfortable. I have my main cabin, three for the crew and two for passengers, each with its own toilet. In a pinch, I can accommodate two additional passengers in the lounge area."

"This sounds very promising for you, Captain," Doc spoke up.

He turned to address her specifically. Seeing her warmed his heart.

"In hopes that you would all be going back to England with me, I have anticipated how we can make this work. The crew will share two cabins, two in each. The third cabin is for the cook and his helper. The two passenger cabins will be for Jane and Mary in one, and Doc and Melinda in the other. I think I can make Sam quite comfortable in the lounge, especially since we won't be at sea more than two days."

"I love it," Melinda responded with a beaming smile.

"Then it's settled. We will get underway at first light in the morning," he commanded. "Now. for today, I have some business to conclude here in Gijón and I have two paying passengers to disembark and see on their way. Please gather your things and meet me back here just before sundown. We'll get you settled in and you can partake of the great cuisine my cook will prepare on board for our dinner!"

>•)|H•··

CHAPTER 31

1585 CE
AT SEA

SUNRISE THE NEXT MORNING OVER THE harbor was perfect for an *en plein air* painter. The azure sky was sprinkled with white cumulus clouds, lit by the golden rays of the rising sun. The tide was receding, perfect for departure of the catamaran and its new passengers.

With formality slipping away between them, Captain Henry insisted on calling Doc by her first name, Ada, and he encouraged her to call him Charles in private, although that did not come easy for her.

She joined him on deck, reviewing with him all that had transpired since they had last seen him two months prior. She decided to see just how open Charles would be to the ways of so-called modern women, explaining their interest in exercise, the martial arts, science, and medicine. She also told him that the local customs for dress did not suit his women passengers. They wanted more freedom of movement and, if problems arose, they wanted to be prepared to take care of themselves. She then removed her skirt to reveal her slim fitting trousers, pockets, wide belt, and buckle. Waiting to see his response—she realized how he handled it would play a big part in her thinking about whether a relationship with him would work or not—made her extremely nervous.

"My, my, Ada," was all he could muster as a first reaction. "I thought you were beautiful but seeing you like this simply assures me I was correct in my thoughts. I like the look, non-conventional as it is. Now, I should tell you a little more about myself that I believe will assuage the nervousness that I sense coming off of you in waves!"

The captain sat her down in his lookout seat and faced her.

"I was married once, as you told me you were. It wasn't meant to last and that became clear fairly soon in the relationship. She was a very nice, respectable woman but her views of the world, I learned, were very different from mine. She was devout in her religion, one I found to be very prescriptive and never to be questioned by me. She was not interested in learning how the world worked. She believed her parents had told her all she needed to know about those things.

"I began to find myself suffocating in the relationship and she found me to be, in her mind, too heretical. We ended up parting ways to the benefit of us both. Struggling to understand how I had gotten myself in that marriage, I have ended up alone for many years now. Ada, I find you, in particular, and your three female companions, to be more interesting than any women I have been around before. What you think might be shocking to me is quite simply the opposite. Your presence is like finally being able to breathe fresh air after a long time struggling in the presence of women who are stifling to me and incompatible with the way I choose to live."

Ada couldn't distinguish which was stronger, her feeling of relief, pleasant surprise, or excitement about what might come next.

"Now," announced Captain Henry, who had asked Ada to continue to address him officially in the presence of others, "I must maintain the presence of command for the crew. Let's gather everyone so I can tell them what to expect on our journey to the harbor at Portishead."

When all were assembled, Captain Henry told them how conditions had deteriorated between Spain and England just in the short time they had been away.

"Don't be surprised if we encounter a privateer ship on our way back. This time, I believe we will not be in the same position when we were attacked on our earlier voyage. In fact, I hope we do run across another band of bumbling idiots. I look forward to surprising them as we leave them behind, sailing away in this swift catamaran which is a rarity in these waters."

* * *

The return to the harbor at Portishead in England proved to be an uneventful trip, much to the disappointment of Captain Henry, who was ready for a little action. When they arrived, Sam said his goodbyes and disembarked, off to find transportation to Paris.

Mary began her journey back to Avebury in the company of a merchant wagon convoy headed in that direction.

That left Melinda and Jane somewhat at a loss for their next moves. It was becoming quite clear to them that Captain Henry and Doc were starting a romance. They knew their admired leader would be sticking close to the captain. Melinda began to share her thoughts about her next move.

"I am serious about my plan to begin my new life in Stratford-upon-Avon. I do not want to lose contact with any of you, so here is an invitation. When I get to Stratford, with my share of the money from this adventure, I plan to buy a place to live somewhere around there. I will make sure I have enough space to accommodate any of you who will come to see me … and I am counting on you to make that happen. I am going to check into an inn and inquire about the best way to get there."

Jane decided to broach a subject that had occurred to her on the short voyage they had just completed from Spain to England.

"I am not inclined to settle in one place right now. Coming here from the future is for me, exhilarating. I have also seen how much I enjoyed the adventures we have had together. What I'm leading up to, Captain Henry, is applying to you to become a member of your crew, for a time at least. As you have seen, I'm fast, strong, a good archer, and pretty good at martial arts. You mentioned earlier about a new business model that includes transporting high value cargo and important passengers. I could be of double service to you in working on the ship and providing protection for your cargoes—merchandise and people."

Captain Henry immediately responded in the affirmative.

"Now that we are back in harbor, I will be losing at least two of my crew and will need to replace them. I have no doubt you could pick up what is necessary to know for the sailing aspects of a crewman's duties, especially under Jones' command. I have been thinking already, after seeing you in action, how valuable you are in hostile situations. I would hate to tell you goodbye. Consider yourself hired. We will work out the details later today or tomorrow."

"Terrific! I won't let you down." Jane displayed a smile so big that it could have caused an injury to her face.

Captain Henry looked at Ada and saw her smiling as well. "What do you think?"

"I think you made an excellent decision. My experience so far with Jane has been exceptional and I have a feeling I've only scratched the surface in understanding her potential. Oddly, I don't believe even Jane understands her true capability, as her life in Avebury did not stretch her as I believe this new life on the sea will."

The captain took her arm and led her away from the others, wanting to settle on one more detail.

"Okay, now to a sensitive logistical question that is actually more of a personal question. We have undeniably forged a bond of mutual trust and admiration, not to mention a romantic attraction that is becoming all I think about. With that, the practical question first, which immediately leads to the real issue. With Jane joining the crew, she will need one of the crew cabins to herself. That gives me one cabin for the other two crewmen and one for the cook and his helper. That leaves my cabin, allowing for two vacant cabins for our paying customers' use.

"Well, Charles, which I will call you since we are alone, you wouldn't be proposing this arrangement if you didn't already know how I feel about you. In listening to you go through the berthing details, I surmise it only works out if you and I share your cabin. So, even though you didn't ask directly, the answer is yes, I think sharing your cabin is perfect! Naturally, it will be quite controversial for some, seeing as we aren't married, but I think we are up for that challenge. Now, I'm changing the subject so that both of our reddened faces can return to normal. Please begin by telling me what you anticipate my seafaring duties will entail!"

CHAPTER 32

1585 CE
ENGLAND

WITHIN TWO WEEKS OF THEIR RETURN to the harbor in Portishead, England, Captain Henry had signed up two other crew members to join Jones and Jane. They were Harrison, second mate, and the veteran seaman, Robby Langdon, who went by Salty. Blackwell, the cook, was assisted by Fletcher, who also filled in as a deck hand. With Jane assigned to a cabin by herself, Jones was more than happy to take up quarters in the lounge by himself and not be disturbed by anyone's snoring.

The training got off to an excellent start for Jane and Ada on their new duties as crewmembers. They had kept up the routines they started in the glade above Gijón while they awaited the arrival of Captain Henry.

Those days seemed a lifetime ago but only about six weeks had passed. Two of the weeks spent in port included day sails out of the harbor to teach Jane and Ada their duties and to acquaint the new seaman with the existing crew, which now included the two women. The remaining time in port was used for serious exercise plus Jane's martial arts instruction continued for Ada. Her lessons now included Captain Henry and Jones, who demonstrated a keen interest and aptitude for the particular fighting skills Jane taught.

"I've got a job for us," announced the captain late one day as he returned from a solo trip into town. Everyone was eager to get underway at last.

"As you know, there is a growing curiosity in trade with colonies in the Americas, some of which has interest for me and some that I am definitely not interested in. There are competing companies venturing into this new world. The Spanish, English, French, and Portuguese trades are possible sources of business for us but the hostilities among them will certainly create some interesting situations. But there is wealth to be generated so we will figure out our best moves."

Ada and Jane listened closely, the wheels turning in their heads, as Captain Henry continued.

"This current customer is an English Lord. He needs rapid passage to a Spanish port in Cuba, a long way off from here. His plan is to complete some business there and return almost immediately from the Americas back to England. His business is twofold. He has some personal affairs to deal with but his primary mission is a task assigned to him by Queen Elizabeth.

"That task is to bring back a shipment of gold bullion—perhaps a mix of bars and coins, they didn't say—that is to be delivered to an emissary of the Queens's treasurer who will meet us on our return. The man who has arranged this particular business for me is someone I have known and worked with over a number of years. He recommended me for the journey, vouching for my honesty, trustworthiness, and frankly, my reputation for successfully dealing with attacks by privateers in the past, never losing my cargo to thieves or pirates."

"This sounds exactly like the type of work you purchased the catamaran for," observed Ada.

"And," Jane added, "it seems as though you may have agreed to my request to join your crew anticipating this kind of job."

"You are both correct. The compensation is generous. However, I won't sugarcoat what we are about to embark on. The voyage will be dangerous with the naval conflicts raging between Spain and England. If our precious cargo becomes known, and we must assume that it will not remain a secret, I have no doubt there will be privateers. And we can't rule out ships of the Spanish Navy coming after us for the gold. Are you two on board?"

"Yes," was the simple reply from both.

Then Ada added, "When will we leave?"

"Our customer should be here in about four days and we will depart quickly after. His name is Lord Walter Dunch, a lawyer. His father, William, was once Auditor of the Royal Mint on a temporary basis. Oddly, he later spent some time in prison, only to be pardoned later. He was a wealthy man who purchased the manor at Avebury in 1548. That is where Lord Dunch lives now. He is in his early thirties and has some of his own ties to Her Majesty. I believe that is why he has been entrusted with this mission to bring back the gold bullion for the Queen."

"We met his wife, Lady Deborah Pilkington Dunch, at the manor when we first arrived here and met Mary!" Ada exclaimed.

"I'm sure Mary is aware of the Lord's mission since she works in the Avebury manor house. I'm sure she will learn he is traveling with us," observed Jane. "I have a feeling we will be reunited with Mary before all of this is over."

As they were awaiting the arrival of Lord Dunch, food, water, and other supplies were purchased and stored. The food was scheduled to be delivered the day before sailing to keep things as fresh as possible. The exercise routines were an everyday occurrence and the time devoted to martial arts training was lengthened.

Captain Henry brought aboard some edged weapons and firearms for the crew. Jane had her bow and a plentiful supply of arrows. First Mate Jones, who had joined their martial arts training, had proved to be a fast learner. All agreed he would be very valuable if they were attacked.

* * *

The four days passed and Lord Dunch arrived on schedule. Jane was able to confirm that he did have a conversation with Mary before he departed for Portishead. Although Ada and her time-travelling companions didn't meet him while they were there because he was away, his wife, Lady Dunch, had told her husband about their visit. She said there was an uncanny resemblance between their Mary and her long lost cousin, Jane. A curious and adventurous man, Lord Dunch was anxious to meet Jane.

The Captain was counting on the speed of the catamaran as the best defense to keep them out of harm's way while at sea. On reaching their destination in Cuba and while stationed in port, he anticipated this would be their most vulnerable time. That meant any fighting that occurred would be at close range.

Ada and Jane had spent a great deal of time practicing their marksmanship with pistol and rifle near the glade where they had been training before. They found a spot on the far side of the hill to reduce the sound of the gunshots that might reach the village and arouse curiosity. Even so, distant gunfire was not a great concern since it was not unusual for others in the village to occasionally test out their firearms away from the inhabited area.

Captain Henry joined their practice sessions when he could and was impressed by their skill, which seemed to grow day by day. During one of their practices, he offered an observation based on his experience.

"Ada has actually fired in the heat of battle, so maybe she can validate what I am about to say. Shooting at a stationary target is one thing. Shooting at an enemy combatant in the heat of battle is another. They don't stand still and they are prepared to kill you if they can get close enough. A pistol is a short-range weapon. With every yard you add to the distance between you and the target, meaning its accuracy is diminished. Add to that, in the excitement of the encounter, the shooter's hand is not as steady. Constant practice will help. Your aim will become automatic and the trigger pull will not hesitate caused by doubts at shooting at another human. You will fire through reflex, not so much conscious thought. I think both of you will be ready if need be."

That night was the first for the crew to meet their esteemed passenger. Captain Henry invited him to dine with them in his quarters, also inviting Ada and Jane. All were assembled a few minutes before Lord Dunch arrived. When he entered the cabin, the Captain first introduced him to Ada. When his next introduction was to Jane, Lord Dunch just stared.

"My God! I caught myself about to call you Mary," he said to Jane. "The resemblance is indeed remarkable. But now that I look more carefully, I see there is a difference but from a distance it would be hard to discern between the two of you. I must say, I have enjoyed knowing your cousin, Mary. She is quite an accomplished woman, although I must admit, a little aloof. I don't believe I've ever really gotten to know her."

"A family trait I'm afraid," Jane apologized. "But be assured, my Lord, she has said nothing but good things about you."

As they were seated and the cook began bringing in wine, the conversation turned to the state of the conflict between Spain and England and the reasons Lord Dunch chose Captain Henry's ship and crew for his mission to the colonies in America.

"Spain is the strongest economy in this part of the world," he explained. "They have ambitions beyond their current national boundaries and, as I readily admit, so does England. These ambitions have led to open hostilities on the seas and there are credible reports that Spain is planning to assemble its armada for an attack on England. This will be an epic power struggle between two powerful nations for domination. I place my allegiance with England and will do what I can for my Queen. That is why I've taken on this voyage with you. The gold I'm charged with bringing back from America will be of great help in financing England's war effort."

"And you have chosen me and my swift ship to help you accomplish this," responded Captain Henry.

"Yes. Your reputation is well known among my peers as a man who is trustworthy and a fine seaman. Not the least of the recommendations has been the record you have of never losing one of your cargoes to privateers, even though you have been attacked more than once. There are stories of your recent voyage, being attacked by superior numbers, yet prevailing and capturing the attacker's ship. The story has it that the ship was a privateer vessel, albeit the captain professing allegiances to England. I understand you sold the ship in Spain before returning to our shores."

"That is right," the captain nodded. "I don't have respect for any ship and its captain that attacks my ship, regardless of the flag they may be flying. Our victory in this particular case was helped immensely by the other guests at my table tonight. Jane, here," he said, raising his glass to her, "was ferocious. In fact, she and another crew member saved my life in that particular fight when I had become overwhelmed by enemy combatants."

Captain Henry omitted the fact that the other crew member was Mary. As far as Lord Dunch and the staff at the Avebury Manor knew, Mary was on holiday in Liverpool visiting her ill relative during that time.

Lord Dunch carried on with his recollection of what he had heard.

"The story I was told was that there were two women archers on your crew at the time, incredible warriors and they were the ones that turned the tide of the battle."

"Stories are just that, stories," Captain Henry scoffed.

Ada was relieved they had told him that particular detail and even more grateful he remembered it.

"Facts are often left aside in the narrative to accommodate a more adventurous version of a tale. The story you heard is partially true in that Jane here was the woman mentioned in the story."

"Well, I'm certainly glad she is with us for this voyage. Above all else, I must return with the treasure I'm to retrieve for the Queen."

Captain Henry used this opening to offer his opinion on tactics to ensure that would happen.

"I can't predict the future but I will say I don't think our biggest danger on this voyage will be while we are at sea. I have great confidence in the speed of this catamaran to keep us out of the reach of danger. What I am concerned about is the spell when we'll be in port in Cuba after we have accepted the precious gold cargo and again when we return to port here. Beyond that, I believe the overland trip from Portishead to Avebury will be another time of vulnerability.

"I suggest that before we embark tomorrow, you send word back to Avebury to have a trusted group of experienced fighting men meet us here on our return to provide escort back to Avebury. Since our schedule is heavily influenced by the varying strength of the winds in our sails, I can't predict exactly when we will return but I think the voyage, heading out, will take about a month, possibly a little more.

"A normal ship would probably take forty to ninety days, depending on weather. But in our faster ship, I'm confident we will be closer to the lower number, thirty to forty days, even with some bad weather along the way. With good weather, maybe thirty days each way but that is too hopeful.

"So, to be safe, if you arrange for your men to be here sixty days from now to meet us on our return, that should be excellent. If we are late, which we may be, they must be instructed to wait. I don't want to arrive without their protection here, and they best be ready for action."

Captain Henry then asked to know more about their destination in the Americas; Baracoa, Cuba.

Lord Dunch responded, "Baracoa is a beautiful town in Cuba, founded by Diego Velazquez of Spain in 1511. We have agreements with several privateers operating in the Caribbean who have been attacking Spanish ships for some time. One of those recently captured Spanish ships was loaded with treasures to return to Spain. A big portion of the wealth captured was gold bullion.

"The captain of this particular ship is one well known to Her Majesty. They have had a transactional relationship for years, not one of mutual admiration or respect. Sometimes, this particular captain's activities have helped the Queen's causes; other times they have been contrary to her wishes. One of those contrary times led to a decree that the captain would be hanged if he ever returned to England. After the captain acquired the trove of Spanish gold, he sent a request to the Queen pleading that if he presented her with the gold, she would revoke the decree for him to be hanged."

Although he thought the story might have surprised and worried the women, he detected no reaction from them and went on.

"The gold will be of enormous help to England in their battle with Spain so the timing of the ship captain's proposal was fortuitous for him. The Queen agreed to his proposal. That led to my assignment to go to Baracoa—a mission being kept secret, mind you—transfer the gold to your superior ship, *The Twin Flame*, and bring it home to England.

"It's important to note there will be one of the privateer captain's agents in Baracoa keeping watch for our arrival sometime in the next month. I have his description and an official letter from the Queen to vouch for my identity. This agent, by the name of Kit Walden, is to be my contact. He will arrange the time and place for us to meet for the delivery."

"All well and good, Lord Dunch," Captain Henry cautioned, "but it seems from what you have related, there are quite a few people who are aware of this *secret* plan. To me, that means when we arrive, it will not be so secret. I suggest at the last possible moment, you announce to this Kit Walden that you have an alternate meeting time to transfer the gold to *The Twin Flame*. That doesn't mean no one will hear of the new time but it may reduce the number who might."

"Agreed, Captain. I have been contemplating something like that myself," Lord Dunch asserted defensively.

Captain Henry then asked, "Tell me, precisely how much bullion can we expect to be loaded on my ship? I'm particularly interested in how much weight I will be taking on."

"My understanding is that the gold has been melted down and poured into molds, resulting in gold bars weighing about twenty-seven pounds each. I have been informed to expect to receive fifteen such bars. So, that will be something on the order of 400 or so pounds."

"That will be the equivalent of taking on three additional passengers in weight," the captain estimated. "It will slow us down a little but she'll manage."

Ada whispered to Jane, "Four-hundred pounds of gold! When I was researching this time period, I read that the supply of gold, largely coming into Europe from the Americas, was increasing, driving the market price down to slightly over the equivalent of $500.00 per *ounce* in twenty-first century dollars. That means 400 *pounds* would bring about three ... three-and-a-quarter million dollars. In this time in history, that is a *lot* of purchasing power!"

Jane gave her a sly look and a little nod.

>•)++··

CHAPTER 33

1585 CE
CUBA

THE NEXT DAY, BRIGHT AND EARLY, *The Twin Flame* sailed out of the harbor at Portishead. They were underway to Cuba.

The weather was mostly good for the duration of the voyage. The time at sea was spent with Ada and Jane learning how to perform tasks that were delegated to them. They were fast learners, earning the respect of Jones, Harrison, and even the weathered Salty. Ada and Jane were in excellent physical shape so the concern the men had about women carrying their share of the load disappeared by the first week at sea. The men did notice with some wonder how effortlessly Jane performed tasks that involved strenuous labor. They were also impressed by her ability to move quickly around the deck at night when visibility was poor.

When they were about two days out from Cuba, a Spanish schooner heading their way appeared in the distance. The safe assumption was that it was a privateer vessel but it was of little consequence as their faster catamaran soon left them vanishing from sight over the horizon.

* * *

Two days later, they saw a smudge in the distance that soon became clear was the coastline of Cuba. Captain Henry slowed their progress, intending to reach the harbor of Baracoa after nightfall.

Lights from the town gave plenty of illumination to be able to navigate the channel and dock. Prior to entering the harbor, Captain Henry called his crew and Lord Dunch together to explain his plan.

"We will dock quickly and without much commotion. When we are secure, Lord Dunch and second mate Harrison here, will disembark and seek out Lord Dunch's contact. The man should be somewhere nearby keeping a lookout for our arrival. Since its dark, he may not be watching for us at this hour but he should be nearby. Lord Dunch should be able to spot him from the description he was given. This is not a particularly big place, so that should be accomplished within an hour."

The captain continued delivering his orders.

"I plan to take us back out of the harbor, circle around, and return an hour later to meet the two of them here. I don't want to be tied up at the wharf and be vulnerable any longer than necessary. When you return, Lord Dunch," he said addressing him, "you, Harrison, and your contact man, Walden, must board quickly.

"Walden will show us where to go to pick up the gold bullion. After the delivery is accomplished, we will replenish our fresh water and take on some new food stores. Walden can advise us on where to go for that. Just make sure it's not anywhere near where we pick up the gold.

"My experience tells me that if we are going to have a problem, it will be when we are loading the gold on the ship at the location you arranged with your man. My guess is that the gold will be taken from some secretive spot and moved to where we will be mooring for the transfer from land to this boat. For anyone watching, and I'll bet there will be some, the gold will be revealed and that's when they will pounce. That's what I would do, anyway, but be prepared for anything to happen."

With the plans made, Captain Henry steered the catamaran to dock in Baracoa. As his boat touched the wharf, Lord Dunch and Harrison leapt over the side and began walking quickly toward town. Captain Henry maneuvered the boat away and set out of the harbor.

An hour later, the catamaran slowly made its way back into the harbor. With eyes peeled for any sight of Lord Dunch, they finally spotted him with Harrison and a man of medium height who looked like a brawler.

"I don't like the looks of this Walden bloke," said Jane, "but looks can be deceiving. Anyway, we need him for what we do next."

Drifting up, as soon as the hull of the catamaran touched the wharf's fenders, Lord Dunch, Harrison, and the contact man jumped on board. Captain Henry again quickly maneuvered out into the harbor while Lord Dunch's contact relayed to the captain the destination for picking up the gold.

When asked his name, the man replied, "Giving names can be dangerous. Just refer to me as the contact."

Their destination, the shadowy Walden explained, was about a mile by sea from where they currently were. He described the location as a private dock serving a plantation house near the mouth of the Rio Miel. The house was recently vacated and the new residents had not yet moved in.

The land on either side of the house was wooded, with fields beyond. The gold had been hidden in the woods days before in a place, he assured them, that would not be found by anyone except the ones who had placed it there. The men Walden had chosen for this mission would come up a road behind the house, head into the woods, and retrieve the gold.

He further confirmed Captain Henry's belief that they would be attacked when they arrived. He indicated Baracoa was a small place and secrets didn't stay secret for long. Walden believed the thieves would stay hidden, letting his men pass but not attacking until they pulled the gold out of hiding and moved the load toward the dock. In the darkness, the thieves would need to wait until they were sure the gold had been taken out of its hidden location—which turned out to be very near the dock.

Captain Henry called Jane aside to discuss his plan on hearing this information. He assumed the thieves would come to the location by boat, stowing it somewhere upriver so it would be hidden from the house and the woods. If that was correct, the thieves would not likely wait in the house. Instead, they would hide in the woods upriver, on the west side of the house, since they would be coming from where they hid their boat.

"So, here's how we will fool them," continued Captain Henry.

"I've learned you are an excellent swimmer, Jane. Jones, I know is excellent as well. I want you two to choose your weapons, wrap them watertight in some oilcloth, attach a cork float or two to the bundles and when we are still a couple of hundred yards from shore, you will slip overboard in the darkness and swim to a point about fifty yards to the east of the dock. Make your way silently and swiftly towards the dock, looking for any men who may be hiding and waiting to attack us. I will loiter in the distance giving you enough time to make your approach before I move to the dock.

"Jane, I'll leave it to you as leader of this mission to use your judgement as to the timing of your attack on any hostiles you encounter. The rest of the crew will keep weapons ready but out of sight here on deck. I don't want anyone on our crew to be surprised if this landing results in a firefight. If so, and I am assuming it will, it is imperative that we bring the bullion on board before we cast our lines and leave.

"Now, for the action on deck here," he continued. "Ada, you are our best marksman. I want you to find a prone, shielded position to fire from."

Pointing to Salty, he said, "I want you to be her loader. That will save time in addition to the fact Ada will be unable to load from a prone position. You will have three muskets loaded and ready, rotating them to Ada and reloading the ones she fires.

"Ada, if it comes to an all-out attack, I want you to fire as fast as you are given a fresh musket. If we are boarded, you and Salty need to drop the muskets and use pistols. Each of us will have a loaded pistol. Once those are fired, each of you will resort to your choice of an edged weapon."

Pointing to Blackwell and Fletcher, the captain told them it would be their responsibility to assist in getting the bullion on board.

"I don't know who will be bringing it to our boat," he said, "and I don't know if they will be reliable, either."

Looking into the cook's eyes, he told Blackwell, "You will be in charge of the bullion loading so improvise as the situation unfolds. Each of you will have a pistol in your belt—you'll need your hands free for loading. I have confidence you will make it work."

Although the danger was well understood, he added, "Lord Dunch, keep an eye on your man, Walden, for any signs of treachery. With this much gold at stake, my circle of trust is pretty damn small."

CHAPTER 34

1585 CE

CUBA

IT DIDN'T TAKE LONG FOR THE catamaran to reach a point about two hundred yards from the dock where the gold was to be loaded. The night was overcast, with a little trickle of moonlight coming through a thin cover of wispy clouds; conditions perfect for Jane.

For Jones, his night vision was not as good but with Jane as a guide, their plan would work. They silently slipped into the water on the far side of the boat with their gear wrapped and attached to cork floats. Swimming quietly with only their heads out of the water and pushing their respective floats ahead of them, they made their way up the far side of the Rio Miel to its shore about fifty yards above the house. Trees came down to the water's edge. Their thick cover and the darkness were perfect camouflage for their approach. It was not long before they were subjected to a swarm of biting insects but they had anticipated that would be the case, so they steeled themselves to endure it.

Quietly moving through the trees toward the dock, Jane heard a muffled cough in the distance. Jane moved close to Jones and whispered in his ear.

"I think men are clustered in the woods near the dock. Number unknown. There may be more in other places. Let's move forward until I can see them and then we will decide how to deal with however many there are. I want us to stay concealed in the woods but close enough to the shore to be able to keep track of *The Twin*

Flame. Don't reveal ourselves until these thieves make their move. Then I'll do what I can with my bow. It will be silent, so they won't know where it is coming from at first. I might be able to get off another shot while they are trying to understand what is happening. So, hold for a few seconds before you start firing. After that, we improvise."

"Got it," whispered Jones.

As Jane moved cautiously through the darkness in the trees, she couldn't help but think about the contrast of what she was about to do: stalking other humans with the intent to do them harm and the life she had been living only months ago in twenty-first century Avebury, waiting on tables, and taking tourists on tours of the henge and stones.

How orderly, living a safe life in a society governed by laws.

Her biggest concern then was being different from everyone else she met and trying to blend in. She never could truly connect with anyone on a deeply personal level.

Life has certainly gotten more complicated.

Pushing those thoughts from her mind, she decided that, if at all possible, she would shoot to disable the thieves rather than kill them. They weren't necessarily evil, just a reflection of living in this time and trying to survive.

The Spanish and the Portuguese had stolen the gold from the Mayans who were here before. Now, she was part of a group aiding the English to steal the same gold from the Spanish.

Am I really any better than they? Their leader has convinced them this is acceptable behavior. Hadn't the Queen convinced Lord Dunch that what he was doing was acceptable behavior? And haven't I convinced myself that following Captain Henry is acceptable? Get a grip. If you lose focus now, you will be a dead woman. Stay alive to think about the morality of all of this at a later time.

These thoughts vanished as Jane simultaneously heard the catamaran bumping up against the dock and a call from the darkness from the party, still hidden, that identified themselves as being the bearers of the gold. She turned to Jones and motioned for him to come closer to her side.

A long thirty seconds passed before a response came from Captain Henry on the boat, followed by Blackwell and Fletcher leaping off the dock and heading for the men coming out of hiding with the gold for the handoff. That's when the anticipated attack came. The thieves broke cover from their hiding place in the trees and a second group of thieves burst out of the darkness from their place of concealment in the vacant house.

Jane let an arrow fly, piercing the thigh of the first robber running out of the trees. Before he even let out his scream of pain, her second arrow hit the next man revealing himself. Her arrow went completely through the bicep of his right arm. As she nocked her third arrow, she saw the flash of Ada's first musket shot from the catamaran, felling one of the thieves coming from the house.

Standing near Jane, Jones fired at about the same time as Ada, bringing down the third man racing from the trees towards the catamaran. That shot from his musket gave away their position as Jane knew it would, so she motioned for him to follow her to a new spot just behind a tree not fifty feet from the dock. She let fly her third arrow, hitting a man rushing toward the gold bearers, bringing him down instantly.

"Looks like the thieves we suspected would be here have split up, one group directly attacking the catamaran and the other group going for the men carrying the gold." Jane was shouting over the chaos now, the need for silence over.

Within a minute of the start of the attack, realization dawned on the thieves that their prey was not as vulnerable as they thought they would be. Confused looks peered toward the trees where Jane's counterattack had come. The thieves were surprised by the furious volley of accurate fire coming from *The Twin Flame* that had broken their advance on the men carrying the gold toward the docked ship. Blackwell and Fletcher had to fire their pistols, bringing two of the thieves down, the third shot missing wide. Still, for cooks, they didn't show any hesitation.

The hesitation on the part of the surprised attackers allowed Blackwell and Fletcher, who had been joined by Harrison and Lord Dunch, time to gain access to the dock. Everyone furiously began loading the heavy bullion onto the catamaran's deck.

More fire came from Captain Henry and Ada on the ship. Jane and Jones were attacking their flank, which led to a panicked withdrawal by the thieves. Taking advantage of that respite, Jane and Jones boarded the catamaran right as Walden and three of his gold bearers also jumped on board. Captain Henry, with the help of Harrison and Salty, pushed off from the dock as a light offshore breeze filled their sails.

As Jones began to get the ship underway, everyone else on board began firing whatever weapon was still loaded in the direction of the thieves. Jane was not shy in letting loose a volley of arrows as others were reloading the muskets.

Soon, they were far enough into the darkness. The raiders on shore were attempting to shoot in their direction but they could not accurately pick out individual targets. The crew on board found positions that partially concealed them.

Salty helped Captain Henry with the sails and rigging, making them unavoidably exposed. One of the shots from shore nicked the mast near Salty's face, causing a flying splinter to draw blood from his cheek.

Once out of range, Lord Dunch's contact, Walden, now appearing to be a frightened man, told them where to sail for the food and water he had arranged for their return trip. He explained that he had understood they would want to move fast after obtaining the gold, so their provisions were loaded in a boat, guarded by one of his men along a rocky shoreline. This man would row out to them after receiving a prearranged signal from Walden. The provisions would be transferred to the catamaran. The men who helped carry the gold at the plantation house, plus Walden, would then use the boat to row their way back to Baracoa.

Captain Henry spoke to Walden and the three men with him who had helped carry the gold on board.

"You four will disembark as agreed after we pick up our provisions at this next stop. Lord Dunch will give you the compensation for your help as we are on our way there."

Then he turned to the others.

"I see all are accounted for. Is anyone injured?"

Salty stepped forward with blood running into his scruffy beard and grumbled that he was alright. One of Walden's men had a flesh wound in the arm and another had a wound from a musket ball that had gone completely through the meaty part of his thigh.

"You two men see Blackwell. He not only cooks for us but he has some skill as a medical practitioner patching up wounds."

It only took about half an hour to reach the pickup point for the return trip provisions. Signals were exchanged and Walden's man on the rocky shore launched his boat into the sea and headed toward *The Twin Flame.*

As it approached near enough to see better, the Captain noticed not one, but two men on the small boat. Turning to Walden, his demeanor hardened as he spoke.

"I see two men, not one as you said coming towards us."

"I guess my man decided he needed help," Walden said quickly. "I'm sure it's fine."

Captain Henry, despite the darkness, noticed the furtive look in Walden's eyes as he spoke. The captain casually moved to stand closer to Jones, who was only a few steps away. The captain noticed Jones' body tighten as he, too, saw the second man in the approaching rowboat.

"Jones," the captain whispered, "I don't like this at all. I sense you have the same feeling. Keep an eye on Walden. I've not had a good feeling about him since he came aboard. I'll watch his men on the boat. Quietly slip over to Jane and let her know our suspicions. We will know their intentions when they first board us."

Jones slowly moved from the railing and walked over to where Jane was standing near the mast.

"The Captain sent me with a message for you."

"I saw you two standing together," she whispered. "I think I know what it is. Two men on the approaching boat; not one. I don't like it."

"That's the message. If something goes wrong, the captain is covering the two in the boat and told me to watch Walden. If something happens, he thinks it will be right when they board our boat."

"Good. I will keep an eye on the men who came aboard with the gold bullion, too, even though two of them are beat up pretty good. The rowboat is about to come alongside. I have my bow here, just out of sight." Then, Jane disappeared from view.

Seconds later, the rowboat bumped up against the catamaran, near a short ladder that was placed there to assist. One of the men in the boat called out, "Permission to come aboard. My mate will begin handing up the provisions to me."

"Granted," Captain Henry called back.

The man started up the ladder and hopped on board. He turned, reached back, but instead of bringing up the first bag of the provisions, he revealed a short musket, similar to the one the captain had seen the highwaymen brandish on their journey from Gijón to Oviedo.

"No!" shouted Captain Henry, as he fired a pistol he had concealed behind his back.

The man with the musket was knocked back into the rowboat, shot in the chest. The captain pulled out his second pistol and shot the other man in the boat, who was starting to raise a musket of his own.

Almost simultaneous with the captain's first shot, on board, Walden pulled a knife and took a step toward an unsuspecting Harrison standing near him. But Walden's surprise attack was caught short as Jones dropped him to the deck with a leg sweep, followed up by a crushing blow to his head with an elbow.

Jane put two of Walden's other men down. She shot an arrow through the good leg of the one with the musket ball wound in his thigh. The unwounded man she hit with an arrow to the shoulder. As she had decided earlier, she aimed to wound rather than kill if possible.

The third man of the shore party, the one with the flesh wound to his arm, was taken down by the knife Jones had retrieved from the hand of the unconscious Walden. Jones hurled the knife with force and accuracy, hitting the target squarely in the chest.

All of the action took place in seconds from the firing of the first shot from the Captain. Ada, Lord Dunch, and the other crew members weren't expecting this sabotage and had hardly moved.

Captain Henry immediately called out to Jones. "Give me a report!"

"No further danger now, Captain," he replied. "None of our people are injured. You killed the two in the boat as far as I can tell from here. Walden is unconscious on the deck. Of the three who boarded with the gold, one is down with Jane's arrow through his good leg, the next is down with an arrow to the shoulder, and the last is lying with a knife in the chest—none dead but all severely wounded."

The captain looked pleased.

"Harrison, Salty, load their casualties in the rowboat after bringing our provisions aboard. When this contact creature and the other unconscious men come around, put them in the rowboat to join their wounded. Then they can row wherever they want. In the meantime, we will shove off and be long gone. Oh, and one more thing. Relieve those men of the payment Walden gave them for their services bringing the bullion on board."

"Aye, aye," Jones said and Jane leapt to help him.

The captain turned to Ada and Lord Dunch.

"This has been an adventure laced with treachery and deception. I think this Walden had somehow gained the trust of the privateer captain to make the delivery of the gold for him but planned all along to betray him and take the gold for himself. He suspected there would be thieves at the delivery point, just as we did.

"So, he planned to keep the cover of being with us until we could pick up the gold, fight off any thieves that we all suspected would be there, and then make his treacherous move at the pick-up point for the return voyage supplies."

Lord Dunch responded, quite stunned from the encounter.

"In hindsight, that is becoming clear. I think when we are back in England I will find a way, probably through the Queen's emissaries, to get word back to the privateer captain of his agent's duplicity and treachery. He will be relieved to know the gold was delivered to the Queen in spite of that turn of events. I am confident that the privateer captain will track down and deal with Walden in a most unpleasant way."

Captain Henry replied, "I have no doubt you are correct. I would not want to be in Walden's shoes. I think his time on earth will quickly come to an end when our message reaches the captain he betrayed."

)•)ııı··

CHAPTER 35

1585 CE
ENGLAND

THE TRIP BACK ACROSS THE ATLANTIC was anticlimactic. The weather was favorable and the few ships they saw in the distance were never close enough to do them any harm. As they approached Portishead in England, about thirty days later, their apprehension began to grow thinking of what might lay ahead as they landed.

Lord Dunch had heeded Captain Henry's warning about the return trip on land. Before they had departed on the voyage, he had sent a messenger back to Avebury to have a small but formidable party estimate the date of their return, travel to Portishead, and wait for them there even if they had to wait a month. Once they safely reached Avebury, the Queen planned to send a contingent of soldiers to meet them and take possession of the gold and transport it the final way to London.

When they sailed into the harbor at Portishead in the early evening and Captain Henry had docked, Lord Dunch went ashore to locate his escort party. The others stayed on board, even though they were anxious to set foot on land after their voyage. They all stayed alert for any suspicious behavior in the area.

It didn't take long for Lord Dunch to return, accompanied by the leader of his escort party. His group had been staying in the nearby inn waiting for *The Twin Flame* to dock. The leader turned out to be John, the building contractor and Mary's friend.

John told Captain Henry that his plan was to have six of his people spend the night on the deck of the catamaran and on the wharf near the boat. He thought it best if Captain Henry's crew stayed with the boat as well overnight. Early the next morning, he would have one of his several wagons come down to the wharf to load up the gold and then join the protective convoy that would depart for Avebury. Captain Henry agreed.

"We have not successfully come this far only to risk losing the gold on the first night back. We will stay here with the gold until it is loaded on a wagon in the morning. However, none of us would object if the men you send down bring us a fresh meal from the inn's kitchen!"

Later in the evening after night had fallen, the men appeared with baskets of food. However, one of them was a woman—it was Mary.

"I knew you would be one of those coming to meet us!" Jane shouted out as she quickly jumped off the catamaran onto the wharf.

"Of course, you did!" Mary exclaimed. "When I learned of this mission to guard the trip from here to Avebury, I naturally suggested that John would be a wise choice to put together an appropriate group of men from town. With that agreed to, it was no surprise to John that I wanted to be a part of the action. In fact, he said he would only have been surprised if I *didn't* want to come!"

"I see that you carried through with your plan to let John know of your feelings toward him," Jane smiled.

Mary beamed. "Yes. He was quick to let me know that he felt the same but was unsure how to approach me since I was certainly giving out mixed signals. The conversation I was so fearful of, one where I would talk to him about who I really am, went much better than I expected. There is much more to John than appears. In town, he is respected as an honorable man, an excellent construction supervisor, and a friend to many. But what I suspected is also there. He is highly intuitive and has read everything he can get his hands on in Avebury and from travelers passing through. He is quite inquisitive and has learned much about the world beyond Avebury from many nights in local taverns meeting and discussing ideas with the people he meets.

"When I told him about my ancestry, he didn't blink, although I could see he was looking carefully at my eyes. I could almost see him thinking about the times he had seen me easily lifting heavy objects in my work at the Red Lion. Once, when a serving plate slipped off my tray, he noticed my reflexes were able to catch the plate before it hit the floor, not even spilling any of the food. He didn't say anything at the time but, apparently, he took it all in then."

"What about the age thing? How did he handle that?" Jane asked.

"He said he would take whatever time we could have together but was more concerned about how I would feel when he began to visibly age more than me. That concern for *my* feelings, not his own, almost made me cry."

"I'm so happy for you," Jane observed, deciding to end the conversation on that note.

The night proved uneventful, possibly because anyone hearing about the gold on board who might be tempted to make a play would have seen John and his guards on the dock, ready to alert the crew on the catamaran and spring into action.

❊ ❊ ❊

A cool, clear morning greeted a rising sun and the activity around the catamaran was already humming, preparing for the wagons in the distance approaching the wharf. Within an hour of first light, John had the convoy of wagons ready to roll, the gold stored and hidden on one and his passengers from the catamaran ensconced on the others.

Jane and Mary were seated together on the second wagon,

having learned on their previous trip by wagon how well that worked if they were attacked. Jane had her bow, and, no surprise, Mary had brought her own with her. Captain Henry and Ada were on the last wagon of the convoy, with loaded weapons just out of sight but in easy reach. Jones and the rest of the catamaran crew remained on *The Twin Flame* to make repairs and get her ready for her next voyage.

At the end of the first day of travel, as the convoy settled into camp for the night, Captain Henry, Ada, Jane, John, and Mary gathered away from the others. Captain Henry spoke first.

"In my bones, I feel that if we are going to be attacked on this trip, it will be sometime tomorrow. John has told me that there are several choke points in the trail ahead that are the favorite ambush points for robbers."

"Yes, from my conversations with travelers resting in Avebury over the years," John confirmed, "there have been stories of bandits attacking travelers along this trail. While infrequent, the convoys mentioned several places along the way where misfortune struck them ... and those places are all along the way we will travel tomorrow."

"Here is my suggestion to you, John," Captain Henry started. "You are the leader of this protective force, so the decision is yours. But here it is. Jane and Mary clearly have exceptional skills. Their night vision is better than anyone's that I have ever known. They are superb archers and have quicker reflexes than any of us. I suggest they leave here tonight and make their way up the trail we will be on tomorrow. With their keen hearing, coupled with what I know is an ability to move silently, they will detect any bandits hiding along the way, well before they might be seen or heard.

"I believe any band like that will set their trap before daylight and wait for us to show up. I will leave it up to Jane and Mary, depending on what they discover, to take preemptive action or to come back to us for reinforcements. This probably sounds like I am putting them in harm's way, which is true, but if we are surprised tomorrow, they will be in even greater danger. I could suggest some of your men go with them but, frankly, they likely would be in the way and hinder Jane and Mary's movements."

Mary spoke next. "I like the plan. It makes sense to me."

Jane agreed. "I'm in. We will be ready to move out around midnight. I'm assuming anyone with plans to ambush us will be in route to their hiding places now, so we will give them time to get there and still allow us about five hours of darkness to find them. The two of us will be moving fast, even though quietly. If anyone is out there, we will find them."

※ ※ ※

Four hours later, Jane and Mary were moving out of the camp, walking up the road the convoy would be taking the next day. Jane broke the silence.

"Let's walk for about twenty minutes and then start a slow run for about twenty minutes, then repeat the process. I'll let you get about fifteen yards ahead of me, so our footfalls and breathing won't interfere with each other's hearing. My sense is that if anyone is out here, they will be off the road but not too far off. We should hear them before they hear us. I doubt they will be very careful now as they should be expecting us in the morning."

"Alright. We will periodically alternate who leads." Mary adjusted the quiver of arrows that she had slung over her shoulder. "Let's go find anyone who may be out there!"

About 3:00 in the morning, Jane, whose turn it was in the lead, stopped abruptly, raising her hand signaling Mary to halt. They both stood dead still for less than a minute, listening intently. Then Mary quietly moved up to Jane's position and whispered in her ear.

"I hear it. I think our target is about twenty yards ahead and maybe ten yards or so back in the trees. Let's leave the road and go into the trees ourselves. We should be able to move in close enough to get a look without them seeing us."

"Got it. Let's go."

The two took about fifteen minutes, moving extremely slowly and silently, to reach a point where they could see ten men sitting in a circle with no fire. A few were lying down, obviously sleeping, while others were talking among themselves, thinking they were alone in the forest. One, his tone of voice suggesting a leadership position, was outlining how they would go about the ambush in the morning. From the attitude of those listening, they were not hearing his plan for the first time but showing deference by allowing their apparently nervous leader to talk.

Close enough to hear the leader talk but not so close that he could hear them if they whispered, Mary summed up the situation.

"There are ten of them. None have weapons in their hands but they're not far out of reach. You move over about five yards from me. While you stay out of sight and cover me, I'm going to give them a little surprise."

Once Jane reached her new position, Mary quickly moved from cover and stood about ten feet from the men, her drawn bow up with an arrow pointed directly at the man who had been speaking.

"Morning gents! Let me introduce myself."

As Mary spoke, one of the startled men reached for a pistol in his belt. As he pulled it out, Mary's arrow pierced his hand and before his dropped pistol reached the ground, she had another arrow nocked and ready.

"Now, that was not very friendly," she jested. "I suggest the rest of you stay still until I finish my say. I'm one of the folks you obviously planned to rob tomorrow. I'm here to tell you that's not going to happen."

One of the men standing near the leader, looking around, and seeing no one else, spoke out.

"She's fast, lads, but there's ten of us and one of her. Well, nine

… now that Joe is whining over that arrow stuck through his hand. I say we go for it and take her down."

No sooner than the last word was out of his mouth did an arrow came out of the woods and lodge in a tree three inches from his head.

"Not so alone," said Mary in a calm voice. "I'm just the only one you can see. I'm losing patience and thinking I should go ahead and shoot you," she said looking into the eyes of their leader.

"Wait, wait," he commanded, "nobody moves until we hear what the lady has to say."

"Now, that's smart," Mary agreed. "It's dark here but I seem to recognize one of you boys. Tom from Avebury, is this your little band of thieves?"

Tom, obviously shocked to be recognized and called out by name, blurted out, "I can't really make out your face but the voice sounds familiar."

Moving a little closer, Mary asked, "Recognize me now, Tom?"

"My god, is that you Mary?"

"Yes, and I'm surprised to see you here and not in the shop helping out the butcher. What's going on with you?"

"I'm confused now," Tom stuttered. "I was told that a shipment of gold was coming through here. Gold stolen from the English to be handed over to the Spanish."

"Couldn't be more wrong," Mary snapped. "Who told you that?"

Tom pointed to one of the men who had been lying down and was now sitting.

"Robert there, he told me and said we could get quite a reward for stealing it back for the Queen!"

Robert, sensing the turn of events were not going to work out well for him, had been slowly pulling his pistol from under his leg. As he quickly raised it to fire at Mary, another arrow sped from the trees and lodged in his shoulder, the pistol dropping away. Jane then stepped forward from her place of concealment, another arrow at the ready.

"Does anyone else want to give it a try," she asserted.

Mary told them to slowly move away from their weapons and then sit back down together a few yards away.

"Not you," she said, pointing with her drawn arrow to one of the men. "You start a little fire so you all can see better and we will talk—or I can just start shooting."

The man she pointed to wasted no time moving to gather a few sticks and limbs that were close by and began the process of getting the pile lighted. It didn't take long for the newly lit fire to provide some light to the group.

"Okay, Tom, here's the deal," bargained Mary. "You have been duped. The man lying there with the arrow in his shoulder, I would wager a month's pay, is a Spanish agent. He knows full well the shipment we are carrying to Avebury is for the Queen. I suspect he has a plan to double cross you at some point. Who are these other men you have with you?"

"Oh, Mary, this is horrible," Tom cried. "Five of these men are cousins of mine from Swindon and the other four are close friends of theirs. I recruited them, for what now looks like fool's work!"

"Here's my offer to you Tom," she announced. "I will take you at your word that the wounded man here tricked you. He has admitted as much by going for his pistol when it became clear his cover was blown. There is probably a reward for him by the Crown. I will allow the reward for him to go to you and your men under the condition that you accompany me and my companions tomorrow as extra protection to Avebury. You will turn Robert over to the Queen's representatives who will soon be there to take the gold shipment to London."

Tom sheepishly agreed. Mary continued.

"The other condition is this: I will not divulge that you were planning to rob the shipment on its way to the Queen but that you had volunteered to help guard the shipment and captured the villain trying to arrange its theft. Since I'm more certain than ever he is a known, wanted man, whatever he says about tonight will be considered nothing more than a desperate man lying to keep from being taken to London to be hanged."

Mary added as an extra precaution, "You, Tom, will never reveal my role in anything that happened here tonight. Remember, I'm only a simple serving lass at the Red Lion Pub and you, a simple butcher's helper. Neither of us would benefit from the tongue-wagging in the little village of Avebury if the true story of tonight came out."

She turned to the others.

"And for the rest of you, as you ultimately head back to your homes in Swindon, remember that your original intent, duped or not, was to steal the Queen's gold. That is a hanging offense, or worse. So, keeping your mouths shut will save your lives. Understand? Do we have a deal?"

The affirmative, vigorous head-wagging would have been comical if the consequences had not been so serious.

"Okay, then," ordered Mary, "Pick up your weapons, put out the fire, and we will begin the walk back to join our group with the wagons."

* * *

The first rays of daylight revealed the band of would-be-thieves, now thoroughly embarrassed for being caught doing dirty work for the Spanish, not to mention being captured and taken in by women. They walked behind Mary with their heads hanging. Tom and Jane brought up the rear with the bound Spanish agent between them.

As the lead wagon rolled into view around a bend in the road, Captain Henry, with John sitting beside him, incredulously peered at the approaching band.

"What's this?" he said to John as he turned in his seat to signal the other wagons to stop.

Smiling as she approached hailing distance, Mary shouted out to them.

"Captain Henry, John, we just recruited an additional escort for the remainder of our trip to Avebury. Found them in the woods just waiting for us!"

Later when she was alone with John, Mary told him of her concerns.

"These men from Avebury and Swindon have seen me do things now that are certainly not ordinary. Unfortunately, I think we need to seriously consider moving away from Avebury in the not-too-distant future."

CHAPTER 36

1586 CE
ENGLAND TO
NORTH AMERICA

THE YEAR 1585 CAME TO A close. Spring of 1586 in Avebury was much the same as the year before but with a few notable changes. Mary and John were married in April in the old Saxon church next to the manor house. The speculation about Mary being different that was beginning to bubble up when her lookalike cousin Jane had mysteriously arrived the year before had all but disappeared. Her marriage to John played a role in bringing some sense of normality to the situation in the public eye.

The couple agreed that Mary should continue her work in the manor house. They both appreciated the insight that position gave her on the comings and goings in the village. The overheard conversations in the manor house, considering the connections of the residents with the Crown, allowed them to stay abreast of the news of the escalating fight between England and Spain. This was augmented with conversations in the Red Lion with travelers passing through having news of other events occurring in England.

John continued with his work overseeing a construction crew, working on projects in and around Avebury as well as some of the smaller villages nearby. Between the two of them, they were doing well financially, plus they had a tidy amount saved from their share of the proceeds from Captain Henry's sale of the captured privateer boat and the gold mission. However, they both had a growing uneasiness being in Avebury, particularly for Mary every time she went to the butcher shop and was in the presence of the butcher's helper. He had kept quiet, but still ....

Ada and Charles had not yet married in a formal sense, although they were committed to each other in every way except by being bound by a legal marriage contract. Theirs was not a union arranged by families to protect wealth or status. Marriage was going through a social evolution at that time, with secular unions between two people being practiced by some. A conflict between the Church of England and the Catholic Church on the particular religious obligations of marriage created problems for many. Ada and Charles did not want to take sides in religious views as their shipping business catered to wealthy clients on all sides. Also, they reasoned, the fact they both had been married before added a little complication to the situation, particularly so in the requirements of Catholic marriages.

Jane had taken on increasingly more responsibilities on Captain Henry's catamaran. With a little prompting from Ada—who explained how women in the future were seen as equal to men as long as they pulled their own weight—the Captain announced that Jane had earned the title of First Mate alongside Jones. Her role was effectively identical to his but becoming second-in-command was an unheard-of assignment for a female in these times. Captain Henry was tickled to upset the status quo.

Jane had the charge of ensuring the safety of the boat, crew, and cargo in the increasingly hostile waters they crossed in service to their clients. She was already regarded by the captain as an equal to Jones, which was evident when he sometimes shouted for his first mate and Jane was quicker to respond. Her new status was actually well received by Jones and the crew of the catamaran. By now, they were well aware of her prowess in a fight and saw her as a smart and capable leader they trusted in the everyday management of the ship.

＊ ＊ ＊

One early spring morning in their home port of Portishead, Captain Henry returned to the catamaran, calling out to Ada.

"Good news! I've got us two passengers for a trip leaving in three days." As he boarded the boat, he explained in a quieter voice, "They want us to take them to America. Not in the South, around Cuba, but further North to an important Spanish colony called St. Augustine. It is a strategic port for Spain as it is near the route Spanish trading ships coming north from the Caribbean take before turning east towards Spain. The area provides a harbor for ships damaged in tropical storms and serves as a base for Spanish Navy ships hunting pirates that prey on Spanish trading ships heading back to Spain loaded with goods and treasure from Spanish settlements further south."

"What is the motivation for our new passengers willing to pay our high rates for the trip when they could go far less expensively on a Spanish trading ship? I'm just curious what we may be getting into," Ada asked.

"Excellent question!" he replied. "The passengers are Spanish with substantial financial interests in St. Augustine. I gather those interests are not sanctioned by the Spanish government. They have unsubstantiated intelligence that Sir Francis Drake is planning an attack on the colony. They want to get one person out of there before the suspected attack occurs with a cargo of roughly 250 pounds—I'm guessing gold. Since the gold is not going to benefit Spain, I'm not troubled by helping out."

"I'm okay with that, too, but I'm worried that our speed, which gives us a margin of safety on a hazardous trip, will be compromised by the weight of the third passenger and the 250-pound cargo," Ada added with a slight frown.

"I think I know a way around that," he suggested. "I've recently been talking to a sailmaker I've known for years. He has come into some rope and sailcloth that comes from China. He was a little vague on what the material is, on purpose, as I think it may be a trade secret. But my guess is that it is either silk or some blend incorporating silk. It's just as strong, maybe stronger than conventional sail and rope but much lighter in weight. The cloth is expensive ... but our boat is not a big trading vessel with many times the amount of sail and rope that our smaller boat has, so it won't be exorbitant.

"I've not finalized the agreement with our two passengers but I think they are desperate for quick passage so I will talk with them about footing the bill to outfit our ship with new rope and sails in addition to our normal fee for transporting them. Speed is every bit as important to them on this trip as it is to us. My sailmaker can start this afternoon, work around the clock with his helper, and get it done in time for us. If that all works, our ship should be about 250 pounds lighter. Not quite enough to cover the full weight of our third passenger but it covers the cargo weight."

"Okay, let's do it!"

"Another fortuitous circumstance," added the Captain, "is we recently had the ship's keel scraped, caulked, and tarred, so all of the barnacles and other growth has been removed. We won't have any drag from that slowing her down on this trip. A small thing but every little speed advantage we can get helps!"

The next few days passed rapidly, with the ropes and sails being replaced and the provisions for the trip acquired and loaded. The morning of the fourth day saw the catamaran leaving the harbor at Portishead heading west.

✳ ✳ ✳

The voyage to Florida took a month. The early spring weather was favorable and it was way too early for the summer wind storms. The passengers told the captain that *The Twin Flame*, having English registration, even if disguised, would be problematic sailing into the harbor at St. Augustine. The passenger to be picked up with the cargo would be waiting at a small village right inside an inlet connecting the Matanzas River to the sea about twenty miles south of St. Augustine.

As the destination came into view late in the afternoon, Captain Henry shared some thoughts with Ada.

"This reminds me of the pick-up at the Rio Miel in Cuba. We will be going into the mouth of a river, looking for our passenger and his cargo and being vulnerable to bandits who may have gotten wind of our plan. However, somehow this seems different. While I'm not expecting trouble, I think we should be ready for anything."

"I agree," responded Ada. "This time, as I understand it, our passenger is not in hiding awaiting our arrival but will be at a modest dwelling having a dock out into the river. I still think, to be on the safe side, we should send Jane and Jones out ahead of us to check out the house."

"I think you are right. I'll tell the two to be ready to swim ashore just after dark."

Staying just in the mouth of the inlet, Jane and Jones dropped overboard in the gathering darkness and began swimming for a point just above their rendezvous spot to quietly go ashore and take a look. What worked against them was swimming into an outgoing tide but they were both excellent swimmers and moved out of the center of the river as quickly as they could and made the rest of the way swimming close to the shore where the current was weakest.

Reaching their destination, they quickly scrambled into some trees flanking the river and found a hidden spot that allowed them to watch the small house where they were to meet the new passenger and cargo. They could see a light in the window from an oil lamp somewhere inside.

No outside movement was detected after a half-hour of surveillance, so the two moved to a vantage point near one of the windows which was open for ventilation. They could hear men talking inside. Giving it another fifteen minutes to see if anything was amiss, Jones called out to the men inside in Spanish.

Knowing they were to be met here was one thing—but not knowing exactly when caused them to be startled as Jones announced himself. One of the two men inside came to the door, cautiously opened it, looking out at the soaking wet Jones standing there. After a minute or so of conversation, the men inside came out and saw Jane. They quickly got over their surprise at seeing a woman there and began asking about the boat.

Jane stepped into the house and grabbed the lantern from the table. Back outside, she picked up a flat board and used it to alternately block the light facing the boat in the darkness, transmitting a signal prearranged with Captain Henry to let him know it was safe to move in.

In about fifteen minutes, the catamaran bumped up against the small dock serving the house and swiftly tied tight to it. Their passengers were relieved to see two men they knew helping to load the cargo. With Jane, Jones, the passengers, plus the two onshore helpers, loading the roughly 250 pounds of cargo, packed in five wooden trunks, took only a few minutes to complete.

Captain Henry wasted no time pushing off after everyone and the cargo were on board. Taking advantage of the outgoing tide, it didn't take long for the catamaran to disappear into the darkness and make its way into the ocean. After being safely away, Captain Henry introduced himself to the two helpers and showed them where they would be berthed on the return trip accompanied by his five trunks of cargo.

Then he called to Ada and Jane to meet with him in his cabin.

"We are safe for the duration of the night but we need to be especially vigilant when the sun rises. We picked up two new men who are now on their way back up the Matanzas River to St. Augustine. I don't know them, so I am not trusting they will not reveal what they just helped happen. They have to know it is a fortune in gold we are carrying. St. Augustine is a Spanish colony and the gold is not bound for Spain. Either man could decide to go to the Spanish authorities there and spill what he knows in exchange for a handsome reward if the gold is recovered by the Spanish Navy."

Jane agreed. "I will get some sleep now and plan to be up just before first light. If we spot them first, our speed should be faster than anything the Spanish have near here. Their caravels and galleons probably sail at about eight knots. A good frigate can go twelve to fifteen knots. Our catamaran is capable of at least fifteen knots and can go faster, possibly exceeding twenty. The wind will affect us all relatively equally. So, if we spot them before they get too close, they'll never catch us."

* * *

Sure enough, at 11:00 the next morning, Jane spotted what appeared to be a frigate on the horizon, heading in their direction. It was a beautiful morning, with blue skies and white cumulus clouds overhead. A pod of dolphins was playfully swimming alongside the catamaran.

"The chase is on!" Jane said with a beaming smile, quite invigorated by the contest. "This far from shore, I doubt they are aware of what happened last night and have no idea that we are carrying gold. We probably just look like a target of opportunity, so they are making chase. It is unlikely their captain has ever seen a catamaran. With a spyglass, he will see our twin hulls, something he won't have seen before. I think that before the afternoon is over, he will be lost to sight and when darkness falls, we will extinguish all light so he will not see us again."

Captain Henry was standing near her as she spoke and added to her plan.

"Long before he loses sight of us, I will slowly adjust our heading more to the southeast as if we are heading to the African coast and keep that direction until darkness falls. Then, I will correct course back to the northeast and Europe. If he stays through the night, tracking the last course he sees us on while it's still light, he will be nowhere near us come morning."

Sure enough, the next morning found the seas clear of any ship other than their own.

During the month it took for them to make it back to Portishead, they saw several other ships and were able to elude them fairly easily. The speedy catamaran was certainly earning its keep. One morning during the voyage, Captain Henry was standing in the company of Ada and Jane.

"I've been thinking about another advantage we might add to our catamaran. It's about these new sails we procured before we left. I was a little disappointed that they aren't a crisp clean white but are sort of dingy gray in color. But now, after our experience eluding other ships, I believe when we are docked, I'm going to have the ship's hull painted the same bluish gray as the sails. From a distance, that color will render us virtually invisible in the early morning and evening twilight, giving us close to a half hour in the dim morning light to spot another ship before they see us plus a little advantage to avoid being spotted late in the day when the sun is down but not yet quite dark."

"I like that idea," responded Ada.

"Here's another thought," he added. "The sailmaker who sold me these sails was telling me a story he heard from his Chinese contact about an experiment in China using copper sheathing on the keel of a ship to repel borers and barnacles. He said this practice was not known in the West but was being experimented with by an unusually smart Chinese ship's captain. If that is true and the ship's bottom stays clear of these things, it should eliminate the rough surface they cause and the accompanying friction, slowing our speed. This story may or may not be true, I don't know, but I do know we will continue to be chased on many of our voyages. Every little advantage in speed we can gain is important. I'm going to try applying copper to the bottom of our ship on our return to see if it will work. My younger brother, Andrew, is in the shipbuilding business, and I can trust him to keep the application secret. If it works, I don't want to lose our advantage to others."

Back in the harbor at Portishead, his two passengers disembarked to arrange their transport to a secret location they did not share. Within an hour after nightfall, they returned to the wharf with a wagon, loaded their cargo, and faded into the night.

As they were clattering off the wharf with their wagon pulled by four draft horses, Charles turned to Ada.

"Well, that trip, after we pay our crew, will net us a very tidy profit, not to mention gaining, at no cost to us, a new set of very strong lightweight sails that proved to be excellent!"

"My, you've been busy," Ada teased.

Jane came up just then.

"Why don't you two go up to the local pub for a dinner on land, served with fresh ale. I'll stay on the boat and keep watch. You can bring me back something to eat that's not fish! After a month of eating fish, I think maybe some good Shepherd's pie would be delightful."

As the Captain and Ada walked up the wharf, Jane turned back to look out over the harbor.

Interesting, she thought, *how in this time in history, not much of the glow of oil lit lanterns spills out from the village to where I am.*

She noticed there was little competition for the light of the countless stars shining down over the harbor, breathtaking in their beauty. A light breeze was picking up, coming off the water toward land. She began thinking about her life in the twenty-first century and how different it was here in this time. True, health care as she had known it was non-existent here. People died from ailments that would have been minor problems in the future. Infection from a cut, an abscess tooth, a compound fracture from an accident and, not surprisingly, food poisoning took a toll on the population.

But, on the other hand, the freedom she felt on the catamaran when it was at sea, the comradery she felt with the crew, and the excitement of the adventures they were undertaking made it all worthwhile. Having kept her true identity secret for so long, living in the small village of Avebury, she was positively euphoric living on a boat with her new companions having to hide nothing, having no secrets. What she was missing she realized was not having a male partner to share her life with. How she could change that and still find the freedom living at sea with all the stimulation that was bringing into her life was a puzzle she was struggling to solve.

What she didn't realize was Jones, who she had gone into the Rio Miel with in Cuba and again on the last mission, couldn't seem to get *her* off *his* mind. He realized she was very different from any woman he had ever known and there was some mystery about her background that he intended to dig into. He, too, had a background that he had not revealed. He went by the name Jones … but Jones was not his real name.

He had gotten caught up in the religious wars between the French Catholics and the Protestants known as Huguenots. He was raised by a Huguenot family and was a very spiritual person but not a particularly devout Huguenot. Jones was, however, very angered by the persecution of his family by the Catholics and joined the fight against them under the French general Francois de La Noue. General de La Noue was captured by the Spanish in 1580 and spent five years in a Spanish prison. After the general was captured and gone from his life, he decided to adopt the name Jones—which sounded English to him—and flee to England to start a new life.

His real surname was Leroux. He further determined not to introduce himself with any first name but to simply go by Jones, as he did a few years later when he signed on with Captain Henry. He did not boast about his fighting skills, which had been honed to a high degree of lethality in his many battles against the Catholics. When minor skirmishes occurred after he joined the captain's crew, he fought well but was careful not to display any particular prowess above that of his sea mates. He did not want to call attention to himself in that way.

When Leroux had seen Jane in action in the early encounter with privateers and witnessed what she was capable of in battle—and then later partnered with her on the Rio Miel adventure—his admiration for the woman grew. Totally intrigued, he decided that, given an opportunity, he would attempt to get to know her a little better, even if it meant revealing a little about himself.

The opportunity presented itself that night, docked at the wharf in Portishead, when he saw the Captain and Ada leave the boat and head to town for dinner. Several of the other crew also headed in that direction, leaving just him and Harrison on duty with Jane to guard the ship.

Leroux, making a little shuffling noise with his feet so as not to startle her, which, considering her keen hearing, was not necessary, he walked up beside her and looked out at the harbor.

"Beautiful night," he said, thinking that was a lame start but he could think of nothing else. A nervousness he was unaccustomed to was beginning to overtake him.

"Yes," she said, without adding anything more or even looking directly at him.

Trying to keep his voice from cracking he added, "Sailing on this catamaran has been a new experience for me. It's a great boat." Then he thought to himself, *are you going to just talk about the boat?*

Jane simply replied, "Yes."

This is going to be very difficult, he thought. *What can I say now?* He decided to simply plow on.

"I didn't really come over here to talk about a boat. I came to admit something to you. We have been together for several months now and never talked about anything other than work-required conversation. I wanted to let you know that I find you a very interesting person and would like to get to know you a little better—that is if you don't mind.

Jane had sensed his nervousness from the start but wanted to string him along with a show of indifference, keep him at a distance. This was automatically something she did when men approached her with more than a sense of duty. But, in his case, she was actually somewhat interested in him, too. She sensed there was more there than met the eye. There was something he, like her, tried to keep from others. She was curious. Jane decided to make a statement rather than ask a question.

"I am an intuitive person. I find I can size people up sooner than most. I have noticed you don't seem to share some of the small talk I see others engaged in and you purposely keep to yourself. Not obnoxiously so, mind you. You are just not overly gregarious. You are hiding something."

Hmm, this is going to the heart of the matter more quickly than I suspected. I think I will take a risk and be truthful, Leroux figured.

"I've seen how you deal fairly with others," he started. "And, of course, the captain places a great deal of trust in you, so I'll take a chance. My name is not Jones. It's André Leroux and my heritage is French, not English."

He stopped there because he could feel his throat tightening up from this brief moment of revealing himself—for the first time to anyone in almost five years.

"I thought as much," Jane replied calmly. "I sensed there was something about you that you keep closely guarded. A natural guess would be you are avoiding the law for some criminal activity but I don't believe that's it. So, please go on."

Leroux opened up. It was as if he could no longer keep his truth bottled up, so it just poured out. He told her about his years of fighting the Catholics, not because of being a religious zealot but because of what they had done to his family and others he knew in his circle of Huguenot friends and acquaintances. He had tired of the seemingly endless fighting and dying in wars where both sides prayed to a seemingly-different god. Their leaders used people like pawns to further their own secular ends in power struggles on the continent.

He told her that because of his choice of allegiance to one side in the religious wars and his participation as a soldier, he would have no peace once he decided to leave. One side would call him a deserter, the other side an enemy. Thus, he made his decision to change his name, leave France for England, and find a new life.

Exhausted from this outburst of emotion and unaccustomed honesty, he leaned against the railing and lowered his head, staring down at the dark water below.

To Leroux's surprise, Jane did not seem uncomfortable with anything he had revealed. She calmly spoke to him with a soft, even voice.

"I appreciate you sharing this with me. It reminds me of something I read about one of my ancient ancestors. Rest assured; I will not reveal anything you said to me. This is your story to tell, not mine. But this explains something I saw in the fight with the privateers some months ago and with the business on the catamaran later. I was busy but I did notice how you handled yourself. You seemed focused, totally alert to all around you, and your movements in battle were economical, powerful, and skilled. I knew you had seen battle many times before … more than me, for I have not seen much. But I am naturally equipped with more strength, quickness, and stamina than others here. So, to me, my adversaries in combat appear to move in slow motion, weak, and dull-witted. This gives me a considerable edge even though I have little experience. There is more to tell but that can come later."

"I look forward to hearing more when you are ready," Leroux replied, relieved that she had not told him to jump overboard.

"I have a feeling I will be ready to share more with you soon," she added. "But for now, I see the captain has sent someone from the pub with the Shepherd's pie and some ale I asked for. Would you care to join me? There appears to be plenty for both of us."

>◆)ᵼᵼᵼ··

CHAPTER 37

1586 CE
AMSTERDAM, NETHERLANDS

A WEEK PASSED AFTER THE CATAMARAN arrived in Portishead. Captain Henry spent the time refurbishing the ship and the crew used the time to regain their land legs and enjoy the time ashore. The captain, Ada, Jane, and Leroux—who had since revealed to the captain his reason for previously going by the name of Jones—found a secluded spot out of the village to continue to hone their martial arts, archery, and firearms skills.

Jane had confided much about herself to the Frenchman during that week. Like others, it was difficult for him to comprehend her alien origins in the beginning but his growing attraction to her provided plenty of incentive for him to believe what he was hearing. Leroux, being an experienced soldier, had his own set of martial arts skills, some different from the skills practiced by the others. In addition to learning from them, he was able to add some new moves to their growing expertise.

Late one afternoon, Captain Henry returned from a meeting with a merchant who needed his assistance with a delivery of time-sensitive financial documents to an investment house in Amsterdam. When he announced the prospect to the others, Jane decided it would be a good time to explore an idea she and Leroux were considering for their future. She began with a reaction to the new opportunity the captain had presented.

"Captain, Leroux and I will be with you on this trip to

Amsterdam. But sometime in the not-too-distant future, we need to branch out on our own. We'd like to continue our relationship with you and Ada, perhaps in some partnership ventures but with our own boat. In the time I have been with you, I have learned to love life on the sea. There is a freedom I don't want to lose. From what you have now learned about Leroux's history, you can understand why he feels the same as I do."

Leroux spoke up then.

"Yes, Jane and I have some different—and some similar—reasons for our feelings about life on the water. As you know, I would be in jeopardy returning to France and I am not an Englishman. The sea gives me a sense of peace and belonging."

Jane added, "I am different than others in this world. There is an almost universal feeling in this age that people who are different are suspect, sometimes feared, and never really accepted as part of society. I know things about life and science, coming from a future age, that are not understood now and will not be for hundreds of years. People believe in witches—in their ability to heal or harm from a distance—without even requiring evidence or physical contact. They are feared and persecuted. Being put to death is not an uncommon occurrence among those suspected of having unusual powers."

Ada nodded in agreement as Jane continued.

"During Elizabeth I's reign, the *1562 Act against Conjurations, Enchantments, and Witchcrafts* legislation was enacted describing minor and capital offenses. Minor acts, as described in the Act, came with a year's imprisonment and quarterly humiliation in the market square—six hours in a pillory to *'openly confesse his or her Erroure and Offence.'* Two minor offenses or any major offense would result in a death sentence. How do I know all of this? It was written in the records of my ancestors, which I have.

"The butcher's helper and his cousins in Swindon saw me and Mary in action in the woods as we thwarted their attempt to relieve us of the Queen's gold. They also saw us dressed in trousers rather than dresses. A woman wearing pants is considered by many to be an abomination before God. If one of them decides to say something against me or Mary in public and we are put on trial, we are in serious trouble. A jury, if that is the body that would hear the case, or a judge, once presented with an allegation of witchcraft and looking closely at our eyes would suddenly be fearful. That would not help at all! Leroux and I have had discussed how we could recruit a loyal crew for our future boat. John and Mary would be perfect. I think we should contact them with an offer to join us before something goes wrong for them in Avebury."

Captain Henry looked a bit concerned but paid close attention to Jane's words.

"Here's another concern of mine," she continued. "The average age in London now is about thirty years. I am eighty-five and have the potential to live to 200. Leroux is not so fortunate in sharing my longevity but because of my knowledge of health, hygiene, and my ability to utilize local herbs, cook certain foods, and along with my fundamental knowledge of chemistry, I can help him live to twice or three times that average age of thirty. If our long lives are noticed by others, their ignorance of these things will be dangerous for us. However, living at sea, not being on one particular land location for too long, gives us an opportunity for a safer life rather than staying in one place. Plus, we are actually good at handling a boat and defending ourselves from pirates!"

Leroux added, "I agree with Jane. Even though I don't understand the things she says she can do for me to add to my years, I believe her. I also know she is the only woman I have ever met who I want to spend my life with. I don't want my time with her cut short through persecution for false claims of her being a witch."

Ada joined the conversation with her observations.

"I had a feeling this day would come, where we would part ways," she sighed. "I do agree with everything you have said about the danger of the common belief in witchcraft and because of that I concur with your decision to find a life on the sea. One consequence I see is that if Mary and John join you, the residents of Avebury will no longer receive their annual supply of the Ghost Flower addition to their annual feast, so their strengthened immune system will wane. On the other hand, we've completed our mission to get the information about the flower to the twenty-first century. This can potentially save countless lives in the future—tens of millions, I think—if Joel and Thomas are successful in finding what we've left for them. The greater good is being served. However, in the present moment, I'm glad to hear that you still want to partner with us on some business ventures."

Finally, the captain was ready to embrace the change that was coming about.

"Okay, you are sharing your general plan for the future. More specifically, you want your own boat. I am assuming you will want a catamaran since this one has served us all so well. That will cost some money to build. I know a great Dutch shipbuilder who will make one for you. Ha! It might even be better than mine, now that we have learned some of its few weaknesses. I'll introduce you to him when we arrive in Amsterdam. I know you both have accumulated some treasure from our recent ventures and this next trip should add enough money to get you what you will need, or at least close enough.

"From what I have learned about the conflict between Spain and England, the war at sea will only grow over the next few years, making the sea a more dangerous place than ever. That danger will give us many opportunities to ply our trade, using our growing reputation for getting people and treasure safely to their intended destinations. There will be a lot of business for two ships rather than just our one and, if we work together, we will make a good living, indeed!"

* * *

A short time after, they were under sail to the Netherlands. Compared to their other trips, the voyage to Amsterdam was comparatively tame. They took great care to avoid other ships they saw in the distance and their speed advantage worked well for them to avoid any contact.

On arriving in Amsterdam, the captain made the delivery of the packet of papers to the financial house as he had been commissioned to do. That mission complete, Captain Henry took Jane and Leroux to meet his shipbuilder acquaintance. After the better part of an hour explaining what they wanted done, aided with some rough sketches of their ideas, they waited for the builder to respond.

"Well," he said in a tone mixed with interest and a little skepticism, "I've never built a ship like this but I'm getting the idea of what you want. I'll come down to the wharf in the morning so you can show me *The Twin Flame* to give me a better idea of what you're asking me to do. I'm beginning to see how the double hull, separated by a space with the deck above raised over the water, would reduce drag when sailing at speed. The updraft should give even less drag as more of the boat volume lifts out of the water. Interesting idea!"

"I thought you would be intrigued," smiled the captain, "And I'll bet you can think of ways to improve our design even further. The idea is to give us berthing capacity for the crew, a small secure space for our clients' cargo and a cabin for two paying passengers, with the speed to outrun any danger we meet on the sea. The boat will be way too small to carry cannons sufficient to fight off a galleon or a frigate and our crew will be too small to fight off a boarding party from a bigger ship. That means we shouldn't sacrifice speed by carrying the weight of cannons that would ultimately be insufficient to do much good anyway. Speed is our weapon. Make it a fast boat!"

"I like the challenge!" the craftsman exclaimed. "My imagination is already beginning to churn out novel ideas to give you strength and speed."

"Let me add two more ideas to your thinking," Captain Henry added. "I was able to obtain sails and rope from a Chinese connection of mine—silk was the secret ingredient I believe—that lessened the overall weight while giving more strength. I also have our boat, as you will see tomorrow morning, painted a light blue-gray to help us fade into the horizon in the low light of morning and evening."

"You have approached me at a good time, Captain Henry," he replied. "I recently finished a commission for a customer so I'm looking for my next project. I have a crew that I can put on it right away and that includes a designer who is superb. It may take three months to complete… maybe more, maybe less. It would be very helpful if your friends could stay here during that time to oversee the work, making sure it is being designed and built exactly as they wish."

"I'll speak for both of us as I can see the look on Jane's face," Leroux jumped in. "Yes, we will stay here in Amsterdam while you are building her. After you see Captain Henry's catamaran tomorrow, you can give us an estimate of what you will charge to build a similar one, knowing we will finalize the price as we go through the design process. Based on your estimate, we will know if we have enough to cover the cost and seal the deal."

"Done. I'll meet you at the wharf tomorrow. From your description, I'll have no trouble spotting Captain Henry's ship."

When they rejoined Ada at the inn where they were staying, Captain Henry told Leroux and Jane why he had not mentioned the copper cladding on the keels of the twin hulls of the catamaran he would build for them.

"Wait until you get your boat and are back in Portishead. I'll have my cousin clad your boat with copper in secret. I don't want this technique to be used by others who may at some point be chasing us!"

Ada chimed in when he had finished.

"I'm not an expert on shipbuilding but I do seem to recall from history that cladding the keels of navy ships became common practice in the 1700s or thereabouts, so it will work for us. It will just be ahead of its time when we do it now—something that will be to our advantage to not speak about to others. Perhaps when our boat, and then yours, Leroux and Jane, are clad, we will add a coat of tar over the copper, or some coating, so that it will not be noticeable when we are at full sail and our keels are riding high in the water and exposed."

They found a suitable messenger, in the form of a merchant planning a trip that included Avebury on his route, to take a letter to Mary and John. Leroux thought it best not to be overly specific, in the event the merchant opened the envelope and read the contents. He also knew Mary did not know his real name was Leroux and didn't want to divulge that information in a letter that might be compromised.

They decided that the letter should come from Jane but not go to the manor house or her cottage. Instead, they addressed it and had it delivered to a John Mallow, a construction manager in Avebury. The letter made it clear that it was imperative that he and Mary travel to Amsterdam as quickly as possible, arriving no later than three months from the date of the letter to meet at the inn specified therein. If they could not manage to arrive in Amsterdam within that time period, they were to meet later in Portishead instead. The message further specified that they consider, after hearing a proposal upon their arrival in Amsterdam, not returning to Avebury. They should plan to have a person they trust to handle their affairs in Avebury should they decide that chapter in their lives was over.

··┅╢╀•╂

CHAPTER 38

1586 CE
ENGLAND

IT WAS A MONTH AFTER LEROUX and Jane sent the message to John and Mary before it arrived via the traveling merchant. The envelope was delivered to John one afternoon as he was cleaning up a worksite in preparation for returning to the cottage he now shared with Mary.

He overcame his curiosity since the exterior of the envelope indicated it was sent by Jane and he waited until he was home with Mary so they could open it together. Sitting at a dining table, lit by an oil lantern as by then it was growing dark, the two of them opened the envelope and read the message.

"This is certainly unexpected," Mary said in a quiet voice. "Jane would not have sent this unless she was very serious. She mentions a partner but gives no name."

"I'm intrigued," offered John.

"Yes, me too. This could not be coming at a better time. Today, I was in the butcher shop on an errand for the manor house cook. When I casually greeted the butcher's helper, as I always do, he suddenly looked very nervous and did not look into my eyes as he usually does when returning my greeting. I believe he either has, or is intending to, reveal to others that there is something suspicious about me. I'm sure he is in it for a reward in some way. My time here is coming to a rapid end. I'm sorry you are in this with me, John."

"I'm not sorry," he brushed the idea aside. "You have made me happier than I have ever been in my life. Where you go, I go. No question about it."

"I love you," Mary responded, with a sudden dampness shining in her eyes.

John then added, "I've been picking up some strange looks from folks in town recently, too, that weren't there for a short time after our wedding. But something is happening now concerning their attitudes about us that is definitely not good. I'm all for taking up Jane's offer and heading to Amsterdam as soon as we can wind up our affairs here."

"I'll write a letter tonight," Mary agreed. "It will be vague on details about our plan but specific enough to let them know I may not be returning from an unexpected trip. I'll make sure to give it to Lord Dunch. Based on what he knows about me already, he won't be surprised and I trust him to follow through on what I'll ask of him regarding concluding my affairs in Avebury. That will include selling this cottage. I'll tell him where to send the proceeds later."

The very next day, John saw some of his construction workers huddled together in conversation. When he walked over to them, the conversation stopped and he saw what appeared to be a guilty look on one or two of their faces. As the day progressed, he knew it was time to go. He told one of the men he needed to leave for the afternoon and put him in charge of finishing the day's work.

On his way to the cottage, he stopped by a friend's place who he knew had fallen on hard times and wanted to sell two horses he owned. Avebury, being a small place and not affluent, meant there had been no offers in the month since he put them up for sale.

"Hey, Avery," John called out with a friendly wave as he approached the gate to Avery's cottage. "Your two horses still for sale? My wife and I have been thinking about buying them from you for some recreational riding when we have the time and I could use one for scouting out additional construction work in the area. I could cover more ground quickly with a horse than I have been doing on foot."

"Absolutely, they are still for sale. I'd almost given up." Avery said and then suddenly realized his mistake in saying that before announcing a price. "But they are fine animals and the tack that goes with them is of the finest quality," he added, trying to recover.

"How about you saddle the two of them and let me take them home to show Mary. If we take a short ride in the morning before I go to work and she likes them, I'll come by and either pay you or return the animals. Tell me your price."

After the expected hemming and hawing over the price, they settled on a number and Avery went about saddling them up for John. When he was finished and John had mounted one of them, he said, "I'll see you early in the morning," and rode off with the two horses.

Getting back to the cottage in the late afternoon, he saw Mary had returned home early from her work at the manor house. She rushed to the door to greet him.

"John, I left early today. I think something is afoot that spells serious trouble for me. Even the servants in the house are looking at me in a weird way. I wrote out the instructions we talked about last night and sealed them up, giving them to Lord Dunch. He is the only one I trust now. I'm sure he is thinking I am about to disappear but he's not asking. Actually, it will be easier on him if I am gone."

John suggested a plan.

"I think we have little time left before we have some unwanted visitors, hysterical in their ignorance looking for you on charges of witchcraft. Pack up what we can carry on the two horses I brought and we will leave no later than dusk. We can go by Avery's house; you stay out of sight. I will ride up to his gate, call him, tell him we are very happy with the horses. I'll explain I want to pay him tonight since I have an early morning commitment at my construction site. Then, I will join you and we will head north for a few hours before finding a secluded spot to camp for the night. I don't think we will be followed but I still would like to put a few hours of travel between us and Avebury right now."

"I agree," Mary said. "I have already packed for both of us, including enough food and water for a few days if we are frugal with it. I've included my ancestry books and my bow and a quiver of arrows, plus your two pistols, powder, and shot. I've packed up the money we have saved as well. I say we leave within the hour."

"Done. I think we can be out of here in less time than that."

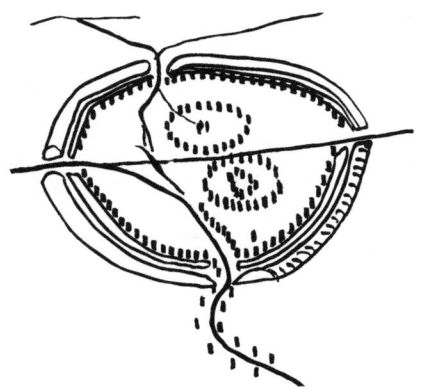

CHAPTER 39

1586 CE
ENGLAND

***

IT WAS LESS THAN AN HOUR before Mary and John were on their way. Unfortunately, it was still light; dusk had not yet come when they neared Avery's cottage. Mary stayed back but there was no vegetation or trees near enough to provide adequate cover. Still, John rode ahead and called for Avery. He came around the cottage from the rear.

"Hello, John, I thought you were coming back in the morning?" he called.

"I was," John assured him, "but something has come up. I do want the horses and will take them off your hands right now."

He leaned down as Avery approached and handed him a small leather bag containing the agreed upon price for the horses. Just as he had handed over the bag, two men burst from around back, one of them pointing down the lane at Mary.

"There she is! There's the witch!" shouted one of the two.

Turning to Avery, the other said, "When you told me of John's interest in the horses, I suspected it had more to do than what you were told. Look at the baggage packed on these horses. They are leaving!"

John recognized one of the men he knew that lived in Swindon and then he saw the butcher's helper peer out of one of the cottage windows.

"Thanks, Avery," John said in a voice dripping with sarcasm, as he wheeled his horse around and raced towards Mary. "Let's go!"

Within minutes they had raced out of sight of Avery's cottage. When they slowed to a canter, Mary let out a sigh of relief.

"John, that was too close. I'm glad we didn't plan to stay in our cottage tonight. I think we would have had some very unfriendly visitors."

"Yes, and since I know how we would have reacted, there would have been casualties. The story would be told that we started it. It would have been very, very bad for us and those we injured or possibly killed."

Mary nodded and took a deep breath.

"I'm looking forward to being in Amsterdam and learning what Jane has to offer. Her invitation could not have come at a better time. Earlier, when life seemed okay, we might not have gone. Now, this offer of something new is a lifeline."

CHAPTER 40

1586 CE AMSTERDAM, NETHERLANDS

THE HORSES JOHN PROCURED FROM AVERY turned out to be decent stock. Traveling at a steady pace and camping along the way, Mary and John made good time at the beginning of their journey to Amsterdam. The most difficult part was navigating the Straight of Dover by ferry. Finding a transport willing to take their horses took nearly three days.

At last, they arrived in Amsterdam and found the inn that was mentioned in the letter and went inside. After they asked about Captain Henry, the innkeeper told them there was a message left for them to meet at his boat. He got them settled into a room and gave them directions to the wharf.

A few minutes later they were riding to the location. They spotted *The Twin Flame* and found the captain and Ada nearby.

"Mary! John!" Ada rang out on spotting them tying up their horses nearby.

Captain Henry chimed in, "We didn't know if you would get here before we departed for Portishead!"

"Captain, Jane's letter was a godsend. We were within a hairsbreadth of personal catastrophe!"

Just then Jane appeared on the deck of the ship, a smile on her face at seeing them as big as Mary or John had ever seen.

After spending time on the wharf and the deck of the catamaran catching up, including hearing Leroux's story and the relationship formed with Jane, the subject turned to the mysterious offer in the letter they had received.

"Jane, I am surprised, honored, and humbled by your offer for me and John to join you and Leroux on your new boat as part of your crew. I just don't know which feeling is the more intense," Mary admitted.

"I think our future together was somehow preordained. I am so happy," exclaimed Jane.

Ada then chimed in.

"Charles—Captain Henry—has been marketing the services of our two boats to some of the financial wizards who work in this town. He was right about the hostilities between Spain and England, not to mention the Portuguese slave ships and their cargo, making the sea a dangerous place and exceedingly risky for shipments of high value to remain safe. The business opportunities this creates for us are enormous. He has just entered into a contract for both of our ships to carry four passengers to the lands north of St. Augustine in Florida."

Captain Henry described the mission.

"Here is the backstory for this particular contract. A majority of Europe is Roman Catholic and a Protestant movement is growing in the Netherlands, particularly Calvinism. Catholic Spain wants to destroy Protestantism, including the movement in the Netherlands. The leaders here in the Netherlands have decided to create colonies in other countries for religious freedom. They are not as interested in exploiting new colonies for gold and silver as others have but they are interested in the growing commercial opportunities in the New World in addition to providing safe havens for Protestants that want to flee Europe.

"This trip we are to undertake is essentially a scouting mission. There is a large, successful commercial enterprise here in Amsterdam that has the support of the country's leadership. They are interested in learning more about the potential for establishing business in the New World, preferably north of the areas controlled for now by the Spanish and Portuguese. They want us to take four passengers, two in each of our boats. The four will be a cartographer, or mapmaker, two ex-military long range surveillance types trained in harsh conditions, and a young man who is a trading specialist with the company hiring us.

"The plan is to head for a position on the American coast well north of the Spanish settlements in Florida. When we arrive, they want to sail up the coast to allow the cartographer to map out potential harbors suitable for shipping and settlement. When we come across such places, the two hardy scouts will disembark for several days to explore the surrounding area. The trade representative will make his assessment on each place to report back to his bosses in Amsterdam when we return.

"We need both of our boats for this ambitious project. For a short mission, we could probably crowd our passengers and crew on one boat. But this trip is going to take the better part of a year. We need room for their equipment and a large store of provisions this long haul will require. Another reason for making this a two-boat voyage is I like the idea of having a backup boat if one of them is severely damaged in a storm or some other unfortunate calamity."

Mary and John were doing their best to absorb all of this new information. The captain continued.

"Considering the time at sea, the risk of sailing in unknown waters, the pirates and privateers roaming the ocean looking for plunder, I've negotiated a king's ransom-sized fee for us. Further, when we return, if all agree, I have also negotiated a very favorable arrangement with the same financial wizards who recommended us for this contract to invest our gains from this trip, and potentially others, to earn us a comfortable living for quite some years to come.

"Ada, with her razor-sharp memory of history that she studied in the twenty-first century has given me some good advice on when we should move our investments from here to a country called Switzerland. She says here, Amsterdam, has the absolute best financial advisors to manage our fortune for now but, later, Switzerland will become that place. I didn't understand her offhand comment about tulips not being great investments but that's okay."

Mary and John agreed with the plan. Mary observed, "Being at sea for a year will actually be the safest place I can imagine for me, Jane, John, and Leroux, despite the danger from pirates or what we may encounter on foreign shores. We are all in!"

"Now," Jane said with a serious look, "Leroux and I need to think about hiring the rest of our crew. In addition to you two, Mary, and John, we will need two more seamen to help sail the boat, and we will need a cook and an assistant cook who is also a deck hand. Of course, Leroux and I will be involved when needed. Four hands should be sufficient for everyday requirements. Remember, the ship won't sail itself at night, so there will be two on and two off for most of the voyage. It will be a small crew but provisions will be needed for everyone. It's not only the weight and space requirements of the crew members themselves but the weight and the storage space for food, water, and other necessities for each person aboard. That augers for hiring the absolute fewest seamen we think we will need."

Leroux had an astute observation. "We need to be careful who we pick for the remaining two members of the crew. We don't want a person who has loyalties to Spain and we don't want to have a holy war aboard ship. That means we can't have Catholics when we are on a mission with Calvinists passengers. Let's stay away from religious extremes. That doesn't mean I don't want a crew with spiritual beliefs, just not ones that are so wed to a particular religion that conflict will break out. We will be together in tight quarters for about a year. That will be hard on everyone, so let's choose our crew wisely. We may find our best recruits here in the Netherlands."

During the time they were in Amsterdam, Captain Henry had been interviewing seamen for potential hire to replace Jane and Leroux since they would now have their own boat. He had selected those he needed and had two other fine applicants that he referred to Jane and Leroux to consider adding to Mary and John.

Captain Henry had also been giving a lot of thought, based on his experience with long voyages, to what they would stock for food to keep healthy. He planned to have the standard hardtack, salted beef, and ale. His stores included sauerkraut, hard cheeses, nuts, and olive oil. To fight scurvy, in addition to the sauerkraut he would add dried fruits, raisins, and dried beans. Ada suggested obtaining dried ground orange peels to add to the food where appropriate. She explained to him the need for the vitamin C that oranges would provide. It was not a great menu but it should suffice. He reasoned they would catch fish along the way and suggested both boats stock some fishing tackle as well as a seine net to their list of supplies for the voyage.

CHAPTER 41

1586 CE
AT SEA

THE SHIPBUILDER FINISHED THE NEW CATAMARAN within the three months as everyone had hoped. With design suggestions from Jane and Leroux, he had added a novel system for remotely opening a port on the underside of the deck between the two hulls. When the boat was sailing, that contraption would effectively flush the toilets he designed for each of the cabins. The design also featured a waterproof weapons locker on the deck near the helm and a small tank that could be filled with seawater when they caught fish to keep alive and fresh for a day or so until needed to support the menu. The tank was constructed so that the water could easily be flushed out if they needed to reduce weight to gain speed.

The time finally came for their departure. It was in the fall, after the high point for summer and early fall hurricanes but not yet bitterly cold. Jane and Leroux had hired two sailors, Hal Hawkes and Nick Thorne, to join Mary and John. The two sailors were young but old enough to have been through more than one encounter with pirates on their previous ships. They were also able to hire brothers, Liam and Finn Jansen, for the galley jobs. So far, they were pleased with their new crew's experience, demeanor, and positive excitement for the adventure ahead.

Sailing out of Amsterdam, they headed southwest, through the English Channel and into the Atlantic. The first part of the journey was dangerous, going through the Channel between England and

France. They saw warships along the way but kept a good distance and with their speed, never allowed a close encounter.

A few weeks later on the open sea, the two boats pulled together as they had been doing periodically so Jane and Leroux could come aboard Captain Henry's boat to talk about common issues, refine their plans for when they reached New World, and to enjoy each-others company.

One of these visits found Jane and Mary standing on the deck looking at the horizon ahead over the sparkling waters of the Atlantic. They were sharing some thoughts about their common Golan ancestry and Jane's life in the twenty-first century compared to Mary's life in the sixteenth century. It wasn't long before Ada, John, and Leroux joined them. Mary thoughtfully observed some common experiences.

"Jane, regardless of the separation in our times, you and I always need to be on guard against people recognizing that in some ways we are different and therefore feeling discomfort in our presence. When those observations lead to fear, our lives actually are endangered."

"Yes, I agree," Jane responded, "and have restrained myself from acting or saying something that will highlight a difference between me and others. I believe it is worse here in 1586 than the time I come from, 2035. Now, we could be accused of witchcraft as a result of ignorant fear and be hanged—or worse. In 2035, I doubt I would have been hung but I ran the risk of being shunned—ostracized from membership in the community. I could have lost my work at the Red Lion and at the manor house. Economically, I ran the risk of dying in poverty.

Ada added her thoughts.

"The twenty-first century still had its strong prejudices against people who seemed different. People, at least in the United States, had dropped the accusations of witchcraft but sadly had shifted their ignorance to so-called culture wars. Blown out of proportion by political campaigns as talking points to stir up the emotions of their respective bases, the results were to marginalize communities that were not part of whatever was considered the mainstream of culture at the time. These culture wars had some basic talking points that I agreed with and others I didn't but none of it, for me, led me to believe that anyone should be put to death, as those are in this time accused of witchcraft. Indirectly, in the twenty-first century, a death sentence did result from the persecution of some in the form of suicide. Ignorance induced fear is a terrible thing no matter the time frame in history. As a human race, we are making progress but we have a long way to go."

Listening intently, John, born in the sixteenth century but wiser than most, spoke.

"Ada, your points are well said. My recent personal experience has broadened my view of the world. I always saw Mary as someone different from other women in Avebury. But I saw that difference as intriguing, interesting. Her uniqueness made me want to be with her and share her experiences. I had no idea, until her recent revelations to me about her ancestry, just how different she really is but that only makes me want to know more, not cower in fear!"

"I have experienced being different," Leroux added. "I was raised by a Protestant family in a predominately Catholic world. I was seen by some as heretical in my views. I fought with the Huguenots against the oppression of the Catholics, so, yes, death was an outcome that was not a foreign possibility to me because of my beliefs and being part of a minority community. When I decided that fighting and killing, as I did, was something I could no longer justify or live with, I left the ranks of the Huguenot warriors. That had me labeled as a traitor by those I considered my own people. I was still an enemy by those I had fought against.

"I think of myself as a spiritual person, I believe in a supreme power. I also am sickened by how the rulers of some of the kingdoms of Europe use religion to further their own aims ... aims driven by their egos and desire for power. They are also driven to war sometimes because if they are seen to be weak in the face of other competing rulers, they will lose their crown—usually followed by either imprisonment or execution. So, they fight and profess they are doing God's will to motivate their subjects."

Captain Henry had walked up on the group.

"I have been listening to what you have been saying. My history has not had me in a position of being persecuted for any beliefs that I have. However, I am an outsider in this world because I do not openly discuss my spiritual beliefs, nor do I argue with others about theirs. The dangers to my life have been transactional. I am a ship's captain, engaged in the economic life of my world. I work to make a profit in commerce, using my skill as a seaman as my tool. Why I consider myself different from others, as you have been discussing, is I struggle to find like-minded people to be around. I question things. I ask myself *why?* about so many things in my relationships with others and about the many mysteries of nature. That was the primary reason my marriage fell apart earlier in my life. My wife refused to open her mind to new possibilities, to respect the beliefs of others that differed from her own. She did not like traveling with me on my many voyages. She said it wasn't the place for a proper lady. Anyway, over time it didn't work out."

Ada placed her hand on his as he continued.

"John, as you described your attraction to Mary, I found an attraction to Ada. On the surface, she is unquestionably a good-looking woman and pleasant to be around. But as I got to know her, I became more interested in the depth that was below the surface. I freely admit I was shocked when she told me about her being from the future. My first reaction was that she was mentally unbalanced, telling such a tale. Then, when I realized the truth in what she was saying, it made my initial interest soar. What an opportunity to be associated with such an incredible human being! No, I didn't experience fear because of ignorance of what she professed but rather an unbounded curiosity to know more."

Ada reacted to the Captain's sharing of his thoughts. "Many of the men I have known are intimidated by strong women."

"Yes," Captain Henry responded, "I have observed that as well. I have been acquainted over the years with strong, intelligent, caring women who find it difficult to establish meaningful relationships with men. I haven't figured it out completely but what I have observed is that many men have been raised to think that they must always be the strong one and be in charge of a relationship. That as a man, that is what is expected of them by society and their peers. They are uncomfortable being around a woman they see as smarter and more capable. It challenges their self-image.

"What they miss is that everyone, men and women, have different ways of looking at the world and different strengths and weakness. Together, a couple can achieve more in countless ways than either one can alone. But it takes a man with a positive sense of self-worth to be comfortable in a relationship of equals or with one that has attributes superior to attributes they possess. Men who understand this and choose a mate on a basis of mutual respect and admiration for the qualities of the other, and not a competition for who is the smartest or most talented know the secret to a rewarding, supportive and satisfying relationship. That is what I have found with Ada."

The group attentively listening to the captain spell out some of his deepest thoughts on relationships were somewhat surprised. But, hearing a ship's captain, a fierce warrior in the face of pirates and a commanding presence in the company of his crew share these wise observations only added to his stature in their eyes.

"Alright," summed up Jane, "I see that a commonality among us is we are open not only to learning about what we don't understand but we are intrigued by the complexities of the world and the living creatures inhabiting it. Our first reaction is not fear but a desire to know."

"Back to the present," announced Captain Henry. "You four

should reboard your boat. I'm seeing some cloud formations in the distance that tell me land is near. That comports with my calculations that we should be arriving at our first destination. We will keep our boats in hailing distance of one another. Once we see a coastline and move closer, we will decide whether we can land or if we need to go farther up the coast to find a suitable spot."

* * *

As they sailed closer to the coastline, Captain Henry began to see the coastline more clearly with the use of his telescope. He then spotted the sails of another vessel. He immediately had the two vessels turn from their westerly heading to a northern direction. He told Ada his thinking.

"I don't know whose ship it is that I see in the distance. It appears to be much larger than ours and I can barely make it out so I doubt they have seen our smaller profile. I want to keep it that way until we determine which way they are heading. It appears they are coming out from the coast. I want to see which direction they turn before we go any closer."

After twenty minutes of watching, Captain Henry saw them turn to the south.

"Let's give them an hour sailing in that direction and then we will return to our westerly direction. I am curious as to what they were up to. The way they sailed out, I suspect they had a landing party go ashore in a small boat. Why, I wonder?"

"Based on the rudimentary charts we have and our present latitude, I suspect we are off the coast of what in the future will be called North Carolina," observed Ada. "The Spanish, in recent times, have concentrated their activities farther south—in Florida, the Caribbean, and South America. My best guess is that is a pirate ship."

"Ada," he replied, "that piques my interest even more to know what they may have been up to on the shore."

After an hour had passed, the mystery ship—possibly a pirate vessel—had disappeared from sight to the south. Captain Henry then gave the word to move toward the shoreline.

As they came closer to land, they could see a bright, sandy beach ahead, with the frothy ocean waves rolling ashore, washing across the sand.

"Our boats have a shallow draft. I believe we can approach the shore fairly closely and then launch the small canoe we have stored away just for this purpose to see what is there. Jane's boat has a similar canoe," said Captain Henry.

"Jane," he shouted over to the other boat, "I will come over and pick you up and we will go in my canoe first. If we want Mary and John to follow, we will signal them to do so once we are there. I want Leroux and Ada to stay here with our respective boats. Take your bow and I'll take my pistols. Our passengers will stay put. I don't want them involved in this."

Shortly after, in a bright sun that was now approaching late morning, Captain Henry and Jane set out. They rode the mild waves in and beached their little canoe, dragging it farther ashore, before heading toward the dunes flanking the beach.

Pointing, Jane said, "Look, over there. Another boat has been dragged on the beach and there are many footprints going from it towards those dunes."

"Yes, I see that now," he agreed. "Let's take a look."

It didn't take long to follow the path where feet had disturbed the sand up and over the dunes and into the wooded area beyond. There was no sight nor sound of anyone around.

"I think it's safe to assume all those who were recently here departed on the ship that sailed away," he announced.

"I agree they are gone, Captain," Jane added. "However, while I don't hear or see anyone, I am sensing that we are being watched. I saw some signs along the way as we walked in here that indicate a presence of others in this area, fairly recently … others who weren't members of the shore party."

"In that case, keep a sharp eye out. However, I do want to see what the sailors from that ship were doing here before we turn back," he ordered.

Cautiously, they moved forward toward a small hillock devoid of the trees surrounding it. Jane was the first to spot movement ahead of them and warned the captain with a gesture.

"Move carefully but in a non-threatening way," the captain whispered. "If anyone watching us wanted to do us harm, it would have already happened."

As they approached the small rise in the ground, they saw what they assumed were native people who appeared to have just finished digging something out of the sand. They were equipped with bows and arrows and several of them carried long, lethal looking spears. They stopped what they were doing when they saw Jane and the captain.

They seemed to notice the non-threatening way they approached. It was obvious they were staring at Jane, a woman accompanying a man. They peered at the way she was carrying her impressive bow, with her quiver of arrows slung over her shoulder. They also noticed she had no arrow in her hands and the captain had no weapons in his hands. Curious, they hung back but were obviously primed to spring into action if necessary.

Jane tried to communicate first. Spreading her arms wide, her left hand still holding her bow but the other hand open and faced towards the nearest one who looked like the leader, she spoke softly but with authority.

"We mean you no harm. We are curious as to what the men who were here before were doing."

She knew they would not understand her words, so she was relying on her calmness and tone of voice to diffuse tension. It seemed to work, except for one man standing just to the left of their leader. He quickly began raising his bow while placing an arrow on the bowstring. His movement was fast but Jane was by far faster.

Even with her arms outstretched and her arrows in the quiver slung over her back, in a blur she had her bow ready with its arrow suddenly pointing directly at the face of the man who just had his bow raised to the level of his waist. He froze.

"Easy now, my friend," Jane said, showing a little smile at the advantage she now had.

After a shocked moment of silence, the leader of the band moved his hand over to the bow, still at the waist level of his companion, and slowly pushed it down, saying something to him Jane did not understand. The other four men couldn't conceal their looks of shock at the speed displayed by Jane and her total absence of fear.

Captain Henry whispered to Jane, "Good work. I think we may be okay for now. These must be the native Indians I've heard about."

The leader of the group then smiled and turned to the others, saying something that seemed to indicate there would be no further hostility. He moved to an area of disturbed sand and directed one of his men to finish uncovering what had been recently placed there and then covered over with sand. It was a chest. When opened, it absolutely glowed from the sun's reflection on a priceless collection of silver jewelry, gold pieces, precious stones, and assorted pieces of what appeared to be religious icons, probably looted from a church.

"Pirates, for sure, were in that ship," muttered Captain Henry.

The band of men, natives to the country, or Indians as they were called by Europeans since the time of Columbus, began going through the contents of the chest, attracted to the jewelry, precious stones, and a few of the icons that seemed well crafted. What they didn't seem to be so excited about were the eight bars of gold included in the chest. The gold bars had no obvious utilitarian or decorative use to them.

After the first excited moments of snatching up the jewelry and loose precious stones, they examined with great interest the religious objects. The religious symbolism had no meaning to them but they were attracted by the obvious artistic skill in their creation and the fine craftsmanship in the metal work and use of precious stones. They decided to take those as well.

The Indian leader turned to Captain Henry as this was going on and motioned for him to share in their find, pointing to the gold bars, of which he showed little interest. He gave a furtive glance at Jane, almost to signal he was not an enemy, *so don't use your obvious skill and speed with your bow on me.*

Captain Henry read the situation correctly. The Indians, as he was now thinking of them, were interested in the jewelry, precious stones, and artfully crafted religious icons. The gold bars were not seen as useful, so the captain wisely only picked up the gold bars. He placed them on his jacket that he had spread out on the ground and then backed away from the chest. This seemed satisfactory to the leader of the native band. Within just a few minutes, the chest was empty and the band of Indians faded into the brush and trees.

"That was unexpected," the captain said looking down at the gold bars. "See if you can find a sturdy stick so we can tie up the gold in my jacket and sling it between us on the stick to carry back to the beach. It will be heavy to carry. I'm guessing this load will be just under 200 pounds but between the two of us we can do it. I'd like to carry it out of here and back to the beach in one trip. I don't want to hang around and get shot from a point of concealment in case the Indians decide to come back."

Jane agreed. "I'm with you on that! I can hold my own when I can see my adversary but if they decide to come back and ambush us, it won't be a level playing field."

After finding a suitably strong stick to hoist the gold-filled jacket, they made their way back to the beach. Captain Henry signaled Leroux, still on his catamaran in deeper water, to break out his canoe and join them on the beach. They were just close enough that when he shouted, John could hear the captain instruct him to come alone. Somewhat surprised at the direction to come alone, leaving Mary behind, he nevertheless launched his canoe.

When Leroux arrived on the beach and learned what had happened, he was awestruck. But he recovered and followed through with the plan. The gold was too heavy to risk taking it back though the breakers in a small canoe already burdened by two people. They put the gold in Leroux's solo canoe and then the two canoes returned in tandem to the captain's catamaran.

When the excitement died down after the adventure was explained to all, Captain Henry said he would pack away the gold for now. When they arrived at their next stop, wherever that turned out to be, they would decide what to do with their unexpected largesse.

"Now," he declared. "We need waste no time moving away from this place. I don't know if or when the pirates will return but I want to take no more chances with the natives we encountered here. We will go back into the sea some distance from the shoreline and head north. As the afternoon wanes, we will find a spot to anchor for the night and then possibly go ashore in the morning. I want to get a fair distance from here while we still have light. I know we have been at sea for a long time and shore rest would be welcome but I want us to wait one more night before we land."

※ ※ ※

As the afternoon wore on, they came upon what seemed like an entrance to a large bay. Looking at the width of the entrance, the captain decided to disembark on the right side of the entrance which gave the added safety of a separation from the body on the left where they had encountered the natives earlier.

Reaching a place where it appeared they could get the two boats fairly close to the shore—but not close enough they could be grounded by an outgoing tide—they double anchored the two catamarans after furling the sails. Then they used the two canoes to ferry everyone to shore and set up a campsite.

"It is cold here now," Ada observed. "I can feel the chill of the fall night air. But our clothes are warm and we will soon have a nice fire and later move into the small tents we brought for this purpose. In the morning, we can see what we find in the way of fresh water to replace our stores and scrounge up any local plants or game we can use to augment our food.

As darkness fell and they were seated around a comfortable fire separate from their passengers and crew who had kindled their own a few yards away, Captain Henry shared what he was thinking concerning the gold they had acquired and asked if they might all chime in with their thoughts.

"My initial thinking is that we should divide the gold among us in this way. We have eight equal pieces. Two for Jane and Leroux, two for me and Ada, and one for Mary and John to share. That leaves three. I suggest we give one to the Dutch company that hired us as a good will gesture … not to mention it is a smart move to encourage them to use us for future business. That leaves two pieces."

"I have been thinking about this," Ada spoke up. "I like what has been said so far and agree with the divisions. Here's an interesting thought to consider for one of the remaining pieces. Captain, you told me about the financial wizards you got to know in Amsterdam who recommended us for this particular contract. You also said you had worked out an arrangement with them to invest our money going forward. What if we took one of these remaining bars, handed it over to their firm which you found to have an excellent reputation for honesty and results, and gave them instructions to convert the gold to financial instruments, investing in commercial enterprises that would allow the original investment to grow over time."

"And then?" he asked.

"And then we authorize the investment company in Amsterdam

to set up an account and name it the Ghost Flower account. They will be given authority to make investments in commercial enterprises on behalf of the fund, taking risks that are moderate, spreading the risk over several commercial enterprises, and reinvesting the earnings. They won't understand this now, of course, but we will stipulate no investment in tulip bulbs. Then, in 1910 CE, the contract with the investment company in the Netherlands will be required to transfer the fund to a comparable investment company in Switzerland."

"Why make the transfer?" the captain asked.

"We don't need to explain it to the financial wizards. Just between us, there will be a very troubled time later in Europe. Switzerland will be the safest place for our fund to survive those troubles."

"Sounds good so far," he agreed. "I will get the advice of a lawyer familiar with financial investments to help us draw up an agreement."

"Good idea. The agreement will stipulate that in 2036 CE, the investment company in Switzerland is to contact Joel Larsen in Boston, which is not even a place at this time, with instructions to tell him we want the annual proceeds from the fund to assist in medical research and development. The lawyer and the investment company representative can help with the exact wording necessary. The original investment with all earnings reinvested over 450 years will provide a tidy little fund to advance medical research."

"Tidy?" the captain remarked. "I'm no financial genius but in that length of time it will be a bloody fortune!"

"Now, we have one gold bar left. What do you propose we do with it?" Ada asked.

"After this voyage," he replied, "I predict both our boats will need significant repair and maintenance. We should use the remaining bar for those expenses."

·⋯⟩⟨⟨·

CHAPTER 42

1586 CE
NORTH AMERICA

OVER THE COURSE OF THE NEXT two months, the catamarans slowly sailed North, stopping periodically at openings to large bays or significantly-sized inland waters that emptied into the sea. Each time, their two passenger scouts disembarked and spent a few days exploring and mapping the area. When they returned, they would describe in detail to the company man what they had seen. He would dutifully scribe their reports in painstaking detail along with his own evaluation of the commercial prospects of each site.

The last stopping place on their northerly sojourn was a large rocky island, flanked by two rivers. The river on the west side was particularly attractive and Captain Henry had the two boats sail upstream for several miles. All were impressed.

In the privacy of their cabin that evening, after they had departed the island and had decided to call an end to their exploration, Ada confided to Charles that history would later show that the site they were leaving would be highly impressive to the Dutch. She told him they would name the place New Amsterdam, a name that even later in history would be renamed New York.

She decided not to share that the daughter of the man they had with them on their Cuban adventure, Lord Dunch, would ultimately be moving to New Amsterdam to be able to worship as she saw fit. She was afraid sharing too much about the future might cause an unpredictable shift in how history might unfold. However, her intuition told her they may end up playing a part in what would unfold nonetheless. If nothing else, their interactions with Lord Dunch in the present might cause him to think of something that would not have crossed his mind otherwise.

Completing the foray up and back on this latest river on their voyage, the passenger who represented the captain's client announced that the goals of the voyage had been met. He was anxious to return to Amsterdam to share what he had learned with his company's leaders.

Captain Henry and, now, Captain Jane, had the crews of their ships go ashore to stock up on fresh water and any other fresh foods they could forage suitable for beginning the return journey.

✸ ✸ ✸

The following weeks passed without incident as they sailed northeast across the Atlantic. That began to change when they neared the continent and the shipping activity began to increase.

After one dark night with very poor visibility, the first glimmers of dawn found Captain Henry on deck scanning the waters for any ships that may have drawn near in the darkness. Sure enough, he made out the silhouette of a Spanish galleon in the distance. No sooner had he roused the others to point out the danger, an English privateer came into view on the east side of the galleon.

Captain Henry assembled his crew to give them instructions.

"It appears we have stumbled upon a cat and mouse game between these two ships, with the dark night aiding one of them, the English ship, to creep up undetected on the Spanish ship. I think fireworks will soon be happening! We will hang here until it starts and then determine if there is an opportunity for us to aid the English ship or if we should move on out of eyesight. We have no cannons so our assistance would be last minute if the privateer has boarded the Spanish ship and the outcome is uncertain.

"It appears based on their direction of travel, the Spanish ship is on its way to Spain from the Caribbean area, so it is probably loaded with treasure. That, I'm sure is the conclusion of the English privateer. There is a slim chance we may profit from what is about to happen ... or if the Spanish prevail, we need to be moving away ... and moving away fast!"

Captain Henry hailed Jane and Leroux and instructed them to come closer so they could develop a plan together. After they were close enough, the captain shared his thoughts with them. They agreed with his assessment. Leroux suggested that if the two ships in the distance joined in combat, they would be totally focused on each other. That might allow the two catamarans to get close enough to the aft end of the Spanish ship without being fired upon and assess what opportunity might present itself.

❋ ❋ ❋

In the months before they had departed on this trip, Ada and Charles had discussed her excellent skills as a marksman. Ada had explained how use of a musket limited her accuracy at any real distance. She talked about how rifles had replaced muskets in the future, improving their accuracy many times over and the effective distance to a target increased substantially.

This conversation led Charles to do some digging into what might be available along the lines of what she described. This led to multiple conversations with other sea captains who were well traveled.

From their conversations, he learned the history of a man, Augustus Kotter of Nürnberg, Germany, who reportedly had developed a rifle sometime around 1500. Another man named Gaspard Kollner from Vienna had built something similar around the same time.

The weapon was fashioned with a bore that had helical grooves, causing the bullet to spin as it left the barrel, resulting in a straighter trajectory and greater distance. Archers had fletched their arrows in a helical pattern to induce spin for ages before that so the concept was not new; only applying it to the bore of a rifle was new. The captain learned that the shop of Herr Kotter was still in operation, now run by his descendants and apprentices after Herr Kotter's passing. The new proprietor of the gun shop was a great grandson of Herr Kotter who was in Portsmouth, England, for a time, seeking special metals for use in the Nürnberg shop.

Charles and Ada made the trip to Portsmouth to meet this man after a friend made him aware of his presence there. The meeting led to the commissioning of a special rifle to be made for Ada.

The man they met with, learning of their interest—and seeing they were able to pay the considerable sum for such a special weapon—also informed them of an experimental bullet he was developing. He had studied the work of one of the Chinese fireworks manufacturers that was obtaining a better powder than the simple black powder currently used in muskets. The gunsmith, curious about how some of the Chinese fireworks used an explosive powder preloaded into a thick paper tube to propel an explosive charge high in the air, he began using that concept to develop a preloaded tube containing powder and shot that could be loaded into a rifle.

He found that by using a brass tube, rather than paper, and installing an impact detonating cap in the end of the shell to be ignited by the strike of the rifle hammer, he could improve the efficiency of the powder used by the tighter fit of the bullet in the barrel. This resulted in less leakage of the gasses when fired, putting more of the energy into the flight of the bullet. The advancement also made loading simpler and more reliable since there was no guesswork in how much powder to use each time. He also experimented with the improved explosive powder supplied by his Chinese connection to reduce the considerable fouling of a rifle barrel caused by the commonly used black powder.

Sometime later, the same man delivered a custom-made weapon to them in Portishead, with 100 rounds of the special ammunition. The result was terrific. Ada found she could accurately hit a target at 300 yards with considerable force on impact. Charles realized why this unusual weapon was unknown to others when he paid the gunsmith. It cost him about a third of what he had paid for the catamaran.

* * *

Now, in the middle of the Atlantic and getting ready for perhaps another battle, Captain Henry gazed at the two ships in the distance and began formulating a plan of action. He thought back on the purchase of the special rifle for Ada. Turning to her as she stood by his side, he told her what he had been thinking.

"Ada, when these two ships begin battling one another, their attention will be focused on that commotion. When they see our two catamarans approaching, I don't believe they will see an immediate threat. With a spyglass, they will quickly observe we have no cannons and no doubt notice we have a very small crew. My idea is to hang back just far enough to be out of the way but close enough to get to them quickly if it appears the battle is going badly for the English ship.

Then, if that happens, we will approach the Spanish ship from their stern, where they have limited firepower available to turn on us. They may well have a swivel gun mounted on the rail at the stern. Its purpose is for close work repelling any surprise boarders. You should be able to take out the crew assigned to it from a distance. The stern of the ship is a weak spot but it is much taller when we will be in the water, so we should position ourselves at an angle to their rear. That will be just far enough to the rear they won't be able to train their broadside cannons on us but close enough to their side so that we will have a firing angle at the fighters along the side preparing to repel the English boarding party. The first priority will be to take out the swivel gun, then focus on their marksmen positioned higher up on the masts or rigging.

"If we engage, I propose I use our spyglass to be a spotter for you. Then, you will be able to use the new rifle to begin fire from its maximum effective range which is about 300 yards. They won't expect that. Their muskets will have an effective range of about 120 yards. They can shoot farther than that but with little accuracy.

As we get closer—but when we are still out of danger of their muskets—Jane and Mary can use their bows to great effect, again beginning to fire arrows from a distance they will not be able to comprehend. We can be a great aid to the English without ever boarding the Spanish ship."

The captain then hailed Jane.

"Captain, bring your boat closer. I have a plan to share."

Minutes later, the plan unfolded as Captain Henry had laid out. There was a light breeze that helped them into position but not so much as to move them too quickly into the range of the Spanish ship. The two ships, English and Spanish, were already engaged in firing at each other with cannons, enveloping the scene in heavy smoke. The marines on each boat were beginning to fire as well. In the smoke and fog of battle, the Spanish ship paid little attention to the two, much smaller boats they noticed approaching, especially since they saw no evidence of cannons on board and what appeared to be a very small crew on each.

However, when Ada's fire started dropping their snipers from the rigging and shortly after, arrows began to pick off the Spanish crewmembers exposed at the railings in preparation for boarding, they definitely took notice.

Unable to train any of the cannons on the sides of the ship on the smaller boats since they were at an oblique angle behind it, their frustration mounted. The marines on the galleon began firing their muskets at the catamarans with no effect. The musket balls were either falling short or going inaccurately wide due to the long distance.

The diversion created by the catamarans' fire continued to help as the two big boats collided. The English boarding party leaped aboard the Spanish galleon, screaming war cries, and slashing with sabers and fighting axes. After several minutes of intense fighting with significant losses on both sides, the remaining Spanish crew surrendered. Their captain had been killed as well as their first mate.

As the fighting subsided and the intense smoke began to clear, the two catamarans came up along the side of the English ship opposite where the two ships were still together, secured by the many ropes attached to grappling hooks that the English had thrown over in the boarding process.

It took a while for the English captain to hail them as he was obviously intent on ensuring all resistance was over and his crew was in control of the enemy ship. The English crew had seen the English flags flown by the catamarans during the battle so they were welcomed to stand by until their captain was able to turn his attention to them and formally accept their presence.

In time, that acknowledgment happened. He welcomed the captains of the two catamarans to come aboard. As they did so, there was some astonishment as the captain and his crew realized that one of the captains was a woman.

Captain Henry smiled at their reaction as he boarded and saluted the English captain. Jane simultaneously did the same.

"Congratulations on your prize, Captain!" he said and then added, "I'm pleased we could offer you some small help, even if you may not have needed it."

The English captain introduced himself as Captain Summers of the Sir Francis Drake fleet. Captain Henry introduced himself and Captain Jane. Following a few more formalities, Captain Summers suggested they return to their ships so he could finish his work in overseeing the condition of his men and the progress in securing the Spanish crew and assessing the damage to both ships.

Captain Summers asked if they would sail nearby his ship until morning and then come back aboard for a more meaningful meeting. He said he wanted to thank them for the assistance they provided at a less hectic time.

Through the night that fell a little later, they saw the English crew working diligently by the light of many lanterns repairing the damage to their ship and doing likewise to the captured Spanish vessel to prepare it for a journey to England. The spoils would either be repurposed for the Queen's fleet or be sold to the highest bidder.

☀ ☀ ☀

The next day, Captains Henry and Jane rejoined Captain Summers on his ship and were escorted to his cabin. Once there, a long discussion ensued, with both sides enlightening the other on their mission and recapping the battle actions. Captain Summers thanked them for the assistance they had given him.

"I am confident we would have prevailed without your help yesterday but your actions saved many of our crewmen's lives. The sniper fire you provided and the amazing accuracy of your archers is very much appreciated. I had one of my men retrieve the arrows from the Spanish dead and wounded. They look to be finely crafted and I am sure you would like to have them back."

"Thank you, Captain Summers," offered Jane, "I hope we won't be needing them again on this voyage but one never knows."

"The Spanish ship that is now ours has a cargo of precious metals and other spoils they amassed in the Caribbean to take back to their King. Those treasures will now be given to our Queen. However, as a gesture of our thanks and appreciation, I'm giving two of these gold bars to each of you."

Captain Summers motioned for two of his men to step forward, each carrying two bars of gold, and offer them to the catamaran captains. Captain Henry looked at the magnificent gift and gave profuse thanks while at the same time modestly saying that it was not necessary.

"Take it. I think you earned it," Captain Summers insisted. "And I have one more item for you."

He motioned to another of his crewmen standing by.

"These pennants are something for you to fly when you are in the presence of other English ships. They designate that you have the recognition of our fleet commander, Sir Francis Drake. It may help if there is ever any doubt about the loyalty of those small ships you have that look like none I have seen before.

"Captain Jane, please don't take what I am about to say as condescending but lady captains are a rarity. Flying this flag will give you respect with some of the more traditional, shall I say, seamen you will encounter in the future. They haven't seen you in action like I have. If they had, the flag would be entirely unnecessary."

"Thank you, Captain, I will fly it proudly," she smiled.

As they left Captain Summers' ship, Captain Henry turned to Jane.

"Now, we can return to our boats and explain to our paying passengers why we took the action we did. I don't believe they were ever in any real danger. But we are going to have to say something about it being our duty to assist another English ship, or something like that, to appease them."

CHAPTER 43

2035 CE
SPAIN

JOEL AND THOMAS HAD FINISHED THEIR search for clues in Avebury. They recognized the *boton charro* painted in the pistil of the flower in the manor house painting, along with the word *aqui* where a signature of the painter would have been. That, with the two bricks bearing the same clue, gave them a satisfied feeling they had what they needed to travel back to Salamanca and the university library there.

Arriving early one morning at the library, they met with the curator of the rare books section who Melinda had introduced to them before. He agreed to allow another look at the illuminated manuscript where they had seen the drawing of the Ghost Flower before.

"Well, here we are, Thomas," Joel said as they entered the room holding the codex they had seen before when they were with Melinda and Doc. "Let's keep our fingers crossed that we are correct in our assumption this is where we will find the secret hidden for all these centuries."

"I don't know which I feel more—fear we will find nothing, or excitement over what we think will be there," nervously responded Thomas.

"Here it is. Put on your protective gloves and let's go to the page we are looking for."

Joel slowly opened the tome, carefully turning the ancient pages until they got to the one they were looking for.

"I don't know ..." he said, discouraged. "I don't see anything that wasn't here before. We must have missed something in Avebury."

After a minute that seemed like an eternity, Thomas, with his intuitive senses working in overdrive, slowly started poring over the book again.

"Let's not give up yet, Joel, I can feel something different. Let's keep looking at this page. Whatever we are looking for would have been here when we looked several weeks ago and we didn't see anything then. But we weren't looking beyond what was obvious on the page."

"Alright, Thomas, but whatever we are looking for certainly isn't jumping out at me."

"No, it wouldn't. It has to be something other scholars looking at these manuscripts over the last several hundred years wouldn't have noticed either. So, what is it we are seeing ... but not seeing?"

"Hmm ...what about this very, very faint indentation in the middle of the page?"

Joel lowered his head so that his eyes were looking horizontally across the page, giving him a better angle to see the relief of the area where there appeared to be an indentation in the calfskin.

"There is definitely something here! I learned a trick once looking at old art work that might work here," Joel exclaimed as he pulled his smart device out of his pocket and took a picture of the faint indentation. Then he used two fingers on the screen to enlarge the picture, making the suspected indentation clearly stand out.

"Wow!" he exclaimed as he held the phone over to let Thomas take a look.

Joel quickly pulled the phone back for a closer look. "Let me say again, wow! It is an oval shape in the center of the page and look at this: I can faintly see the word *aqui* in the center!"

"Okay, now I see that," Thomas said excitedly. "At a glance, it doesn't look like it is anything of note, just an anomaly in the calfskin—until you make the connection that the indentation is there on purpose!"

"What else might be here?" Joel wondered. "Let's read through the page. Or rather, you translate it out loud to me since you are the one fluent in Latin!"

Thomas started at the top. With the artwork taking up some of the room on the page and the ornate flourishes of the penmanship, the text was not overly long. When Thomas translated one sentence halfway down, Joel said, "Stop! Read that line again."

Thomas slowly read it again. "The answers you seek are in this page and on those following. Read carefully and find enlightenment."

Joel's eyes grew wider. "That sentence could easily be interpreted as referring to the subject matter being written about having nothing to do with what we are looking for. That's very clever."

They looked at each other and said simultaneously, "Doc!"

With his face contorted in concentration, Thomas pointed out that the choice of one word in particular was odd.

"Why is it written that the answers are 'in' this page rather than 'on' this page?"

Joel's face brightened up.

"Could it refer to the oval indentation in the center of the page? Let me feel this page."

He lifted the page between a thumb and forefinger and gently rubbed them back and forth. Then he went to the next page and repeated the rubbing.

"The page we are interested in is thicker than the others. Not a lot, not even really noticeable unless you are looking for something odd like I am right now."

"Good observation," Thomas agreed. "The sentence does not stop with that inference but goes on to say 'and on those following.' Let's move on to the pages after this one and look for something that possibly only we would notice."

Turning to the next page, nothing immediately jumped out at

them. But when they turned to the next and the next, Thomas's intuition continued on high alert.

"Look at this artwork at the bottom margin," he said pointing to a flourish that seemed a little more complex than necessary to just end a page. Embedded in the flourish was what appeared to be a chemical symbol.

"I see it!" Joel exclaimed. "And another on the following page and on the ones after! I'm no chemist but I'll wager that Sam left his chemical analysis, symbol by symbol, letter by letter on each of the following pages, disguised as simple artistic adornment. Very smart, indeed! Sam, you are a genius! Or maybe I should say *were* a genius since he did this 450 years ago."

"Now what do we do?" quizzed Thomas.

"Now," Joel confirmed, "we get the right authorities involved. That would be the World Health Organization, the president, or whatever that person is called for the University of Salamanca, the Secretary of State for the U.S., and their counterpart in Spain. We will need a pharmacologist from both the States and Spain and someone they all recognize as an expert in conservation who can oversee whatever we need to do to this one page to extract what I believe may be remnants of a true Ghost Flower embedded in the page. This won't be easy but we can get it done. Maybe the two of us won't get it done but with the horsepower back at the black site, they can make it happen, I'm certain."

Nodding in agreement, Thomas continued looking at the page with the Ghost Flower drawing in the margin.

"I remember when we looked at this page before. Did we not notice what we are seeing now because we weren't looking for it? Or, was it not there but is now because Doc, Melinda, Sam, and Jane went back and changed history? Is what we are seeing today different from what we saw or is it the same?"

"My sense is that it is the same," Joel offered. "The pages didn't change. It's always been like this because Doc's team went back and created this original. Now the question in my mind is what if they didn't go back? I think the answer is that we wouldn't be looking here today at this version with the thick page, the indentation, and the chemical symbols. They wouldn't be here. What happens, happens. What doesn't happen, just doesn't happen."

* * *

Two weeks later, the officials at the black site flexed their political muscle and a team with all of the necessary skill sets was assembled in a sterile laboratory at the university in Salamanca examining the codex.

The desiccated flower was removed from its 450-year resting place, sandwiched between the two thin sheets of calfskin parchment. A phytochemist examined the flower and seeds and announced that he would be able to run an accurate chemical analysis using equipment supplied to him by the lab research scientists. He said he may not have been able to be as accurate thirty years ago but the capabilities of the equipment available to him today had advanced considerably since then. He was also pleased to have the rough analysis Sam had provided all those years ago from a fresh flower and impressed that his analysis has been disguised in the artwork at the bottom of each page.

Between his examination of the centuries-old dried flower and Sam's notes from examining a fresh one, he was confident he had what was needed to be able to develop a vaccine that would allow the world to tame the current pandemic and possible future ones. He had no way of knowing how long the effects of a vaccination would last but time would give that answer. His initial thought was that a vaccine could be produced in pill form, rather than liquid needing to be stored in a refrigerated environment prior to being injected into a subject. If this proved feasible, then distribution could be made worldwide at far less cost.

Joel and Thomas were properly suited up to prevent contamination and were present during all of the examinations of the flower. In the last day of the examinations, Joel shared a concern with the phytochemist.

"Just as a matter of background, I spent several years working for a large pharmaceutical company. This is not a philanthropic industry. They are definitely for-profit and have shareholders to answer to. We need their resources to finalize the design of the vaccine, get the FDA and other similar agencies in the world to review and approve the efficacy and safety of the product, and after all of the necessary approvals are gained mass produce it for distribution.

"There is a significant cost involved in making all of this happen. I believe from conversations with the government folks who are involved with us now, that these initial costs incurred by pharma conglomerates will be covered with government funding. Then, the pharmaceutical companies should be allowed to charge a price that covers their raw materials and distribution expenses and garner a reasonably small profit, say ten percent. A few of the companies won't necessarily be happy with this arrangement but I believe they will do it, as societal pressures will be too great for them to resist.

"The bigger concern for them will be the fact that this vaccine, if it proves to provide immunity from both bacterial and viral infection, will render many of the drugs they currently market obsolete overnight. This will be a very, very big loss of revenue for them."

"But," Thomas opined, "that is something beyond our control. Such decisions and policies will be up to the governments around the world to deal with. It will trigger billions of dollars in pharmaceutical lobbying fees being spent attempting to have national governments offset the profit losses of big pharma. However, a side benefit I see is the pharmaceutical companies will reorder their research budgets with the dollars freed up to concentrate on other serious health concerns—dementia, diabetes, cancers, and birth defects just to name a few. In time, pharma will be fine."

The phytochemist said he understood and then asked, "What do you think happened to Doc, Melinda, Jane, and Sam after they completed their part of this amazing adventure? I hope they found happiness in their new lives all those centuries ago."

"We will never know," Joel answered. "But considering who they were, I'm certain they lived good, fulfilling lives."

Little did he know there was still more in store for him and Thomas to discover, thanks to their friends who had lived 450 years in the past.

CHAPTER 44

2036 CE
BOSTON, MASSACHUSETTS

IN THE FEW SHORT MONTHS AFTER retrieving the secrets from
the ancient illustrated manuscript, Joel and Thomas were making
great progress working with the stakeholders in converting what
they had extracted from the Ghost Flower remnant into a viable
vaccine capable of stemming the tide in the pandemic which had
reached a true international crisis.

Fortunately, they were able to accomplish this without
mentioning the team that had traveled back in time—the disbelief
they would have encountered would have been too much to deal
with in the short time needed to move ahead with the production
of a vaccine. Their story simply stuck to current research on ancient
documents leading them to this particular document with the
embedded flower and encoded chemistry. That latter part had
been tough to explain but they were successful in intentionally
muddling through.

One fine autumn day back home in Boston, Joel and Thomas
had retreated to an office they had set up in the downtown area
to assist in the ongoing coordination of the vaccine development
efforts.

"Joel, I think we are nearing the end of our part in this project,"
Thomas announced. "The pharma scientists and research teams
have done a remarkable job in successfully taking what we provided
in order to develop a vaccine that is getting regulatory approval

worldwide. There are some tough financial issues coming to light on distribution and speedy production methods. Government subsidies are coming but at a pace that is too slow, given the way governments work, and that is costing additional lives to be lost."

"You summarized the situation quite well, Thomas," Joel agreed. "I wish we could do more. We have done what we're capable of so far in terms of developing a vaccine for this virus. What we know, based on our experience, is this pandemic is not the only health issue in the world. There are so many others that exist now and more will be coming at us in the future, different cancers, for example, that are attacking an aging population.

"Another health crisis is currently stemming from the mass movement of people from the heavily populated coastal areas around the world as a result of rising sea levels. This is a new crisis, long predicted but not acted upon beyond hand-wringing. Rising waters are already forcing millions of people out of their homes and destroying the resources needed for economic survival. The infrastructure in the areas that are receiving the evacuees can't handle the load. Water resources, aging and undersized distribution systems, on top of overflowing sewer systems are fostering disease at an unprecedented rate. The electrical grid in coastal areas that are serving communities are useless. Agricultural lands that are now inundated with salty sea water are no longer producing the food needed for the population."

"It's very depressing. I wish we could do something," Thomas worried. "And you don't need to remind me that a wish is not a plan. I just don't know how we can help."

"True. I don't have a plan either," Joel admitted. "Let's pack up for the day and have a drink at the bar downstairs before heading home for the night."

※ ※ ※

The next morning found Thomas and Joel back in their office, contemplating what they needed to do before terminating their lease on the office. An almost palpable gloom had settled in. Around 10:00, the building receptionist rang their office phone. Joel answered and was told there was a representative from a Swiss financial company who wanted to see him. She asked if she should allow him access and send him up.

"Sure, why not," Joel told her.

Within two minutes, the door to their suite opened. A man dressed in a dark business suit, with a touch of color added by a deep red tie, entered. His silver hair and confident bearing led them to believe he was probably a senior member of the financial firm the receptionist said he represented. He was carrying a small briefcase. Briefly looking around the small reception area, flanked by the three offices for Thomas, Joel, and an administrative assistant, he smiled and reached out a hand to Joel.

"Thank you for seeing me," the man said, introducing himself as Jonathan Wright, vice president for Zurich Financial Services, a Swiss corporation with an office in Boston. Shaking Thomas's hand next, he began.

"I have something for you that has been the subject of much curiosity in my firm for many years now. Do you have a place we might sit?" He requested this as he simultaneously lifted the briefcase to indicate he wanted to share the contents with them.

"Sure, we can use my office. I have a small conference table there," replied Joel.

Once they were inside and seated around the table, Wright looked around the room as he began to speak.

"I can tell from your reactions that my purpose in coming to see you is completely unknown. I'm not surprised. Let me start the conversation by saying that what I have to relate to you will be hard to comprehend at first but once you look at these documents, I think you will believe my fantastic story is a true one."

Joel and Thomas were silent.

"First, let me ask, is there anyone in the adjoining office? What I have to say next is for your ears only."

"No," answered Joel, "our admin assistant is away today, so it's only the two of us."

"Excellent," Wright continued. "Let me begin by giving you the executive summary of my story, then I will show you detailed documents to verify what I say. This story begins 450 years ago with a woman named Dr. Ada Sendall."

Joel and Thomas sat straighter in their chairs; their eyes wide with anticipation of what might come next.

"This is good," Wright nodded. "I can see by your expressions that you know of whom I speak. Dr. Sendall established an account with a financial investment firm in Amsterdam in the year 1587. The initial deposit was a single bar of gold which, at the time, was probably valued at $480 or $500 dollars in U.S. currency. As required in the original 1587 contract, that account was transferred to our firm in Zurich in 1910.

"The agreement governing the invested funds stipulated that any disbursements of annual earnings were to be reinvested, with no withdrawals of principal or interest other than for reinvestment over the years. Now comes the shocking part of the story. Imagine the compounding effect over four-and-a-half centuries on an original investment made in various commercial enterprises over that time period. The earnings varied from year to year depending on many factors, one of the most important being the astute investment acumen of the investors. I must tell you, the financial house in Amsterdam that managed the account until 1910 was one of the best. We didn't fare poorly either with our management of the funds when we took over."

"I can only imagine," commented Joel.

"Well, you don't need to imagine because I will tell you the result. Dr. Sendall's investment is now worth three billion dollars."

Stunned silence followed.

Then Joel asked, "Since you are here, telling us this story, I assume we are involved in some way?"

"Oh, yes," Mr. Wright replied as he pulled a sheaf of papers from his briefcase. "This paper names you, Joel, as executer of the fund, effective as of the date of delivery of this document to you. And, Thomas, you are named as the associate director. Dr. Sendall specifies that the fund be used to promote world health."

Joel and Thomas looked at each other in disbelief. Wright went on to explain more details.

"She has some non-binding recommendations included in the papers here. She recognizes that times change and needs that cannot be anticipated will arise occasionally, so she didn't want to restrict the use of the fund in that regard. Dr. Sendall trusts that you two will make wise decisions. She suggests that you continue to use a Swiss financial firm as a home base for the fund for two primary reasons.

"First, she believes in the integrity of our financial system and our reputation for outstanding fiduciary responsibility. Second, she did not know—and could not know—the magnitude of the fund's worth today when she made the initial investment all those years ago. However, she correctly assumed it would be substantial. She knew considerable wealth creates great interest, including notice by criminal elements in society. The Swiss have a well-founded reputation for keeping investments we manage secret if that is the desire of the client. She believed that secrecy will serve you well as you administer the fund going forward."

"I'm overwhelmed," exclaimed Joel, quickly followed by a similar statement from Thomas.

"Well, that's understandable," Wright said matter-of-factly. "The documents express Dr. Sendall's desire for the two of you to be fairly compensated as she believed your time going forward will be consumed by the administration of the fund. There is also provision for expenses incurred managing the fund be covered as well. Finally, I will stop talking for now, leaving these papers with you to absorb. I suggest we meet again tomorrow so I can answer the questions I know will bubble up as you go through the information here. My sincere warning to you is that you do not share this information with anyone other than your spouses, if you have them, before we talk again."

With that, Mr. Wright rose to leave.

"Wait ... before you go," Joel started, "I have a request for you pertaining to our meeting tomorrow."

"Of course, what is that?" he asked.

"Tomorrow when we meet, I would like to hear your recommendations regarding who we might retain for legal representation," Joel said, "someone with experience in both Swiss and United States laws that affect the fund. This person, logically from your firm, will, at least in the short run, bring us up to speed on the fund's investments and begin a conversation with us on how to make future disbursements from the fund while keeping the need for secrecy. And we'll also require a tax expert who can advise us on what will inevitably be required to be paid on the taxable expenses of the fund, again protecting the anonymity, that seems to be a prudent way of operating."

Smiling, Mr. Wright agreed, "I will do what you ask. I can see from your requests that Dr. Sendall's appointment of you as directors of the fund was well founded. Can I plan to meet you here in your offices tomorrow, say at 1:00 in the afternoon?"

"Yes, that will be perfect," Joel confirmed. "You have not met our administrative assistant, Gail, but I can say unequivocally that she is trustworthy and will keep what she hears to herself. Thomas and I will definitely need her help right away. I will have her join us. I'm excited!"

><)+++··

CHAPTER 45

1586 CE
ENGLAND

SITTING ON THE DECK OF *THE Twin Flame*, Ada, Captain Henry, Jane, and Leroux, were watching a glorious sunset reflecting off the waters of the marina where they had leased a spot on the wharf in Portishead. Mary and John had left for the evening to see what they could discover in town.

Captain Henry had arranged leases that gave them four, six-foot-wide docks, each jutting out from the wharf along the sides of the two boats. On the wharf itself they had constructed two very sturdy twelve-by-twelve-foot secure storage lockers, one for each boat, for equipment they could choose from as needed for different voyages. They had clothing for different seasons, fishing gear, spare rope, sails, and carpentry equipment and supplies for repair and maintenance of the catamarans.

Charles and Ada had just completed a short contract for a client who needed swift passage from Portishead to London and back and they were discussing some other potential business that seemed imminent. After a bit, the conversation drifted to something else Ada had on her mind.

"I've been thinking about Melinda lately," Ada said, as she looked out over the water, a glass of cool white wine in her hand. "Our recent trip to London started me wondering how she is doing. I know she planned to see if she could meet William Shakespeare in Stratford. Now is the time the historians called the 'lost years' in his history, believing he spent much of that time in either Stratford or London. Perhaps we could plan a trip to see her. Maybe even tie it into a lucrative business venture for us."

Sipping on her own wine, Jane agreed that she would like that very much. Charles didn't have quite the same history with Melinda but was interested in the trip nonetheless. He offered to see what he could arrange.

"Since we don't know exactly where Melinda is now, maybe we could do an overland trip to Stratford-upon-Avon, then go on to London if that is where we discover she might be. If you and Leroux are up for it," he said to Jane, "you could meet us in London and bring us back here to Portishead at some predetermined date. I'll see if I can get us a paying customer at least for the Stratford piece of the journey. Perhaps with a fee that is at least large enough to cover our need for a wagon and some horses with a little profit left over."

As their conversation began winding down and their attention turned appreciatively up at the stars beginning to appear in the night sky now that the sun had disappeared, Captain Henry's nephew, James the farrier, hailed them from the wharf.

"Uncle, permission to come aboard!" he said with a grin at his own wit in using such formality.

"Permission granted! What brings you out tonight, James? Bored with the nightlife in Portishead?"

Reaching the catamaran, James leapt aboard and began explaining.

"I just met a woman who had checked in to the inn nearby. She asked the innkeeper if he knew a man called Captain Henry. The innkeeper sent her to me. She told me she had a message of utmost importance for you and that she had come a long way to see you. Her English is almost non-existent, so I could hardly make out what she was saying. However, I got the gist of it and told her I would tell you of her presence and ask if you would meet her at the inn."

"Did she give you a name?" the captain inquired.

"Sophia, she told me," James answered.

A look of alarm spread across the faces hearing this.

Puzzled, he said to James, "Yes, come with me to the inn now. Strangely, I've never met the woman but I heard about her from Ada and the others. You can introduce me. I want Ada, Jane, and Leroux to come as well."

"You seem quite agitated, Uncle. I'm surprised," his nephew observed.

"No time to explain now ... it would take too much time."

With that, all five left the catamaran and headed toward the inn in the light of a moon beginning to appear over the horizon. Reaching the establishment, they went in. James took the stairs up to Sophia's room to alert her to their presence. He returned quickly for them and they were ushered into Sophia's small room.

"*Mia dios*, it is you I've looked for," Sophia blurted out to Ada and the captain in her broken English.

"Well, here we are and I can already see the news you bring is not good," he replied.

Sophia launched into an emotional outburst in Spanish, complete with tears running down her face. Ada took over the communication in Spanish with the captain looking on in dismay. His nephew had accompanied them into the room and was looking on with an obvious expression of puzzlement, too.

The captain wanted to know why Sophia had asked for him, as they had never met. Ada asked the woman and an animated conversation revealed that after they had departed Salamanca, Brother Francisco had done some digging to find where they had gone. He learned that they ultimately had met with a sea captain and sailed to England. His instinct told him that it would be easier to track down a known sea captain than the ones he had met with, so he instructed Sophia to find them through Captain Henry.

After a few minutes of back and forth over the details of the story that was unfolding, Sophia, apparently exhausted, fell onto her bed, weeping with relief that she had successfully delivered her message.

"This is serious!" Ada turned to explain. "I have just heard remarkably tragic news from Salamanca. I'll translate her Spanish to English and give you the short version of what she said. King Philip II has long championed Catholicism in Spain against inroads being made by the Protestants. His government has also recently, though not for the first time, began suffering financial setbacks. One of his supporters in Salamanca, a quite greedy fellow, has convinced Philip that the wealthy resident of Salamanca who commissioned the illustrated manuscript from Brother Francisco, has secretly been funding a planned Protestant rebellion against the Crown. Brother Francisco knows this is a lie, a lie perpetuated by this evil man to gain control of the wealth of the purchaser of this manuscript."

Sophia had relayed more, Ada explained.

"This is what she said from what I can translate. Brother Francisco confided in her that the wealthy man who had commissioned his work told him of his action to prevent the manuscript Brother Francisco had created from being included in a politically-theatrical show of burning heretical books, even though there is absolutely nothing heretical in it. His patron secretly donated his several illustrated manuscripts, including the one we worked on together with the Ghost Flower for Thomas and Joel, to the library at the University of Salamanca. He retained in his home collection a number of less important and less valuable books for the seizure he knew was to come. He believed the ones he had donated would not be missed."

"Well, at least we know how this manuscript ended up in the library at the University of Salamanca," the captain said, "that must be a relief to you."

Sophia roused herself, wiping tears from her cheeks.

"Brother Francisco knew how important this work is to you, so he asked me to come here to let you know. He also wanted you to know that even though the Spanish Inquisition is not aware of the exact works the Brother produced for his patron, just the fact that he is known to have a relationship with him put him in mortal danger. Right before I left to come here to find you, Brother Francisco disappeared. I fear the worst. As for me, since I worked for him, I am considered a heretic as well and so cannot return to Spain since my life is now in danger. I am at a loss as to what to do. At least I have delivered the message that was so important to Brother Francisco."

Ada translated for the others. Hearing this, Captain Henry gently put his hand on Sophia's shoulder.

"I'm sure we can do something for you, just let me consider it. You were very brave to come here. Thank you. Ada, please tell her what I just said."

After more conversation with Sophia, Ada told her they would return to see her in the morning at the inn.

They departed to the wharf, with two problems to consider. One was how to assist Sophia. The other was now that James had overheard something about their recent adventure, whether to bring him totally into the fold, or to explain what he had heard in Sophia's room as an isolated adventure without bringing up all of the rest of it. They said goodbye to James with a promise they would meet in the morning to explain what had just happened.

Back on the catamaran, Charles asked Jane and Leroux to join him and Ada in their cabin.

"First," he said, "I would like to offer a suggestion for helping Sophia and, hopefully, at the same time helping us. Ada and I have been talking about purchasing a cottage somewhere near here as a home base when we are not at sea. Ada, you and Jane have taught me enough to know the dangers to our health spending our shore time in a public inn and eating in public places. I have had my eye on a property near here that I just learned is going to be offered for sale. It is a fairly large cottage on a hill with a view of the sea.

It's on a fifteen-acre piece of land that would give us privacy and a place to have a garden and raise a few chickens and perhaps a cow or two. Maybe we could even have a horse to pull a wagon. Since our sojourns at sea cover long periods of time, what if we offered Sophia the job of taking care of the place in our absence in exchange for room and board?"

Ada quickly spoke up. "I like the idea very much. We have talked about having a land base for some time. I know the property you mentioned and if we can get it, that will be ideal. I just didn't know how we would maintain it when we are away so often for long periods. Sophia could be the answer. The catamaran is already getting overcrowded with our ever-growing possessions and the storage building we have on the wharf is full. I really like the idea of having a garden, too. It would be fantastic if I could teach Sophia how to can fruits and vegetables that we could take on our voyages. She could even do that when we are away. I'll explain canning later but it's a good thing!"

"I like the sound of it," Jane offered, "I think that will suit the two of you very well. But what do we do about James? Let me say at the outset, I find him an interesting man and he seems considerably smarter than many here. I sense a restlessness in him. I believe he would jump at the chance to join us. He could make a very valuable addition to one of our crews."

Captain Henry spent a minute absorbing this and then looked to Ada.

"What do you think of this idea of bringing James into our group? He comes around quite a bit when we are here. It's going to be increasingly difficult to keep secret who Jane really is, Mary, too, for that matter, and our activities hidden from him."

"From the little I've seen of James," Ada replied, "I certainly like him but you know more about your nephew than any of us."

"Yes, I know him and I know he is of strong moral character and as honest as the day is long. I also have had thoughts about taking him along on some of my merchant trips in the past but he couldn't leave his job for a month and then come back and continue."

Ada, deep in thought as the captain spoke, suggested an idea for consideration.

"Let's assume we buy the cottage property here in Portishead and Sophia agrees to staff it for us. There will be work maintaining the land, taking care of the livestock, fields, and garden. And there will be inevitable maintenance work that goes with owning a small estate. We could employ James to assist Sophia. He could keep his farrier business in town and act as our representative while we are away ginning up new business for us and for Jane and Leroux. With that additional work and the revenue that would come with it, he should be able to hire someone to occasionally take his place and allow him to accompany us on some of our voyages. Having someone here in Portishead while we are away to look after our interests is going to become necessary, I strongly believe."

"I like that line of thinking, Ada," Charles agreed. "I'll talk to him tomorrow to see if he is interested. I think he will be. Indeed, it will be good to have someone here when we are away."

Ada and Charles said their goodnights and Jane and Leroux retired to their boat. Ada was still considering their plans for later times.

"Charles, we have been talking about our future and what happens when we have amassed enough wealth to take on fewer contracts. I'm not going to mention aging in any of this but that is a reality!"

"I'll pretend you didn't even bring that age thing up. But I've thought about it, too. Jane is a partner with us, now with her own boat. She and Leroux will enter more contracts without us as we begin to slow down in years to come. But I believe there will still be contracts in the future for the four of us with our two boats. Don't count us out just yet, missy," he teased.

···ᵐᵐ❰•❰

CHAPTER 46

1586 CE
ENGLAND

THE NEXT MORNING ARRIVED WITH ANOTHER beautiful sunrise over the waters of the harbor. Charles and Ada were up early and enjoying a sumptuous breakfast prepared on a grill they had placed on the wharf adjacent to the catamaran.

"Just think," mused Ada, "if we are able to acquire the property we were talking about last night, we may soon be having breakfast in our own kitchen. But I will miss this view," she added as she looked around the harbor, bathed in the early glow of the rising sun. "But we will still be having many meals on our boat at sea."

Just as they were finishing, Jane and Leroux joined them on the wharf. After wishing them good morning, Ada brought up Melinda.

"If my memory of history—some of which is yet to happen— serves me, William Shakespeare could be in London beginning sometime this year. If Melinda is still following her dream of meeting him and perhaps talking her way into getting a part in one of the plays Shakespeare is thought to be acting in now, she may be in London, not in Stratford."

"As I see it," chimed in Jane, "we have a choice to make. We are beginning to run low on our supply of the Ghost Flower herbs. If we are going to London, we may well need to strengthen our immune system. That city is definitely not the healthiest place on the planet right now. Additionally, Melinda could probably use a resupply as well. Avebury is nearly straight west from here, on the way to London—almost anyway. We could stop there on the way to London at the old stone circle in the woods to pick some more Ghost Flower plants, if they are still growing there. We could avoid trouble by never going into Avebury itself. Another choice is to sail from here, Portishead, around the southern tip of England and go directly to London. By sea would take far less time but we don't pick up our herbs and we don't know if Melinda will be there."

"There is a third choice," offered Captain Henry. "If I can get a merchant to engage Ada and me to take a wagonload of supplies to Swindon, Bath, or some other destination midway between here and London, that could pay for the entire trip. Then, Jane, if you and Leroux sailed to London and met us there, we could all come back here together. If Melinda is, in fact, in London and not Stratford, we could all have a reunion before we return. If it turns out she is in Stratford, we will visit with her and then still go on to London and meet you there.

That suggestion was met with hearty approval by all. Jane quickly said, "I'll see if we can arrange for a paying passenger or two to go with Leroux and me, one way, to London. That will pay for our trip with a little to spare for what we might choose to do in London."

The captain added, "I can see where bringing James into our group here in Portishead will be of benefit already. There will be a lot for Sophia to do setting up a household for Ada and me and in our absence, James will be a great help to her."

Before the sun had reached its zenith on that beautiful day, the captain struck out on foot to meet with James and make him the offer they had discussed. He found his nephew busy putting a new shoe on a horse that seemed to be acquainted with the process. The mare was quietly standing there as James held her back left hoof between his knees, hammering in the last nail.

"Hello, James. Busy as usual I see," he hailed.

"Hi, Uncle," James looked up to greet him. "Yes, this one is about done and I have two more horses yet to work on. What are you up and about to on this nice day in Portishead?"

"I have a business proposition for you to consider," Captain Henry replied.

With that preamble, he explained he and Ada were planning to buy some property nearby. To do this, they had the idea of hiring Sophia as a caretaker who would need his assistance in maintaining the place. He said the proposal included using James to be his business representative when he and Ada were away at sea and possibly including him as a part of the crew on some of their future voyages. He made a compensation offer that James indicated was very generous. After a few more questions regarding some of the details, James happily agreed.

"Very good!" exclaimed his uncle after receiving his decision. "I want you to join us for dinner tonight aboard my boat. There are some things you need to know about my crew."

This last bit he said with a slight smile of amusement as he anticipated James's reaction when heard the stories of distant worlds and time travel.

CHAPTER 47

1586 CE
ENGLAND

A FEW DAYS AFTER CAPTAIN HENRY had secured the arrangements with James and Sophia—who took little convincing to stay on with them—he approached the owner of the cottage and land he and Ada had decided to buy. After some customary haggling over the price and what furniture and equipment would be included in the sale, an agreement was struck. He informed the owner that his nephew, James, would be his representative in completing the transaction and that he had a solicitor drawing up a paper giving James the full authority to act on his behalf.

That action complete, the captain turned his attention to the idea of traveling to Stratford-upon-Avon to seek out Melinda, with a stop at the old stone circle near Avebury to collect Ghost Flowers.

Another week passed as arrangements were made with James and Sophia to take on the responsibilities of Ada and Charles's new home and to find a paying customer who needed their services to take him and a wagonload of merchandise overland to Stratford.

Returning to the boat one afternoon from town, Captain Henry seemed in a particularly good mood.

"Ada, I have some good news for you. I found a better proposition for us rather than taking a wagonload of supplies to pay for our travel to Stratford. I mentioned our upcoming trip to the solicitor I have been working with ... the one who is arranging for the legal authorizations for James to act on my behalf and to secure the property we are buying. When he heard of our planned trip, he asked me if I would be willing to take a sheaf of documents to a barrister in Stratford. As it happens, a client of his needs these documents to be in the hands of the Stratford barrister as quickly as possible. Before I arrived, he was at a loss as to how to accomplish the delivery with speed. He said his client was willing to pay handsomely to make it happen."

Ada thought for a minute and replied, "I think we can accommodate that request. All we will need are two good horses. We won't need to fuss with a wagon and all that entails. Now that James and Sophia are lined up to take care of our responsibilities here, we could leave tomorrow."

Later that day, they confirmed the plans with Jane and Leroux to meet them in London after estimating the time it would take to get to London via Stratford. They decided that whoever got there first would leave a message at the closest mooring place near the bridge across the Thames in London as a way of communicating, since it was impossible to plan a simultaneous arrival. Ada mentioned it would be called London Bridge in the future.

✳ ✳ ✳

Just as Ada suggested, she and Charles were able to leave Portishead the next day on two sturdy horses they bought from James. With the provisions they packed for the trip and supplies for sleeping off the road along the way, they traveled the first fifty miles of their journey in a little over a day and a half reaching the outskirts of Avebury in the afternoon.

"Okay, Ada, now that we are approaching Avebury," Charles said, "you lead the way to the old stone circle in the woods you told me about."

"Gladly," she called as she nudged her horse ahead. "Let's hope there are still Ghost Flowers to be had there!"

A half hour later, Ada guided them into the small stand of woods around the ancient stone circle.

"Oh, no," she gasped as they rode up to the circle, startling a small herd of deer that had been grazing in the circle. "They are eating our flowers along with everything else there!"

Captain Henry pulled back on his horse's reins, stopping to get a full view of the area.

"I see a few white flowers near the edge of the circle. If that's what we are looking for, we may be in luck."

Urging his horse forward with Ada by his side, they rode into the stones, many of which were scattered around the few still standing.

"Whew," Ada exclaimed as she came closer to the flowers to get a good look at them. "These are what we came for. Another few days and I think we may have been out of luck. Mary told me that the flowers went extinct sometime around now for various reasons. We just saw one of those reasons ... hungry deer!"

Dismounting, Charles produced a leather bag for the two of them to fill and they began picking every flower they could find.

When finished, Ada, looking over their new stash, offered the opinion that they had enough to dry and store to supply them with their powers of immunity for at least three years, even after sharing some with Melinda.

"Now that we have achieved this goal, I would like for us to camp here for the night. Since we are here, Ada, I'd like to explore the site of these mysterious stones," Charles suggested.

Overnight, they saw no other people in the area but did notice a healthy population of rabbits. Charles noted that deer were not the only inhabitants of the area that seemed to enjoy adding the flowers to their diet.

❊ ❊ ❊

Leaving the Avebury area the next morning, they resumed their journey to Stratford. Two days later when they arrived in Stratford, they went straight to the barrister's office to deliver the package of documents as they had agreed.

Before leaving his office, they inquired as to where William Shakespeare might live. They were told he and his wife, Anne Hathaway Shakespeare, lived in William's father's house on Henley Street.

"That was easy enough," Charles chucked. "This is a small town, so let's ride over there before we find an inn for the night."

The two of them found the house in a matter of minutes and knocked on the front door. The door was opened by an attractive woman who introduced herself as Mrs. Shakespeare. While no big deal to Charles, Ada was almost dumbstruck in the presence of a woman she had read about in the future. Before her was Anne Hathaway. Taking a chance, Charles said they were looking for a friend of theirs, Melinda Ramsey, who they thought might be an acquaintance of hers as well.

"Yes, of course, I know Melinda Ramsey," Anne replied. "She is an ardent student of the theatre, and wanted to talk with my husband who is an actor here in Stratford. William told her he hadn't much experience but was eager to learn himself and had been writing some scenes for inclusion in potential plays that he was pleased to share to get her reaction."

Ada and Charles looked relieved.

"You both look like tired travelers. Come inside and I'll get you something to drink," Anne offered.

In the background, they heard some crying and Anne explained. "Those are our twins, Hamnet and Judith. And this," she said as a small girl curiously came up to her mother's side and clutched the side of her dress, "is Susanna, our other daughter, who is now four!"

Ada had regained her composure and leaned over to say hello to Susanna. Anne led them into a parlor, inviting them to sit.

"We don't mean to inconvenience you," started Ada, "but we

hope you can tell us where to find Ms. Ramsey. Is she here in Stratford?"

"She was but an opportunity came up for her to accompany William and two other young men to London in hopes of finding work in one of the theatres there. Women are not allowed to act in plays but William, being an adventurous—and a fearless I must say, young man—was sure they could get her a part by having her pretend to be a boy and play that role. As a woman, she has no beard but with her slim build and the right clothes, they believed she could pull it off. They have been gone now about a month."

Showing disappointment that they would still have more travel ahead to meet up with Melinda, Ada asked, "Do you know where they might be in London?"

Anne explained the difficulty of being an actor with so many political, legal, and religious objections to that form of artistic expression.

"My guess is they are probably at one of the theatres William mentioned that are located outside of the London city limits where there is not as much scrutiny or legal problems with the plays that are of the type my William is interested in. He mentioned two places to me. One is The Theatre and the other is called The Curtain."

Charles asked Anne if there was an easy route to reach these theatres. She produced some paper and a quill pen from a sideboard and drew a rough map.

"After crossing the bridge over the Thames River into London, take Grace Church Street, heading north. Leave the city through Bishopsgate and stay on that road until you find those theatres on the left, just past Finsbury Fields. It's a rough area, so be careful when you go there. Pickpockets, thieves, and prostitutes are everywhere, I hear. But that environment of lawlessness out on the fringes of London gives William and other actors some degree of freedom to exercise their creativity without fear of the certain retribution they would find in the city."

When Anne had concluded, Ada expressed her gratitude.

"Thank you so much for your assistance. I think Charles and I have taken too much of your time already so we should move on and find a suitable inn for the night."

"Nonsense," she protested. "I would love to have your company tonight and we have plenty of room here in this house. You can tell me news of your part of the world over dinner. That would be a real treat for me."

Ada couldn't believe she was really present in the Shakespeare household during a time she had only read about in history books. Without giving away too much, she intended to satisfy so many questions that were popping into her head.

✻ ✻ ✻

They spent the afternoon attending to their horses and settling into a guest room that Anne had been busy sprucing up for their stay. Ada enjoyed a long bath while Charles shaved. They felt renewed when they returned to the kitchen to find Anne and the cook preparing an early meal for her children.

"Is there anything I can do to help?" Ada offered.

"No, thank you, but please join us for a cool glass of mint tea," the cook replied, pouring each a measure from a large pitcher on the table.

"If you don't have to leave straight away in the morning, I think you would enjoy taking our row boat out on the Avon tomorrow," Anne suggested.

"Well, a little bit of water would do me good," Charles laughed, "I'm not so well-suited on four legs."

"That sounds like fun," Ada agreed. "My riding has improved but floating is much more enjoyable."

After the children had been fed and put to bed, Anne and her guests moved to the dining room. The cook served a lovely meal with wine and their conversation touched on many lively topics. Anne was especially interested in knowing more about how Ada and Charles had met and what life was like on a long sea voyage.

With the dishes cleared and the day growing dark, Charles admitted the long horseback journey had left him quite tired. They said their goodnights and retired to the comfortable guest quarters in the Shakespeare home. As Ada was getting ready for bed, she chatted away.

"I can't believe what just happened," she said to Charles. "I know everything that impresses me about Anne Hathaway and William Shakespeare hasn't even happened yet but, take my word for it, those two will go down in history to be read about for ages. You haven't experienced any of it yet but as our life goes on, trust me. You will hear about the accomplishments of William Shakespeare!"

As she looked over at her beloved companion for a reaction, he was already deep asleep and snoring lightly.

CHAPTER 48

1586 CE
ENGLAND

VERY EARLY THE NEXT MORNING, BEFORE the light had even begun to rise over the Stratford house on Henley Street, Ada was dreaming.

She was driving a car in Boston with a sense of urgency to get to the airport, fearing she was late to catch her flight. The traffic was thick and confusing and other large cars and trucks were extremely close to hers, causing a sense of panic. Ahead, she could see a large pleasure boat being towed on a trailer. The trailer had fishtailed somehow and lodged horizontally across two lanes, completely blocking any way through. She heard horns honking all around her and tried repeatedly to press her hand on her steering wheel but no sound was coming out. Looking down on the passenger seat, the steering wheel was broken in two. She screamed, trying to roll down her window with an old crank-style handle to no avail.

Suddenly, she woke, feeling someone's hand on her shoulder. Still groggy, she opened her eyes to see Charles, on his knees at the side of the bed.

"I need help," he moaned, clutching his stomach.

Coming to, Ada climbed down from the bed and knelt beside him. He was wringing wet with fever as she felt his back and forehead. She helped him up and settled him back in bed. She lit a lantern on the nightstand and tried to take stock of the situation. His pulse was steady and she gauged his temperature to be about 100 or a little more—serious but not yet critical. She lifted his nightshirt and felt around his abdomen and back.

"Charles, can you hear me?" she asked. "Tell me what you are feeling."

He licked his lips. "It's my guts inside," he managed. "They have tightened up and feel on fire. I woke about two hours ago, made it outside and retched. I thought it must have been something I ate for dinner. But the feeling is still there and won't pass."

In her mind, Ada quickly reviewed the meal Anne's cook had prepared for them last night. It was quite possible something was contaminated. *Am I feeling sick?* she wondered. She poured water from a pitcher on the nightstand into a cup and raised it to his lips.

"It's important to stay hydrated," she told him. "Try to take a sip."

Charles turned away and rolled on his side, bringing his knees up to his chest in a child's position. She could see he was in agony. She wasn't sure of the time but it was still very dark out and the house was quiet. Deciding she would likely wake everyone else up but knowing she had to get into action, she grabbed the lantern, whispering as she left, "I'll be right back."

Finding her way through the house, she located the kitchen and tried to quietly rummage around in the cupboards for any type of tea that she could make.

Ginger, peppermint, licorice, fennel, or even any green or black tea would do. I could use a cup myself, she thought.

As she searched, her mind raced. She felt she could rule out appendicitis since she could not detect any sharp pain in the lower right side of the abdomen or back and he didn't show any serious signs of stomach bloating. Considering his symptoms, her guess was an intestinal infection or some type of viral gastroenteritis. Finding a small sack with green tea, she filled the kettle from a bucket of water and lit the fire.

Ada made her way back to their room and found Charles still in the fetal position, rocking himself slowly.

"Damn it to hell," he cried, "what anguish is this?"

Ada poured cool water on a hand cloth and pressed it to his head.

"There, there, we'll fix you up in no time," she assured him.

But she hid her worry, knowing there would be no effective treatment for gastroenteritis, if that was what was ailing him. After harping on the preventative precautions she insisted they all take— avoiding food and water that may be contaminated and reminding everyone to wash their hands thoroughly and often—there was little more she could do but wait and pray.

Anne appeared at the door. "Ada?" she called quietly. "Is everything okay?"

"Oh, Anne, I'm so sorry to have disturbed you. I hope I didn't wake the twins. Charles woke up ill and I'm trying to help but he's in terrible agony," Ada replied. "I started to make some tea but we'll need something stronger."

"Just stay with him now and I'll tend to things," Anne reassured her. "Don't worry, my dear. I'll send someone for the doctor."

Over the next few hours, Charles' fever worsened and he became delirious. He mumbled vague orders as though he were at sea. Ada changed his clothes and bedding twice to try to keep him dry and comfortable.

The doctor finally arrived by midday and provided a laudanum tincture, which helped Charles drop into a deep sleep.

✳ ✳ ✳

With very little change in the captain's condition over the next three days, Ada became increasingly anxious. She wondered if he could recover. It was difficult to get any fluids into him and she wished she could magically manifest even the simplest medical setup.

The first night he fell ill, when she rummaged for tea in the kitchen, she had forgotten about the fresh batch of Ghost Flowers they had picked. It wasn't until dawn that she remembered them and quickly sprang into action grinding them. She marveled at how fortuitous their stop in Avebury had turned out to be. The cook helped her make a meat broth with their powder and Ada fashioned a type of straw that she used to drop the warm liquid into his throat.

Will the Ghost Flower make any difference, she wondered.

Only leaving his side momentarily to take care of essentials, she was exhausted. Anne encouraged her to take short walks and small meals but Ada resisted, not wanting to leave him alone for even a minute. She held his hand for hours on end, longing for any connection that might help him heal.

The doctor stopped in again but he was basically useless. Ada understood his indifference, considering the magnitude of the disease and death he had seen recently in the area. She knew better than try to offer any therapeutic advice to him lest he think she was a witch.

Anne had arranged a small cot for Ada in order not to disturb Charles any more than necessary. She pulled it as close as possible to him so she could hear his breathing and reach out to touch him. She recalled many of their intimate moments together and reflected on how she loved the sound of his voice which was so soothing to her.

At night, she read to Charles from a bible she found in the nightstand drawer. Often through tears, she squinted in the dim light to read New Testament passages she hoped comforted him, continuing until her voice disappeared.

With hours dragging on, Ada became lost in thought.

I am so connected to him now. How could I go on without him? This is surreal ... I've come from another time and place and yet I can't imagine ever being anywhere else. I believed our life together would continue forever ....

❋ ❋ ❋

On the fifth morning, Ada stirred on her cot to find Charles partially sitting up with a cup of water in his hand.

"Charles!" she exclaimed. "You've come back to me."

Charles managed a weak smile and teased, "You didn't think you could get rid of me so easily, now, did you?"

Ada rushed over to him and kissed his lips.

"I never doubted it for a moment."

"How long have I been down?" he asked.

"Five very long days," she answered.

After fetching him some fresh water, Ada bounced out to find Anne and the cook to tell them the good news.

"His fever has broken and he's sitting up!" she exclaimed. They hugged and Anne immediately began barking orders to get some broth heated up.

"Do you think he could manage a potato in it?" she asked.

"I think so," Ada beamed.

Over the next few hours, Charles was able to get a small bowl of broth and potatoes down. Ada opened the window and let some fresh air and sunshine reach his face.

"Ada," Charles said with a serious tone. "Sit down. I want to tell you something."

She rushed to his side and brushed his hair off his forehead.

"I'm not sure I'm well enough to move on," he began. "You've already lost the better part of a week and I think you should go on without me to find Melinda and meet up with Jane and Leroux. There is our new home and property to see after as well. And we can't be a burden to Miss Hathaway any longer. You can help move me to a local inn and then I can follow as soon as I'm able," he said.

"Nonsense," Ada scolded him. "I wouldn't dream of leaving you for a moment. Home is where you and I are together. Now, I'll hear no more. We've always agreed on how to approach things and we always do everything together. This isn't any exception."

"Well, I won't argue with you there," he said. "But some things are going to be different now. Not once, but twice, I had a vision like no other; perhaps it was the fever. I saw Jesus opening a door and I felt connected with God in a new way. I had a sense that all along I had missed out on the grace that I could find in faith. You remember that I was not always keen on the overly religious ways of others but, if you agree, I would like for us to start going to church together when we can."

"My dear, dear, Charles, I am also renewed in my faith," Ada assured him. "I don't know if you were aware that I was reading stories of Jesus to you often while you lay here but they touched me deeply, too. I am ready to explore this wonder with you and make a new start … together."

※　※　※

Later that evening, Ada took Anne aside and relayed Charles' message.

"Anne, I can't begin to tell you how grateful we are to you for opening your home and heart to us this past week. I can't imagine what we would have done without your help. But Charles and I both know it's time we get out of your hair and we'll move to a local inn tomorrow."

"Don't be silly," Anne scolded. "You'll stay here as long as it takes for Charles to be well enough to travel. Frankly, your company has been a blessing since William has been away. We have more than enough room and you are no bother at all. So, it's settled?"

"Well, I won't protest too much," Ada smiled and breathed a sigh of relief. "But knowing Charles, he'll want to get back on the road as soon as possible. You can't keep a good man down for long!"

CHAPTER 49

1586 CE ENGLAND

AFTER ANOTHER FIVE NIGHTS AT SHAKESPEARE'S home, Charles was getting fidgety. But Ada wasn't so sure it was time to leave just yet. As a way to test the waters, she brought up the idea of taking the row boat ride on the River Avon that Anne had suggested the first night they arrived and before he fell sick.

"It looks like a lovely day," Ada said as she opened the curtains that morning. "What would you think about taking that row boat down the river that Anne mentioned?"

"I see," Charles teased, "you want to test my sea legs, is that it?" He came up behind her at the window and took a deep breath. "I suppose I could pull my weight and then some," he grinned.

Anne was delighted to hear that they were going. She asked the cook to pack them some lunch, which Ada strictly oversaw to be sure nothing would cause Charles anymore grief. Anne then led the couple down the road a bit to a shed. Together, they pulled the boat out and carried it to the bank.

Charles and Ada set the small wooden rowboat into the water, its oars smooth and well-worn from years of use. The boat bobbed gently on the River Avon as Charles steadied it for Ada. She stepped in gracefully, her skirt brushing the water's surface. Charles, a bit tipsy getting in himself, chuckled as he sat on the bench to take stock of his vessel.

As he slowly rowed, they glided past a bevy of swans, their white feathers glowing in the warm afternoon sunlight. Ada reached over the side to touch the water, her fingers creating small ripples that danced around the birds. Undisturbed, the swans were at peace as they dipped their beaks into the water, searching for food.

On their route, they passed under the town's stone bridges with their arches casting long shadows over the water. From beneath the bridges, they could hear the faint echoes of townsfolk walking above. Ada smiled as she spotted a small group of children on the banks, waving enthusiastically as the rowboat drifted by. She closed her eyes for a moment, etching the scene into her mind so she would never forget it. She gave thanks for Charles's recovery and the joy she felt knowing he was near her.

As they approached Holy Trinity Church, its spire reaching towards the sky, Ada pointed out the intricate stained glass windows that glittered in the sunlight. The church stood as a silent guardian over the town, its ancient stones weathered by time. Ada realized this was the place that would one day become famous as the burial place of William Shakespeare. Charles paused in his rowing, allowing them to drift for a moment while they admired the church's reflection on the water's surface.

Continuing their journey, they saw small boats moored along the banks, fishermen tending to their nets, and traders loading goods for transport. Charles and Ada smiled at one another, the tranquility of the Avon wrapping around them like a comforting embrace.

After returning to their starting point, Charles helped Ada out of the boat. They secured the boat back in the shed and then walked hand-in-hand back to the Shakespeare house. The row boat ride held a special significance for them now. They realized their bond had grown much deeper—they were now like one—because of the events that had taken place at Stratford.

✳ ✳ ✳

The next morning they decided it was time to move on and they made their preparations for their ride from Stratford to London. Still cautious about eating the food at pubs in the villages they passed through, Ada and Anne's cook had prepared some dried pemmican bars and she would need to carefully select vegetables and meat along the way. Both had lost considerable weight but she hoped the fresh Ghost Flower powder would strengthen their immune systems and prepare them for the next several weeks away from home.

Sleeping under the stars, Ada sensed Charles was nearly recovered. He gazed in the night sky and excitedly pointed out constellations and asked questions as he had done many times before. Ada explained that in this time, a young Italian math student named Galileo was still forming his early theories about the planets but in the near future, he would vastly improve telescope technology. Charles loved to hear about the discoveries that would someday be made. He often asked Ada to tell him the story about men walking on the moon.

Coming into London early one morning, they were assailed by the smells of the sewage in the narrow streets and the body odors of the poor who only bathed once a year, if then. The houses they passed were built very close together they noticed, allowing little ventilation in crowded spaces. This was not unnoticed by Ada, who understood how easily disease can be transmitted in such an environment.

"My God, Charles, I couldn't live here. I'm wearing the standard woman's clothing so as not to attract attention and that is making riding this horse very uncomfortable. I'm trying to blend in! Of course, I've noticed that being a woman riding a horse isn't helping but I certainly don't want to walk. Let's get through London as quickly as possible following the directions given to us by Anne. My impression is the two theatres she told us to check out, being on the outskirts of London may offer us some respite from the smells and crowding here in the city. I'm not inclined to spend too much time visiting Melinda. We should attempt to get on Jane and Leroux's boat as soon as we can."

"I've visited here before on business but only for short periods," Charles said. "The city is growing fast, probably nearing 200,000 people now, with a majority being poor. I'm agreeing with you that the sooner we leave the better."

Moving at a good clip, they reached the northern edge of town and soon came across a building called The Theatre, which was across the road from a common sewage ditch.

"Let's go inside and start our search for Melinda," suggested Ada.

"Agreed. I'll go in first," Charles said. Before Ada could protest, he had dismounted and she quickly followed him.

As the two of them went in, they saw a production being rehearsed in preparation for a show that afternoon. Light was coming from overhead as the structure was essentially an amphitheater, in the shape of an octagon, with three covered galleries facing a thrust stage. The middle area of the octagon was open to the sky above, below which was a cobblestone floor, covered with straw.

"Doc!" came a shout from a woman standing near the stage. "What a surprise!"

Ada and Charles turned in the direction of the shout and saw Melinda standing near the stage with a look of happy surprise. She began quickly walking toward them and when close enough, gave them a big hug. Ada tried to conceal her surprise at the pungent body odor but knew it was so common in London that the people living here no longer noticed it among themselves.

"Let's go outside and talk so we don't interrupt the rehearsal," Melinda suggested. "I can't believe you are here. How did you find me?"

"We were in Stratford looking for you and Anne Hathaway told us where we might find you," Ada replied. "How are you?"

"I'm quite well, thanks, primarily because I still have immunity from my last meal some time ago sprinkled with the Ghost Flower garnish. Without that, I think I might not have survived in these conditions."

"Which one of the actors on stage is Shakespeare?" inquired Ada, unable to hide her curiosity at meeting the Bard.

Melinda described which one he was and then went on to say that her dream of acting with him was achieved one afternoon in a play where she was costumed as a boy. She described the culture preventing women from acting. Not only that, women her age who were not married were looked on with great suspicion. She explained that while she was with the current group of actors, they found it very amusing to have her accompany them when they went out, with her dressed as a boy.

"However," she added, "what has been a joy for me is to work with Will in writing plays for us to sell to The Theatre for our performances. He is really good at it. It's not uncommon for the plays to be put together as a collaborative effort among the actors to earn money to live. Will isn't yet at the point of going solo and writing the plays he will become famous for. But I know he has been forming ideas for them in his head. You know, this play creation is a competitive business for the revenue it generates, meager as it is. So much of what we create is never put on paper, or at least after we have written something in private, we memorize the lines then destroy it, lest it be stolen and sold without us. There is no copyright protection for us here!"

In a voice dripping with sarcasm she added, "I do love this time." Then, becoming serious she added, "However, I do not want to stay in London much longer. I long to return to Stratford, which I really like. That's where I plan to stay after satisfying this dream of working with Will and getting to know him."

Ada chimed in, "Charles and I are going to find a place further away from here to spend a few days until Jane and Leroux meet us near the bridge over the Thames. We have a prearranged date for meeting them and it appears we are on schedule for that in two days' time. Perhaps you and Will can meet us there and visit with all of us before we leave."

"That will be great! I'm sure Will would like that. In the meantime, several of us in the acting company are staying at a small inn north of here that is away from the city. I think they have a vacant room the two of you can rent. I'm sure it's cleaner than what you might find in the city proper. So, if you decide to stay there, you can join us for supper tonight. Sound good?"

Ada thought it best not to tell Melinda about Charles' illness until later when they were alone.

"I like it. We will let you get back inside and we'll head for the inn after you give us the details. Our conversation can resume then!" Ada said, looking at Charles, who was nodding in agreement. Shortly after learning where the inn was located, they rode away, not unhappy about not going back into the city limits of London.

That night at the inn was a treat. While careful about what they ate and drank, Ada and Charles thoroughly enjoyed the company of the actors and were very entertained by Shakespeare's humor and wit. Melinda seemed happy but it was evident that, other than the time spent with Shakespeare, she was longing to get back to a quieter and, frankly, safer life in Stratford.

She explained she had met a young man there who she was finding herself missing more each day. He was very entrepreneurial and he enjoyed her company immensely. He had inherited a beautiful little cottage situated on a property just across the River Avon from the village of Stratford. Rowing on the river with Anthony, as she said his name was, seemed like a fairy tale dream.

✳ ✳ ✳

The next days passed for Charles and Ada enjoying evenings in the inn sharing time with the actors and Melinda. One afternoon during this time, they went to The Theatre to see a play where Shakespeare would be one of the actors. Melinda accompanied them, regaling them with commentary as the play unfolded.

Choosing to each pay an extra two pennies above the penny required for general admission, allowed Charles, Ada, and Melinda to be in one of the galleries with a rented stool for each of them to sit on rather than stand. From that higher vantage point, they were better able to see the action than those standing at floor level, some five feet below the stage.

Melinda explained the audience on the floor, or in the pit as some called it, was generally less sophisticated than the audience in the galleries. The price of admission being higher for those in the galleries seemed to create an economic division between the groups. Those standing on the floor were typically less educated and sophisticated. Both groups, however, shared a common desire to be entertained. But what entertained one group did not necessarily appeal to the other quite as much. This led to the players needing scripts that allowed them to satisfy both groups.

The audience standing in the pit, who were eating and drinking ale while watching, were often short on attention span. They especially wanted action, sex, and bawdy comedy. If those parts of the play were too far apart, they would boo and sometimes throw fruit or food at the players to show their displeasure. The audiences in the galleries seemed to better understand and appreciate the more cerebral lines, sophisticated word play, and the influence of earlier Greek tragedies. However, the theatre experience was much more interactive in those days. Singing, dancing, booing, and applauding became acceptable behaviors as did eating and drinking ale while watching the actors on stage. Overall, the plays were written and acted to appeal to the entire audience. In the end, the players were more often applauded as opposed to being run off stage.

Absorbing what Melinda explained to them about the diverse expectations of the audience, Ada began to have a better understanding of the reasons behind the construction of the scenes in Shakespeare plays that she had not quite grasped in her twentieth century theatre experiences. She realized some of the scenes as she saw them then seemed a little discordant from other scenes and didn't have quite the same emotional appeal for the modern audience sitting quietly and politely in their seats as opposed to dancing, singing, and shouting at the actors as the audience she was part of now behaved. Keeping such a varied audience happy at that time when the plays were being written was no easy feat. But the actors and playwrights understood their customers and successfully met the challenge, resulting in theatre being a very popular pastime, entertaining thousands each year in the theatres around London.

When the appointed day to meet Jane and Leroux arrived, Melinda and Will rented a small carriage to ride along with them. Arriving late in the afternoon at the wharf near the bridge over the Thames, they spotted Jane and Leroux lounging on the deck of their catamaran. After Jane recovered from the shock of meeting Shakespeare and the excitement of seeing Melinda again, she invited them to dine with them that night on board the boat, with their cook preparing a fabulous meal, served with several bottles of excellent Pinot Noir.

During dinner, many stories were shared, evoking much laughter mixed with surprise at some of the events that had taken place since they had last seen each other. A highlight for them all was to hear tales told by Will, as they now all addressed Shakespeare. At one point, thoughtfully looking around the boat and hearing some of the adventures involved with their many voyages, he remarked that he might want to write a play involving sailing, with perhaps a shipwreck in a stormy sea. Melinda smiled and said she thought that was a wonderful idea.

Will also mentioned that Anne had written to him about Charles and Ada's stay in Stratford. She was especially impressed with their complete devotion to each other and insisted that Will think about writing more love stories.

Before the evening was over, Ada managed to have some time alone with Melinda and told her about Charles' illness and Anne Hathaway's kindness.

"My experience in this time has been the best of my life," Ada confided. "I have thought many times about what I am missing in the modern world we left behind—the advanced medical care, grocery stores, safe clean drinking water, air-conditioning, and all that we accepted as normal in our lives. However, here I am finding life with Charles something I never had there. Given the opportunity, I would not give up the positive excitement and renewed sense of purpose I've found here if I were offered the opportunity to return to the twenty-first century. I know that would not be the way I would feel if my life had been different before—but it was not."

Melinda listened thoughtfully before responding.

"I feel the same. I would not want to return either but some of the reasons are different. Before we came here, I was involved in research into the past and have been intrigued for years about what life in the times I studied was really like. I am now able to see these times first hand, to live in them, and become associated with historical characters like Will. For me, these are wonderful, irreplaceable experiences.

"Yes, I know I have given up a great deal of all that came with my life in the twenty-first century but those sacrifices pale in comparison with what I am gaining as a person in my life here. Yes, I also know that without the medical care I left behind and the relative safety of modern living conditions, my years of remaining life here will undoubtedly be less than the alternative. But for me, the quality of these remaining years will be much more fulfilling. The choice I have made is good for me."

Ada closed the conversation mentioning Joel, Thomas, Sam, and Jane.

"We all make choices in our lives. I think my choice to come here, and it seems yours as well, were good ones for us. On the other hand, I don't think Joel and Thomas would feel the same if they had come on this journey back in time. They were in a good place in their lives before, and where we felt no great loss in leaving our circumstances there, I think they would have regretted coming with us if that had been their choice. The two of us, it seems, made the right choice. As for Sam, I don't know. He left for Paris and I have heard nothing from him since."

After a moments reflection on what she had just said, Ada smiled and added, "All you have to do is look at Jane over there with Leroux and you don't even have to speculate about her feelings about choosing to travel into the past with us."

Their time in London came to an end. Ada and Charles sailed off with Jane and Leroux for their home in Portishead. Melinda promised to get them a message when she was back in Stratford. She also agreed to let them know the progress of her romance on her return.

CHAPTER 50

2038 CE
BOSTON, MASSACHUSETTS

IN THE YEAR THAT HAD PASSED since Joel and Thomas had received the largesse left to them by Ada, they had been able to use it very strategically to hasten the development of an immunization utilizing the Ghost Flower information. The vaccine that resulted was now being distributed worldwide with amazingly good outcomes. The pharmaceutical companies had been able to produce it in pill form which did not require refrigerated storage prior to use. This was extremely helpful in serving underdeveloped countries.

The worldwide spread of the virus had slowed almost to a stop. Unfortunately, millions of people had already died but without the secrets of the Ghost Flower being unlocked as expeditiously as they had been, the toll on human life would have been exponentially greater.

At the end of a particularly long day, Joel was relaxing in a chair in their office lobby talking with Thomas and their administrative assistant, Gail.

"Can you believe all that has happened since those days when we first started this adventure? I'm still struggling to get my head around it. It all started with a dinner conversation years ago with cousin Melinda about some research she had done in Spain and her casual mention of a white flower drawn in the margin of an obscure, ancient manuscript. That simple conversation led to all that followed, bringing a pandemic, the likes of the historic Black

Death, to its knees."

Thoughtfully, Thomas ruminated on a conversation they had not long after Doc, Melinda, Thomas, and Jane had gone back in time to 1585 CE.

"I'm still wondering what happened to them as they lived out their lives, never to come back. I hope they found happiness and purpose. We will never know."

"Don't be too sure of that, Thomas," responded Joel. "I heard a rumor about a multi-billionaire science geek who is extremely interested in time travel. Word is he is assembling a team to restart the time travel program for which the government has refused to authorize further funding. Should we volunteer to partner with him and his new team?"

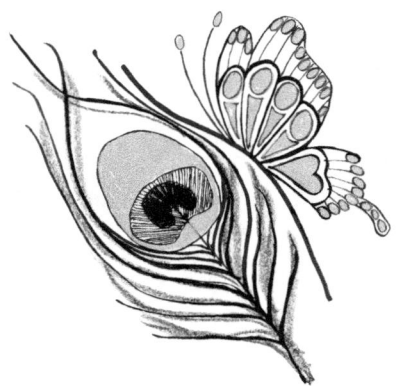

2024 CE
ORLANDO, FLORIDA

THE STORY YOU'VE JUST READ WAS nearly finished before my husband, Bill, died after a short and unexpected illness. He planned several spin-offs and frequently mused about the Ghost Flower characters and what might become of them. Their fate is now in your minds and hearts.

After he passed over, I embarked on a spiritual journey; I did not know where it would take me. And it is still evolving. I can feel our connection becoming stronger daily. Through many spiritual advisors, I began to learn of the Twin Flame, the mysteries of the Pleaides, and our soul's purpose. It all makes perfect sense.

Bill and I talked every day about his writing. The plan all along was for me to paint the cover of Ghost Flower and Bill mentioned specific items to include. During his illness and final days, we both felt closer to God, to each other, and to all those who were praying for us.

As I read through the book after the first round of edits, there were moments when I was smiling—then crying—as I recognized so many stories were about us. Bill wove in personal details about our experiences that covered centuries of history. His words inspired me such that I felt we were embarking on publishing this book together.

He has been with me as I made refinements to the text, drew, and painted the images for the cover, worked on the layout, and sketched the chapter vignette drawings. His motto was, "use everything" and it inspired me to deliver a range in my artwork to complement the range in his writing. The art became my time to connect with him in a deeper way, and I cherish it greatly.

Of course, there are questions of who are we, where did we come from, and what is our purpose? Some have said this is a labor of love—but to me, it is love.

As I continue on my spiritual journey to heal and go forward, I believe this book tells the real story of our life together.

I know Bill is continuing his humanitarian mission. I hope you are as inspired by his work as I am.

Thank you to my family and friends for the love and support and space during this healing time…

And to Jain Lemos, our editor, thank you for believing in Bill and for a wonderful and joyful collaboration. I look forward to our next project.

My best to all of you,

—Ksenia J. Merck
October 2024

WILLIAM F. MERCK II
1944-2024

WILLIAM F. MERCK II (BILL) WAS born in Waycross, Georgia on October 14, 1944. He was the oldest of four boys. His parents owned a building materials business where he began working at a young age. Bill acquired his Associate degree in Arts from South Georgia College in 1964. He also graduated from Georgia State College (Georgia State University) with a BBA in Management and subsequently earned an MBA in Finance. He served as an officer as First Lieutenant in the United States Army from 1969 to 1972. For two of those years, he was stationed in Germany.

After the military, Bill started his career in higher education at James Madison, then known as Madison University, as the Director of Housing. He went on to serve as the Vice President for Business Affairs at James Madison University. He then went to the College of William and Mary where he served as VP for Administration and Finance.

He served for twenty-two years as Vice President for Administration and Finance at the University of Central Florida where he held management responsibility for the following administrative units: Business Services, Environmental Health and Safety, Landscape and Natural Resources, Parking and Transportation Services, Facilities, Operations, Sustainability and Energy Management, University Police, Resource Management, Emergency Management, and Procurement. He was later promoted to Chief Financial Officer.

In his fifty-year career, Bill led the building programs for the three universities, transforming the campuses to create spaces for learning and living to benefit all the students, faculty, and administrators. His work involved more than just building campuses and leading administrative departments; it was rooted in his ability to lead through listening, conversation, and truly grasping what was required to address challenges. He connected with individuals at every level to effectively resolve issues. He cared about people and worked with integrity to do the right thing. He mentored and promoted many people of diverse backgrounds as he encouraged their potential and helped them succeed.

Bill volunteered in each community where he lived and served on the professional boards of several organizations including the United Way in Williamsburg, Virginia, and Orlando, Florida. He was on the board of the Eastern Association of College and University Business Officers (EACUBO) and served as the citizen representative on the Orlando Orange County Expressway Authority (OOCEA). While in Virginia, he served on the board of the Rockingham Memorial Hospital and on the Finance Committee of the Williamsburg Community Hospital. He also served on the board of the public television station, WVPT, in Harrisonburg, Virginia.

When faced with adverse situations, Bill handled these with grace, dignity, his even-keel delivery, and a caring spirit. He was solid in his judgment and stood by his decisions, especially those impacting the health and safety of people.

Bill was creative, too, and not only in problem solving. He had a wide range of interests and was a great storyteller. He was interested in so many aspects of life and he wanted to hear each person's unique story. Bill loved to travel and was curious about different cultures and about how things came together and why. He loved to draw portraits and was an avid photographer. He loved nature and the beauty that God created. He was a hard worker; both in his career and in his personal life, tackling many projects.

After retiring, Bill pursued writing. He is the author of *So, You Want to be a Leader: Secrets of a Lifetime of Success* and *Breadcrumbs: Finding a Philosophy of Life*. The two books work hand-in-hand with engaging personal stories to inspire readers to think about how their philosophies shape who they are. To find out more about these books, please visit williamfmerck.com.

His third book, *Ghost Flower*, published posthumously by his wife, Ksenia, is a science fiction novel set in the future but requires the characters to time travel to the past to find a cure for a disease.

Bill was a beautiful soul in so many ways. He loved his family and friends. He influenced so many people in a positive way with his warm, kind heart, and his depth, wit, charm, and compassion.

During his short illness, Bill connected with God and was at peace.

Bill had a great life.

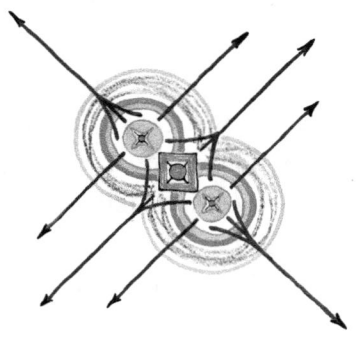

Goodbyes are only for those
who love with their eyes.
Because for those who love
with heart and soul
there is no such thing
as separation.
—Rumi

GHOST FLOWER
SPACE ✳ TIME ✦ DESTINY

WILLIAM F. MERCK II

BREADCRUMBS
Finding a Philosophy of Life

WILLIAM F. MERCK II

SO, YOU WANT TO BE A
LEADER

Secrets of a Lifetime of Success

WILLIAM F. MERCK II

◄◄M‖►►
MERCK II PRESS
◄◄◆►►

GHOST FLOWER
SPACE ✳ TIME ✦ DESTINY

COMPANION JOURNAL

KSENIA J. MERCK

www.ingramcontent.com/pod-product-compliance
Lightning Source LLC
Chambersburg PA
CBHW070759030726
47504CB00003B/618